006

REKI KAWAHARA   ABEC   BEE-PEE

SWORD ART ONLINE
phantom bullet

SWORD ART ONLINE

"I...don't want to admit that there are VRMMO players who would commit not PK, but actual murder."

Sinon § A player in *Gun Gale Online*, an MMO of guns and steel. She dispatches her foes with the massive Hecate II sniper rifle.

"I'm going after Death Gun.
I can't let him shoot
anyone else with that pistol."

Kirito § A boy infiltrating *GGO* to investigate Death Gun. In an MMO of guns and steel, he's the only swordsman.

"Even Kirito wouldn't do something like that...I think."

Asuna § Kirito's girlfriend. In *ALO*, she plays an undine magician.

"Ha ha ha, that sounds about right. And he went out of his way to use a sword in a gun game."

Lisbeth § A girl who upgraded Kirito's swords in *SAO*. In *ALO*, she is a leprechaun blacksmith.

"Yes, it's quite a surprise. Knowing Kirito, I figured he would be raising hell from the very start."

Silica § A girl Kirito saved in *SAO*. In *ALO*, she plays a beast-taming cait sith character.

"They sure aren't showing much of Big Brother."

Leafa § Kirito's little sister. Real name: Suguha. She plays a magic fighter sylph in *ALO*.

"Always check
your six."

"———!!"

"You cannot do anything.
You will fall here, sprawled into
the dust, and have no choice
but to watch as I kill the girl..."

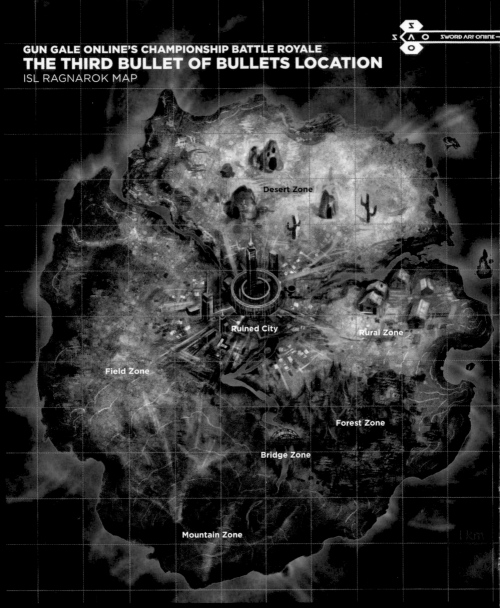

GUN GALE ONLINE'S CHAMPIONSHIP BATTLE ROYALE
THE THIRD BULLET OF BULLETS LOCATION
ISL RAGNAROK MAP

Desert Zone

Ruined City

Rural Zone

Field Zone

Forest Zone

Bridge Zone

Mountain Zone

1 km

ISL RAGNAROK
The island that serves as the map for the final match of the third Bullet of Bullets tournament in the VRMMO *Gun Gale Online*. In this battle royale finish, the thirty gunners who won their preliminary rounds face off all at once on the same map. The last surviving player becomes the champion.

The setting of the fight is ISL Ragnarok, a circular island measuring ten kilometers across. It has a composite environment with mountains, forests, and deserts, with the player avatars being placed randomly somewhere on the island at the start.

All players are automatically given an item called a Satellite Scan Terminal. Every fifteen minutes, an overhead satellite passes over the island, capturing the coordinates of all players and sending them to all terminals. In other words, fifteen minutes is the maximum amount of time to effectively camp out for an ambush.

In the center of the map is the ruin of a city from a once-flourishing civilization. A large river dissects the southern half of the map, over which lies a steel bridge. There are forests in the southeast, plains in the west, rural settlements in the east, and deserts in the north. Aside from sand, the desert also features rock formations and caves.

Map Illustration: Fuu Midori

SWORD ART ONLINE phantom bullet

VOLUME 6

Reki Kawahara

abec

bee-pee

YEN ON

NEW YORK

SWORD ART ONLINE, Volume 6: Phantom Bullet
REKI KAWAHARA

Translation by Stephen Paul

SWORD ART ONLINE
© REKI KAWAHARA 2010
All rights reserved.
Edited by ASCII MEDIA WORKS
First published in Japan in 2010 by
KADOKAWA CORPORATION, Tokyo.
English translation rights arranged with
KADOKAWA CORPORATION, Tokyo,
through Tuttle-Mori Agency, Inc., Tokyo.

English translation © 2015 by Yen Press, LLC

Yen On
1290 Avenue of the Americas
New York, NY 10104
www.yenpress.com

Yen On is an imprint of Yen Press, LLC.
The Yen On name and logo are trademarks of Yen Press, LLC.

First Yen On Edition: December 2015

ISBN: 978-0-316-29645-8

10 9 8 7 6 5 4 3

BVG

Printed in the United States of America

"THIS MIGHT BE A GAME, BUT IT'S NOT SOMETHING YOU PLAY."

—Akihiko Kayaba, *Sword Art Online* programmer

SWORD ART Online
phantom bullet

Reki Kawahara

abec

bee-pee

7

"Big Brother!"

That a cheerful smile from my beloved sister—at a lunch table on a beautiful Sunday afternoon—would cause me to sense impending disaster should tell you just how guilty I felt about my present actions.

I stopped my fork just before the cherry tomato reached my mouth. "Wh-what's up, Sugu?" I asked, only to find the premonition come to fruition when my sister—nay, cousin—Suguha Kirigaya picked up something from the seat next to me.

"Listen, I found this article on the Net this morning."

She shoved a full-sized A4 printout into my face. It was a hard copy of the news column from the nation's biggest VRMMO gaming website, MMO Tomorrow, typically abbreviated to M-Tomo.

The bold headline proclaimed: THIRTY FINALISTS ANNOUNCED FOR 3RD BULLET OF BULLETS BATTLE ROYALE FINAL IN GUN GALE ONLINE.

After a short lead, the article ran the list of names. Right beneath Suguha's neatly clipped index nail, it said "F Block, 1st Place: Kirito (Debut)." I tried an empty bluff.

"W-well, well, funny that someone else is using a similar name."

"Similar? It's the exact same name."

Under Suguha's trimmed bangs was a grinning face with forth-right, crisp features, the very image of a healthy, athletic girl. In real life, she was a talented kendo practitioner, who helped her team reach both the high school nationals, known as the Inter-High, and the Kendo association tournament nationals at the high school level, striving for what was known as the *Gyokuryuki* prize—all in just her first year of high school. In comparison, my spindly, scrawny figure was no match for her physical stamina. In the virtual world of ALfheim Online, where skill reigned supreme, she was the fairy warrior Leafa, whose graceful, hardy sword occasionally overpowered my own self-taught style.

So I'd have to give up and apologize immediately if I ever got into a fight with Suguha in real life or VR, but fortunately for me, that never had to cross my mind. In the year since I'd come back to the real world, we were closer than we were before we'd grown apart. Even my dad, who temporarily returned during summer vacation from his transfer to America, was jealous of us.

So for lunch today—Sunday, December 14, 2025—with my mother stuck in the editor's office, Suguha and I went out shopping for groceries so we could fix poached egg Caesar salad and seafood pilaf. We sat across from each other at the table to eat our lunch in blissful peace—until the article entered the picture.

"Uh...yeah. So it is," I noted, tearing my eyes away from the printed "Kirito" and tossing the tomato into my mouth. As I chewed, I mumbled, "B-but it's not such an uncommon name. I mean, in my case, it's just an abbreviation of my real name, Kazuto Kirigaya. I bet this Kirito in GGO has a name like, um... Tougorou...Kirigamine. Yeah."

The baldfaced lie to my trusting sister prickled at my heart. After all, the Kirito that Suguha was singling out was 100 percent me, without a doubt.

The reason I had to hide that fact was that in order to enter the Bullet of Bullets tournament in the first-person shooter MMO Gun Gale Online, I had to convert my Kirito avatar from its home world of ALO into the world of GGO.

Character conversion was a feature made possible by the Seed platform, the engine on which all VRMMOs ran, which allowed a player to move a character they'd built up in one game to another game while maintaining the same level of strength—a system that was unthinkable just a few short years ago.

There were limitations, of course. The biggest one was that only the character itself transferred, not any items or money. Because of that, conversion was useful only for permanent transfers, not for the tourist desire to check out a different game for a week or two.

I knew that if I told her I was leaving ALO for a different game, Suguha would be terribly shocked; she loved the fairy realm with all her heart. Not to mention that I very much did not want to explain the reason that I had had to convert Kirito to GGO. The seedy underbelly of the VRMMO world was deeply involved with the move.

Seijirou Kikuoka, a government official, had asked me to investigate something in GGO. He was once a member of the government's SAO Incident Team, and was currently situated in the "Virtual Division"—the Ministry of Internal Affairs' Virtual Network Management Division.

The previous Sunday, Kikuoka summoned me for a meeting and described a very odd event that had happened.

In the main city of GGO, an avatar shot at another avatar, claiming the work of some kind of "judgment." It would be unremarkable, a simple stunt, if that was all that happened. But the two players whose figures were shot by the avatar in question both died of heart attacks at the very moment they were shot in the game.

It was just a coincidence—I was 90 percent sure of that.

But that last 10 percent possibility in my mind was something I just couldn't shake. So I agreed to Kikuoka's bothersome, dangerous request: that I log in to the world of GGO and make contact with the mysterious shooter myself.

I didn't have the time to build up a new character from scratch, so I converted Kirito from ALO and entered the BoB preliminary competition yesterday in an attempt to catch the shooter's eye. While I struggled mightily with learning to adapt to the unfamiliar gun battles, the good fortune of finding an extremely helpful player right off the bat got me through the preliminary round somehow—and I even made first contact with the gunman I believed to be my target.

Whether the man calling himself Death Gun truly had the power to kill players from within the game was unknown still.

But one thing became very clear. There was a completely unexpected connection that tied me and Death Gun together:

Just like me, Death Gun was a survivor of Sword Art Online, the game of death. And beyond that, we had crossed swords in a battle for our lives—

"Big Brother, you look scary."

My body jolted with surprise. My eyes focused on a single point again to see Suguha's face, her eyes full of concern. She put the hard copy down on the table, clasped her hands together, and stared at me.

"Um, listen…I'll be honest. I already know that you converted Kirito from ALO to GGO," she admitted out of the blue. My eyes bulged. There was a grown-up, understanding smile on my younger sister's lips. "Do you really think I wouldn't notice that you were gone from my friends list?"

"B-but…I was going to convert back once this weekend was over…and people don't check their list every day…"

"I don't have to look to be able to feel it," she stated confidently. There was a strange light in her big eyes. Oddly enough, I was struck by her femininity in that moment. I looked away with the shyness of that realization and the guilt at trying to hide my conversion.

Suguha said softly, "I noticed that 'Kirito' was gone last night, and logged out so I could barge right into your room. But you wouldn't leave ALO without telling me for no good reason. I realized there must have been a reason, so I contacted Asuna."

"Oh…great," I muttered, wincing.

I had only related my secret conversion from ALO to GGO to Asuna Yuuki and our "daughter," the AI named Yui. That was because Yui had limited access to the game's system and would know if I disappeared from ALO for two measly seconds, let alone two days. There was no hiding it.

Yui didn't like it when I kept things from Asuna. She might have accepted it if I explained that I had a very good reason for it, but I certainly couldn't cope with the thought of placing undue stress on Yui's core programming.

So I told Asuna and Yui—and only them—that I was leaving for GGO at Seijirou Kikuoka's request, explaining that it was "to investigate the Seed Nexus." I just couldn't tell them what that investigation actually entailed: contact with Death Gun, and the connection between his in-game shootings and two real-life deaths…

It was all preposterous, but its absurdity was eerie enough to eat away at me. That was the biggest reason that I hadn't told Suguha or my other friends about the conversion.

I looked down and didn't explain any further. I heard the sound of a chair scraping. Soft footsteps. Then hands on my shoulders.

"…Big Brother," Suguha whispered, leaning onto my back, "Asuna told me, 'He's going to go on a little rampage in GGO like he always does, and then he'll be back.' But I think she was secretly worried about it. I am, too. I mean…when you came back so late yesterday, you had this terrible look on your face."

"Oh…I did?"

Suguha's short hair brushed my neck. She breathed out directly beside my ear.

"You're not…doing anything dangerous, are you? I don't want you to wind up someplace far away again…"

"…I won't," I said, loud and clear this time. I put my hand on the one pressing my left shoulder. "I promise. When GGO's tournament ends tonight, I'll come back. Back to ALO…and to this home."

"...Good."

I felt her nod, but Suguha's weight stayed on me for a while.

For the two years I was trapped in SAO, my sister had been stricken with terrible grief. And now I was putting her through the possibility of something similar happening. It was unconscionable.

I had the option of messaging Seijirou Kikuoka and canceling the whole operation. But after having been through yesterday's prelims, two reasons made that choice very difficult now.

For one, I promised a rematch to Sinon, the sniper with the preposterously huge rifle who kindly taught me all about the game while I let her assume that I was a female player.

For another, there was a score to be settled between me and Death Gun.

I had to face the gray-cloaked man again and be sure. I needed to know his former name within the game—and those of his two comrades who I killed with my own sword. That was my primary responsibility, after coming back to the real world...

I patted the hand on my shoulder and reassured Suguha: "Don't worry, I'll be back. Now let's eat, before this food gets cold."

"...Okay."

Her voice was a little more forceful than before, and she squeezed my shoulder tight for a moment before letting go. When she trotted back around the table to her chair to sit down, Suguha's face was wearing its usual energetic smile. She shoved a huge spoonful of pilaf into her mouth and chewed for a moment, twiddling the spoon.

"By the way, Big Brother..."

"Hmm?"

"From what Asuna tells me, the job you're doing this time is going to pay you *really* well."

"Urk."

In the back of my brain, the image of the 300,000 yen Kikuoka promised me, and the cutting-edge PC it could build, sprang to life, complete with an old-fashioned cash register sound effect. I told myself that a slightly smaller hard drive wouldn't be the

worst compromise for Suguha's cooperation, and thumped my chest clear.

"Y-yep! A-and I'll buy you whatever you want with it."

"Yay! Well, you see, there's this nanocarbon kendo *shinai* I've always wanted…"

…Maybe I'd have to make do with less RAM, as well.

I left the house on my crappy old motorcycle during at three PM, to avoid rush hour traffic. Making my way east along the Kawagoe Highway, I passed through Ikebukuro and headed down Kasuga Street for the center of the city. I turned south at Hongo to go from Bunkyo Ward to Chiyoda Ward. In minutes, the general hospital that was my destination appeared ahead.

I was here only yesterday, but my memories of that trip seemed so distant now.

The reason was obvious. When I slipped into my bed last night, I couldn't fall asleep. I lay there in the darkness, eyes wide open, thinking about the past. Reliving the memories that had been dormant in my mind so long—the destruction of the PK guild in SAO known as Laughing Coffin.

Just before four in the morning, I gave up on sleep and put my AmuSphere on to dive into a local VR space. I called up my "daughter" Yui from her PC, which was hooked up via LAN, so we could have a chat that would eventually get me to fall asleep. It worked, but I never hit truly deep sleep, and the dreams I found instead were long.

Fortunately, I didn't remember most of them, though there was a voice that had been continually ringing in my ears from the moment I woke up until now.

Are you Kirito?

It was what the player I took to be Death Gun whispered to me in the midst of the BoB preliminaries yesterday. And it was also a question from a member of Laughing Coffin, two comrades of which I killed with my own sword. Three, if you included the man who was Asuna's sworn guard.

Is it you? Are you the Kirito who killed us?

Whether it was in the BoB waiting hall or in my dreams, my only answer could be "yes."

At today's final, which began at eight, I was sure I would come face-to-face with that ghost of a man again. If he asked me the same thing, I had to respond in the affirmative. But at this point in time, I didn't have the confidence to do that yet.

"If I'd known this would happen…"

…I wouldn't have converted Kirito from ALO. I'd have started a brand-new GGO character from scratch.

I grimaced at my own stubbornness to accept what had happened to me as I stopped the bike and headed for the inpatient lobby.

I made sure to message before I left the house, so Nurse Aki was already set up in the same room as the previous day. Her hair was adorned with the same braids, but there was a pair of rimless glasses on her nose this time. She was sitting on the chair next to the bed, long legs folded as she read an anachronistic old paper book. When I opened the door, she looked up and shut the book quickly with a smile.

"You're here early."

"I'm sorry to put you through this chore again today, Miss Aki," I said, bowing. The clock on the wall said it wasn't even four yet. That meant I had over four hours until the BoB started, but it would be foolish to wait until the last second and rush to the event in a panic again. It would be a much better use of my time to log in early and get some shooting practice in.

As I hung up my jacket on a hanger, I told Nurse Aki, "My event doesn't start until eight, so you don't need to monitor my heart signals until then."

The nurse, dressed in her white uniform, shrugged. "It's fine, I'm on the graveyard overtime shift tonight. I'll be here as long as needed."

"Uh…i-in that case, I feel even worse…"

"Oh? Well, if I get sleepy, I might just borrow your bed here," she remarked with a wink. As a VRMMO addict with zero real-life skills, all I could do was mumble and look away. She laughed at that. She'd seen what a pushover I was during my post-SAO physical therapy. There was no winning against her.

I hid my embarrassment by plopping down on the bed and looking at the imposing monitoring equipment and the silver, double-ringed AmuSphere headgear lying on the pillow.

The unit Kikuoka prepared for me was still brand-new; the aluminum polish and the artificial leather interior were spotless. Compared to the crude helmet that was the NerveGear, the AmuSphere was much more refined and resembled a fashion accessory more than a piece of electronics.

In keeping with its promise of "absolute safety," it didn't even look like a machine capable of the lethal microwaves that the NerveGear produced. It was designed to send only the faintest possible signals.

So common sense said that it wasn't at all necessary to be strapped to a heart-monitoring device in a hospital with electrodes on my chest and a nurse on watch around the clock. No matter what anyone tried to do, the chances of anyone being able to harm me through this AmuSphere were zero. Nil.

But.

Zexceed and Usujio Tarako, two of the best GGO players around, were dead.

And I knew that Death Gun, the man who fired virtual bullets at their avatars, was once a red player in SAO—someone who knowingly, intentionally, killed other players.

What if there was still some unknown, dangerous effect of full-dive technology?

What if a player who had committed murder in the abnormal realm of SAO learned how to unleash murderous intent and hatred in a digital form that could be transmitted through the AmuSphere as data, traveling online and eventually reaching the nerve center of the target...with the signal to stop his heart?

If that hypothesis were true, it might be possible for Death

Gun's virtual shooting to have real, fatal effects. And at the same time, it could be possible for Kirito's virtual sword to kill Death Gun or someone else.

After all, I had killed other players in Aincrad. And my kill count might have been higher than most of the red players who partook in the activity.

Until this point, I'd been trying to forget about the lives that I ended with my sword. But yesterday, the lid that sealed those memories away had been opened.

Then again, I'd never be able to forget those things anyway. All I did for the past year was look away, pretending I couldn't see them. I tried to hide from the weight of the sin I ought to bear and pay the price for...

"What's wrong, kid? You look like hell."

The toe of a white slipper poked my knee. My shoulders twitched and I looked up to see the gentle gaze of Nurse Aki through her rimless glasses.

"Uh...er, nothing," I muttered, shaking my head, but I couldn't stop myself from biting my lip. Just a few hours earlier I'd made Suguha uneasy for the exact same reason, and now I was doing it to Nurse Aki, who was stuck at this annoying duty for my sake. I felt pathetic.

She gave me that same grin that had cheered me up so often during physical rehab and got up from her chair to sit next to me.

"C'mon, this is your big chance for some free counseling with a pretty nurse. Lay it on me, kiddo."

"...I'm guessing I'll be in trouble if I don't take you up on that," I noted with a long sigh. I looked down at the floor for a bit and asked, "Um, Miss Aki, you were in the surgical department before rehabilitation, right?"

"Yes, why?"

"Well, this might be a rude or completely insensitive question, but..." I glanced quickly to my left and mumbled, "How much do you remember about the patients that...didn't make it?"

I was expecting to be scolded or get a dirty look. If I was in her position, I'd be annoyed having to listen to the opinion of a kid who thought he knew what it was like to work in medicine.

But the gentle smile never left Aki's face. She looked up at the white ceiling and said, "Well, if I actually sit back and try to remember, I can see the names and faces, all right. Even the patients who were only in the same surgery room for an hour… It's strange, given that I only saw them while they were sleeping under anesthesia."

She must have meant that patients had died during operations where she was present. I knew it wasn't something I should touch upon lightly, but I couldn't keep myself from asking.

"Have you ever wished you could forget?"

I don't know what she saw when she looked into my face. She blinked twice, but the smile never vanished from her lightly reddened lips.

"Hmm…good question. I don't know if this answers it for you or not, but," she prefaced, her voice husky, "when people are meant to forget something, they will forget it, I think. They don't even have to want to forget it. After all, the more often you think you want to forget something, the stronger you're making that memory, aren't you? It means that deep in your heart, in your unconscious, you believe it's something you shouldn't forget."

I took in a short breath. It wasn't the answer I expected.

The more I wished to forget something, the less I was meant to forget it…?

The words sank into my chest and brought a bitter taste to my mouth. Eventually that turned into a sardonic smile.

"Then I guess I'm a real bastard…"

I looked down at the floor between my feet so I didn't have to see the questioning look in Aki's eyes. My arms squeezed together around my knees, pressing the words out of my chest.

"Inside of SAO, I…killed three players."

My dry, croaking voice echoed off the white walls, sounding distorted when it reached my ears. Maybe it was actually the inside of my head producing those echoes.

Aki was my personal nurse when I attended this hospital for physical rehabilitation—November and December of last year. So she knew that I'd been trapped in a virtual world for two whole years, but I'd never told her a word about what happened in there until now.

Her job was to save people's lives; there was no way she'd be happy to hear about someone taking them, no matter the reason. But I couldn't stop the words from tumbling out of my mouth now. I hung my head and let the dry cracking voice flow.

"They were all reds—murderers themselves. But I had the option to pacify them without killing. And I killed them anyway. I let my anger and hatred and vengeance do the dirty work. And for the past year, I forgot all about them. Even as I'm telling you this now, I don't remember the two men's names or faces. So you see…I'm a guy who can even forget the people he's killed himself."

A dense silence filled the room. Eventually, I heard the rustling of clothes and felt the shifting of the mattress. I figured Aki was standing up to leave the room.

But she didn't. I felt her hand reach around my back to my shoulder and squeeze me close. I froze with alarm as the left side of my body was pressed against her white tunic. Her gentle whisper hit my ear.

"I'm sorry, Kirigaya. I know I said that I would give you counseling, but I can't erase the weight on your shoulders, or bear it with you." She lifted her hand off my shoulder and ruffled my hair. "I've never played any VR game, much less Sword Art Online, of course…so I can't measure the weight of this 'killing' you're talking about. But…I do know this much. You did that— you had to do it—to save someone, didn't you?"

"Uh…"

Again, I hadn't expected that answer.

To save someone. Yes, that might have been part of the equation. But that didn't mean…

"In medicine, there are times when you have to choose lives. To abandon the baby to save the mother. To abandon the brain-dead to save those who are waiting for organ donors. When there are huge accidents or disasters, we have to set up a triage to determine the priority of patients. That doesn't mean that we can kill people if we have the right reason, of course. The weight of a life that's lost never changes, no matter the circumstances. But the people involved have the right to consider the lives of those who were saved. So do you. As long as you think about the ones you're saving, you have the right to be saved as well."

"The right...to be saved?" I repeated in a husky voice. I shook my head fiercely with Aki's hand still resting on it. "But...but, I *forgot* about the people I killed. I abandoned that weight...my responsibility to them. So I don't have the right to be saved..."

"If you really forgot about them, you wouldn't be agonizing like this now," she stated firmly. She put her hand on my cheek and forced my face in her direction. Beyond the rimless glasses, her sharp eyes were glowing.

When her neatly trimmed thumb brushed the outer corner of my eye, I realized that I had been crying.

"You *do* remember. When the time comes to remember, it all comes back. And when that happens, it *all* needs to come back, including the people you fought to protect and save."

Aki bumped her forehead against mine. The chilly contact seemed to quell the raging weight swirling around my head. I let my shoulders drop and eyelids close.

A few minutes later, with my bare midriff covered in sticky electrodes for the heart monitor, I laid back on the bed with the AmuSphere in my hands.

Fear and self-condemnation, a cold weight in my stomach that had plagued me since last night, felt distant now. But I was certain that if I ran into Death Gun again in the world of Gun Gale Online, it would rush back in moments.

The VR interface felt as heavy as cast iron in my hands as I slipped it over my head and turned it on. It made a soft ping to indicate it was out of standby. I turned to where Miss Aki stood on the other side of the monitoring equipment, and spoke.

"Thanks for watching over me. And also for…well, just thanks."

"Of course, dear," she said kindly, tossing a thin blanket over my body. I breathed in the clean, soapy scent and shut my eyes.

"I don't think you'll see anything until after eight o'clock…and I should be out by ten. Here goes… Link start!"

A dazzling rainbow array appeared before my eyes and swallowed me whole. Just before all of my senses were shut out entirely, I heard Nurse Aki's voice:

"Have a good time then, Kirito the Hero."

……What?

But in the next moment, my mind was ripped from reality and transported into a wasteland of sand and gunpowder.

8

"So irritating—"

Thunk.

"—that guy!"

Shino Asada seethed, kicking the steel support beam of the swing set with the toe of her sneaker. She was in a small playground fairly close to her apartment. The navy-blue sky above stretched over a single sandbox and two pieces of equipment; it was a lonely little place, especially without any children on a weekend as it was.

Next to Shino, Kyouji Shinkawa was sitting on one of the swings, his eyes wide.

"I-it's strange to hear you speaking so...forcefully."

"Well, I mean..."

She shoved her hands into the pockets of her denim skirt and leaned back against the sloped beam, pouting.

"He was such an arrogant, harassing, show-off loser...I mean, who goes into GGO just to fight with a *sword*?"

With each grumbled insult, she kicked a little pebble at her feet. "On top of that, he pretended to be a girl at first, and convinced me to guide him to the best shop and pick out his equipment for him! I almost lent him money, even! Ugh, and I even gave him my personal card...'Would you mind resigning,' indeed!"

She had to stop grousing when there were no more stones of the right size to kick. When she glanced over, Kyouji was staring at her with an odd expression, somewhere between surprise and concern.

"…What, Shinkawa?"

"Nothing… I've just never seen you talking about someone else like that…"

"Oh…really?"

"Yeah. Most of the time you don't seem to have any interest in other people, period."

"…"

Perhaps he was right. On any given day, she made no proactive effort to interact with others. When people came to contact her, such as Endou and her gang of bullies, Shino found it irritating, but didn't think anything more of it. She believed it would be a waste of her emotional energy.

In fact, Shino already had her hands full with her own problems, so she didn't spend any time worrying about others. And yet somehow, that one guy had gotten under her skin. Even now, over twenty-four hours after their first contact on Saturday afternoon, he ruled over a significant portion of her mind.

But that was only natural.

It had been half a year since Shino started playing the VRM-MORPG Gun Gale Online. But not a single player there had approached her as directly as he had. And that wasn't all. When he clutched her hand in his vulnerable state after the first round of the tournament, she was so shocked that she missed two easy shots at medium range in the second round.

"You might be surprised to learn that I get angry easily."

She stretched out a leg to scrape more pebbles into range so that she could kick them toward the planter.

"Oh…is that so?" Kyouji murmured, examining Shino. Eventually he thought of something and hopped up off the swing. "So…will you camp out in an open area and hunt him? If you want to snipe, I can be a decoy. But if it's for revenge, you'd probably prefer a direct battle. I can get us two or three good machine gunners. Or you could use a beam stunner to arrange an MPK..."

Shino blinked in surprise. She eventually raised her right hand to interrupt Kyouji's fanatical PK planning.

"Um...hang on, it's not like that. He's irritating, but he fights very honestly. I want to crush him in a fair fight. I might have lost yesterday...but now I know his style, and I'll get a chance for a rematch."

She pushed up the bridge of her noncorrective glasses and pulled her cell phone out of her skirt pocket to check the time.

"The BoB final starts in just three and a half hours. I'm going to blow a giant hole in that misleading avatar while everyone's watching."

She pointed a finger into the eastern sky. The red rising moon was right in her sights.

The preliminary tournament for the third Bullet of Bullets, GGO's championship tournament, began on the evening of December 13.

As Sinon, Shino had easily advanced through Block F until a supposed beginner appeared before her—and yet, despite "that man" being a beginner, it was a confrontation she felt had been inevitable, somewhere deep in her heart.

His name was Kirito. He was a player who had used the Seed platform's unique conversion function to transfer from an unfamiliar VRMMO over to GGO.

On her way through the city of SBC Glocken to the regent's office to enter the preliminary tourney, Sinon had run into Kirito the moment after his initial dive. When he had asked the location of a gear shop, she had rather surprisingly offered a personal tour, instead of her typical style—an unfriendly point in the right direction.

The only reason she did that was because she had thought Kirito was a girl.

From what she learned later, GGO's male avatars contained a

series called the M-9000s that on first glance looked like F-models instead. They were very rare, so many people who won them sold their entire accounts for huge sums. At any rate, Kirito's avatar was quite beautiful, with lustrous black hair, big eyes like the night sky, wintry smooth skin, and a delicate build. He looked much more feminine than Sinon's actually female avatar.

Through her six months of GGO, Sinon had never met a true female beginner to the game. She knew other women in the game, of course, but they were all veterans with more experience than she had. She'd traded more gunfire with them than words.

So when Sinon saw the lonely, confused girl—secretly a man—she remembered the girl she had been when she started, and she volunteered to act as a guide.

She had outfitted him with weapons and armor at a major shop, had taught him about bullet lines and other GGO features, and had even explained how the tournament worked at the regent's office. Then they had gone into the underground waiting area beneath the tower and had entered a changing room to put on their battle gear. Just at the moment Sinon had unequipped all of her gear except for underwear, Kirito finally, and extremely belatedly, revealed his name and gender.

In her shame and rage, Sinon had slapped him across the face and made an ultimatum: *Win your way through the prelims and face me. The last thing I will teach you is the taste of the bullet that spells your defeat.*

But at the time, she hadn't thought it would actually happen that way.

Kirito was a newbie who had just converted to GGO. For whatever reason, he didn't choose a rifle or machine gun for his main weapon, but the ultra-close-range lightsword.

But a sword couldn't possibly beat a gun, Sinon sensed. She had been on the verge of forgetting all about Kirito.

But somehow, he had kept his word to her. He had made his way through the sixty-four-player Block F from the first to fifth round with nothing but his lightsword and a small-caliber handgun, proceeding toward the block final against Sinon.

On the sunset highway that served as their stage, Sinon had witnessed Kirito's terrifying ability for herself. He had blocked her Ultima Ratio Hecate II's deadly .50-caliber bullet—an antimateriel sniper rifle round—with his narrow energy blade; he had cut the round in half, in fact.

Kirito had charged through the trajectories of the two halves of the bullet and pressed the blade of the lightsword to Sinon's throat.

"Would you mind resigning, then? I'd prefer not to slash a girl in two."

"~~~~!!"

Just remembering it brought the humiliation back as fresh as when it happened. She swung her fist down away from the direction of the moon. Shino looked around on the ground for more rocks to kick, but she'd already booted all of them toward the planter. She smacked the metal pole behind her with her heel instead.

"Just you wait. I'll pay you back twice over for this," she vowed. Kyouji stood up from the swing and examined her, an even more concerned look wrinkling his brows.

"…Wh-what?"

"Is everything…okay? That isn't going to, y'know…"

Kyouji looked down at her hand. She noticed that her clenched fist had the index and thumb extended to form the shape of a gun.

"Ah…"

She quickly straightened out her hand and shook it. Normally, the action would have recalled the image of a gun in her head and caused a panic attack. For some reason, that didn't happen this time.

"Uh, yeah. I guess…I was fine because I was so mad."

"Oh…"

Kyouji raised his head and looked Shino right in the eyes. He reached out and grabbed her right hand in both of his. She automatically looked down at his warm, slightly sweaty palms.

"Wh...what's this about, Shinkawa?"

"I'm just...worried. You're not acting like the usual you...If there's anything I can do to help, I want to do it. I can't do anything but cheer for you on the monitor tonight, but if there's anything else...just say the word..."

For just a moment, she glanced back at Kyouji. While his face was delicate and naïve, the eyes in the center of it burned with smoldering emotion.

"I...I don't know what you mean by the 'usual me,'" Shino mumbled. She couldn't even picture what her ordinary self was like.

Kyouji squeezed harder, the words tumbling out of his mouth. "You're always very cool and reserved...and in control, and never fazed by anything...You've suffered the same things I have, but you didn't stay home and refuse to go to school. You're strong; really strong. I've always admired that about you. You're...you're my ideal."

Alarmed by Kyouji's enthusiasm, Shino tried to pull back, but the solid metal support of the swing set blocked her way.

"B-but...I'm *not* strong. You know that. I have panic attacks just from looking at guns..."

"But Sinon doesn't." He took a half step closer. "Sinon uses an enormous gun without a problem...She's one of the greatest players in GGO. I think that's your *true* self, Asada. Someday, you'll be like that in real life. Which is why this worries me, when I see you raging and losing composure about this guy. I...I can help you..."

The problem is, Shinkawa, she thought to herself, looking away from him, *even I laughed and cried like a normal person years ago. I didn't turn the way I am now because I wanted to.*

Yes, it was Shino's deepest wish to be as strong as Sinon in real life. But that was only in the sense of overcoming her fear of guns. She didn't actually want to eliminate all of her emotions.

Maybe, deep down in her heart, she just wanted to talk and laugh with friends, like anyone else. Maybe that was why she felt such a strong connection to the unfamiliar girl who needed a helping hand in SBC Glocken, and was so angry when it turned out to be a man instead.

Kyouji's confession made her happy. But she couldn't help but feel that something was slightly out of focus within her heart.

What…what I really want is…

"Asada," came a sudden whisper in her ear. Shino's eyes went wide. She hadn't noticed that he had wrapped his arms around her and the steel pole behind her.

The empty park was almost completely dark now, but there were people passing in the street on the other side of the barren trees. Anyone who saw Shino and Kyouji in the park like this would assume they were young lovers.

She instantly, instinctively pushed Kyouji back.

"…"

He looked at her, hurt in his eyes. She came to her senses and apologized.

"I-I'm sorry. It's very nice of you to say these things…and I think you're the only person in this city who actually understands me and who I can share these things with. But…it's not like that for me, not yet. This is a problem that I have to overcome on my own…"

"…Oh…"

He slumped sadly, and guilt filled her breast.

Kyouji must have known about her past, and the incident that shaped her present. Before Kyouji had stopped attending school, Endou's group had informed the entire campus of Shino's background. It occurred to her that if Kyouji knew that and still opened himself up to her, she ought to accept his affection and return it. If he grew disheartened and left her…that would make her very lonely, indeed.

But for some reason, the face of Kirito crossed a corner of her mind. His extreme confidence. His utter belief in his own strength. She wanted to fight him and beat him, to wring out every last ounce of her own power in the process.

She wanted to break out of the thick dark shell of her terrible memories so that she could be free. That was all she wanted. And she would fight in the sunset wasteland and win for that sake.

"So…will you wait until then?" she asked timidly. Kyouji stared back at her with silent eyes swirling with emotion. Eventually, he nodded and smiled. He mouthed a word of thanks, and Shino smiled, too.

She left Kyouji at the entrance of the park and rushed home, stopping at a convenience store on the way for some mineral water and the aloe yogurt she would eat for dinner. Normally she cooked for herself, trying to keep her meals balanced, but for a variety of reasons, it wasn't a good idea to stuff herself before a long dive of three hours or more.

Shino trotted up the steps, plastic bags rustling, and entered her apartment. She impatiently relocked the electronic lock, crossed the kitchen, and headed for the back room, checking the clock on the wall.

There was still plenty of time before the BoB final at eight o'clock, but she wanted to log in soon so she could check her equipment and ammo, and get in plenty of meditation to focus her instincts.

She ripped off the denim skirt and cotton shirt she was wearing, placing them on hangers. She hurled her underwear top into the hamper in the corner and changed into a more comfortable tank top, a loose sweater, and short pants, shivering at the chill in the room.

Shino set the AC to a reasonable temperature and switched on the humidifier before leaning back onto the bed with a sigh. She grabbed the plastic bottle out of the grocery bag, twisted the cap and downed a small gulp of its cold water.

Through experience, she had learned that while the AmuSphere's sensory interruption feature shut out 99 percent of real stimuli, there were still things a user could do to maintain a comfortable dive for optimum game play. One needed to hold off on big meals and take care of the bathroom before the dive, of course, but also manage the temperature and humidity, and wear comfortable, loose clothing. She once drank a huge cup of freezing water in midsummer, and found herself afflicted with terrible stomach pain in the midst of battle. The AmuSphere picked up abnormal signals and engaged in an emergency extraction. Once she had settled her stomach and logged back in, her avatar had died in battle and spawned back in town.

Some wealthy, hardcore MMO gamers set up their own isolation tanks to completely remove all outside stimuli from their experience. The luxury net cafés equipped with relaxation facilities were already offering tanks as part of their service. Kyouji had even treated Shino to a visit to one of them last month.

They had their own private chambers where you logged in. It had its own shower, after which the user stripped naked and entered a capsule that took up half the room. The interior of the capsule was surprisingly spacious, and it was filled with about sixteen inches of a dense, slimy liquid.

Once she was lying down, her body floating in the liquid and her neck supported by the gel-based headrest, there was almost no skin sensation. She put on the AmuSphere connected to the wall and closed the heavy hatch. The interior of the tank was filled with dark silence.

In truth, just that experience alone was extremely fascinating to her, but she was supposed to be meeting up with Kyouji in GGO, so she had to log in to its VR space.

Upon diving, she was surprised to find that the VR signals she received *did* seem clearer than usual. Because there was an absolute minimum of bodily feedback going on, Kyouji claimed that the experience blocked out the signal noise that occasionally leaked through the interrupter. In any case, it was such a pristine experience Shino felt like she could even hear the fine scraping of enemy boots in the sand. Maybe it was worth its high cost, after all.

But at the same time, Shino felt an unease that she couldn't quite put into words.

Being completely removed from her real flesh made her worry about her body on the other side. Going inside a VR world carried a faint feeling of danger, knowing that one's actual body was a helpless rag doll at that moment—and the tank only amplified that sensation.

Compared to the NerveGear, the "tool of the devil," the Amu-Sphere was almost absurdly safe. That the isolation tank method had any effect at all was a result of the AmuSphere disallowing real-world signals to dampen at a full 100 percent. It was built with safety systems that could easily pull the user back to reality if a level of light, sound, or vibration was reached.

Still, a diver's body was defenseless. It wasn't far off from being asleep, but when Shino was in the isolation tank, she couldn't shake the prickling fear in the back of her neck. In the end, she decided that even if the signal noise was higher, the best place to dive was in her own room, the place where she felt safest in the world.

The spoon dipped repeatedly into the yogurt while her mind mulled over these concepts, until she realized the carton was empty. She washed it out in the sink and tossed the container in the recycling bin. After a quick teeth brushing, she washed her hands and face and returned to her room.

"Here we go!"

She smacked her cheeks and rolled onto the bed. Her cell phone was set to blink-only mode, she'd locked the door and windows, and she'd already finished Monday's homework earlier in the day. She was ready to purge all thoughts of her real life from her brain.

Her AmuSphere was on and the lights were dimmed. The faces of the players she would defeat flashed against the darkened ceiling before disappearing.

The last one to appear was the lightsword user with the shiny black hair and red lips: Kirito. He had a handgun on his left side and a photon sword on his right, and a cocky smirk on his face as he stared at her.

The flame of competition grew within Shino. This had to be the ultimate foe, the one whom she crawled the deadly wasteland to find. The one who would grant her the power to destroy that awful past—in a way, the one who was her final hope.

She would fight with all of her being. And she would crush him.

A deep breath in, then out. Shino shut her eyes. When she said the phrase that shifted her soul into gear, her voice was stronger and clearer than ever.

"Link start!!"

The gravity that tugged her body downward disappeared, replaced by a floating sensation. Next the world rotated forward ninety degrees so that she was no longer lying down. Like descending from a soft slide, her toes touched down on hard floor. Sinon waited for all of her senses to adjust before opening her eyelids.

The first thing she saw was an enormous neon holo-sign floating under a starless night sky. The crimson letters read BULLET OF BULLETS 3, burning down through the gaps between buildings.

She was in the square before the regent's office, at the north end of the main street that ran through the center of Glocken. It was normally a rather secluded area, but players were packed cheek by jowl today, carrying on with food and drink. This was only natural, as, thanks to the excitement around the BoB, a majority of the currency in GGO was actively being wagered on the tournament results.

The oddsmaker, with his flashy holo-window displaying the current odds (who was, surprisingly, not a player but an official system-controlled NPC), and the shady information venders selling hot tips were both swarmed with eager visitors. She wandered over to the NPC bookie and checked out the window to see that her own odds were quite low. That defeat in the preliminary final yesterday must have done it. But when she looked for Kirito's name, he was also considered quite a long shot.

She snorted and wondered if she should place all of her money on herself, then changed her mind when she realized that this would tarnish the purity of her goal. She left the crowd. Naturally, people recognized her as a regular BoB finalist, so the stares followed her as she went. No one bothered to approach her, however. Sinon was known as a wildcat girl, someone who would mercilessly rip anyone to shreds once she'd identified them as a foe.

She started toward the regent's office, planning to get into the waiting dome early and hone her mind, when a voice called out to her from behind.

"Sinon!"

There was only one player in GGO who dared to address her this way. Just as she expected, when she turned around she saw Spiegel, the avatar of Kyouji Shinkawa, whom she'd just left minutes ago in the real world, waving and racing up to her. His tall male avatar, clad top to bottom in urban camo, was red-faced with excitement.

"Took you long enough, Sinon. I was worried. Is...something up?" he asked, noting the faint smile on her face.

"No, nothing. Just thinking, it's weird to run into someone here that you just saw in real life less than an hour ago."

"Yeah, sure...I'm not as cool as this in real life. More important, how's your plan coming along? Got any good strategies?"

"Strategies? Nothing aside from doing my best...It'll probably just end up being a cycle of searching, sniping, and moving."

"Ah, good point. But still...I believe that you'll win."

"Uh, thanks. What are you going to do now?"

"Hmm...I figure I'll watch the match from a pub nearby..."

"Then after it's done, you can buy me a round there in celebration or commiseration," she said with another weak grin. Spiegel looked down for a brief moment. Suddenly, he grabbed her arm and dragged her away to the corner of the plaza. Just when they were out of sight of all the other players, Spiegel faced her in a huff, his face desperate. She blinked.

"Sinon...I mean, Asada."

She was stunned. He'd been playing MMOs long enough to know what a taboo it was to refer to a player by their real name.

"Wh...what?"

"Can I trust what you said earlier?"

"'Earlier' meaning...?"

"You said to wait, didn't you? If you manage to confirm your own strength, will you...y'know..."

"Wh-what are you asking?!"

She felt her cheeks growing hot, and buried her face in her muffler. But Spiegel took another step forward and clutched Sinon's wrist again.

"I...I really mean it when I say that I lo—"

"Stop it, not now," she said, firmly this time, and shook her head. "I want to focus on the tournament. This isn't a battle I can win unless I wring out every last ounce of strength I have..."

"...Oh. Good point." His hand pulled away. "But I believe in you. And I'll be waiting."

"Th-thanks. Well...I should be getting ready now. Bye."

She pulled away, thinking that if she spent any more time around him, that confusion would carry over into the event.

"Good luck. I'm rooting for you," he returned fervently. She smiled awkwardly and turned away, leaving the shadow of the building and hurrying over to the entrance of the regent's office. All the way, she felt his gaze burning into her back.

Only when she passed through the glass doors and into the suddenly empty, quiet interior did she finally feel the tension leave. She leaned back against a large stone pillar and wondered if she'd been leading him on too much.

She did like Kyouji, she thought. But she was too busy handling her own matters for now.

Due to the accident that took his life, Shino had no memories of her late father. The most memorable male face inside her mind was the culprit of the post office shooting from five years ago that still caused her to go into panic attacks when she relived it. Those lightless eyes so like bottomless swamps lurked everywhere in the darkness around, watching her.

She was like any other girl—she wanted to have a boyfriend that she could talk to on the phone every night and visit on the weekends. But if she went out with Kyouji, she might one day find *those eyes* within him. That terrified her.

What if it wasn't just guns that triggered her panic attacks? What if she started feeling fear of men in general? That would make it almost impossible for her to live, period.

She had to fight. That was all she could do for now.

Sinon strode across the entrance hall to the elevators, her boots smacking against the floor. But once again, someone called out to her. Not Spiegel's smooth baritone, but a cool, husky voice that called her name. She closed her eyes.

When she reluctantly turned around, she saw the hated man himself.

9

I touched down on a street corner close to the regent's tower at the north end of SBC Glocken, the hub city of GGO.

Crowded neon holo-signs floated against a backdrop of the gloomy sunset sky. Most of them were advertisements for real companies; in ALO, such advertising tie-ins would be protested for ruining the immersion of the world, but in the setting of a ruined, futuristic city, it seemed oddly appropriate. But most visible of all the neon signs was the one for the Bullet of Bullets final, which was just about to start. The instant I saw the thick red font, a shiver ran through my body. I told myself that it was a shiver of excitement, not fear.

With a puff of breath, I faced forward and unconsciously pushed the long hair resting on my shoulders toward my back. When I was finished, I realized what I'd done and felt disappointed, then chalked it up to growing familiarity with my new avatar.

I figured I would get registered for the final first, and headed for the regent's office. It wasn't long before I attracted stares from both sides of the main street. I only barely resisted the urge to glare back.

They weren't trying to intimidate me. The avatar I inhabited now looked just like a girl—a very pretty one, in fact. If I were in their position, I'd be staring, too.

You'd figure that a few of them would extend past staring and call out to me, too, but as I approached, the men scurried away to keep their distance. I thought I knew why—stories must have spread about my berserker nature after the mad charging strategy I used against my opponents in the prelims.

Only the names and prior tournament appearances were made public in the contestant listings, not gender. Kirito could be taken for male or female. If I had to guess, my reputation in GGO was "the psycho-killer girl who went out of her way to use a blade, rather than a gun."

I wasn't taken with that categorization myself, but it would be helpful if it meant that some of the other contestants in the upcoming final avoided me during the fight. I wasn't trying to win—I just wanted to make contact with Death Gun again, the man in the tattered cloak.

There was no "Death Gun" among the thirty finalists. But he had to be there. If his goal was to display his strength within GGO, there wasn't a better chance to do that than the Bullet of Bullets. All eyes would be trained on it. Death Gun's real name—or at least, his character name—had to be something different.

I needed to find out that name, speak with him again during the tournament, and figure out what his SAO name was. From there, I could gain his real name, via Seijirou Kikuoka, who had access to the confidential player account data from SAO. Once we had his real name, we'd be able to tell if he killed Zexceed and Usujio Tarako—if he was *able* to, that is.

But in the process, I'd have to face my own sin again.

The fear hadn't left me. But it was a necessary emotion. I had to make sure I didn't choose the escape route of forgetting again.

I strode down the street with clenched fists, my assault boots clacking against the pavement. The enormous tower of the regent's office was up ahead.

In ALO, and even in SAO, I fell prey to the excitement of a good

PvP tournament. To think that I'd enter into one with nothing but dread...

I snorted at my own timidity and headed up the long stairs toward the tower. Just outside the glass doors of the entrance, I spotted a familiar sand-colored muffler waving like the tail of a cat.

I didn't need to see the pale blue hair or the legs extending from the hem of her jacket to know that it was Sinon the sniper, my opponent in yesterday's preliminary block final. She was the only person I knew in GGO, but I wasn't sure if I should approach her or not.

After all, when I got lost right off the bat upon logging in to GGO for the first time yesterday, I brazenly asked the bystander Sinon for help, chose not to correct her obvious assumption that I was a girl like her, acted like a newbie girl to elicit all kinds of advice and explanation about the game's systems and what equipment to buy, then took a trip into the changing room to get a solid look at her underwear.

And that wasn't even everything.

After an unexpected encounter with Death Gun himself in the middle of the preliminary round, I was stunned by the revelation that he was a fellow SAO survivor, and a member of the killer guild Laughing Coffin. In my shock, I abandoned the final round against Sinon. As soon as the battle started, I simply walked forward without a strategy, ready to receive her fatal shot so I could lose on purpose.

But Sinon didn't shoot me.

She shot six rounds of pale, burning fury, all of which missed me. When she abandoned her advantage and came face-to-face with me, she screamed, "Screw you, die on your own time. Don't get me involved in your view; that this is just a game, just a single match."

Those words tore deep, deep into my chest.

Much, much earlier, I'd spoken very similar words to someone else.

It was nearly four years ago. Just as I started my second year of middle school, to my incredible fortune (or misfortune) I was selected to join the Sword Art Online closed beta test. At the end of each school day, I plunged into the still-free world of Aincrad until the next morning.

At the time, I was a Kirito with an almost embarrassingly typical hero look, and I made a bit of a name for myself by placing highly in PvP events. Because I was even feebler at personal skills back then, I didn't have any real friends. One of the few who I thought I might one day be friends with was a person I saw often in duel tournaments, a swordsman with plain brown hair.

He possessed both a logical mind and an innate talent for swordsmanship. I secretly hoped that I might cross swords with him at an event, and when that moment finally came, I was in for a shock. At the very end of a pitched battle, he intentionally chose to take an attack that I knew he could avoid. I suspected that he threw the match for the sake of a huge payday from the oddsmakers running the market, and I confronted him about it—using the same words that Sinon said to me just yesterday.

It was the pain of being shamed by myself from four years ago, and I immediately apologized to Sinon. Though we faced off in a classic duel to settle the fight, I was sure that Sinon had to be unhappy about the result. She was a sniper, and her strength lay in firing an unstoppable single round from long distance. No doubt she was burning with the desire to place that bullet between my eyes in tonight's final competition.

Thanks to the above complications—almost entirely my own fault—I wasn't sure if I should approach Sinon, even though she was just a few feet away. After a few seconds, I made up my mind and raced up the stairs to greet her.

"Hey, Sinon. Good luck today."

The tail of the muffler came to a stop and the blue hair seemed to arch just like a cat's. The sniper girl spun around on her right heel with a tremendous glare on her face. She snorted, "What do you mean, *good luck*?"

The dangerous glint in her dark blue eyes told me immediately that this was a mistake, but I had a reason to talk to her. I had to choose my words carefully so that she didn't shut the door in my face before I could get to that point.

With my best serious face, I said, "I just mean, let's both do our best and see what happens."

"You're shameless."

Right off the bat, I was not doing good. I soldiered onward.

"Anyway, you're sure diving in early. We've got three hours until the event."

"Gee, I wonder whose fault it was that I nearly failed to register on time yesterday," she shot back, turning away even as she shot me a sidelong glare. A cold sweat broke out on my face. "And besides, you're here early, too. Don't act like I'm some kind of loser with nothing better to do."

"Sh-shall we find a meaningful use of our time? While we're waiting for the event to start, maybe we could get some tea…er, trade some intel…"

I could never say this to her in the real world. In fact, given that I had Asuna, I shouldn't even be saying it in the virtual world. But this was, cross my heart, hope to die, not a VR come-on, but a necessary step for not just my own duty and fate, but Sinon's safety as well.

Naturally, Sinon couldn't have known all of this, but after several seconds of a very probing look, she snorted and made the smallest of nods.

"Fine. It'll probably end up with me giving you all the advice again, anyway."

"Th-that's not my plan…Well, not entirely," I mumbled, hurrying after Sinon as she strode away.

After we concluded our tournament check-in process at the ground floor terminal with plenty of time to spare, Sinon took me to a large tavern zone on the first-basement level of the tower. The gamma levels were so low that the faces of the players milling at the countless tables were nearly indistinguishable. The only light in the room came from the large panel monitors hanging from the ceiling, spitting out bright, primary colors.

Sinon slid into a booth in the back and examined the metal menu placard, eventually pushing a small button on the side corresponding to an iced coffee. A hole opened in the center of the metal table, and a glass filled with a black liquid emerged. It certainly wasn't as warm and friendly as the Aincrad system, where NPC waiters took orders and brought the food themselves, but it suited GGO's general atmosphere better.

I pressed the button for a ginger ale and downed half of the glass in one go when it appeared. Once the virtual carbonation stopped tickling my throat, I initiated the conversation.

"Tell me if I have the battle royale straight: Thirty players are placed randomly on the same map and open fire once they find each other, until the last remaining survivor is crowned the winner?"

Sinon glared at me over her coffee glass and said, "I knew you were just trying to get me to explain things to you. All of these details are laid out in the e-mail the developers sent to the contestants."

"Y-yeah, I read it, but…"

In truth, I skimmed through it once, intending to read it in detail once I was in the game. But when I saw Sinon the veteran right in front of me, it seemed that asking her in person would be quicker…not that she wanted to hear it. I coughed uncomfortably.

"I was just hoping that you might, um, confirm my understanding…"

"It's all in how you say it," she noted in an exceedingly chilly voice that froze my spine. Fortunately for me, she was nice enough to launch into a quick explanation of the rules once she'd returned her glass to the tabletop. "Basically, as you said, it's a battle between thirty finalists on the same map. The starting locations are random, but you're guaranteed to be at least a kilometer away from any other player, so you don't have to worry about spawning right in front of someone."

"A k-kilometer? So the map must be pretty huge, then," I interrupted. Her blue lasers cut me off.

"Did you really read the message? It says right at the very top. The battle takes place on a circular map ten kilometers across. It's a composite stage with mountains, forests, and valleys, so there's no overall advantage or disadvantage to any one loadout or character build."

"Ten kilometers?! That's huge…"

It was the same size as the first floor of Aincrad. In other words, an area that ten thousand people were able to comfortably inhabit and hunt in was now the exclusive domain of just thirty, spaced entirely apart.

"Will we…even find each other? What if the entire event passes without anyone seeing anyone else?"

"First of all, it's a shooting game—you need that much space. A sniper rifle's range is close to a kilometer, and an assault rifle can hit a target nearly half that distance. If you had thirty people in a tiny map, they'd start firing the moment it started, and half the group would be dead in moments."

"Ahh, good point…"

She continued her patient explanation. Behind the gruff posturing, it seemed like there really was a helpful, considerate girl—one who would be furious if I ever let on that I was realizing this. I shut up and listened.

"But as you say, there's no point if nobody manages to make contact. On the other hand, someone's going to get the idea to hide until the very end, right? So all of the contestants are given an item called a Satellite Scan terminal."

"Like…a spy satellite?"

"Yes. An observational satellite passes overhead every fifteen minutes. At that point, it sends locational data on all players to all of the terminals. If you touch the blip on the map, you can even see their names."

"Hmm… So you only get fifteen minutes at best to camp out in any one location. Once your location is shown to the others, they could sneak up on you anytime."

"Exactly," Sinon nodded.

I grinned and asked, "But doesn't that rule hurt a sniper? Isn't it your job to hide in the bushes like a potato with your rifle held still?"

"Enough about potatoes," she snapped, tossing navy-blue sparks in my direction before snorting confidently. "Fifteen minutes is more than enough time to fire a shot and kill a target, then move a kilometer."

"Oh…I see."

I took her word for it. Anyone trying to use the satellite data to ambush Sinon would end up sniped from long distance anyway. I committed that warning to memory and cleared my throat, hoping to sum up everything I'd learned.

"So basically, once the match starts you stay on the move, spotting enemies and trying to stay alive until you're the last one standing…right? And every fifteen minutes, each player learns the locations of everyone else on their map. Which means that you also know who's still alive at the time. Is that correct?"

"Essentially, yes." Sinon downed the rest of her iced coffee and set it down on the table with a high-pitched clank. She got to her feet. "Well, that's all. The next time I see you, I'll be pulling the trigger without—"

"Hey, hang on! I'm just getting to the point," I yelped, reaching out to pull on Sinon's sleeve in a gesture that reminded me of a certain government official I knew.

"…There's more?"

She shot me the dirtiest glance and checked the military watch on her wrist, but I was too close to back down now. Sinon sighed heavily and sat down again. She put her elbows on the table, rested her chin on her folded hands, and prompted me to continue with her eyebrows.

"W-well, um…this might be an odd question, but," I prefaced, waving my left hand to bring up the menu window. All VRM-MOs built on the Seed's engine shared nearly identical menu systems, so I knew exactly how to make my window's contents visible to her.

After flipping through a few tabs, I showed her the message from the devs containing the list of names of all thirty finalists for the BoB. Around the middle was *Kirito*, first-place finisher in Block F, and *Sinon*, second-place in Block F.

Sinon looked at my window. The bridge of her nose wrinkled up like a cat's—a jaguar's, if anything.

"What is this? Are you bragging to me again about the results of yesterday's prelims?" she hissed.

I took a deep breath and shook my head, trying to sound as grave as possible. "No, absolutely not."

She sensed the change in my attitude and squinted with her shapely brows. "Then…why are you showing this to me?"

"Are there a few names on this list that you don't recognize?"

"Huh…?" She glared at me with open suspicion. I ran a finger down the short list.

"Please, tell me. This is important."

"…Oh, all right…"

Sinon looked down at the purple holo-window floating over the table, though she was still clearly suspicious. Her navy-blue eyes flicked right and left.

"Let's see, this is the third BoB, so I would recognize most of these people. The ones that I don't recognize, aside from a certain cocky lightswordsman…are three."

"Three. Which names?"

"Hmm… There's Musketeer X, Pale Rider, and…I think that's supposed to be 'Steven'?" Sinon read awkwardly. I checked the names for myself. "Musketeer X" was displayed in kanji, while the other two names were in the Western alphabet. I closed my eyes and repeated the three names to myself.

Sinon turned to me with equal parts suspicion and irritation. "So what's your point? You keep asking me these questions, but you're not explaining what's going on."

"Yeah...um..."

I let the moment drag out, thinking frantically. She had singled out three names...

One of them, if my hunch was correct, was the character name for Death Gun—the reason that I was here, a survivor of SAO and former member of Laughing Coffin, related to two unexplained deaths.

This suspicion stemmed from the fact that Death Gun must have taken considerable care to hide his true identity. He probably wanted to go with "Death Gun" for a character name, except that it would open him up to all kinds of spam messages, and he would have gotten involved in trouble during the preliminaries. On the other hand, if his actual character handle was spread around, it would dim the "Death Gun" image he'd gone to so much trouble to build. Instead, he'd kept his identity a secret from everyone. It was no wonder Sinon didn't know it.

The problem was, which of the three was Death Gun?

A white hand passed through my view as I pondered. The nail of the index finger tapped on the tabletop. I looked up to see Sinon glaring at me through narrowed eyes.

"...I'm really getting mad now. What's going on? Is this an elaborate setup to irritate me and get me off my game in the battle?"

"No...no, it's not that..."

I bit my lip in the face of that ultrahot stare. I wasn't sure if I should explain everything or not. In the world of GGO, most people knew the rumors that there was a player calling himself Death Gun who performed public shootings in crowded places, and the people who were shot hadn't logged in since. However, very few of them seemed to actually believe that he'd really killed them. Sinon was in the majority on that one.

In truth, I wasn't completely convinced, either. In my recent conversation with Kikuoka, we determined that no matter what logic was used, killing a player in real life with virtual bullets was absolutely impossible.

But at the same time, I couldn't just laugh off Death Gun's power. If he was indeed a central member of Laughing Coffin, that made him a homicidal player who had actively conspired and acted to end the lives of multiple people in Aincrad. I couldn't discount the possibility that someone with such an extreme background could find some logic that transcended the common sense that Kikuoka and I followed.

If I confessed everything that I knew to Sinon, told her that Death Gun's power might be real, that she might die if he shot her, and that she should cancel her appearance in the final, would she accept my word for it? Absolutely not. I thought of the desperation in her face yesterday, when we were racing against the clock to get to the entry desk in time after she helped me with shopping. She had to have her own very serious reason for competing in this tournament...

The dark blue eyes stared holes in me as my silence continued—but eventually, they softened. Her thin-colored lips barely moved as she spoke.

"...Does this have something to do with the sudden change that came over you during the prelims?"

"Huh...?"

I looked up, straight into Sinon's eyes, lost for words. Within seconds, I forgot all the logic and calculations running through my head, and simply nodded. The words were whispering out of my throat before I knew it.

"...Yeah... That's right. I was greeted out of the blue in the waiting dome by someone who played the same VRMMO as me, years ago... I'm sure he's going to be in tonight's match. One of the three names left has to be his..."

"Was it a friend?" Sinon asked.

I shook my head violently, hair spinning. "No. Just the opposite—an enemy. I'm pretty certain that we tried to kill each other once. And yet...I can't even remember his original name.

I have to remember. I need to make contact again during the battle…and find out why he's here, what he's doing…"

At that point I realized that Sinon was not going to understand anything I was saying. In a normal VRMMO, even rivals in competing guilds were still comrades in a way, fellow enthusiasts of the same game. Calling him an "enemy" was a bit dramatic.

But the blue-haired sniper didn't laugh at me, or do anything other than widen her eyes a bit. She spoke with the bare minimum of vocalization, just loud enough for the system to recognize it as speech. "Enemy…tried to kill…each other…"

She continued by asking me a question that shot deep into my mind, despite the same nearly silent volume. "Do you mean… your play styles didn't match? Or you had a falling out in your party, that kind of in-game thing? Or was it—"

I interrupted, shaking my head. "No. An actual fight to the death, with both of our lives on the line. He…his group did something unforgivable. Peace and understanding weren't an option. We had to settle it with the sword. I don't regret that part. But…"

I knew that the more I revealed, the less Sinon would believe me, but I couldn't stop. I clutched my hands together on the table, stared into those navy-blue eyes across from me, and urged the words out of my choking throat.

"But…I've tried to hide from the responsibility I bear. I haven't been thinking of the meaning of my actions. I've been trying to forget them. So escape is no longer an option. This time, I have to face it head-on."

These words were meant for myself. Sinon couldn't have understood. I shut my mouth, and she looked down. No doubt she was cursing herself inwardly for getting involved with such a head case.

"Sorry for being weird. Forget about it. Basically, it's an old score," I summed up, trying to put on a wry smile. But Sinon interrupted.

"'If that bullet could actually kill a player in real life, could you still pull the trigger?'"

"...!"

I sucked in a sharp breath. She'd just quoted an emotional question I'd posed to her in the final battle of the preliminary tournament block last night. Even now, I didn't know why I asked her that. I'd shot that question back to her when she asked me how I'd gotten my strength.

An attack in a virtual game that could kill a real-life player. Common sense said this was impossible—it was why no one really believed the rumors about Death Gun. There was only one world where that statement was true, and it didn't exist anymore.

I held my silence as Sinon stared into me with her sharp eyes. Her mouth finally opened. "Are you saying, Kirito...that you were in *that* game...?"

The question, barely more than a breath, melted into the dry air of the tavern. Her navy-blue eyes wavered and looked down, and she shook her head. "I'm sorry, I shouldn't have asked."

"...No, it's okay," I responded to her surprising apology. A hard, uncomfortable silence settled between us as we maintained eye contact.

I hadn't planned to reveal my background as a Sword Art Online survivor to Sinon. But she would never understand what I was talking about earlier if I didn't explain that part.

Sinon understood what I meant now. When I said the word "enemy." When I spoke of a "battle to the death."

I waited for her eyes to fill with fear and loathing. But...

Sinon never looked away, and didn't stand up to leave. Instead, she leaned over a bit and stared right into me. Those sapphire eyes were filled with something. Was she...seeking help from me, or was my mind playing tricks on me?

The next moment, she squeezed her eyes tight. Her lips trembled, and she bit them hard. Before I could even marvel at this change, her tension loosened. The sniper girl let out a long breath, then smiled wanly.

She whispered, "We ought to move over to the dome. We're going to run out of time for checking gear and warming up."

"Uh…yeah, good idea," I agreed, and stood up after her. According to the simple digital watch on my wrist, it was nearly seven o'clock already. There was only an hour left until the event began.

Sinon pressed the DOWN button on the unremarkable elevator in the corner of the massive tavern. The mesh door creaked open, revealing a metal box. We filed inside, and I pressed the bottom button.

As we stood in the cramped elevator, surrounded by metallic sounds and a virtual dropping sensation, Sinon mumbled, "I understand that you have your own baggage."

I sensed her take a step closer to my backside. Something poked me in the center of my back. Not a gun barrel—but a finger.

A little bit louder, she said, "But our agreement is a separate matter. I'll get you back for what happened yesterday. You're not allowed to get shot by anyone else."

"…Understood," I agreed.

My greatest reason for diving into GGO was to contact Death Gun and solve a mystery. Not only was I hired by Seijirou Kikuoka for the job, it was now personal to me. So thinking rationally, I knew it was in my best interest to avoid the dangerous sniper Sinon and prioritize my primary goal.

But in coming here, meeting, and fighting with her, I'd forged a new personal connection. I couldn't just ignore that now. No matter which virtual world I was in, "Kirito" always had to be a swordsman. Even if that sword happened to be made of light without substance.

"…I'll survive until I run across you again," I announced. The fingertip left my back.

"Thanks."

Before I could ask what she meant by this, the elevator came to a violent halt. The door opened onto a darkness that surrounded me with the odor of steel and gunpowder—the smell of battle.

10

A long, slow breath in. Once the virtual lungs were full of cold air, they expelled it at the same slow pace.

With each relaxed breath and the rhythm of the heartbeat, the green bullet circle expanded and contracted in time.

Within the rifle scope, a single player moved through the brush in a low crouch. In his hands was a compact Jati SMG. While no sidearm could be seen, his entire body seemed to be oddly rough and bulging. He probably kept the weapon weight to a minimum and decided on a high-powered, anti-optical defense field, plus effective live-ammo composite armor to fill out his weight limit. The thick helmet with custom face guard made him look just like a giant boar. His name was Shishigane, a Vitality-first defensive player; he had appeared in the last tournament, but she'd never faced him.

At nearly twelve-hundred-meter range, even her super-powered Ultima Ratio Hecate II would have difficulty breaking through that armor to deliver a fatal shot. Landing two hits would do the trick, but he was no rookie. As soon as she shot him, he would find cover to hide behind, and she wouldn't see him again anytime soon after that. And if she waited around for him to emerge, other players would wander over to investigate the sound of her first shot, and she'd be pumped full of machine gun bullets.

Sinon was on her stomach between a large boulder and some shrubbery, finger on the trigger. She delivered a silent challenge: *Come on out.*

If her target came within eight hundred meters, she knew for a fact that she could hit him on the face, where his armor was weak and the damage modifier was much higher. She'd knock him clean out of the stage.

But her telepathic message didn't reach him. He moved in a different direction and steadily distanced himself from her. Even his back was fully armored—there was no weakness to exploit. She'd have to give up on him and wait for the next target to approach. Just before she took her eye off the scope, Sinon noticed something round hanging from the man's right hip.

A large plasma grenade. Two of them, in fact. Possibly a good-luck charm in lieu of a sidearm. It would be a handy weapon in a short-range battle with plenty of cover, but in this game, every cheap but effective item had its risks. Sinon felt the tension return, and she squinted into the scope.

She moved the pointer slightly down and to the right from the man's back. The reticle caught the waving, metallic orbs.

Breathe in. Breathe out. Breathe in—hold it.

All of her distractions disappeared. The moment the metal in her arms became a part of her, the bullet circle shrank abruptly to a pinpoint of light. Her finger pulled the trigger without her thinking about it.

A shock stung her body. For an instant, the muzzle flash turned her vision white. Her eyesight recovered at once, and through the scope, she saw one of the grenades on the man's waist explode. Sinon pulled her head away from the gun.

"Bingo."

A brilliant blue fireball erupted from the center of a distant hill, flattening the brush around it. After a few seconds, a blast like thunder reached her ears. She didn't need to check to know that the man's HP was entirely gone.

Sinon was already on her feet, bipod folded up and Hecate over her back. The few minutes after a shot were the most dangerous to a sniper, given the revealing nature of the gun's tremendous sound and exhaust flare. She checked left and right and took off running down the route she'd chosen ahead of time.

There was thick brush around her that made visibility difficult. She told herself that any nearby foes would be more distracted by the boar-man's explosion than her gunshot, and the possibility of a sneak attack was very low, but she didn't slow down either way. After more than a minute of sprinting, she finally reached the roots of a massive, dead tree and stopped for a breather. When she looked up, she saw a blood-red sun passing through a gap in the heavy clouds.

Nearly thirty minutes had gone by since the start of the Bullet of Bullets final match.

The boar-man was the second of Sinon's sniping victims so far. But the total number of survivors at this point was unknown until the satellite data updated every fifteen minutes. She pulled the thin Satellite Scan terminal out of her waist pouch, brought up the map indicator, and waited for the locational update.

When the chronograph on her left wrist showed the real-life time as 8:30, a number of blips appeared on the finely detailed map. There were twenty-one in all, which meant nine had been eliminated already. She stared closely at the map, hammering the details into her brain.

The special stage for the final was a circular island about ten kilometers across. The north side was desert, while the south was forests and mountains. Sitting in the center was the ruin of a large city. Sinon was presently at the foot of a rocky mountain looming over the very southern end of the map. A large river ran to the north of her, cutting between the mountainous region and the forests.

There were three dots within a kilometer of her. She touched each one to check their names. The closest was Dyne, about 600 meters northeast, moving westward. Following slightly from the east of him was Pale Rider. And blinking quietly nearly the peak of the mountain 800 meters to the south was Lion King Richie.

Richie was a high-firepower type with a Vickers heavy machine gun. He'd found the highest point on the map, and was going to stake out that point and clean out anyone who came after him. He had tried the same strategy last time and ended up dying because he ran out of ammo—a very lame ending. He probably had some trick up his sleeve this time, though. At any rate, she could ignore an enemy who refused to move.

The problem was Dyne, who seemed to be fleeing at top speed, according to the movement rate of the dot, and the pursuing Pale Rider. Dyne was the leader of the squadron that Sinon had recently been active with, and a veteran soldier who'd placed in the final of all three BoBs so far. With his excellent SIG SG 550 assault rifle, he was a master of midrange combat. She didn't respect him much as a person, but he couldn't be discounted in battle.

Meanwhile, this Pale Rider who had Dyne running like a timid mouse was someone Sinon had never fought, much less seen in person. Was he really that good, or did he have an advantage based on terrain or equipment? At that moment, the aerial satellite passed out of range, and the dots on the map began to blink. In another ten seconds, the information would be gone.

Sinon instinctually lifted her right hand and started to tap on the other eighteen, more distant blips, one after the other. But just before her finger brushed the screen, she clenched the hand into a fist—she realized that she'd been about to search for one name in particular.

"…Forget him," she muttered. She had no obligation to be worried about the present fate of Kirito the Despicable Lightswordsman. All that mattered was the prey within her Hecate's range. If Kirito appeared in her sights, she would aim, fire, and destroy him without emotion. That was all.

The blinking lights turned off. Sinon returned the terminal to her pouch and stood up, taking note of the surroundings. On the other side of the gentle hill facing her was a thick forest. Dyne and Pale Rider were making their way through from her right-hand side to the left. In the direction they headed was the great river that split the map, and a bridge spanning it. Cautious Dyne probably preferred the open, clear views from the bridge as a setting to fight Pale Rider to the risky and unpredictable forest.

Sinon was closer to the bridge than they were. If she ran now, she could set up in sniping position before they got there. She would observe their battle and take out the winner in the moment that he let his guard down.

She shouldered the Hecate, crouched down, and dashed again through the brush.

When Sinon made it through the reddened hillside and leaped under the last bush at the edge of the zone, she was met with a red ribbon of reflected light.

It was the river. It flowed from the southern mountains, winding its way through the center of the map to the north, and vanished in the distant ruined city. On the far bank was a forest of massive, ancient trees. A narrow, stone-lined path could be seen twisting away beneath the thick branches. The path hit the river just 200 meters to the north of where Sinon hunched, forming one end of a crude metal bridge. The two players should be racing at full speed down that path toward the bridge.

Just at that moment, a figure burst out of the shadow of an especially large tree at the forest's edge, very close to the bridge. She hurried to place the Hecate on the ground, impatiently flipped up the scope's cover, and peered through it.

Woodland camo, top and bottom. Square chin beneath the helmet. SIG in his hands. It was Dyne. He raced down the stone path with smooth, veteran form. Within a few seconds of leaving the forest, he was on the rusted bridge. Just as he was finished crossing the fifty-meter bridge to the riverbank where Sinon hid, he threw himself to the ground and took up a firing position.

"I see what you're doing," Sinon noted, impressed. He was well situated to blaze down any target who tried crossing the bridge.

On the other hand, his sides were defenseless. His back was wide open to anyone on this side of the bridge.

"Check your six at all times, Dyne," Sinon muttered into the scope, catching the side of his face in her reticle. She could just shoot him now without waiting for the end of his fight with Pale Rider. Although her shot would alert the other player to her presence, he'd have to cross the bridge to attack her. It was only 200 meters to the bridge, so even were he to run at full speed, she knew she could hit him.

I'd feel bad for the audience watching on the screen, she added silently, tracing the Hecate's trigger.

Suddenly, Sinon felt a cold shiver run down the back of her neck. Someone was right behind her.

You idiot! You were so wrapped up in your own chance to snipe that you neglected to check your own back! she mentally screamed at herself, taking her hand off the Hecate. She sprang 180 degrees and pulled her MP7 sidearm over. Even in the process of that smooth movement, her brain was working. *But nobody can be here. When I checked the Satellite Scanner a few minutes ago, the only person behind me was Lion King Richie. He wouldn't leave the peak of the mountain, and I couldn't have missed his approach with that heavy machine gun.*

On the other hand, no one aside from Richie could have snuck up on me in such a short time. So how—and who?

She raised the MP7 to point behind her, stunned with shock, at the same moment that the black gun barrel appeared. It wasn't her imagination—someone had pulled up right behind her.

At this point, escape was impossible. She just had to keep spraying bullets until someone's HP was gone or their magazine was empty. Sinon depressed the trigger—

—but just before the firing pin could strike the first bullet, the attacker held up a hand to stop her and murmured, "Wait."

"…?!"

Her eyes went wide, and traveled from the point of the gun to the enemy's face.

Shiny black hair down the back. White skin, even in the setting sun. Stunning, shiny, slender black eyes.

Her archenemy Kirito was leaning over her, Five-Seven gripped in his left hand. A number of conflicting emotions rose within Sinon and burst apart. She forgot about the muzzle pointed at her face and bared her teeth in a snarl, ready to open fire with her MP7.

But again, Kirito whispered, staying Sinon's trigger finger at the last moment.

"Wait. I have a plan."

"You can't be serious," she whisper-snarled back, seething with fury. "There are no plans or compromises at this stage! Someone dies, and that's that!"

"If I wanted to shoot you, I could have done it anytime!"

The surprisingly desperate note in Kirito's words caught her off-guard. What could be more important than the present situation, where their guns were drawn at one another?

Though it frustrated her to admit it, Kirito's statement was truth: If he was good enough to sneak into point blank range against her, he could have shot her in the back or sliced her up with the lightsword.

"…"

She waited in silence for him to speak again.

"I don't want to go blasting now, and have them hear us." For just a moment, Kirito's glance leaped up over Sinon's shoulder to the scene by the metal bridge, which would soon turn into a firefight.

"…? What do you mean?"

"I want to watch what happens in the battle on the bridge. Don't interrupt them until it's over."

"…What are you going to do after watching? Please don't be an idiot and say we resume our gunfight."

"Depending on the situation…I'll be leaving this spot. I won't attack you."

"Even if I snipe you in the back?"

"If you do, that's your choice. Do me this favor; they're about to start!"

Kirito looked back at the bridge again, clearly distracted. To her surprise, he lowered the Five-Seven and put it in his waist holster, even as she had her submachine gun pointed at his forehead.

More exasperated than angry, Sinon slumped back. If she put just the tiniest bit more pressure on the trigger, the MP7's 4.6 mm, twenty-round chamber would eliminate all of Kirito's HP. But even Sinon had to admit she didn't want the battle against her archenemy to end with such an absurd, one-sided result.

She'd been thinking of strategies so hard, steam shot out of her ears—Kirito might be able to evade the Hecate's shot, even without a visible bullet line. She'd rather deal with all of the other finalists until it was just the two of them, and she could focus on expending every last ounce of energy on beating him.

"If we regroup, will you fight me properly next time?"

"Yeah," he said. Sinon stared into his eyes for about half a second before lowering her SMG. She didn't take her finger off the trigger, just in case he did start swinging at her, but he only straightened up and laid down in the shadow of the bush next to Sinon. He pulled a small pair of binoculars out of his belt pouch and looked through them.

She was both furious and annoyed that she seemed to be a secondary, if not tertiary, concern to him now. Why would he bother observing someone else's battle? And where did he appear from in the first place? When she checked the Satellite Scanner just minutes ago, Kirito's name didn't appear within a kilometer of her.

But Sinon chose to sit on these concerns for now and returned the MP7 to her waist. She put her arms around the Hecate and looked through the scope.

Dyne was still down in firing position on this side of the long bridge. The way he held the SG 550 straight, without a single twitch, belied an impressive level of concentration. Despite having chased him here, Pale Rider wouldn't be able to just pop out of the forest on the other bank.

"Maybe the battle you were hoping to see isn't going to happen at all," Sinon remarked drily to Kirito. "Dyne's not going to just lie around there all day. If he gets up to move positions, I'll shoot him first."

"I don't mind if you do…Wait a second." Kirito's voice went sharp. Sinon pulled her eye out of the scope and scanned the bridge herself.

On the far bank, a player had just loomed out of the thick forest along the path. He was tall and thin, with an eerie pale-patterned camo suit. His face was invisible, thanks to a helmet with a black shield on the front. The only visible weapon was an ArmaLite AR-17 shotgun at his right side. This was probably—no, it had to be—Pale Rider, the man who chased Dyne here.

Dyne's shoulders stiffened on the other side of the bridge. Even at a distance, Sinon could sense the tension in the scene. On the other hand, there was no hint of unease in the way Pale Rider stood there. Slinking, he approached the bridge, showing no fear of Dyne's SIG.

"He's good…" Sinon muttered to herself. Kirito's body shifted. She looked over for a second to see his girlish face painted with an alarming strain. It was Pale Rider he was concerned about. Sinon had never seen the name or avatar before, but his skill level was clear from the way he moved.

In the world of GGO, there was a future-predicting assistance system called the "bullet line," which would be impossible in real life. But even with that, it was not easy to approach an enemy with a full-auto machine gun. The typical method was to run at a sprint from cover to cover, zigzagging to close the distance.

But Pale Rider left himself completely defenseless, sliding forward toward the bridge. There was no terrain to hide him from gunfire. Even Dyne was visibly confused by this action, and this was exactly what he *wanted* to happen.

But as the longtime leader of a PvP squadron, he clicked back into gear quickly. A second later, the sound of his precise Swiss SG 550 assault rifle rattled across the river.

He shot at least ten 5.5 mm rounds, but Pale Rider evaded the shots with a very unexpected method—he leaped up onto one of the countless wire ropes supporting the bridge and began to climb it using nothing but his left hand. Dyne hastily followed his course, but it was difficult to aim upward when on all fours. His second burst of fire went wild, and Pale Rider used the momentum of the wire to launch into a long jump. He landed quite close to Dyne's end of the bridge.

"For a Strength-first build, he kept his weight total low to boost his three-dimensional movement ability…and his Acrobat skill is really high," Sinon whispered at the same moment that Dyne got to his knees, determined not to fall for the same thing again, and pulled the trigger three times. But Pale Rider read that one ahead of time. The pale silhouette dove headfirst, just underneath the upward-facing line of fire. And not a clumsy dive, but a skillful, compact somersault using his left hand to push off the ground. When he stood up again, he was barely sixty feet from Dyne.

"Son of a bitch!" Dyne growled in a familiar way, and moved to switch out his empty thirty-round magazine. But before he could, Pale Rider's ArmaLite spat fire with a stomach-churning *thud*.

There was no way for a shotgun to miss entirely at that distance. Several bullet-hit effects sprang up on Dyne's body, and he flew backward with the force of it. But he was too skillful to give up on changing his cartridge, and was just pulling the gun up to his sights when another blast rang out.

The second shot from Pale Rider, delivered closer than the first, knocked Dyne off balance even further. That was the danger of a shotgun: The damage was bad enough, but the movement delay was so powerful that its victims were helpless to prevent further shots from landing true.

He should have sprayed fire from the hip, rather than trying to hold the SIG steady at eye level, Sinon thought, but it was too late for Dyne to make use of that advice, even if he could somehow hear it. Rider handily reloaded the AR-17 as he approached and pulled the trigger a third time, right in front of Dyne's face. The twelve-gauge shotgun blasted a hail of shot that eliminated his remaining HP.

Dyne fell backward, limbs splayed, and stopped entirely. A large red indicator reading DEAD appeared over his body, rotating slowly. Dyne was now out of the battle royale. In order to prevent any players from sharing information, he was prohibited from logging out during the tournament, and was forced to remain in the dead body, watching the rest of the battle play out as it aired on the stream.

"That blue guy sure is tough," Kirito whispered. Sinon nearly nodded, but frowned when she heard what he said next. "Is he the one inside the cloak...?"

Sinon was momentarily confused until she recalled that Pale Rider was one of the three names Kirito had demanded from her. In other words, he might be the one whom Kirito had fought to kill in that other VRMMO. And the name of that game might be—no, it had to be—the stuff of legend...

She forced herself to stop thinking about it right then. Kirito had his reasons for this, but the weight of his past was his alone. She couldn't shoulder the burden for him, and even if she could, she shouldn't.

Sinon turned off the Hecate's safety to distract herself from that hesitation and whispered, "I'm going to shoot him."

Without waiting for a response, she put her finger to the trigger. Pale Rider had already left the scene of his victory and headed north along the river. She caught his slender back in her crosshairs and fine-tuned based on wind and distance.

At last, Kirito croaked back, "Yeah...I get it. But if he's really the guy..."

If he is? He's going to dodge a sniper's first shot, sans bullet line, from just 300 meters, while facing away?

You must be joking, she mouthed, and started to pull the trigger without hesitation, when—

To her utter shock, Sinon caught a sight through her scope she hadn't expected.

Pale Rider's right shoulder, clad in pale blue camo, burst with bullet fire, and his slender form lurched and fell to the left.

"Aah—!" exclaimed both Sinon and Kirito, who was watching through his binoculars.

He was sniped—and not by Sinon. From the deep forest on the far bank of the river.

Despite her shock, she instinctually put all of her concentration into listening. She needed to figure out the direction and type of rifle blast that took down Pale Rider. But no matter how hard she strained, all she heard was the dry rustling of wind and the flowing of the river.

"Did I miss it?" she wondered.

Meanwhile, Kirito had the same idea. "No, there was no sound at all. What does it mean?"

"The only possibility is…one of the quieter laser rifles…or maybe a live-ammo gun with a suppressor, but…"

"Sapresser?"

She glared at Kirito, wondering how many things she needed to teach the idiot before all was said and done, then gave in and explained, "It's a noise canceler that goes on the end of the gun to keep it from being too loud."

"Ohh…a silencer, you mean."

"That's another word for it. Whatever you want to call it, a rifle with one of them equipped can cut down on the sound a lot. It does negatively affect accuracy and range, plus it's ridiculously expensive for a disposable item."

"I see," Kirito muttered, nodding. He looked to the tip of Sinon's Hecate II. All that he saw was a muzzle brake, and even a beginner like him could tell there was no suppressor attached.

Before he could say anything, she added, "It's not like I'm cheaping out by not using one. It's just not my style."

She returned to the scope with a snort. Pale Rider was still prone on the ground. But it didn't seem to be a one-hit kill. If it was fatal, the DEAD marker would be floating above him, as with Dyne nearby. Why wasn't he running or fighting back, if he wasn't dead?

There were other questions, too. Sinon knew from checking the Satellite Scanner map that no one else was within a kilometer. That meant whoever this mystery sniper was, they were shooting from very far away. It also had to be quite a high-caliber rifle. But the larger the gun in GGO, the less useful a suppressor was, and the worse its downsides. It didn't sit right with her that she didn't hear the gunshot.

At this point, Sinon remembered that she'd felt the same suspicions about the player right next to her, just minutes before. Without turning her head, she asked, "By the way, Kirito, where did you come from? You weren't around this mountain when the satellite passed over, ten minutes ago."

"Huh? Well...I was tracking that Pale Rider guy from about half a kilometer, so I should have shown up on the scanner...Oh, no, wait. I get it."

"What?"

"Actually, about ten minutes ago, I might have been swimming across the river. I was going underwater at the time, so I guess the satellite couldn't detect me..."

You swam across?! she nearly screamed.

There was nothing in the game that prohibited swimming in rivers or lakes, and a fall into water didn't spell instant death. But HP dropped continuously while in water, and a full set of equipment was too heavy for swimming. On top of that, a river of this size was impossible to cross alone without a frogman-style breathing apparatus.

"H-how did you...?" she barely managed to squeak out. Kirito just shrugged casually.

"I took off all my equipment first, of course. When you remove it in your status window, it goes into storage and doesn't require holding in your hands; that's a common rule to all Seed VRMMOs."

"..."

She was dumbfounded. Getting the idea to swim across the river was one thing, but having the fortitude to remove all his defensive gear in the midst of a battle was unbelievable. With a heave of disgust, she said, "Well, if you were showing off your avatar's undies, at least the people watching on the stream must have gotten a kick out of it."

"But doesn't the livestream only show active combat?" he returned confidently. She snorted.

"...At any rate, it seems that being submerged in water means the satellite can't pick you up. That's good to know. On the other hand, you went all that way to chase Pale Rider, and while he was tough, he wasn't all that. If taking one good shot was enough to freak him out and paralyze him, he won't..."

Last, she was going to finish, but Kirito cut her off, binoculars pressed to his eyes again. "Actually, it doesn't look like he's freaked out... Look closer. There's some kind of weird lighting going on around his avatar..."

"Huh?"

She increased the magnification on her scope. It was hard to tell in the intense light of the setting sun, but it did appear as though pale blue sparks the same color as Pale Rider's camo were crawling over his body. She'd seen that effect before. It had to be—

"An electrical stun round?!"

"Wh-what's that?"

"Like the name says, it's a special kind of bullet that runs a high-powered current that stuns its target. But you need a really high-caliber rifle to load one, and each round is prohibitively expensive, so no one uses it for PvP. It's only useful when hunting major mobs with a party."

Even as she delivered this explanation, the sparks holding Pale Rider prisoner were fading. In less than a minute, the effect would be gone. But since it barely hurt his HP, it didn't make any sense why someone would pull off such a difficult, long-range snipe…

"—!"

In the moment, she couldn't tell if the shock that ran through came from her own body, or Kirito next to her.

About 200 meters to the north of the bush in which they hid was the metal bridge, spanning the river from east to west. At the west end of the bridge was the confirmed corpse of Dyne's avatar. About five meters north of him, Pale Rider fell over, having been shot by a stun round from the eastern forest. He would soon be getting to his feet.

Just between them, a black silhouette bloomed from the shadow of the metal bridge's support pillar.

At first glance, it didn't appear to be a player. The outline of the avatar was strangely indistinct. She stared at it hard, and finally understood why. Not only was the player wearing a tattered, gray, hooded cloak, the breeze was blowing it in chaotic directions, like some kind of swarm of vermin. Rather than a classic sniper's ghillie suit, it was more like a "ghillie cloak."

"When did he get there…?" Sinon murmured unconsciously. It was almost certain that the cloaked figure was the one who sniped Pale Rider. But when did he leave the forest and cross the bridge? Even with the hiding bonus of the cloak, she would have spotted him if he crossed the empty bridge. Or did he swim, like Kirito had? If that was the case, she wouldn't have missed him opening his window and manipulating his equipment.

In the next instant, a new shock eliminated all of those minor questions from Sinon's mind.

The tattered cloak slowly moved forward, revealing the main weapon that had been hidden in the body's shadow until now.

"Silent Assassin," she moaned.

It was a massive rifle, nearly as long as her Hecate. The barrel was slightly thinner, but the many bolt holes crossing the body of the gun, the one-piece stock with advanced thumb hole grip, and the dark gray matte finish gave it a chillingly cruel appearance.

But most notable of all was the long sound suppressor attached to the end of the barrel. No, it wasn't attached—this gun was designed around the use of a silencer to start with.

The proper name of the gun was the Accuracy International L115A3. It fired .338 Lapua Magnum rounds—weaker than the Hecate II's .50 BMG rounds, but the L115 was not an antimateriel rifle. As one might guess from the default implementation of the silencer, it was built for sniping human targets. Its maximum range was over 2,000 meters. Those shot by it couldn't see the shooter, much less hear the gunshot before they died. Thus giving rise to its nickname: the Silent Assassin.

She'd heard that the fearsome rifle could be found in GGO, but had never seen one for herself. In fact, Sinon didn't know of any snipers who could fight solo aside from herself. But the person in that tattered cloak had shot Pale Rider from deep within the woods on the far bank of the river. That wasn't possible without the technique and willpower to control the expansion of the bullet circle, which was linked to one's pulse.

Who is he?

She looked at the watch on her left wrist: 8:40 PM. There were still five minutes left until the third satellite flyover. That was a very long period of time for the current situation to hold.

Through her scope, she saw the cloaked man set the L115 on his shoulder with lifeless precision. She squinted to see if his rifle might bear a sticker from his squadron, but aside from a thick cleaning rod attached below the barrel, there was no customization. As she watched him, he carefully slid over to the prone Pale Rider.

Pale Rider had defeated Dyne without taking damage, and was clearly a talented player in his own right. Sinon hadn't heard of him before this, but she figured that he was well known in the distant northern landmass, like Behemoth the minigunner. But based on first look, the cloaked man had even more presence. Sinon felt a chill prickling her entire back, perhaps even more visceral than when she beat that enormous boss monster on her own to win her Hecate.

But in order to be sure of the cloaked man's strength, there was still one question to answer. If he had such a rare rifle and the sniping skill to match it, why did he bother with stun rounds, rather than live ammo? A single .338 Lapua shot to the head or heart would tear the lightly armored Pale Rider apart. Certainly, stunning him first to allow for a fine-precision kill shot would work, but the cloaked man stunned him and then walked right out of the forest, exposing himself to his still-healthy target at close range. It rendered the success of that high-difficulty shot meaningless.

Sinon bit her lip, disturbed by the fact that she couldn't even begin to guess what he was after. Meanwhile, Kirito was oddly silent. She wanted to check on him, but she couldn't pull her eyes away from the tattered cloak.

He was standing right in front of Pale Rider now, L115 still on his shoulder. He reached into his cloak, convincing Sinon that he must be pulling out his sidearm for the kill. It might be a small submachine gun, a full magazine at point-blank range would be enough to take down all of the target's HP.

"...Huh?" she muttered, startled once again.

Instead, he removed what looked like a plain old handgun. She couldn't identify it, because the gun moved into the shade of his body against the setting sun, but the silhouette made it look like a perfectly unremarkable automatic pistol.

A bullet from a handgun was just as powerful as that of a submachine gun, but it wouldn't have full-auto fire if the trigger was held down. It would take too long to empty enough bullets to eliminate all of the enemy's HP, and Pale Rider was just about to recover from his paralysis. As soon as he was able to move, he'd fire his shotgun, and it would be the man in the cloak who died.

Yet the mysterious player showed no signs of haste, his trailing ghillie cloak flapping in the setting sun. He pointed the handgun

down at Pale Rider and withdrew his left hand from the cloak as well. It was empty. For some reason, he touched his hooded forehead with the fingers of his empty hand. Then to his chest. Then left shoulder, then right.

He was making the sign of the cross; a last tribute to a dying foe, perhaps. But his time was running out. Was he certain that he could avoid a shotgun blast at close range? Or was he just a fool who got a lucky gun and didn't know when to rein in his act?

Sinon couldn't unclench her teeth from her lip, it was all so confusing. A whisper reached her left ear.

"Fire, Sinon."

It was Kirito. But there was a desperate tension to his command that she hadn't heard before. She asked him, "Huh? Who?"

"The guy in the cloak. Please, shoot him now, before he fires!!"

His intense plea was passionate enough to move her finger to the Hecate's trigger. Normally she would have argued back out of habit, but she broke that pattern and trained her crosshairs over the back of the cloak. She estimated the wind and humidity from the level of visible dust effects. When she put pressure on the trigger, a green bullet circle covered the target.

Theory said that she should wait until they were done fighting and shoot the victor. If she shot the tattered cloak now, Pale Rider would recover from his paralysis and dart off for the bushes, and she wouldn't get a second chance to snipe him.

But even knowing that, Sinon didn't relax her finger. She just had a feeling that she needed to shoot him. She held her breath and gathered cold virtual air in her lungs. The chill slowed her heart. *Ba-bump...ba-bump...* The circle expanded and contracted with the beating of her heart. When it reached its smallest size, covering the center of the target's back...

A blast.

Flames shot from the large muzzle brake like the breath of dragons. She was just 300 meters from her target. Sinon couldn't have missed—she could already see the avatar flying, a giant hole in its back.

But…

At the exact time that Sinon pulled the trigger, the player in the tattered cloak dramatically bent over backward, like a ghost without a solid form. The deadly bullet grazed his chest and ripped an enormous hole in the earth past him.

"Wha…"

Stunned, Sinon suddenly felt the player's face turn toward her and stare right into her eye through the scope. The mouth, hidden in darkness, sneered at her. Without realizing she was doing it, Sinon moaned, "H-he knew…he knew we were here all along…"

"No way! He never even looked toward us!" Kirito exclaimed, equally shocked.

She shook her head. "He couldn't possibly have dodged like that unless he could see the bullet line. In other words, he must have registered me by sight at some point, which the system remembered…"

Even as she spoke, Sinon was automatically loading the next bullet into Hecate's chamber. But she wasn't sure what she should do, even as she entered firing position. It was 99 percent impossible for her to hit a foe with that kind of reaction speed when there was a visible bullet line to utilize. She could try firing the four remaining bullets in the magazine in quick order. But if they all missed and he was able to close the distance, she'd be in trouble. What to do…what to do?

The cloaked man regained his balance, as though sensing Sinon's hesitation. He turned the handgun on Pale Rider again, cocking the hammer with his thumb. He steadied the grip with his left hand and pulled the trigger, facing his target at an incline.

There was a small flash, and a moment later, a dry *klak* gunshot.

"Ah!" Kirito gasped.

The bullet caught Pale Rider in the center of the chest. It was a critical point, but no matter where a 9mm Parabellum bullet hit its target in this game, there could be no one-hit kills. If anything, Pale Rider probably still had 90 percent health left. For some reason, the cloaked player didn't bother to shoot again. He stood in place, holding the gun in the Weaver stance. He had to know that Sinon was aiming for him, but he made no effort to hide. He was certain that he could dodge any of her shots.

One, two, three…

The electric stun that immobilized Pale Rider wore off at last. His camo-clad body leaped up off the ground, and the AR-17 shotgun rose so fast it looked like a blur, pointing directly at the cloaked player's chest. It was literal point-blank range. Every projectile in the shot would hit the heart. Unlike the pistol, this one *could* be a one-hit kill.

Sinon, Kirito, and most likely everyone else in GGO and the outside world watching the live stream of the event held their breath.

There was no echo of return fire.

Instead, all Sinon heard was a small crumpling *thump*. The AR-17 had fallen out of Pale Rider's hand onto the red dirt.

Next, he fell to his knees, like a lifeless rag doll with broken joints. The avatar leaned slowly, slowly to the right, and collapsed on its side.

From Sinon's position, she could see only the mouth poking out from beneath Pale Rider's helmet visor. It was open wide, as though caught in a silent scream, or perhaps gasping for air.

His left hand rose, eerily weak in contrast to his earlier confidence, and clutched at the center of his chest—

And the pale camo body erupted with scrawling, irregular light like static noise, and vanished. All that was left of the light was a small, floating DISCONNECTION message, which soon evaporated into the setting sun as well.

"…What was that?" Sinon finally said, several seconds later.

The player in the tattered cloak had shot Pale Rider just once with a handgun. He still had HP left at that point; that was clear.

Just after that, Pale Rider's paralysis wore off, and he tried to shoot back with his shotgun, but something happened to his connection, and he was cut off from the game.

That was the logical explanation for what she had just seen.

But what was the likelihood of his connection going bad at that exact moment? And how would the cloaked player know that he'd emerge triumphant from that dire predicament? It was less that he got tremendously lucky, and more that he knew the connection would occur at that precise moment. In fact, it was like…

…It was like he had *willfully disconnected Pale Rider himself.*

But that was impossible. There was no way to interfere with another player's connection from inside the game. Yet, the cloaked player showed no surprise at Pale Rider's disappearance. He smoothly returned his left hand to his side, while he raised his right hand and pointed the pistol up to the sky. Sinon realized what he was pointing at right away: the virtual camera lens that was capturing their footage for the stream. It was represented within the game world as a pale, glowing object, to let the players know they were being filmed. He was pointing his gun for the sake of all the people watching. But why? His battle with Pale Rider was irregular, a victory by disqualification—not something to be proud of. Or was the cloaked man saying that this disappearance was his victory? Meaning…

"He can knock other players…off the server?" she rasped.

Kirito's voice was calm and quiet, as though he wasn't even thinking about what he was saying. "No. Not quite. I wish it was that benign…"

"Benign? What do you mean? That's a huge deal. He's basically cheating his way to victory. What does Zaskar think it's—"

"No!" He grabbed her arm suddenly. She automatically tried to shake him off, but what he said next turned her blood to ice. "He didn't knock him off the server. He *killed* him. Pale Rider… the actual player who was controlling Pale Rider, just died in real life, right now!"

"…Wha…"

What is he talking about?

Before she could respond, Kirito continued, "That's it. That's him. *That's Death Gun.*"

She recognized that name. The vague knowledge floated up from the depths of her memory. "Death...Gun...Is that the guy with all the weird rumors? The one who shot at the last tournament's champion, Zexceed, and one of its high-rankers, Usujio Tarako, and they never logged in after that..."

"That's right," Kirito said, and stared right at Sinon. There was unfathomable shock and fear wavering within his deep, black eyes, as well as something else. "At first...I thought it was impossible, too. Even after meeting him in the waiting dome yesterday, I tried to deny it. But there's no denying it now...He can kill players somehow. Zexceed and Usujio Tarako's players both turned up dead..."

"..."

How do you know that? Who are you? And what happened between you and that cloaked player? Sinon wondered, holding her breath. The questions for Kirito were even more at the forefront of her mind than the shock of learning the Death Gun rumors were true.

In fact, she couldn't believe it right away. Killing someone from within a game? It was so absurd...if not downright contradictory. If real lives were on the line, they were no longer playing a "game." But Kirito's deadly serious expression, tone of voice, and gaze were so realistic and so pressing that she couldn't just laugh it off as nonsense. So who was he...?

Kirito finally removed his piercing gaze from the confused Sinon and turned back to the metal bridge. She followed his eyesight.

The mysterious cloaked player finally lowered his gun and looked over at Dyne's body just to the south. The DEAD tag still floated above his stomach, which meant he should still be online, but he obviously couldn't say anything or show any reaction. There was no way to know how he was feeling about the bizarre battle that had just unfolded nearby.

The cloaked player returned the pistol to its holster and reshouldered the L115, then started clanking off in Dyne's direction. Sinon held her breath, wondering if he was going to shoot Dyne's body next. Kirito went still, clearly thinking the same thing. He seemed ready to leap out of the bush.

Fortunately, the cloaked player did not pull his pistol back out. He passed Dyne's body and continued toward the bridge. However, he did not cross it but, similar to how he appeared, simply swung around the side of the large pillar and vanished—probably because he leaped down to the lower bank. That put him out of sight temporarily, but there was only north or south to go from there. Once he started moving, he would be visible very soon...

"...He's not emerging," Kirito grumbled. Sinon nodded. There was no sign of the cloak after ten seconds. That meant he was still hiding in the shadow of the bridge. He had to be wary of Sinon's sniping.

At that moment, she felt an alarm vibration on her left wrist, and she looked at the clock: 8:44:50. In another ten seconds, the third satellite scan would happen. She pulled the terminal out of her pouch and watched the screen.

"You keep an eye on the bridge, Kirito. I'll use this to find out his name."

"Got it," he responded.

She waited for the map to update. Three seconds, two, one, scan. Far above, a spy satellite from the space-exploration era passed over. Its electronic eye would see through any meager cover. He wouldn't escape its gaze unless he hid in a cave, or, as Kirito had proven for himself, deep water.

A number of blips popped up on the map. Richie was still comfortably situated on top of the mountain to the south. He wouldn't be coming down until the tournament was over.

About 800 meters to the north of that, lined up above the cliff of the brushy area were two dots, Sinon and Kirito. Any distant player would assume from the map that they were in battle. They wouldn't assume the two were lying down next to each other under a bush…she hoped.

There was a faintly glowing dot another 200 meters to the north. That was the deceased Dyne. Pale Rider's dot ought to be close by, but it wasn't displaying. And to the east of Dyne, just under the bridge, was…

"Wha—? Nothing?!" Sinon exclaimed, staring a hole into the high-tech terminal screen. No matter how hard she looked, there was no dot around the bridge except for Dyne's. The cloaked player was already on the move. But if he ran along the river bank, they would have seen him. For a moment, she felt terrified, but she promptly corralled her thoughts to order.

There was one possibility. Like Kirito, he dove into the river and swam downward to escape the satellite. Which meant…

"This is our chance," she whispered. Kirito frowned. He looked at her for clarification, which she provided. "The cloaked guy isn't on the radar. He's in the river. That means he has to have all of his gear off. It's going to take him at least ten seconds to open the window and put all of it back on once he's on dry land again. If we strike then—"

"With one pistol? He can still swim with that equipped, can't he?" Kirito interjected. Sinon thought briefly before responding.

"I've never tried it myself, but if you have enough STR or VIT, I suppose it's possible… But still, we can easily overpower one measly handgun—"

"No!" he hissed suddenly, clutching her arm. "You saw him erase Pale Rider with that black pistol! If you take one hit from that thing, you might die, too!"

She couldn't pull her eyes away from those sparkling black orbs. It was only with great force of will that she could look away and shake her head in disagreement.

"But…I just can't accept that. How can you die for real, just because you were shot in a game…? And more than that, if it's true, that means the guy in the cloak is killing people at will, right? It's impossible…I don't want to believe that someone in GGO—in a VRMMO—would do something like that…"

Even in the desolate wastelands of Gun Gale Online, Sinon found it to be a comforting place.

True evil and malice didn't exist here. What looked like bullets and gunpowder was a pure expression of willpower, of desire to best one's opponent and be tougher than anyone else. After all, dozens of bullet wounds never caused anyone here to bleed a drop of blood. There was no pain, no injury. So while battle could cause frustration, it never caused hatred. In a recent pitched battle, Sinon's left leg was blown off by the minigunner Behemoth, and she destroyed his entire body with her Hecate. But when it was done, all she was left with was confidence, reflection, and respect for her worthy foe. Sinon believed that it was the same for him, as well.

That was why she had chosen GGO as a buffer zone between her weak real-life self and the horrors of her past. If she kept fighting here, she hoped that the wealth of Sinon's confidence would one day outweigh the depth of the hatred that plagued Shino.

True malice must not exist in a VRMMO. It would no longer be a virtual world. It would be the darkness of reality that Shino feared and shied away from…

"I…don't want to admit that there are VRMMO players who would commit not PK, but actual murder."

Kirito replied to her comment with deep pain in his voice. "But there are. The guy in the cloak, Death Gun…once killed many people in the VRMMO that I played. He swung his sword, knowing that they would die. Just like he did now, when he shot Pale Rider. And…so did…"

He looked down and let go of Sinon's arm. He didn't finish his sentence.

But based on the fragments of his past that she'd gleaned from past conversations, Sinon felt she could fill in the blanks.

The Incident that shocked all of Japan three years ago, in 2022. Even Sinon, who had no interest in VRMMOs at the time, knew quite a lot about it, thanks to the considerable press coverage it received. There were over ten thousand young people taken prisoner at the start of the game. When they were released to the world again two years later, only six thousand emerged. That meant that four thousand lives were lost over the course of the Incident.

There was no doubting now that Kirito was one of the survivors of that world. And if his statement was true, so too was Death Gun. But Kirito's words hinted at an even darker truth:

In a world where in-game death meant true death, Death Gun had killed many players of his own accord. He had done it knowing that their bodies in real life would perish. He was the very thing Sinon claimed she didn't believe in: a VRMMO player who would commit murder.

And he was in GGO now, logged in to the map of the third BoB final battle—using some mysterious means to kill players just as he had in the past. That was what Kirito claimed.

When the picture coalesced in Sinon's mind, she felt her entire body go as cold as ice. Her vision went dim, blackness spreading out from the center. Something was in its midst, watching her. That gaze—the lifeless, empty, but close, clinging gaze.........

"...non. Sinon!"

She opened her eyes with a start. On the other side of the vanishing shadow was Kirito's worried face. Only the disgust that flooded up within her at his pristine, bewitching beauty kept the panic down.

She exhaled and said, "I'm fine...Just a little startled. To be honest...I'm not sure if I can believe all of your story just yet... but I don't think all of it is made up."

"Thanks. That's enough for me," he said, right at the moment that the dots on her terminal map started to blink. The orbiting satellite was going out of range. She quickly set the map to display its full width so she could count the dots. There were seventeen dots still bright—the survivors. Eleven dim dots were deceased players. That added up to twenty-eight.

"The numbers don't add up…"

There were thirty when the match started, which meant that if you included Pale Rider's missing dot due to disconnection, there was one more dot still unaccounted for. That had to be Death Gun, who was evading detection at the bottom of the river. Even there, he could still be on the move—either approaching or distancing himself. If it was the former, he might appear from the water just to the east of their cover and attack at any time…

All of the dots disappeared from the screen. She'd have to search with nothing but her five senses for another fifteen minutes.

Sinon glanced down to the east, but nothing was moving. The cloaked player was probably going north. His Silent Assassin, the L115A3, was a deadly weapon, but like her Hecate II, it was a bolt-action sniper rifle, which made it unsuited for mid- and close-range combat. He was probably choosing not to attack the two of them at once, but to take distance so he could hide his location data.

Sinon sighed and muttered, "At any rate, we should move from this spot. All the other players who assumed you and I were fighting are bound to come snooping in to clean up after the battle."

"Good point," Kirito murmured. He stared right into Sinon's face. "I don't suppose it would work to ask you to find an absolutely safe location to hide until the end of the battle royale, would it?"

"O-of course I won't!" she hissed back, just as loud as was safe. "Do I look like Richie the Camper to you?! Besides, there's no safe place on this entire island. I know there are caves in the desert region to the north that won't show up on the scan, but all anyone has to do is toss a grenade inside to finish me off!"

"…All right. Let's part ways here, then."

"Uh…" She hadn't expected that. After a couple of quick blinks, she regained her cool. "Wh-what will you do?"

"I'm going after Death Gun. I can't let him shoot anyone else with that pistol. Besides, I feel like…I might remember, if I meet him face-to-face. What his old name was. And then…"

Kirito's smooth lips shut tight. He took a deep breath and faced Sinon directly. "Sinon, I want you to stay away from him as best you can. I'll keep my promise: The next time we meet on this island, I'll fight you for real. Oh, and…thank you for hearing me out without shooting me."

He bowed briefly, and the black-clad swordsman slid out from the bush.

"Ah…hey!" Sinon yelped, but he was already standing on the reddish dirt in his assault boots, running for the bridge to the north without a backward glance.

She followed his slender, retreating back for a few moments, then shut her eyes tight.

"~~~…"

With a silent *argh!* Sinon let out a long breath and forcefully jumped up from her spot under the bush. The terrain object was destroyed by her violent action, the branches and leaves scattering through the air before they disappeared entirely.

"Wait, you!" she screamed. His figure stopped, a good forty paces away. She picked up the Hecate without looking at it, slung it over her shoulder, and dashed after Kirito. She didn't so much as look at the expression of pure, undiluted suspicion on his face.

"I'm going with you."

"Huh?"

"You're going to fight Death Gun, aren't you? He's clearly really tough, even without the power of that gun. If you lose before I get to fight you, I'll never have the chance for a rematch. Though I'm not exactly happy about it, I'll fight at your side temporarily… which gives us the best chance at knocking him right out of the BoB," she announced quickly, rattling off the lines she came up with while chasing him down, only to then shoot a sidelong glance at him. The lightswordsman's brows were knitted, but his lips were curled into a slight smile—a very odd expression. But his concern won out, and he shook his black hair.

"No…that's not good enough. You saw how he fights, Sinon. He's dangerous. If you get shot, you could suffer real-life harm…"

"We don't know where Death Gun went, so whether we're separate or together, the danger of encountering him is the same. And don't give me that crap about being worried for my sake, when you're such a noob that you ran right out into the open without looking around you."

"...Okay, maybe you have a point..."

After a few seconds' hesitation, Kirito finally slumped his shoulders and nodded—when suddenly, his hand flashed, moving in a blur. She didn't even process that he had pulled his lightsword from the carabiner on his belt until after the blue-purple energy blade had extended from the handle.

No way, is he going to ambush me and pretend he's done with our promise? Sinon wondered in a panic. But Kirito looked away to the west. She followed his gaze to see a number of red lines extending from the shadow of a large rock about a hundred meters away. Bullet lines.

Their mystery attacker's gun barked full-auto fire, while Kirito's lightsword ducked and waved, leaving glowing afterimages and knocking down the storm of gunfire bullet by bullet. Sinon stood dumbly in place for a good second, blown away by a show of skill the likes of which she'd never seen in GGO, before recovering and lurching into motion. She dropped to the ground with her Hecate, getting into firing position and planting its bipod in the sand.

Though she was already certain of this based on the full-auto fire, a peek through the scope confirmed that it was not the ghillie cloak of Death Gun shooting at them. She recognized the oddly shaped open helmet with a fluffy tassel on the crown, and the accuracy-improving eyepatch device. It was Xiahou Dun, an assault rifle gunman who had appeared in the previous two tournaments. He used a Norinco CQ rifle. Though he was a grizzled veteran, the gruff avatar's jaw was agape, and for good reason— he never would have expected that an entire magazine of ambush fire could be deflected perfectly by the novelty weapon that was a photon sword.

"No way, man!" wailed Xiahou Dun, an extremely inappropriate action for someone who looked so much like a stately, whiskered ancient Chinese general. He ducked behind the boulder.

Kirito glanced down at Sinon and shrugged. "Might as well start with him. I'll go in, you cover me."

"...Roger that."

It was an odd turn of events. How did it come to this?

Sinon pressed her cheek into the familiar wooden stock of her gun.

11

"They sure aren't showing much of Big Brother," Leafa noted to Silica, her golden-green ponytail rustling over her back.

Silica's triangular cat ears twitched as they poked out of her light brown hair. "Yes, it's quite a surprise. Knowing Kirito, I figured he would be raising hell from the very start."

"Nah, that son of a bitch is crafty, if anything. He might be hiding out in a safe spot while the crowd thins itself out for him."

That line came from Klein, who was manning the bar counter in the corner of the room. Leafa, Silica, and Asuna—on the sofa in the center of the room—couldn't help but giggle a bit.

"Even Kirito wouldn't do something like that…I think," Asuna added softly. On her shoulder, the palm-sized fairy—Yui the AI, "daughter" to Asuna and Kirito—flapped her tiny, fragile wings.

"That's right! Papa is sneaking up and ambushing his enemies so fast, the camera can't even follow him!"

To her left, Lisbeth couldn't contain her laughter. "Ha ha ha, that sounds about right. And he went out of his way to use a sword in a gun game."

For a moment, everyone visualized that image. The room filled with cheerful laughter, and Pina, the little dragon familiar, perked up her ears from her resting position in Silica's lap.

This group of six people and one animal were not gathered

in a real location. They were within the team's favorite VRM-MORPG, ALfheim Online, or ALO for short. Yggdrasil City was a settlement atop the massive World Tree that loomed over the center of the game's map. The room that Asuna and Kirito rented together was host to today's gathering.

The 2,000-yrd monthly rent on the place bought them plenty of space. The large sofa set was in the center of the immaculate wooden floor, and there was even a home bar built into the wall. The countless bottles on the shelves had been gathered by the hearty drinker Klein from the home territories of all nine fairy races, and even Jotunheim below. According to him, some of them were as fine as thirty-year scotch, if you didn't mind not getting drunk from it. As a minor, Asuna wouldn't know the difference.

The entire south wall was made of glass and offered them a stunning view of Ygg City whenever they wanted, but there was no view of the night skyline today. The glass also acted as a giant screen, and it was now showing them a different world entirely—courtesy of the net channel MMO Stream. It was the livestream of the Bullet of Bullets' battle royale final, the tournament to determine the greatest soldier of Gun Gale Online.

They had gathered to either cheer on, or criticize, Kirito's sudden and unannounced appearance in this tournament. Unfortunately, the massive axe warrior Agil was not present. It was a busy hour for the real-life café/bar that he managed. On the other hand, Asuna was actually diving here from the second floor of that very business, Dicey Café. It was a convenient location in the middle of Tokyo for her, from which she could rush over and give Kirito a piece of her mind once the event was finished.

"Why do you suppose Kirito would go to the lengths of converting from ALO, just to enter this tournament?" Lisbeth wondered, swirling a mysterious emerald-green wine. To her left, Leafa shot a look at Asuna. Only Asuna, Leafa, and Yui knew that Kirito was undertaking this GGO mission for the sake of their fellow ALO player, the undine mage Chrysheight—who was actually Seijirou Kikuoka, Virtual Division official for the Ministry of Internal Affairs. Asuna took Leafa's glance to mean that it was up to her how to respond, so she took a second to think.

"The thing is...it seems he took on some kind of weird job. Something about researching the current state of VRMMOs—the Seed Nexus, in particular. GGO's the only game with a real-currency-conversion system, which is why he's there."

That was exactly what Kirito had told her. But Asuna didn't think for a second that it was the entire story. She didn't think that he was lying, but there had to be something he was leaving out. It was obvious from his facial expression, voice, and demeanor when he explained that he was converting after their recent date.

But Asuna didn't press him for more at the time. There had to be a reason why he wouldn't tell her. And she firmly believed that the reason was not a betrayal of any kind.

So she wished him good luck and sent him on his way, then gathered up their friends to watch the event from their distant world. But she couldn't deny that in the last few days, something odd was eating away at her.

It wasn't distrust of Kirito, but more of a vague premonition. The feeling that something was going to happen, or was already happening. It was a shapeless unease, the same sensation she felt in Aincrad when surrounded by a large group of monsters just outside of the radius of her Search skill...

Lisbeth's sixth sense of friendship seemed to pick up the worry that Asuna had kept out of her voice and expression. "A job, huh...Well, either way, if anyone can grasp the essentials of a game in no time, it's him..."

"But why's he jumping right into this PvP tournament, then? If it's just for research, couldn't he simply walk around and talk to players in town?" asked Klein.

All four of them had this same question.

Eventually Silica suggested, "Maybe...he wants to win the tournament and earn a lot of money so he can convert it back into cash? I've heard that the minimum value to make use of that feature is really high..."

Yui instantly piped up from Asuna's shoulder with more detailed information. "The rate isn't listed on the official site, but according to online articles, the minimum value is 100,000 in-game credits, and the ratio is 100 credits to 1 yen, which would mean 1,000 yen. It seems that the player's registered e-mail address receives a code with the electronic cash already deposited. The top prize for the tournament is 3,000,000 credits, which would be 30,000 yen when cashed out."

It all sounded very fluid and comfortable coming from Yui's lips, but she was pulling down the information and compiling it from the Net as she spoke it aloud. Her search-and-filter speed and precision were greater than any human's. Kirito had frequently—and the girls, every now and then—called upon her ability to put together his homework reports.

"Thanks, Yui," Asuna said, rubbing the little fairy's head with a finger. "It doesn't sound like the cashing-out system itself is very complex. After all, we already trade electronic cash codes through e-mail ourselves. You wouldn't think Kirito would need to confirm the process for himself..."

"Though I can definitely see him getting lured in by a 30,000-yen pot!" Klein japed. Everyone grimaced.

"No, he's not *you*," Lisbeth remarked immediately. "But in most PvP battle royales, it doesn't work to hide somewhere and wait until there's almost no one left. In ALO, they have automatic Searcher spells that reveal your location if you try to hide in the same location for minutes at a time, don't they?"

"Plus, it doesn't really fit Big Brother's personality. He's not the type to sit still while listening to the sound of other people fighting. He wouldn't be able to resist," Leafa commented, with the convincing wisdom of one who'd lived with him for years. It made perfect sense to the group, so they resumed their pondering.

As they did so, the enormous 300-inch screen-wall was positively jittering with flashy graphics. Because it was a gun-based game, most of the shots came from over the shoulder of an individual player. As the virtual camera followed them, the bottom of the screen displayed the name of the player being viewed, but none of the sixteen segments of the screen showed the name KIRITO. As a general rule, it didn't show players not in battle, which meant that in the thirty minutes since the event started, Kirito hadn't been involved in a single fight.

Perhaps he was just being cautious, having transferred from a world of swords and magic to an unfamiliar gun-centric setting. But the Kirito that Asuna knew would face his foes headfirst, no matter the circumstance—he would find a way. Like Leafa said, it didn't make sense that Kirito would appear in a big event and hide for thirty minutes. She could see him getting into an immediate battle with one of the heavy favorites right off the bat and dying with style—but the list of contestants on the right edge of the screen showed his status as ALIVE.

"Does that mean...his purpose isn't to make a splash in the tournament...but something more important?" Asuna wondered, right about the moment that one of the battles on the sixteen-segment screen reached a climax.

The camera was from the perspective of a player named Dyne. He was set up with a simple machine gun at the base of a rusted-out bridge, spraying bullets. But his opponent, dressed in pale blue clothing, leaped up onto the bridge supports as nimbly as a cait sith to approach. He fired a big, mean-looking gun like a criminal in some Hollywood blockbuster, and Dyne was done for in moments.

Lisbeth was watching the same fight among all of the different views, and she whistled softly. "Ooh, he's good. Y'know, watching like this makes GGO look pretty fun. I wonder if you can craft your own guns..."

Following her experience in SAO, Lisbeth had chosen to be a leprechaun blacksmith in ALO. Asuna couldn't help but smile.

"Don't tell me you're converting to GGO next, Liz. We've still got a long way to go to beat the New Aincrad."

"That's right, Liz! Remember, there's going to be that new update when we reach the twenties!" Silica piped up from the other end of the sofa. Lisbeth raised her hands in surrender.

"All right, all right. I'm just remarking about how every game has its worthy opponents. I bet that blue guy's one of the favorites to win it all…"

Just at that moment, the "blue guy" collapsed on screen. The frame swung around, taking the viewpoint of the blue-clad man who'd just fallen. The name PALE RIDER flashed beneath the image.

He was down, but not dead. Fine sparks shot from his damaged shoulder and crawled over his body, a visual sign that the avatar's movement was contained.

"It looks like that wind spell Thunderweb," Leafa remarked. She was a sylph warrior.

The salamander swordsman Klein shook his red hair, which was pinned behind an ugly bandana. "I hate those things. The homing's way too good on them."

"Because every kind of debuff is bad for you! You need to raise your resistance skills already."

"Bah! A true samurai doesn't take a single skill related to magic. You don't do it!"

"Don't you know that for decades, the samurai class in RPGs has been basically just warriors with black magic?!"

Asuna grinned at their argument and reached out with her right hand to focus on the window in question, spreading her index finger and thumb apart. The feed of the prone Pale Rider expanded and pushed the other windows to the sides of the screen.

He'd been paralyzed for over ten seconds, but no other player had entered the frame as of yet. There was only the reddened earth, the bridge, the river beneath it, and the forest on the other side, hazy through the dust...

Flap.

All five twitched at the same time. A black fabric came into view from the left side of the frame. The camera steadily pulled back so that a new figure came into full view on the screen.

"A ghost...?" someone whispered in a hoarse voice, possibly Lisbeth or Silica—or Asuna herself.

A dark gray cloak, tattered and waving in the breeze. A hood that shrouded what lay within in total darkness. And glowing like floating hellfires, two red eyes. It was eerily similar to the ghostly enemies that had tormented them so often back in the original Aincrad.

She squeezed her eyes shut and looked again. Of course, it was a real player, a contestant in the tournament, not a ghostly figure. There were two legs sticking out of the bottom of the cloak, and a very large hunting rifle on the player's right shoulder. This cloaked man must have been the one who had stunned Pale Rider. Even in ALO, the magic warrior who ensnared foes with capturing spells and approached to finish the job with physical attacks was a very popular build.

Sure enough, just as Asuna imagined, the cloaked man reached to his waist and pulled out a black pistol. But if that was supposed to be his main source of damage, it seemed...kinda...

"...Kinda wimpy, ain't it?" Klein said, giving voice to her curiosity. He was scratching at his bearded chin in the way he always did. "No way that peashooter does more damage than that huge rifle on his shoulder. He should use that, instead."

"Maybe the ammo costs a bunch? High-level spells in ALO take expensive reagents, after all," Leafa noted. The group went back to thinking, while the hooded figure cocked the pistol and aimed it at the fallen player.

But he didn't pull the trigger yet. It seemed he wanted to tease his opponent—and the viewers. Instead he raised his left hand and did something unexpected. The index and middle fingers went together and tapped his forehead, chest, and left and right shoulders in quick succession.

The next instant, something prickled inside of Asuna's head.

It wasn't a new gesture by any means; she recognized the classic sign-of-the-cross motion. It featured prominently in many Western films, and even within VRMMOs—some healers liked to do it as a role-playing motion. Perhaps a proper Christian would not enjoy seeing the motion coopted in this way, but Asuna was not a Christian, and it wasn't anger or displeasure that hit her just now. It was more like her fingertip had caught against a string that wasn't to be touched...

Her entire body went tense, and her eyes were wide. The cloaked player finished making the sign of the cross and put that hand to the grip of the pistol. His right foot drew back and he assumed a firing position, ready to shoot Pale Rider at last...

"Wha—?!"

Everyone in the room exclaimed at once.

For some reason, the cloaked player had bent over backwards at an extreme angle. The reason for this came to them a split second later. From outside the frame, an enormous orange bullet shot past and grazed the hem of the splayed-out cloak, tearing through the spot where the player's heart had been just a moment before, then passed out of frame.

Someone must have sniped at the cloaked player from a great distance away. It looked to Asuna like the shot had come from behind him and to the left. It clearly took tremendous skill for him to evade an attack at that angle and speed so deftly. Even in an unfamiliar game, she was certain of that.

The cloaked player regained his balance with an eerie, lifeless smoothness, and turned back to his left for just an instant. Asuna felt like his invisible face smirked beneath that dark hood.

Something in her head twitched again.

What? What is this? Is it...a memory? But that can't be true...
I've never been to GGO, or even seen footage of it in action...

The cloaked player raised his pistol again, ready to fire it straight through Asuna's confusion. This time, he unceremoniously pulled the trigger at the paralyzed foe on the ground.

There was a high-pitched gunshot. An empty brass casing flew out and skittered onto the dusty ground.

The bullet hit Pale Rider in the center of the chest with a tiny flash. It certainly wasn't the kind of enormous attack that would eradicate all his HP at once.

Pale Rider himself bore that impression out a second later when his paralysis effect finally wore off, and he instantly leaped up and pointed his large gun at the chest of the cloaked player.

"Yikes, what a turnaround," Lisbeth murmured, and Asuna could see it coming, too.

But there was no blast, no flash, no clicking of a trigger. The gun fell out of Pale Rider's fingers and clattered on the ground at his feet.

Next, he leaned slowly to his right, kept leaning—and fell stiffly to the ground once again.

Below the smoke-gray visor of his helmet, his narrow nostrils and lips were visible. His mouth trembled, then gaped wide. Silent furor shot out from within. Asuna understood intuitively that this was the shock and fear of the player within the avatar.

"Wh...what the...?" Leafa gasped, her hand to her mouth. Then something even more surprising happened. The fallen, writhing form of Pale Rider went as still as if someone hit the pause button, then faded into a crawling static pattern and disappeared.

The visual effect hung in the air for a while after the avatar vanished, eventually clustering into letters that spelled out DIS-CONNECTION. They were scattered by a pair of matte black boots as the cloaked player strode forward, pulling his hand back behind his cape.

The location of the cameras must have been visible within the game, as he pointed his gun straight toward the screen. Asuna felt a shiver run down her back at the sensation that he was pointing from GGO to ALO—no, from virtual reality to actual reality, at her flesh-and-blood body.

The red-glowing eyes flickered from the darkness of the hood. A mechanical voice rasped out of the screen.

"My true name, and that of this weapon…is Death Gun."

The instant she heard that voice, the sound of raw, twisted emotion shrouded in cold artificiality, Asuna felt the biggest crack yet in the depths of her memory.

Her breathing stopped. Her pulse quickened. The hidden face grew to cover the entire center of the screen. The voice came again.

"One day, I will, appear before, you too. This gun, will bring, true death. I have, that power."

The black gun creaked slightly. Asuna couldn't prevent a shiver at the thought of the trigger being pulled, and a bullet flying straight through the virtual screen at her. The cloaked figure seemed to smile from the darkness, mocking her fear. Again, the voice came:

"Don't forget. *It's not, over. Nothing, is, over…* It's showtime."

The last two words were delivered in halting English. The final, biggest shock of all.

I know him.

She was sure of it. She'd met him before. Traded words with him. But where…?

She already knew the answer. It was in the floating castle… Aincrad. Not the safe replica floating in ALO's sky, but the true alternate world that had trapped her for two years: Sword Art Online. The "it" that wasn't "over" referred to the name of that game.

Who is it? Is someone I met in that game controlling the avatar under that cloak?

Despite her daze, Asuna's mind worked frantically. A sudden hard sound from behind caused her to leap up onto the sofa. She turned around to see the source of the sound—a crystal tumbler that had fallen onto the floor and shattered into tiny polygonal shards, which were quickly disintegrating. It had fallen out of Klein's hand as he sat on a stool at the bar counter. His eyes were wide under the bandana; he didn't even realize that he'd broken the expensive player-made glass.

"What the hell are you doing back th—" Lisbeth started, but Klein's hoarse rasp cut her off.

"N-no way... That can't be..."

Asuna stood up from the sofa, turned, and shouted, "Do you know him, Klein?! Who is he?!"

"I-I don't remember his old name...but...I know one thing for sure..." The warrior turned eyes etched deep with fear onto Asuna. "He's a Laughing Coffin member."

"...!!"

Lisbeth and Silica joined Asuna in sucking in a sharp breath. The name Laughing Coffin was vividly painted into their memories—the red guild that had committed numerous atrocities on their fellow players in Aincrad.

Asuna steadied herself with a hand on her two friends' shoulders. She asked Klein, "Y-you don't think...he's their leader, the one with the cleaver...?"

"Nah...it ain't PoH. The attitude and way of speaking is totally different. But...when he said, 'It's showtime,' that was PoH's catchphrase. Musta been someone close—another guy real high up in the organization," Klein moaned. He glanced at the screen again. Asuna and the three girls followed his gaze.

In the expanded feed at the center of the screen, the cloaked man had put his gun away and was retreating. He slid away to the distant end of the frame as smoothly as a ghost toward the bridge, but rather than cross it, he passed around the far edge of the bridge girder toward the riverbank. The dark gray cloak melted into the shadow of the bridge against the bright contrast of the sun and disappeared.

Leafa's quiet voice broke the heavy silence that filled the room. "Um...what's Laughing Coffin?"

"Well," Silica started, then proceeded to briefly explain the threat and elimination of the murderous guild to Leafa, the only person present who hadn't lived through SAO. When she was done, Leafa bit her lip and looked right at Asuna her with jade-green eyes.

"Asuna, I think that Big Brother must have known this person was in GGO."

"What?!"

"Something was wrong with him when he came back late last night. I think...he must be playing GGO to settle some kind of score..."

This time it was Lisbeth who held Asuna's hand as she grappled with shock. She squeezed reassuringly and shook her head, pink hair bobbing. "But...what about the job he's doing? Didn't he jump into GGO to prepare a report for someone, or something?"

Yes, that was true. Seijirou Kikuoka from the government's Virtual Division had hired Kirito for the job. But even as the man in charge of the SAO Incident Rescue Task Force, Kikuoka couldn't possibly know the details about the rift between Laughing Coffin and the front-line team. But at the same time, she couldn't imagine that Kirito's conversion and the existence of the cloaked player were a coincidence. Something was going on. Something that caused Kikuoka to focus on GGO and hire Kirito to investigate it.

Asuna took a deep breath, squeezed Lisbeth back, and said, "I'm going to log out and try to contact the person who hired Kirito."

"Huh?! You know who it is, Asuna?!"

"Yes. In fact, we all do. I'm going to bring him here to grill him. He must know something. While I'm gone, Yui will search all GGO sites and try to find any data corresponding to this cloaked player."

"You got it, Mama!"

The little black-haired pixie leaped from her shoulder and

landed on the table. Yui shut her eyes and began the process of extracting useful information from the chaos of the Net.

"Okay, everyone…just hang on a bit!" Asuna cried, leaping over the back of the sofa with blue hair flying as she called up her menu window. With a purposeful nod at the group, she hit the LOG OUT button.

Rainbow light enveloped her body, sending her soul flying from the top of the virtual tree to the far-off real world.

12

The game of Gun Gale Online did not feature the "class system" traditional to most RPGs, with warriors, mages, and rogues.

Every player had six base stats such as Strength, Agility, Vitality, and Dexterity, as well as the ability to freely choose and level up hundreds of skills such as weapon mastery, better bullet trajectory predictions, First Aid, Acrobatics, and so on. These combinations allowed a player to make their own unique "build." In other words, that effectively meant that the game had as many classes as there were builds.

The downside was that a poorly designed build—say, STR too low to carry large weapons, plus a focus on heavy arms mastery—limited one's battle ability. So naturally, a number of basic build patterns emerged, as players learned that using *this* weapon effectively required *that* stat and skill. While every player's detailed skill choices were different, this broke down their general builds into a number of broad "class" patterns such as attacker, tank, medic, scout, and so on.

Sinon's "sniper" class was one of those, albeit a rare one. She prioritized Strength so she could equip her massive rifle, along with Dexterity to improve accuracy, and a fair amount of Agility for disengaging and retreating after every sniping attempt. In exchange, Vitality was her dump stat—if she got caught, she was dead anyway, so why bother increasing health? As for skills, Sniper Rifle Mastery was obvious, and she took everything related to accuracy. Again, no use for defensive skills. The tricky part was that even with all the improvements to accuracy, the pulse-measuring system demanded a basic level of player skill for success regardless.

That feast-or-famine build actually put her at a serious disadvantage in the populous battle royale format. It was all too easy for someone to sneak up and ambush her while she was trying to snipe at someone far away. And a sniper was helpless when set upon by close-range attackers with SMGs or assault rifles. She might get off one desperate shot from the hip—which probably wouldn't land—and be pumped full of holes before she could shoot a second time.

For that reason, if Sinon was on her own and fell prey to a high-accuracy midrange attacker like Xiahou Dun with his Norinco CQ, she would lose.

But this time, it didn't play out like that. Through unexpected circumstances, Sinon was accompanied by probably the only lightswordsman in the entire game of GGO.

And when it came to high-risk builds, a sniper had nothing on someone using a photon sword, which was inserted as nothing more than a fun gag by some programmer on Zaskar's development team.

Its range was four feet, the length of the blade itself. That was even shorter than the twenty-foot range of the Remington derringer pistol, the smallest gun in GGO. However, the pale, glowing energy blade contained unfathomable power—it split her point-blank .50 BMG round in two.

If it could cut any shot, then in a way, that made it the greatest defensive weapon in the game. But using a blade just an inch wide to defend against a hail of supersonic bullets, even with the predictive bullet lines, was just about impossible. It required the precision to identify the paths and order of an onslaught of projectiles, the deliberation to quickly and accurately move the sword to deflect, and most of all, the sheer pluck to stare down automatic rifle fire without shrinking.

Sinon couldn't imagine what kind of practice would be necessary to gain all of those skills. They might be beyond the bounds of a VR game to begin with. It demanded the experience, will, and soul power of the player behind the avatar.

Xiahou Dun finished reloading and opened a second hail of fire with his CQ. As she watched Kirito cut down just the on-target bullets out of the storm of glowing lines, Sinon couldn't help but reflect on these concepts.

Strength that transcended the wall between reality and virtual reality. That was the exact boundary that she sought herself. She needed the sniper's precision and bloodless cruelty to crush the weakness of Shino Asada that dwelled within her. She had wandered these wastelands for the last six months in search of targets who would bring her that strength.

If she summoned everything she had to fight and defeat the powerful foe named Kirito, she might get there. This was Sinon's overriding thought ever since their meeting yesterday.

But at the same time, a different feeling was growing within her heart.

I want to know. I want him to tell me. About the place he was before GGO. How did he live there, what did he feel, and how did he survive? In fact, she even wanted to know what kind of person he was in reality. And she had never felt that about anyone before...

"Sinon, now!" Kirito shouted, snapping her back to the situation at hand. He had just finished deflecting all of Xiahou Dun's shots.

Her trigger finger squeezed the Hecate. It would be a sloppy shot with her concentration as affected as it was, but the target was less than a hundred yards away, and her accuracy was maxed out. The bullet struck right in the center of Xiahou Dun's medieval body armor.

In a normal battle, an avatar that lost all its HP would shatter like glass and disappear, but in the BoB final, different rules were in effect that kept the body in place. Xiahou Dun flew through the air, helmet tassel flapping, and landed, limbs splayed, on the dirt. A red DEAD tag began to rotate over his prone form.

She stood up with a sigh of relief and switched out the Hecate's magazine for a fresh one with the full seven rounds. With her trusty friend resting on her shoulder, she turned to her temporary partner.

The side of his face against the setting sun looked somehow mysterious as he twirled the lightsword in his hands and returned it to his waist carabiner. Sinon took a deep breath to suppress a feeling much like her previous urge to know more about him, and said, "The sound of that battle's going to draw more of them. We ought to move."

"Right," he replied, casting a sharp gaze toward the nearby river. "Death Gun must have headed north along the river. He's probably going to hide out and pick his next target when the satellite passes over again at nine. I want to stop him before there are any more fatali—victims. Got any ideas, Sinon?"

She blinked, surprised that he would asked her, then shook her head. She figured that given all the unexpected adjustments she was being forced to make, no good ideas would come to her, but to her surprise, the words emerged quickly.

"…Weird powers or not, Death Gun is essentially a sniper. That means he'll be vulnerable in open space without cover. But if you go north, the forest on the other side of the river fades out pretty quick. All that's left until you reach the ruined city at the center is a wide-open field."

"Meaning that it's quite possible he'll choose that city for his next hunting spot," Kirito muttered, glancing at the faded silhouettes of the high-rise buildings far, far to the north. The distance effects made them look incredibly distant, but it was less than two miles away in actuality. With enough agility and caution, it could be traversed in just ten minutes.

"All right, let's head for the town. If we run along the river, they won't see us from the sides."

"...Got it," Sinon replied. She turned back for a moment. At the foot of the bridge still lay Dyne's body. Oddly enough, the fact that his dead body was there proved that he was still alive. The one who was actually—potentially—dead was Pale Rider, who was gone entirely.

She wasn't ready to believe it just yet. But at the same time, she couldn't accept that it was all a lie.

There was one thing Sinon was certain of, however. This Bullet of Bullets was going to change her. Whether it was in a way she wanted or not, and whether the one who changed her was Kirito or the mysterious cloaked player, was still unknown.

All she could do was trust her instincts. Inspiration was the one skill that no player build could boost.

While she didn't have as extreme a build as Spiegel, Sinon's Agility was far from low. Numerically speaking, she ought to be around the same as Kirito, who claimed to be a Strength-first player.

But as they sprinted together, Sinon found that it was everything she could do to keep up with that long, fluttering black hair. Something about the way he carried himself was different. Kirito leaped over every countless rock and sudden crack at the water's edge, as though he had their locations memorized. The way that he occasionally looked back to check on her and seemed to be slowing down to match her pace filled her with spite.

On the other hand, they reached the flatlands of the southern half of the island much faster than she expected, thanks to the way Kirito found the easiest route to run. Eventually the riverbed beneath her feet turned to concrete, and the skyscrapers of the city were just ahead. They finally reached the ruined city, the main battlefield of the map.

"We never caught up to him," Sinon noted to Kirito as he

rested his legs. She'd been hoping that they might catch Death Gun emerging from the river in an unarmed state, so they could pick him off easily. "You don't suppose we passed him at some point, do you?"

Kirito turned back and grimaced at the river behind them. "No, definitely not. I was watching the water while we ran."

"Oh…"

For one thing, without an Aqua-Lung, he couldn't stay submerged in the water for more than a minute. Death Gun was already carrying the massive L115 rifle, so he couldn't have the weight capacity for another big piece of equipment. He must have sunk into the water, followed the current north, then gotten out somewhere out of sight and run off.

"Then he must be hiding out somewhere in town already. The river ends right over there," she pointed out, indicating the culvert beneath the city that the water flowed into. Thick metal bars blocked the pipe, making it clear no player could slip in. Obstacles like that were programmed to be indestructible, even to a hundred plasma grenades.

"Good point…Only three minutes until the next scan. And as long as he's in this city, there's no way to hide from the satellite's eye, right?" Kirito asked. Sinon thought for a second before nodding.

"Right. In the last tournament, you showed up even on the first floor of a high-rise building. The only places to hide are the water or the caves, both of which have major risks. There's no other place to hide from the scan."

"Okay. Then once we learn his location in the next scan, we'll rush him before he can shoot anyone else. I'll go in directly, and you back me up."

"Fine," Sinon shrugged, "but there's one problem. Death Gun isn't his character name, remember? We can't confirm his location on radar if we don't know which name refers to him."

"Oh…g good point," Kirito murmured, his pretty eyebrows wrinkling. "Well, there were three names you didn't recognize on the list of thirty, right? I was chasing after Pale Rider, and that wasn't him. Which leaves two…Musketeer X and 'Steven'… If one of the two is in the city, then we'll know for sure."

"But if they both are, we don't have time to think it over. We need to decide which one to attack right now. Oh, and by the way…" She cleared her throat. "I couldn't help but notice that a musket is a type of gun, and if you turn the X diagonally, it becomes a cross, like the sign he was making. I don't know, maybe that's a little too convenient…"

"Hmm…Well, I think everyone's character names in MMOs are generally pretty cliché. I mean, mine is just a wrinkle on my real name. What about you?"

"…Same."

They shared an awkward look, then cleared their throats simultaneously. Kirito clearly wasn't able to decide yet. He mentioned, "Meanwhile, if this 'Steven' is a foreigner, like his name suggests, that would settle the matter. Are there any foreign players in the BoB?"

"Umm…"

She checked her wristwatch—under two minutes until the scan. Sinon tried to explain as quickly as she could. "For the first tournament, you could choose either the US or JP server, and I understand that a few non-Japanese players were on the JP server, with the Japanese interface and all. I wasn't playing GGO yet at the time, but from what Spiegel told me, the first BoB champion was one of them. Supertough, just slaughtered all the Japanese players with a knife and handgun alone."

"Huh…What was his name?"

"Um, Sub…Subti-something. It was a weird name. But by the time I started playing, you could only connect to the JP server if you were actually located in Japan, so all of the players in the second and third BoB have been Japanese…or at least residents of Japan. So even though 'Steven' was written with the alphabet, it must be a Japanese person."

"I see," Kirito muttered, blinking hard, then made up his mind.

"Okay, if they're both in the city, we'll go after Musketeer X. If I get hit with a stun round like Pale Rider, don't panic. Just get into sniping position. Death Gun will emerge and try to finish me off with that black pistol. Shoot him then."

"Uh…"

Sinon forgot that there was only a minute left. Her eyes went wide, staring into his big black pools. "Why…would you…"

…*trust me so much?* she finished without saying. "I mean, what if I shoot you in the back, rather than Death Gun?"

Kirito's eyebrows shot upward in surprise. He grinned very slightly. "I already know you wouldn't do that. C'mon, it's time. Let's do this, partner." The lightswordsman dressed in black patted her arm and starting trotting up the stairs from the riverbed to the city.

The spot he touched got the same odd, warm tingle she felt in her fingertips yesterday. She followed him up the stairs. She had already lost count of how many times she'd reminded herself since yesterday that he was an enemy she needed to defeat.

They lined up near the top of the concrete steps, crouching just below the spot where they could be seen from the city, waiting for the fourth satellite scan of the day.

She had the satellite terminal in one hand and the chronograph on the other. In real-world time, it was 8:59:55…56… If the battle was going at the same pace as the last time, they'd be in the latter stages, with less than half the combatants remaining. In fact, just moments ago they'd heard gunshots and explosions from the city overhead. The sounds temporarily stopped—they were all in hiding, watching their terminals now.

Eight seconds, nine seconds…Nine o'clock.

A number of white and gray dots appeared on the terminal map.

"Start from the top, Kirito!" she commanded, touching the two dots next to each other on the west bank of the river at the south end of the city. The names that appeared were, of course,

KIRITO and SINON. Since no close-range battles would take fifteen minutes, the other players had to realize by now that they weren't fighting, but working together. It wasn't against the rules, and players had cooperated this way in the past, but they had to be thinking, *Sinon? Of all people?* All she hoped was that none of the stream cameras caught her in the act of working with him.

She kept all of this distraction at bay as she touched all the northern dots, dead or alive, checking the names. No-No, Yamikaze, Huuka, Masaya...all famous, recognizable names. If neither of the two names they were searching for showed up in town, it meant their theory was wrong from the very start...

Wait.

"...There!" they both shouted in perfect synchronization.

At the outer edge of a round, stadiumlike building in the center of the city. The name popped up at the perfect sniping location with a great view: MUSKETEER X.

She and Kirito shared a look, then returned to their terminals. They cross-checked, Sinon from the north and Kirito from the south. Five seconds later, they looked up again and nodded.

"Musketeer X is the only one in the city," Sinon whispered.

"And 'Steven' isn't," Kirito rasped. "That means Musketeer X is Death Gun. And he's probably aiming for..."

He placed a finger on a dot over a building to the west of the center stadium—the name was Ricoco. In order to move to another spot, he would have to expose himself to Musketeer X.

Even as Sinon noted this, Ricoco's dot started heading for the building exit. The instant he stepped out into the street, he'd be hit by that L115's stun rounds. They had to stop Death Gun before he approached and shot his victim with that pistol again.

Kirito stashed his terminal away and faced Sinon. He was about to say something, then closed his mouth, followed by a simple, "Cover me."

"You got it," she replied, getting up. She walked up the stairs in front of Kirito, checked the area, then waved him onward, bouncing up the last stair herself.

The ancient ruined city at the center of the island known as ISL Ragnarok seemed to be modeled after New York City in the real world. Soaring towers that combined practicality with traditional beauty split the evening sky, while English signboards and advertisements covered the street-level surfaces. Naturally, they were all cracked with age and covered in vines and sand.

Sinon and Kirito sprinted down the street that ran over the river as it went underground. Aside from the two of them, Death Gun, and his target, the city contained at least five or six other players, but there was no time to worry about them now. Fortunately, the previous scan showed no one close enough to reach their street at a moment's notice. There were also rotted-out yellow taxis and large buses here and there that served as excellent cover. The pair ran north, weaving through the vehicles.

With their AGI-aided sprinting, they raced 700 meters in less than a minute—half the length of the city—until the large round stadium appeared before them. Sinon motioned Kirito over to the shadow of a nearby bus. They peered out through its cracked panorama window.

The outer wall of the stadium was about three stories high, with entrances at each cardinal direction. If Musketeer X hadn't moved since the satellite scan, he would be just above the western entrance. Sinon stared up at the top of the wall. Thanks to her Hawkeye skill, the distance effects faded away, bringing the distant objects into focus. At the lip of the crumbling concrete, there was a little triangular split, just like an arrowhole...

"...Found him. Up there."

She'd seen the glint of a rifle barrel in the light of the setting sun, and so had Kirito. He responded, "Looks like he's still waiting for Ricoco to emerge...Let's attack from the rear now, while we have the chance. You get into sniping position from the building across the street."

"What...? But I'm going with you into the stadium," she started to protest, but he cut her off with a look.

"This is the best way to make use of your ability. I'll be able to fight him freely, knowing that you'll back me up with your gun if I get into trouble. That's how a team works."

"..."

She had no choice but to agree with him. He grinned the tiniest bit and checked his watch. "I'll start combat thirty seconds after splitting off from you. Will that be enough time?"

"...Yeah, more than enough."

"Good. Let's do it, then."

The black-haired swordsman pulled away from the bus, faced Sinon directly for a moment, then took off running for the stadium's south gate without a sound.

Sinon felt a strange feeling in her chest as she watched his slender back race off. Nerves? Concern? It was similar, but different. Was it—could it be—forlorn loneliness...?

What a stupid thing!

She clenched her teeth, cursing herself.

I'm acting entirely rationally, all in an attempt to win the BoB and prove that I am the greatest player in this world. I want to get rid of Death Gun so that he stops sowing chaos with his mysterious system-transcending power, and temporarily working with Kirito is a necessary step to achieving that. As soon as we succeed, the lightswordsman becomes my enemy again. We will split up, and the next time I meet him, I'll pull the trigger without hesitation, defeat him, and forget him. I'll never see him again after that.

She ran, ignoring the prickling sensation around her heart. Some buildings in the city could be entered and some couldn't, and those that could had very obvious entrances. For instance, the building to the southwest side of the wide, barren circle surrounding the stadium featured a gaping hole where the wall should be.

If she climbed up to the third floor, she'd be able to see over the outer wall of the stadium. It was too close for proper sniping; the target would almost certainly see her. But if Kirito creeped up on Death Gun, the player would be too distracted to notice her.

She'd wait for an opening and shoot. Then she'd leave the city and Kirito behind. That was the plan...

Sinon believed she was acting as calmly and rationally as she always did. But she couldn't deny that a considerable part of her was dominated by a very different, uncharacteristic thought.

She recognized this just as she was about to pass through the crumbled part of the building wall, and felt a powerful chill in her back. She started to turn around, but couldn't even do that before she fell right into the street.

What...just...?!

At first she couldn't tell what had happened.

A shiver ran up her back...something shone on the left side of her vision...she automatically raised her left hand, and a violent shock ripped through the outside edge of her arm. She was about to leap forward into the nearby building, thinking she'd been shot, but her legs wouldn't move, and she sprawled out onto the street.

Once all of that had properly registered in her brain, Sinon tried to sit up, but her body wouldn't listen. All she could move was her eyes. She tilted them down at her extended left arm, to check the forearm for damage.

But it was not a bullet piercing the sleeve of her desert camo jacket—more like a silver needle. It was about a fifth of an inch wide, and two inches long. The base of the needle made a high-pitched whir and glowed, while little stringlike sparks traveled from her arm to the rest of her body.

An electric stun round.

It was the exact same projectile that had paralyzed Pale Rider—noncompatible with assault rifles, machine guns, or handguns, but usable only with certain large-bore rifles. And she hadn't heard a shot.

There weren't many players using large rifles with suppressors.

But even after accepting all of this, Sinon couldn't bring herself to accept that it was *him* who had shot her. After all, the stun round hit her from the south. But he was *in* the stadium to the north. He was supposed to be aiming for a different target, unaware of Sinon's presence. And she was certain that no player would be able to attack her from the south this early, based on what she'd seen in the Satellite Scan. No-No, Huuka, and Yamikaze were all on the other side of the severely collapsed region that would take time to navigate.

She couldn't understand. Why? Who? How?

It wasn't words that answered her, but a single sight.

Little dots of light fizzled into life in a space about sixty feet to the south, where there should have been nothing. Someone appeared out of thin air, like a chunk had been cut out of the world itself.

Her paralyzed throat opened in a fierce, soundless bellow.

Optical Camo!!

It was the ultimate camouflage material, sending light itself through the surface of the armor and making the wearer invisible. But that skill was supposed to be available only to a small subset of extremely high-level unique boss monsters. Did they throw some mobs into the map of the BoB as a new experiment? They hadn't announced any such thing.

With a flap in the wind, the dark gray cloth cut through the chaos of her racing thoughts.

A long, trailing cloak, the surface in tatters. A hood of the same color that entirely covered the head. To her shock, her attacker turned off the Optical Camo and revealed himself. It was the cloaked player, who should not have been there.

Death Gun.

The silent assassin who had erased Pale Rider just minutes ago, and possibly killed the previous champion, Zexceed, and the major squadron leader, Usujio Tarako.

On the inside of the wavering cloak, she could see the barrel of the massive rifle stretching nearly to his feet, and the sound suppressor fixed to the end. If the large cloak had camouflage abilities, it could cover the entire rifle and allow him to snipe while invisible. Even better, in fact—he could hide from the Satellite Scan. It was the only explanation for why there hadn't been a dot near the road on the latest scan.

Did that mean Death Gun wasn't Musketeer X...?

...*Kirito.*

Sinon called the name of the swordsman in the back of her head, realizing that he was somewhere in the stadium behind her, about to attack the wrong player. She didn't hear his voice respond, of course.

Instead, she heard only a soft, scraping footstep. The cloaked player was sliding closer. In the depths of his dark hood, two glowing red points blinked at irregular intervals.

The eerie, ghostlike presence stopped about six feet away from Sinon's prone form. A hissing, creaking whisper came from his hidden face.

"Kirito...This will tell, if you are real, or false."

The cloaked player knew that Kirito was in the stadium, and yet was speaking to him, not her. The halting voice was metallic, and nearly without emphasis of any kind, though it seemed to be hiding some kind of enormous, burning emotion on the inside.

"I remember, seeing you, fierce with rage. When I kill this woman...your partner, I will know, you are real, if you go mad again. Now...show me. Show me, your anger, your bloodlust, your madness, once again."

Sinon didn't understand a word of what he was saying. But the cloaked man's terrible announcement actually had the effect of lowering her shock and fear somewhat.

Kill? Me? A guy who has to skulk around and hide behind camouflage?

Anger burst forth within her. The heat of that feeling overrode the numbness in her body.

The stun round was still sparking madly, but because it hit her in the left arm, she could just barely manage to move her right hand. Fortunately, the grip of her MP7 SMG was just within reach. She might be able to hold it, point it up, and pull the trigger. If she could fire a whole magazine into him, she just might win.

Move. Move!

The commands Sinon sent from her brain through the Amu-Sphere somehow overcame the game system's paralysis effect, and her right hand began to crawl. Her fingers brushed the familiar grip of the MP7.

At the same time, Death Gun removed his empty left hand from his cloak and lifted it slowly, ponderously. Two fingers touched his hooded forehead. Though she hadn't noticed it before, there was a three-layered, pale blue circle in the air behind Death Gun's head with a blinking red [•REC] in the middle—the stream camera. Countless viewers within and without GGO were watching footage of Death Gun in the midst of his triumphant cross gesture, with Sinon collapsed miserably on the ground in front of him.

His bony hand, clad in black leather, crossed his breast to the left shoulder. Meanwhile, Sinon had the grip of the MP7 in her palm at last.

The guns in GGO had safeties, of course, but nearly all players left them off in battle, prioritizing the increased quickness to fire over the infinitesimal chance of firing accidents. Sinon was one of them. She just had to aim and pull the trigger. She had time. She would make time.

Death Gun finished his cross, stuck his right hand into his cloak, and began removing it just as quickly. Sinon did her best to raise the MP7 with her numbed hand. She nearly fumbled it several times, but recovered desperately in each case. The ultrasmall, three-pound SMG was impossibly heavy. But Death Gun would still need to cock the hammer before he fired. She would surprise him by firing at that moment…

But the instant he removed his hand and she saw the automatic pistol, Sinon's entire body turned to ice, gun hand included.

Why? It was just an ordinary pistol. She'd been face-to-face with much bigger Desert Eagles and M500s in the past. She shouldn't be intimidated by this one. She just had to grip the MP7, point it at the enemy, and pull the trigger.

But before she could jolt her arm into motion again, Death Gun put his left hand against the slide, and she caught sight of the left face of the gun. In particular, she saw the all-metal grip with vertical serrations, and the little logo in the middle.

A star inside a circle.

A black star.

The Black Star. Type 54. *The Gun.*

Why…? Why now, why here, why *that* gun?

The SMG that was her final hope slipped out of her powerless hands. She didn't even register the sound of it hitting the ground.

The hammer cocked with a click. His left hand enveloped the grip, and he took aim at Sinon with the sideways Weaver stance. Suddenly, the darkness under the hood of the cloak twisted eerily. It wavered and dripped like a viscous liquid, revealing two eyes.

Bloodshot whites. Small black irises. Dilated pupils that looked like deep holes.

It was him. The man who had barged into the post office at that little northern town five years ago with a Type 54 and tried to shoot Shino's mother. Little Shino had leaped onto the gun in a mindless panic, wrested it away, and shot him with it—they were the eyes of that very man.

He's here. He was here, hiding in this world, waiting for his moment of vengeance.

She had no more sensation in any part of her body, not just the right hand. The red sun and gray of the ruins was gone, leaving only two eyes in the darkness and the barrel of the gun.

The sound of her heartbeat was huge in her ears. If she passed right out, the AmuSphere's safety measures would automatically log her out, but her mind stayed intact, waiting for the moment he pulled the Black Star's trigger. The trigger creaked. Just a fraction of an inch more, and the hammer would hit the firing pin, releasing the .30-caliber full metal jacket. It wouldn't deliver

numerical, game damage. It was a real bullet. It would pierce Shino's heart, turn it off, and kill her.

Just as she did to that man.

This was fate. There would be no escape. He would have tracked her down and found her, even if she hadn't chosen to play GGO. It would have happened one way or another. Everything was pointless. She shouldn't have even bothered trying to cut herself free from her past.

Amid that torrid whirlpool of resignation, there was one tiny feeling like a single grain of sand.

She didn't want to give up. She didn't want this to be the end. She was finally about to understand the meaning of strength. The meaning of fighting. If she stayed with him and watched him go, one day, it would all click…

The gunshot cut that line of thought short.

She didn't know where she'd been shot at first. Sinon closed her eyes, waiting for the moment her mind turned to nothing.

But…

It was the cloaked player who lurched forward. The eyes inside his hood vanished, returning to red glowing points. An orange damage effect was gleaming on his right shoulder. Someone had shot Death Gun. Before another thought could penetrate her mind, there was a second shot. This bullet grazed the left shoulder of the cloak from behind. Based on the impact of the sound, it was a very high-caliber gun. The cloaked man crouched and promptly ducked through the hole of the nearby building to hide.

Sinon could still see Death Gun from her angle. He put the Black Star back in its holster and pulled the L115 down from his shoulder, exchanging the magazine—from the stun round to its deadly .338 Lapua rounds, she guessed. Even Sinon, as a sniper herself, had to admit that his movements were quick and precise as he pointed the lengthy rifle, looked through the scope, and fired without hesitation.

The silenced *shunk* of his shot happened at the exact same moment that a third attack came from behind. But this wasn't a gun. An object like a small gray can of juice rattled into the street between Sinon and Death Gun—a grenade. Death Gun withdrew further into the building.

She shut her eyes tight. She'd take massive damage if a grenade went off this close to her. Still, that was better than being shot by the Black Star. In fact, dying normally was much preferable. She'd bow out of the tournament, then leave GGO and VRMMOs entirely, living quietly in the real world. Living in fear of when the man would track her down again…

But once again, things did not play out as Sinon expected.

The grenade that exploded half a second later was not the popular plasma type, or ordinary gunpowder or napalm—it was a smoke grenade that emitted harmless gas.

"…!"

Sinon held her breath as her entire vision was shrouded in white smoke.

If she was going to escape, this would be her final chance, but the stun effect hadn't worn off yet. If she could pull the stun dart out of her arm, she'd regain mobility at once, but she couldn't even get her right arm to move around that far. More important, she no longer had the spirit to stand.

She lay there on the ground, mind essentially nonfunctioning, her eyes wide open—when someone grabbed her left arm.

She was dragged upward. Whoever it was dropped the large, unfamiliar gun and pressed a hand to Sinon's back. Before she had time to topple over, she and the Hecate on her shoulder rose up into a pair of arms.

After that, she felt acceleration nearly crush her body. The wind whipped in her ears. Eventually the surrounding smoke thinned out, and as her vision returned, she caught sight of the player who was running with her in his arms.

Pure white skin. Eyes black as obsidian. Long hair trailing in the wind.

Kiri…to.

She couldn't form the sounds. His girlish face was too beautiful, and the expression on his features too serious—no, desperate—for her to speak. She could tell that he was giving the commands to his avatar so fiercely and intently that his nervous system was practically charring itself.

It made sense. Even if Kirito was a STR-first player with only a lightsword and handgun for equipment, adding Sinon and the Hecate had to put him just at his weight-carrying limit. The fact that he could run this fast in those circumstances was nothing sort of miraculous. And on second examination, he wasn't unharmed. There were fresh damage splashes on his right shoulder and left arm. The brightness and volume of light said that the cause was very high-caliber bullets. As an American VRMMO, GGO was programmed with a fairly low pain-absorption level, so while serious wounds like this wouldn't actually *hurt*, there would be significant numbness.

It's okay...Put me down and go.

But she couldn't say it aloud. Her entire body, her whole mind, was numb.

So when the high-caliber round came screaming just past her face from behind, Sinon did no more than blink. In its sloweddown state, her mind processed the details. She didn't hear a gunshot, which meant the bullet came from Death Gun's L115. It was way too close and precise a shot to have passed through the smoke, which meant he was pursuing them. She didn't know what kind of build Death Gun had, but he had to be at least as fast as Kirito. He'd catch them eventually.

Kirito had to understand that as well. But the lightswordsman never slowed down or made a move to drop Sinon. He just gritted his teeth, panted heavily, and kept sprinting.

They circled around the east side of the stadium, trying to pass into the north half of the ruins. Just as on the south side, a main street went straight north. There were more abandoned cars and buses here, but not enough for them to stay out of sight until they left the city. Where was Kirito taking her...?

That question was answered by a half-busted neon sign that appeared on the side of the road.

The blinking sign, barely visible in the evening light, advertised RENT-A-BUGGY & HORSE. It was an unmanned rental vehicle business, just like the one in Glocken. Nearly all of the three-wheeled buggies in the parking lot were destroyed, but there was one that seemed like it might still be functional.

But that wasn't the only vehicle. As the sign advertised, next to the buggies were several large, four-legged animals—horses. But these were not living creatures. They were robot horses whose metal frame and gearworks were exposed to the air. Once again, there was one that might be functional.

Kirito raced into the parking lot and waffled for just a second between the three-wheeled buggy and the robot horse. Through her stiffened jaw, Sinon was just able to grunt, "No…horse. It moves fast, but…too difficult to ride."

Very few people could master the manual-shift buggy, either, but the robot horses were even harder. It was more of a player skill issue than a statistical numbers game, so lots of tedious practice was necessary to master it. With less than a single year in the books for GGO, no player had had enough time to dedicate to learning such a task yet.

Somehow, her advice didn't make up Kirito's mind for him, but he eventually gave in and trotted over to the surviving buggy. He touched the start-up panel and turned on the engine, put Sinon on the rear step and hopped into the seat, kicking the accelerator on. The thick rear wheels screeched, and the buggy turned hard, sending up a cloud of smoke.

Once he had the vehicle pointed north with the street, Kirito shut off the machine for a second and shouted, "Sinon, can you blow up that horse with your rifle?"

"Huh…?"

As movement finally started to return to her right arm, she pulled out the stun round at last. Only when she turned back to look at the robot horse did she understand. Kirito didn't want Death Gun chasing after them with it. That seemed quite unlikely to her, but she nodded anyway.

"F-fine, I'll try…"

Her arms were still trembling as she tried to hoist the Hecate back up. She pointed the gun toward the cold, gleaming horse barely twenty yards away. That was close enough that her skill level would automatically hit the target, even without looking through the scope. She put her finger on the trigger to bring up a pale green bullet circle, then focused it tight on the horse's flank. She squeezed…

Click.

Her eyes went wide. It didn't give.

She couldn't pull the trigger. She looked down at the side of her trusty gun to make sure she hadn't somehow turned on the safety, but that wasn't the case. She squeezed again. But the sensation was as tough as if the trigger was welded into place.

"Huh…? Why…?"

Click. Click. It was still the same. She looked down at her finger and saw something she never expected: her finger wasn't even touching the trigger. Between her pale fingertip and the smooth steel was empty space a fraction of an inch wide. No matter how hard she squeezed, she couldn't close the gap…

"I can't…pull it… What the…? I can't pull the trigger!" she wailed in a little squeak. It wasn't the voice of Sinon, the sniper with ice in her veins, but the whimpering of Shino Asada in the real world.

Just then, a black figure came into view through the haze of smoke around the east end of the stadium.

It wore a tattered cloak that flapped and kicked violently in the wind. A massive rifle in the right hand. It was Death Gun—or the man who had always tormented her, taking Death Gun's form.

Her vision went dark. Her legs went limp. Her body was cold.

No…no, it's the onset of one of my spasms. I've never had one while I'm here, while I'm Sinon. And I was even fine on my very first dive, when they shoved a pistol into my hand...

"Sinon! Hang on!" came a loud voice, and a hand gripped her arm hard. She clutched Kirito's torso as he guided her. A moment later, the ancient fossil-fuel engine roared. The front lurched up into a wheelie, and the buggy shot forward onto the road.

Each time Kirito stomped on the shift pedal, the corresponding lurch in acceleration threatened to pull Sinon off the vehicle. She just barely kept her wits from surrendering to terror and clung to the skinny body with all she had. Only the faint bit of body heat she felt from him kept the encroaching darkness from swallowing her entirely.

Now in top gear, the buggy's screech echoed off the walls of the ruins as it raced up the main street.

Are we going...to escape?

She didn't have the courage to look around and see. It was at this point that she realized her whole body was shaking.

Sinon moved her shaking fingers and pushed the Hecate back up onto her shoulder just before Kirito shouted nervously, "Crap, not yet! Stay alert!"

She turned around out of habit to see the robot horse she'd failed to destroy leaping out of the now-distant parking lot. Her eyes went wide with disbelief, but she didn't need to check who was riding it.

The rider's cloak billowed out like the black wings of an ominous raven. The L115 was slung over his back, and his hands clutched the wire reins. The way he stood up in the saddle and bucked with the movement of the horse was that of an experienced rider. The heavy rumbling of its hooves as it galloped churned up the innermost part of her brain.

"But...how...?"

He shouldn't be able to ride it. She'd heard that even experience with real horses didn't prepare one to ride these mechanical horses. But the black knight smoothly steered around the husks of cars in the street, leaping over one on occasion, pursuing the buggy at the same pace.

He no longer looked like a player to her, but an incarnation of the fear that poured out of her. She wanted to look away, but she couldn't help but focus on the face of the rider over two hundred yards behind them. It was too far a distance to make it out on sight, but even still, Sinon saw two eyes and a large, leering mouth in the darkness of the hood.

"He's going to catch us… Go faster…faster…faster!" Sinon shouted shrilly, nearly a shriek.

Kirito responded by gunning the gas even harder. But just as he did, one of the rear wheels went over a piece of debris and lost its grip, causing the buggy to slide to the right.

Sinon screamed and leaned left, trying to regain her balance. If the buggy spun out here, Death Gun would be upon them in barely ten seconds. Kirito desperately tried to control the lurching vehicle, swearing at it with all he had.

After several seconds of high-pitched tire squealing and snaking back and forth, Kirito had it under control and speeding up again. But in that short delay, Death Gun closed much of the distance.

More and more obstacles appeared on the highway that split the city, taunting them and forcing the buggy to corner to the best of its ability. On top of that, small piles of sand formed here and there on the road, making it harder for the wheels to maintain their grip. It swayed to the sides with each little dune, causing Sinon's heart to skip a beat each time.

These conditions applied to their pursuer as well, but the obstacle course was more of a handicap for the buggy than the four-legged mount, and Death Gun smoothly piloted it around the broken vehicles, gaining ground all the way. On top of that, he had one absolute advantage.

Both the three-wheel buggy and robot horse were meant to seat two. One of them was carrying two people, while the other had a single rider. The buggy's acceleration was clearly slower than the horse's.

Each time it passed behind cover and showed up again, the rider's silhouette grew steadily larger. Though it was much too far away to reach her, Sinon felt the hissing, grating breath against the back of her neck.

Just when he closed the gap to about a hundred yards, Death Gun took his right hand off the reins and pointed it at them. In his grip was the black handgun: the Type 54 Black Star.

Sinon stared at the gun, her body frozen, unable to hide on the back step of the buggy. Her teeth trembled and chattered irregularly. Without a sound, a red bullet line touched her right cheek. Sinon's neck craned to the left on its own, without her willing it to move.

The next moment, the barrel of the gun flashed orange like a demon opening its jaws...

Clang! The deadly bullet passed about four inches to the right of Sinon's cheek with a high-pitched roar.

Even after the bullet raced in front of the buggy and hit a wrecked, old car in front of them, tiny little particles of light hung in the air and touched her cheek. She felt a sharp, cold pain, as if she'd just touched dry ice to the spot.

"Aaaah!!" she screamed, turning away from the grim reaper behind her and burying her face in Kirito's back. A second bullet hit the rear fender of the buggy, sending a hard shock through her legs.

"Oh no, oh no...help...help me..."

She shrank up like a baby, whimpering. The gunfire stopped, but the hoofbeats grew steadily louder as Death Gun switched to a new strategy that would get him a better shot.

"Sinon... Can you hear me, Sinon?!" Kirito shouted, but she couldn't respond. She could only crouch down on the buggy's rear step, moaning to herself.

"Sinon!!"

This final, fierce bellow caused her to stop at last. She slowly craned her neck until the rear view of Kirito's flowing hair came into sight. He was staring straight ahead and gunning the gas, his voice calm despite the obvious tension.

"Sinon, he's going to catch up with us at this rate. You need to snipe him."

"I...I can't..."

She shook her head like a sulking child. The weight of the Hecate II pressed into her shoulder, but instead of the usual drive to fight, the sensation brought her nothing.

"You don't need to hit him! Just keep him at bay!" Kirito continued, but she could only shake her head.

"I...can't... He...he's..."

Sinon knew that even if she put a 12.7 mm bullet in the heart of the ghost from her past, he would not stop. A warning shot would produce nothing.

Instead, Kirito turned around, his black eyes flashing. "Then you take over driving! I'll shoot that gun instead!!"

That shook something tiny that still remained within Sinon—a meager amount of pride, perhaps.

The Hecate...is part of me. No one else...can use it...

The fragmented thoughts sent a tiny pulse through her trigger hand. She ponderously took the massive rifle off of her shoulder, set it down on the roll bar across the buggy's rear, then hesitantly got up and peered through the scope.

Even at the minimum magnification level, the short distance to the target—less than a hundred yards—made Death Gun and his robotic horse take up a third of the view. She reached up, ready to bump up the zoom to get a better shot at the center of his body, then stopped.

It occurred to her that if she zoomed in any further, she'd get a good view of the face under the hood. Her fingers stopped moving. Sinon moved her right hand to the grip and entered sniping position.

Death Gun should have noticed what she was doing, but he did not stop or show any signs of evading. He kept coming straight for them, hands on the reins. She knew he was disrespecting the threat she posed, but she didn't feel any anger—all she felt was fear at the possibility that he might once again pull out that cursed reincarnation of the Type 54 that once attacked Shino.

One shot. Just one shot. Even if he saw the bullet line, she might be close enough that she couldn't dodge in time. It was a weak, passive hope, but that was all Sinon had to scrape together at this point. She moved her index finger to the trigger, ready to pull.

But once again, that strange stiffness crept into her finger and prevented it from working.

No matter how hard she squeezed, her finger would not touch the trigger. It was as if the Hecate itself, her trusty partner, was rejecting her...

No, that wasn't it. *She* was rejecting *it*. Inside of Sinon, Shino was refusing to fire the gun.

"...I can't shoot," Sinon/Shino rasped. "I can't shoot. My finger won't pull the trigger. I...I can't fight anymore."

"Yes, you can!" a stern voice belted, right into her back. "Every one can fight! The only choice is whether to fight or not to fight!"

Even with that challenge from the man she chose as her greatest rival, the vanishing flame within Sinon's heart barely wavered.

A choice. Then I choose not to fight. I'm tired of feeling this pain. Every time I thought I found hope, it was taken away and destroyed; I'm tired of it. It was an illusion that I could be stronger through this game. I have to bear my hatred for that man and fear of guns for the rest of my life. I have to look down at the ground, hold my breath, don't look, don't feel...

Suddenly, a burning flame enveloped her frozen hand.

Sinon's eyes opened wide.

Kirito had turned his body around on the front seat of the buggy and leaned over her back. He stretched out his arm as far as it could go and grabbed her hand just before she could pull it off the Hecate's grip, squeezing it tight.

He must have fixed the pedal to keep the buggy going at top speed, because they weren't slowing down, but sooner or later they would hit an obstacle in the road if he didn't turn back around to steer. Kirito paid no mind to any of that. He shouted in her ear, "I'll shoot with you! So just move that finger once!"

Sinon didn't even know if the game would allow two people to fire one gun together. But she did feel a blazing warmth where Kirito's palm touched her, slowly thawing her frozen fingers.

The index finger twitched, the joint creaked, and her skin touched the metal of the trigger.

A green bullet circle appeared ahead, but it extended well past Death Gun's body, bouncing and pulsing wildly with the racing of her heart and the rattling of the buggy. At this rate, Death Gun wouldn't even need to worry about dodging.

"It's n-no good...There's too much shaking to aim," she groaned weakly.

His reassuring voice sounded in her ear. "Don't worry, the shaking will stop in five seconds. Ready? Two...one...now!"

There was a sudden bounding noise with a terrific shock, and the rumbling simply stopped. The buggy had climbed up something and jumped into the air. She caught sight of the ground out of the corner of her eye and noticed a wedge-shaped sports car stuck in the ground like a primitive ramp. Kirito must have pointed the buggy straight for it before he turned around.

How can he stay so calm in these circumstances? Sinon wondered for just an instant. But she denied it just as quickly. *No... it's not being calm. He's going all out. He's not making excuses, he's choosing to use every ounce of ability he has to fight. That's it—that's his strength.*

The previous day, in the final of the preliminary bracket, she asked Kirito if he had that much strength, what could he possibly be afraid of?

But that question itself was a mistake. True strength was facing forward *despite* fears, troubles, and suffering. There was only one choice there: to stand or not to stand. To shoot or not to shoot.

She couldn't imagine herself doing what Kirito did. But, if not forever—at least now.

Sinon tried with all of her mind and body and soul to pull

the trigger of her beloved gun. The spring, tuned to be light, felt unbearably heavy. But with the help of the warm hand doubling hers, her finger steadily sank into it. The bullet circle shrank just enough to make her feel a bit better, but the enemy's silhouette didn't even fill half of the sphere.

It probably—definitely—won't hit him, she thought as she pulled the trigger, the first time she'd ever made a shot as a sniper with that attitude.

The Hecate II positively exploded, releasing its pent-up dissatisfaction in a blinding flash from the muzzle.

Her uneven support prevented her from eliminating the recoil, knocking her backward, but Kirito was there to keep her steady. As the buggy passed the peak of the jump and began to descend, Sinon kept her eyes wide, watching the course of the bullet. The projectile cut a spiral in the evening air, just barely passing to the right of the reaper's horse behind them.

I missed...

There were more bullets in the magazine, but Sinon didn't even have the willpower to pull the bolt handle anymore.

But perhaps because the "goddess of the underworld" had too much pride to miss entirely, the enormous antimatériel round did not just open a harmless hole in the asphalt; it rammed into the side of a large truck stretching across the highway.

Nearly all of the man-made objects placed around the GGO environments could be used as cover for players to hide behind. But since this was taking as many cues from an FPS as an MMORPG, there were certain risks involved with that. When objects like barrels and large machinery took enough damage, they might explode. Every once in a while, a decrepit old car rotting in the road still had gas in the tank, and if a bullet struck true...

A small flame licked out of the side of the large truck. Death Gun noticed this as he was about to pass around it, and tried to have the robot horse jump to the other side of the street.

But an instant before he could, an enormous fireball erupted, bathing the truck and horse in blinding orange light.

The three-wheel buggy landed at last and jolted off the ground at the same moment that the shock wave of the explosion rumbled the street below. She didn't see the explosion itself, because it was blocked by the sports car they'd jumped off of, but there was no missing the resulting jets of flame and spraying metal parts of the robotic horse.

Did we beat him? she wondered for just a moment, then stamped out that ray of hope. There was no way a simple explosion would kill that grim reaper. At best, they had bought some time. Still, even that felt like a tremendous miracle at this point.

Kirito was facing forward again, regaining control of the buggy and accelerating once more. Sinon slumped over the rear step, staring at the black smoke cloud rising in the purple sky of evening. No thoughts came to her mind. She simply gave in to the rumbling of the racing buggy.

The density of rusted-out vehicles and buildings began to thin, replaced by more rocks and odd-looking plants, until she realized the three-wheeled buggy had passed out of the city and into the desert to the north.

Even the road steadily turned from cracked asphalt to simple sand that had been hardened into furrows. The rumbling of the tires got much fiercer, so Kirito slowed down and drove them between the dunes at a more moderate pace.

Sinon started counting the number of big cacti on either side for no good reason, until it occurred to her to check the watch on her left wrist. The fine needle pointed to 9:12. To her surprise, the string of events from leaving the river bed at the south end of the city until now had taken barely ten minutes.

But in that small span of time, Sinon's perspective on the BoB final—if not the entire game of GGO itself—had changed dramatically.

Now that she could think with some level of rationality again, there was no way that the player behind Death Gun could be the same man as the one Shino had shot in the attempted postal office robbery years ago. The gun that had put that idea in her head in the first place—the Type 54 Black Star—was a minor but reasonably common gun in GGO. In fact, it had a pretty low price on the market. It wasn't impossible that Death Gun would happen to choose it for a sidearm.

The problem was that seeing the gun had shocked and frightened her, nearly prompting one of her fits. One of Sinon's goals in this game was to fight against an enemy using a Black Star. She had believed that if she came face-to-face with The Gun, she would deal with it without shrinking, just as she had dispatched countless other targets in this world.

But in reality, *this* had happened. The effects of the stun round had worn off already, but her whole body still felt dull, and her hands wouldn't stop shaking. Even the comforting weight of the Hecate in her arms was painful.

It was all a lie. An illusion. The massive kill score I built up over these weeks and months and the strength I thought that number represented meant nothing in the end...

As she hung her head, the tires slid over the sand and came to a halt. She heard Kirito's calming voice. "Well, the view's nice... but there's not much in the way of places to hide..."

She dimly recalled that when Kirito saved her from her paralysis, he was heavily damaged already. He probably wanted to find a safe place to hide out in the desert so they could use the auto-distributed first aid kits to regain some HP. But the healing speed on those items was significantly slow. If they were going to recover safely, they'd need more than just sand dunes and cacti to hide behind.

Sinon lifted her heavy head and looked around. She noted some reddish rocks off in the distance and pointed them out. "There... We'll probably find a cave over there."

"Oh, good idea. I remember you saying that the caves in the desert area were hidden from the Satellite Scan," Kirito replied quickly, turning the buggy off the path and into the thicker sand. In less than a minute they were there, circling around the rocks. As she expected, there was a large cave mouth in the north face of the rock. Kirito slowed the buggy down and drove it right in.

It was fairly spacious on the inside, with a dozen or so extra square feet of space, even after they rolled the buggy into a spot hidden from the view of the entrance. It was dark in the back, but thanks to the faint bits of sunset reflecting off the walls, it wasn't totally black.

Kirito turned off the engine and stepped onto the sand, stretched, then turned back to Sinon. "Let's stay here for now to avoid the next scan. Oh, but wait—does this mean we won't get the satellite data on our terminals, either?"

She couldn't help but smirk at the impertinence of his question. Sinon got off the buggy on lifeless legs, made her way to a wall and slumped down against it. "Of course not. And if someone happens to be nearby and tosses a grenade in here on a hunch, we'll both be blown up."

"Good point. Well, it's still better than disarming entirely to hide underwater. Speaking of hiding," Kirito said, wandering away from the buggy and glancing toward the entrance, "he just *popped up* right next to you. Does that ripped-up cloak of his have the ability to make him invisible? When he just vanished at the bridge, and didn't show up on the satellite, maybe it wasn't because he was in the river…"

"I think you're right. That was an ability called 'Metamaterial Optical Camo.' They said it was only something bosses used… but I suppose it's possible that some equipment can make use of it," she explained, then realized what Kirito was worried about. She glanced at the mouth of the cave and added softly, "I think we're fine here. It's rough sand below. He can go invisible, but not silent, and we'll see the footprints. He can't just pop up the way he did earlier."

"Good to know. We'll have to keep our ears open," Kirito said, convinced, then sat down to her right a few feet away. He rummaged in his belt pouch and pulled out a tube-shaped medical kit, then clumsily pressed it to his neck and pushed the button on the far end. It made a little hissing sound, and his avatar was briefly consumed with a red visual effect that indicated healing. A single kit would heal about 30 percent of one's HP, but the full effect took three minutes, so it wasn't much use in combat.

Sinon looked back to her watch. It was just now nine fifteen, the time of the fifth satellite pass. But as she had told Kirito earlier, the signal wouldn't reach them, so there was no point in checking the map.

At the last tournament, the battle royale had started at eight o'clock, just like this one, and it had taken a bit over two hours for the final showdown between Zexceed and Yamikaze. If this one played out at that pace, there would be around ten people left right now. Last time, Sinon was the eighth fatality, just twenty minutes in, so she'd improved on her record considerably not that she was in any mood to celebrate it.

Sinon lowered her hand, leaned back against the wall of the cave, and mumbled, "Hey...do you think, maybe...Death Gun died in that explosion...?"

In her heart, she knew the likelihood of that was incredibly low. But she couldn't help but ask. After a long silence, Kirito answered, "No...I saw him jump off the robot horse before the truck blew up. It was close enough that he got hurt...but I can't believe he'd be dead from that."

It was true that an explosion at that close range normally caused considerable damage.

Normally. To a normal player.

But he wasn't normal. He used that Black Star to kill Zexceed, Usujio Tarako, and probably Pale Rider as well. Maybe the cloaked man really was a ghost, wandering the network. She couldn't say that out loud, of course. All she did was grunt in understanding, place the Hecate in the sand next to her, and clutch her knees.

Head pressed downward, she asked, "How did you save me that quickly when you were in the stadium? Weren't you up on the outer walls?"

She thought she detected a wry grin from him. Sinon turned her head to see the lightswordsman leaning against the wall, hands folded behind his head.

"I could tell at first glance that Musketeer X wasn't the guy we were looking for after all..."

"...How come?"

"Because she wasn't a guy, she was a woman. A proper one, not my fake F-model kind."

She murmured in surprise. Kirito shook his head and looked a tad bitter.

"That was when I realized we'd missed something big...and when it occurred to me that Death Gun might go after you alone, I rushed up and cut down Musketeer X while she was still giving me her name. I'll have to apologize to her later about that..."

Sinon grunted again, but couldn't help but wonder if he intended to apologize for rushing his opponent rudely, or simply because his opponent was a woman. But before she could say anything, he continued:

"I took a hit, too, but I still won, and when I looked to the south, I saw you collapsed in the street...It looked like trouble, so I grabbed Musketeer's big rifle, as well as a smoke grenade, and jumped down from the walls. Then I started shooting and tossing and charging and..."

He shrugged, as if to say, *You know the rest.*

Which meant one of the two bullet wounds in Kirito's body was from Musketeer X's rifle, and the other was from Death Gun's L115. He made it sound like no big deal, but she'd seen his defensive capabilities in the battle against Xiahou Dun. The fact that he'd taken two shots was a sign of how desperate he had been to save her.

On the other hand, you could say that this showed Sinon was just holding Kirito back. Perhaps, even with Death Gun's unexpected Optical Camo gear, she might have paid more attention to her surroundings and sensed him coming, avoiding the stun round properly. If she'd been able to regroup with Kirito sans paralysis, they might have been able to take down Death Gun right then and there.

Assuming he was just a normal player and not a vengeful ghost, of course.

Sinon bonked her forehead against her knees, plagued by indecision and a feeling of powerlessness. She felt Kirito lean closer. He murmured, "You don't have to take it out on yourself like that."

"..."

She took a small breath and waited for him to continue.

"I didn't realize he was hiding in wait, either. If we'd taken the opposite roles, it could have been me who got stunned. And if that was the case, you'd save me, right?"

That peaceful, sensible voice pierced Sinon's heart deeply. She closed her eyes, feeling it throb with pain.

He's consoling me. I thought he was my rival...I thought I'd be fighting him on equal footing. And all this time, he saw my inner weakness. He's been cheering me up, like I was a child in need of encouragement.

And even harder to bear, harder to forgive, was the realization that somewhere within her, just as strong as her humiliation, was a desire to give in to his comfort, physically and mentally.

Sinon...no, Shino knew that if she admitted to the fear and pain that agonized her and reached out just a few feet, the mysterious but honest and simple lightswordsman would accept her and buoy her with all of his feelings and words. He might even give her the forgiveness that Shino had always sought but no one had ever given her since the post office attack five years ago.

But if she did that, the other part of Shino, that icy sniper, might disappear for good. And even before that, she didn't know how she could reveal her innermost thoughts to a person she had just met the day before—a person whose real name or face she didn't even know. Shino hadn't truly spoken her mind even to Kyouji Shinkawa, who'd been her friend in the real world for six months.

Trapped between desperation, helplessness, hesitation, and confusion, Sinon could do nothing but clutch her knees.

Long, long seconds passed.

Eventually, Kirito spoke again. "Well, I'm going. You should stay here and rest a bit more. I really wish you'd just log out, but…it is the tournament, after all…"

"Huh…?" She automatically perked up and looked over. Kirito had stepped away from the wall and was checking the battery level on his lightsword. "You're going…to fight Death Gun…on your own?" she rasped.

He nodded, just barely. What he said next was not an assurance of victory, but just the opposite. "Yeah. He's tough. Even without the power of that pistol, his other gear, stats, and his skill as a player put him head and shoulders above the rest. In fact, it'll be nearly impossible to keep him from firing that gun at least once. It was half a miracle that we got away from him just now. The next time that gun is pointed this way…I don't know that I'll be able to stay standing. I might actually abandon you and run away this time. So I can't force you to take part in this any longer."

"…"

This caught her by surprise; she assumed the swordsman had ultimate confidence in his ability. She stared at his face. The light in his big black eyes seemed to be wavering with a sudden lack of will.

"Even you're afraid of him?" she asked.

Kirito snapped his lightsword back onto the carabiner and grinned weakly. "Yeah, I am. The old me…well, he might have fought him, even knowing it could be fatal. But now…I've got things to protect. I can't die, and I don't want to die…"

"Things to…protect?"

"Yes. In the virtual world…and the real world."

She felt like he was referring to a connection to someone else. Unlike Sinon, Kirito had forged close bonds with many different people. Her heart throbbed again, and words poured out of her mouth before she could stop them.

"Then…just stay hidden in this cave. You can't log yourself out of the BoB, but if we let the event proceed, and it's down to us and one other person, we can escape. We'll commit suicide and let whoever else win. Then it's over."

Kirito's eyes widened. He grinned in understanding briefly, then shook his head. It was what Sinon expected of him.

"You're right, that's an option. But…not one that I can take. Death Gun's probably recovering his HP somewhere else right now, but if we let him reign free over this event, there's no telling how many more he might shoot with that pistol…"

"…I see."

You really are strong.

Even after claiming he had something to protect, he hadn't lost the courage to risk his life standing up to that angel of death. When she had been ready to give up both.

Sinon smiled a lifeless smile and thought about what would happen to her once she left this island.

When Death Gun had pointed his black pistol at her in the street of the ruined city, she was completely lost. Her bones turned to ice. She screamed and shrieked while on the escape, and couldn't even pull the trigger of her beloved Hecate. Sinon, sniper of ice, was on the verge of obliteration.

If she stayed hidden in this cave, she'd never be able to trust her own strength again. Her heart would shrivel, her fingers would stiffen, and every shot would miss its mark.

Not only would she not overcome her memories, but even in the real world, she would quiver in fear of the man's appearance from every shadowed corner, through every door or window. That was the fate that awaited Sinon and Shino, virtual or real.

"…I…" She looked away from him and mumbled, "I won't run."

"…Huh?"

"I won't run. I won't hide here. I'll go out there and fight him, too."

Kirito squinted a bit and leaned closer to her. "You can't, Sinon. If he shoots you…you might actually die. I'm a red-blooded close-combat fighter with defensive skills, but you're not. If he sneaks up on you and strikes from point-blank range, you'll be in much greater danger than me."

She clamped her lips shut, then found one simple conclusion.

"I don't care if I die."

"...Wha..."

His eyes went wide again. She explained slowly, "I...I was terrified earlier. I was afraid of dying. I was weaker than I was five years ago...so I acted pitiful, and screamed...and that's not going to cut it. If I'm just going to keep living life that way, I'd be better off dead."

"It makes sense to be afraid. Everyone's afraid of dying."

"Well, I don't like being afraid. I'm tired...of living in fear. I'm not asking you to help me with this. I can fight on my own," Sinon claimed, willing strength into her limp arms to get up. But Kirito leaned over and grabbed them. His voice was tense and quiet.

"So you're saying you'll fight alone...and die alone?"

"...Yes. That's probably my fate..."

Shino had never suffered any judgment for her grievous crime. That was why the man came back for her. To punish her for what she'd done. Death Gun was not a ghost—he was fate. An ordained result.

"...Let go of me. I need to leave."

She tried to shake him off, but Kirito only held on tighter. His black eyes glittered. Those small, elegant lips formed uncharacteristically harsh words.

"You're wrong. It's not possible for people to die alone. When someone dies, they also die within others around them. There's already a Sinon within me!"

"I didn't ask for that. I've never put myself within anyone!"

"We're involved right now, aren't we?!"

Kirito yanked Sinon's hand upward until she was right in front of his face. In that instant, the raging emotion that had been held in place at the very bottom of her frozen heart erupted. She clenched her teeth so hard they might crack, and used her free hand to grab Kirito's collar.

"Then..."

Her weakness in search of soothing and her urge for destruction brought forth an emotion that she had never held toward anyone, and forced words she had never said before from her mouth. With all of the fire in her eyes that she could summon, Sinon shouted at Kirito, "Then protect me for the rest of your life!!"

Her vision warped suddenly. Her cheeks felt hot. Sinon didn't realize at first that it was because tears were spilling from her eyes. She yanked her hand out of his grasp, made a fist, and slammed it against Kirito's chest. Twice, three times, she pummeled him with all of her strength.

"You don't know a damn thing about me... You can't do a thing for me, so don't act like you know! This is...this is my fight, and my fight alone! If I lose and I die, no one has the right to criticize me for it! Or are you going to bear my burden all of your life?! Are you..."

She thrust her clenched fist in Kirito's face. The hand that had pulled the bloody trigger of a gun and stolen a human life. The filthy hand that still had the tiny spot from where the particles of gunpowder had infiltrated her skin.

"Are you going to hold...this murderer's hands?!"

A number of voices from Shino's memories emerged, accosting her. In the classroom, when she accidentally touched other students or their belongings: "Don't touch me, murderer! I don't want blood on me!!" She was tripped and pushed away. Since then, she had never actively touched another person. Not once.

She smacked him with her fist one more time. There was no system-provided protection here; the entire island was a battlefield. So each blow had to be doing some tiny bit of damage to Kirito's HP, but he did not budge an inch.

"Ah...aah..."

The tears kept coming, without end. She turned her face away,

not wanting him to see her cry, and her forehead thumped against his chest.

She squeezed her face against him, still gripping his collar, sobs escaping between her clenched teeth. Even as she was wracked with uncontrollable childlike gasps, she couldn't help but marvel that this kind of energy had been within her all this time. She couldn't even remember the last time she'd cried in front of someone.

Eventually, she felt Kirito's hand on her shoulder. But Sinon batted it away with her clenched fist.

"I hate you…I hate you!" she shouted, her virtual tears falling one after the other, fading into Kirito's thin shirt.

She couldn't tell how long she stayed like that.

The tears dried up at last, and Sinon felt as empty and powerless as if her soul had left her body and evaporated into the air. She leaned with all of her weight against the swordsman. The sweet pain that took hold in her chest after her cathartic explosion of emotion felt comfortable now. She kept her forehead against his shoulder, breathing in and out.

Eventually, it was Sinon who broke the long, long silence.

"I still hate you…but let me lean on you a bit longer," she mumbled. He murmured in the affirmative. She budged, leaning over atop Kirito's jutted-out legs. She still didn't want him to see her face, so she turned her back to him, and saw the three-wheeled buggy, its rear bumper punctured with bullet holes, and the last dying light from outside of the cave entrance.

Her head felt dull and fuzzy, but unlike the lack of thought when she was under attack by Death Gun, this felt more like the floating liberation of removing tight, heavy clothes. Eventually, the words found their way to her lips.

"The thing is…I killed someone." She didn't wait for Kirito's response. "Not inside a game. I killed a real person, in real life. Five years ago, there was an attempted robbery of a post office in a small town in Tohoku…The media reported that the culprit shot one of the employees, then died when the gun backfired. But that's not what happened. I was there. I stole the robber's gun, and shot him with it."

"Five years ago…?" Kirito whispered. She nodded.

"Yes. I was eleven at the time…so maybe it was only because I was a child that I could do it. I broke two teeth, sprained both wrists, bruised my back, and dislocated my shoulder, but other than that, I was unharmed. My injuries healed right away…but some things don't heal."

"…"

"Ever since then, I've vomited and passed out whenever I see a gun. Even on TV and in manga…even when someone makes a gun gesture with their hand. When I see a gun…I see the face of the man I killed…and I get scared. Terrified."

"But—"

"Right. But I'm fine in this world. Not only do I not have the spasms…" She looked over at the graceful design of the Hecate II on top of the nearby sand. "I've even learned to love some guns. So I thought, if I can be the strongest person in this world, I'll be stronger in reality, too. I'll be able to forget that memory… but when Death Gun attacked us earlier, I nearly had an episode. I was terrified…somehow I had gone from 'Sinon' back to my real self…That's why I have to fight him. I have to fight him and win…or Sinon will be gone forever."

She clutched herself. "Of course I'm afraid of dying. But…but more than that, I'm tired of living in fear. If I run from Death Gun and my memory without fighting…I'll be weaker than I was before. I won't be able to have a normal life anymore. So…so…"

She shivered suddenly, struck by a terrible chill.

"Me too…" Kirito mumbled, the weak cry of a little lost child. "I've killed someone before, too."

"Huh…?"

This time it was Kirito's body, still stuck to her back, that shivered.

"I told you earlier...that I knew the cloaked man...Death Gun, in a different game."

"Y-yeah."

"The name of that game was...Sword Art Online. I assume you've heard of it?"

"..."

It was largely what she expected to hear, but she couldn't help but turn her head to look up at him. He had his back against the wall of the cave, his dim eyes staring out into space.

Sinon recognized the name, of course. There couldn't be a VRMMO player in Japan who hadn't heard of it—the cursed game that trapped ten thousand people inside of it for two years, ultimately stealing four thousand of those lives.

"Then, you're—"

"Yes. They called us SAO Survivors on the Net. And so is Death Gun. I'm positive that we fought there, each trying to kill the other." Kirito's eyes floated in space, seeing only the distant past. "He was a member of a red guild named Laughing Coffin. In SAO, based on the color of your cursor, we called criminals 'orange players,' and groups of thieves 'orange guilds.' Those who actively pursued and enjoyed killing were 'red.' And there were lots of them...lots."

"B-but...didn't you actually die in that game, if your HP went down to zero...?"

"That's right. But that was exactly the point. A number of players found killing to be the ultimate pleasure. Laughing Coffin was a group of them. They attacked parties in the fields and dungeons where the system wouldn't protect them, stealing their gold and items, then killing them. The other players started to watch out for them, but they came up with ways to continue finding victims..."

"..."

"So finally, we formed a giant party to vanquish them, and I was in the group. When I say 'vanquish,' we weren't hoping to

kill the members of Laughing Coffin, we just wanted to neutral-
ize their threat and send them to jail. We found their hideout at
great pains, got together players that we knew could handle them,
level-wise, and ambushed them at night. But…the info got out
somehow. They trapped their lair and waited for us. We managed
to rebound, but it was a terrible battle…and at some point, I…"

His body trembled again, eyes wide and breath short.

"I killed two of them with my own hands. I chopped…one's
head off with my sword. The other, I stabbed through the heart.
The plan was just to imprison them, but I forgot about all of that.
My mind was racing…but…that's just an excuse. I could have
stopped, if I'd thought of it. But I let my fear and anger drive me.
At heart, I'm no different from them. In a way, my crime might
be even worse. I mean…"

He took a deep breath, let it out slowly, then continued, "I
mean, I completely forgot about what I did. Ever since I came
back to the real world, I never once thought about the face or
name of the two I killed then, or the one other I killed much later.
Not until I met Death Gun…in the dome beneath the regent's
office yesterday…"

"So you're saying Death Gun was one of those…Laughing Coffin members…"

"Yeah. He must have been one of the members who survived
and was taken to prison. I remember his attitude, the way he
talked. I can almost…*almost* remember what his name was at the
time…"

He shut his eyes tight and pressed his knuckles to his forehead.
Sinon just watched him, her back pressed against his knees.

The boy named Kirito was a player of Sword Art Online.

For two years, he had fought with his actual life on the line,
and survived.

She'd had her suspicions about him. But until he told her in his
own words, she hadn't appreciated the weight of those facts. She
recalled his question during the preliminary final yesterday.

If that bullet could actually kill a player in real life…and if you

*didn't kill them, either you or someone you care about would die,
could you still pull the trigger?*

That was the exact dilemma that Kirito had traversed. In a way,
it was extremely similar to the incident that befell Shino in that
post office five years ago.

"Kirito…"

Sinon got up and grabbed his shoulders. The boy's gaze was
just a bit out of focus, staring at some point in his past. She stuck
her face in his anyway, looking right into his eyes.

She rasped, "I can't say anything about what you did. I don't
have the right. So I really don't have the right to ask you this,
either…but I want you to tell me just one thing. How…how did
you overcome those memories? How did you beat your past?
How can you be so strong right now?"

It was such a careless and self-centered thing to ask someone
who had just spelled out his own sins for her. But she had to ask
him. Kirito claimed that he forced himself to forget, but Sinon
couldn't even do *that*.

And yet…

Kirito blinked two or three times, then looked right into her
eyes. Slowly, he shook his head.

"…I haven't overcome them."

"Uh…"

"Last night, all my dreams were about the battle against Laughing Coffin, and the three people I killed with my sword. I barely
got any sleep. I'll probably never forget the looks on their faces,
their voices, their words…in the moment they disappeared…"

"B…but…" Sinon stammered. "But…wh…what am I supposed
to do, then…?"

Will I be like this my whole life?

It was too cruel a sentence.

Was it all pointless? If she left this cave, fought Death Gun and
somehow won, would Shino's real-life pain continue forever—
regardless of everything…?

"The thing is, Sinon," Kirito said, raising his right hand to softly cover hers as she squeezed his shoulder, "that's probably the right way of things. I lost my rational mind and killed people. And I wasn't blamed for it; I was hailed as a hero. No one punished me, and no one taught me how to make amends for what I did. So I took advantage of that, and avoided examining what I'd done. I tried to forget. But that was a mistake. I cut them down myself, ended their lives, and I should have taken on that weight and continued to think about it. That was the very least I could have done to make amends, and I didn't..."

"...Accept it...and...think about it. But...I can't do that..." she mumbled.

"No matter how hard you try to keep it at bay, you can't erase the past, and your memories never disappear. So...all you can do is look them straight in the face and fight, so that you can one day accept their burden."

"..."

The strength went out of Sinon's arms, and she slid back down over Kirito's legs. With her back and head resting on him, she gazed up at the ceiling of the cave.

Accept the memories, and fight. She couldn't possibly see herself as capable of that. The path to salvation that Kirito found belonged only to him, and she had to find her own way of coping, she felt. But even still, his story might have cleared up one of her troubles. She glanced at his pale face in the gloom and mumbled, "Death Gun..."

"Hmm?"

"You're saying that under that tattered cloak is a real, actual person."

"Well, of course. He was a former officer of Laughing Coffin, that's for sure. If I could just remember his name from SAO, we'd be able to find out his name and address in the real world. To be honest, *that's* why I'm here in this game."

"...Oh..."

So that meant that at the very least, the cloaked man was not a ghost from Shino's past. She squinted and thought it over. "Then you're saying he can't get over what happened in SAO, and came here to GGO…so he could keep PK-ing?"

"I think it's more than that… When he shot Zexceed and Tarako, then Pale Rider in this event, he chose situations where lots of eyes were on him. Same thing with making the sign of the cross—he's doing all of this to convince a greater majority…that he has the power to kill people from within the game…"

"But how can he do that…? The AmuSphere's not like the original…NerveGear, they called it? It can't emit those dangerous microwaves, right?"

"Supposedly. But according to the person who hired me to come here, the cause of death for Zexceed and Tarako wasn't brain damage, but heart failure."

"Huh…? Heart?"

The moment she heard that word, something chilly crawled up her back, and Sinon couldn't help but shiver. Though it seemed impossible, she put her thought into words. "Meaning…he killed them with…some kind of curse, or supernatural powers…?"

As soon as she said it, she was afraid he would laugh at her, but all that came back was Kirito's tense gaze.

"To be honest…unless we find the real person controlling that cloaked avatar, I couldn't begin to guess how he's killing them. I want to imagine that there's no way for someone firing virtual bullets to stop the heart of a flesh-and-blood player…but, wait… now that you mention it…"

He stopped and rubbed his narrow chin with his fingers, which seemed to be his habit when thinking hard. Sinon looked at him askance from her position atop his knees. He murmured vaguely, "That's…weird…"

"What is?"

"When we were in the ruined city, why did Death Gun switch over to his rifle to shoot me, rather than using his black pistol? He was certainly close enough, and in terms of sheer power, the pistol should be higher—one bullet is literally lethal, after all. On top of that, I failed to avoid the rifle shot. If he used the pistol, he could have killed me for sure..."

She found it stunning that he could rationally analyze the chances of himself dying like that. Nevertheless, Sinon offered her own thoughts. "Maybe because he didn't have time to make the sign of the cross? Or the Black Star...oh, I should point out, that gun is called a Type 54 Black Star..."

She momentarily had to stifle the unpleasantness of saying the name aloud before continuing, "Maybe he thinks he has to make the sign when he shoots that thing. Or perhaps the cross is necessary for him to do the killing?"

"Hmm...but when we were escaping on the buggy, he was shooting at you with the Black Star. How could he be making the sign of the cross while riding horseback?"

She glanced over at the three-wheeled buggy. The bullet hole in the rear right bumper clearly belonged to a 7.62 mm round, not the much larger .338 Lapua Magnum bullet. And she had witnessed for herself that Death Gun pulled out the Black Star while on horseback and shot at her without making the sign of the cross.

"Yes...you're right. That's true."

"Meaning that Death Gun could have killed me, but didn't. Yet he shouldn't have a reason to let me go. I was the one who won the prelim block...and to be totally honest, I stick out more than you..."

"Sorry for being so plain," she said, elbowing him in the side.

He cleared his throat and continued, "Fine, let's say we're about the same. At any rate, maybe it wasn't that he *couldn't* shoot me, but that he had some other reason *not* to shoot me..."

"Hmm."

Sinon rolled over, so that she was facing downward atop Kirito's lap. She folded her hands over her head. Her suspicion of and resistance to the boy hadn't disappeared, but she felt that the warmth of their avatars' contact helped keep the black sensation away. She was surrounded by a pale glow of reassurance, and her head was slowly regaining its sense, thinking faster and faster.

"By the way, you were right when you said something was weird…"

"I did?"

"I'm talking about the bridge. He shot Pale Rider with the Black Star, but totally ignored the helpless Dyne right next to him. I was sure he was going to shoot Dyne, too."

"Oh…but he was already dead at that point, wasn't he?"

"He was only dead in that his HP was gone and he couldn't move. But his avatar was still there, and his mind was still logged in. If his power transcends the game, why should the presence or absence of HP make any difference to him?"

Kirito grunted. "Good point. That's exactly right. Same as in the city, in that original scene, Death Gun had some kind of reason for shooting Pale Rider, but not Dyne…"

"Meaning…this? Between you and Dyne, and me and Pale Rider, there's some kind of common element, marking some players as targets, and some players not," Sinon muttered. She felt Kirito nod.

"I think we can assume that's the case. And going back to earlier, I feel like Zexceed and Tarako must have shared something with you and Pale Rider, too. Maybe it just comes down to strength, or ranking, or whatever…"

"Pale Rider was tough and all, but he wasn't in the last tournament. Dyne's much higher when it comes to BoB rankings."

"Then maybe…it has something to do with a special event?"

"Not the case. I was in Dyne's squadron until just recently, and we ventured out on several expeditions together. I hadn't met Pale Rider, or even heard his name before this."

"What about Zexceed and Tarako?" Kirito asked. Sinon grimaced and turned over again. She looked up at the pretty face and shrugged.

"Those two were celebrities within the game a rank above people like me and Dyne…Zexceed was the previous champion, and

Usujio Tarako was fifth or sixth, but also ran the largest squadron on the server. I'd only talked to him once or twice."

"Hmm…Maybe it's equipment, then…or build type…"

"Everyone has different gear. I'm a sniper, Pale Rider used a shotgun, Zexceed had a superrare XM29 assault rifle, I think. Usujio Tarako used an Enfield machine gun. As for build…oh."

"What?" Kirito asked. She raised her eyebrows in apology.

"I wouldn't call it a common connection…but if you really wanted to stretch, you could say that none of us played particularly AGI-heavy builds. But even that's kind of wind. Some of us were more STR-based, others more VIT…"

"Hmmm…"

Kirito's pretty lips curled up, and he scratched at his head. "Maybe he's just choosing his targets without a good reason… I dunno, it feels like there's got to be something there, though. You said you'd spoken to Usujio Tarako, right? What did you talk about?"

"Umm…"

She tried to revisit her weak memory of the event, placing her hands between her head and Kirito's legs, so that she was using him for a pillow. It occurred to her that this was formally known as a "lap pillow," and felt a sudden embarrassment rising within her, but punted it away under the guise of emergency circumstances.

As a matter of fact, she hadn't made lengthy contact with another person like this for several years. An odd comfort buoyed her heart, as though he was supporting some of her mental weight with the physical. When it occurred to her that she'd like to maintain it for a bit longer, the weak smile of Kyouji Shinkawa floated into her head, and she felt guilty for some reason. If she got back to the real world safely, maybe she'd work on tearing down that wall between them…

"Hey, Sinon? What about Tarako?"

"Oh…uh, right." She blinked to clear her thoughts and revisited the distant memory. "I mean, it really was just for a moment.

I think…it was after the last tournament, when we went back to the first-floor hall of the regent's office, just outside. We talked about what the prize would be for two or three minutes… but I didn't fight him directly in the battle, so it was just idle chatter."

"I see. And Death Gun wasn't in the last tournament…He couldn't just be holding a grudge about not winning a prize…It sounds like it's just a waste of time conjecturing about unlikely causes."

Kirito sighed. He blinked a few times, trying to change his mood, and looked down at Sinon. "By the way, I didn't look it up beforehand…What *is* the prize?"

Impressed that in their dire situation, he had the ability to care about what the event's grand prize was, Sinon answered, "You get a choice. The options vary depending on where you place… but we seem to be lasting pretty long here, so it might actually be good stuff. Assuming we survive the ordeal in one piece."

"Like what, for example?"

"For starters, guns or armor…maybe hair dyes you can't buy in the market, or clothes. But they won't have special capabilities, they'll just stand out from the crowd. Also, it's kind of weird, but they'll send you model guns based on the ones in the game."

"Model guns? So, like…not in-game items, but actual physical replicas?"

"Yep. I placed poorly last time, and none of the in-game items were very good, so I chose that option. In fact, I think Tarako chose a model gun, too. I mean, yeah, it's a toy, but they use metal, so it's actually quite realistic and fancy. At least, that's what Shin—er, Spiegel said. As for me…"

She recalled the travesty of what happened when she pulled the model gun out of her desk drawer a few days earlier, and grimaced. "I shoved it away in my desk, and haven't really looked at it."

But Kirito seemed to have latched on to something, and he didn't notice the look on her face.

"A prize...in real life?" he muttered, his expression surprisingly serious. "And did the company itself send it to you? From America?"

"Yes, through EMS—international mail. That's actually a pretty expensive service. I wonder if Zaskar makes a fortune on this game," she smirked.

But when she looked at Kirito again, she blinked in surprise. The lightswordsman was biting his lip, staring intently at a point in space. It was not the look of one considering what he might receive as an award.

"Wh-what...? What's wrong?"

"EMS... But listen, I just made a GGO account the other day, and the only things they asked for in terms of player info was an e-mail address, age, and gender. How did they get your address?"

"Did you already forget?" Sinon asked, exasperatedly spreading her hands. "Remember how there was an address field when you registered for the BoB prelims in the regent's office yesterday? There was a warning there: If you leave it blank, you can still enter, but you might not be eligible for certain prizes. You didn't enter your info, did you? You can't fill it in later, so you won't be able to get a model gun...wait, what?!"

She yelped as Kirito put a hand on her shoulder and lifted her face up toward his own. She froze, thinking he was about to do something inappropriate, but of course, that wasn't the case.

His face was more serious than she'd ever seen, right up in hers. But she couldn't fathom what was so important about what he was asking her.

"What did Dyne pick in the last tournament?"

"Umm...I-I think it was in-game gear. He showed me once; it was a really ugly-colored jacket."

"And Zexceed?"

"I-I don't know...I've never talked to him. But...he was all about efficiency, through and through, so I don't think he'd have any interest in a purely cosmetic item. So maybe he picked the model gun. I heard that the winner and runner-up can get huge rifle replicas. But…why do you ask?"

Kirito didn't answer her. He stared into her eyes, but she could see his mind was afloat on a sea of thoughts.

"Not a virtual item…but a real model gun…If that's the connection between you, Pale Rider, Zexceed, and Tarako… EMS addresses…regent's office terminal…That's the place where…" he mumbled, barely forming fragments of sentences, "Optical Camo…but if it works…not just outdoors…"

Suddenly, the grip on her shoulder went as hard as stone. His eyes were gaping wide, the tiny black dots trembling. Was it… shock? Or fear?

Sinon got up just a tiny bit and shouted, "Wh-what? What is it?!"

"Oh…oh, my God…This is crazy," he croaked, out of luscious red lips. "I…I've been making a terrible mistake…"

"M-mistake?"

"When you play a VRMMO…the player's mind goes from the real world to the game world, and you're talking, running, and fighting there…So I just assumed that Death Gun was choosing his targets and killing them from here…"

"He's…not…?"

"No. The player's body and mind aren't going anywhere. The only difference between the real world and the virtual world is the amount of information the brain processes. A player wearing an AmuSphere only sees and hears digital sights converted into electron pulses."

"…"

"So you see…when Zexceed and the others died, they were in their own rooms. Along with…the real…killer…"

"What…? What are you saying…?"

Kirito clamped his mouth shut for a moment, then opened it again. The breath of his next statement emerged on Sinon's cheek as freezing mist, as if chilled by his own fear.

*   *   *

"*There are two Death Guns*. The first one, the avatar in the cloak, shoots the target in the game. The second one, who is already in the target's real-life room, kills the player as he lies defenseless and unaware."

At first, she didn't understand what Kirito meant. Sinon lurched upward, her mind a blank. She shook her head back and forth.

"But…then…that's impossible. How could they find their…"

"You just said it. They got model guns."

"Then…then the *company* is doing it? Or did they breach the database somehow…?"

"No…that's very unlikely. But even an ordinary player can figure out the address of the targets. Only if they appeared in the BoB final, and they chose a model gun for their prize, however."

"…"

"The regent's office. Anyone who elects to receive a model gun uses the terminal there to input their real name and address. I wondered about it when I was filling out the prelim entry form… Remember how they didn't put the terminals into booths or private rooms, but right in that wide-open hall space?"

Sinon finally caught on to what Kirito was getting at. She gasped and shook her head in tiny, trembling bursts.

"No…you mean he spied on the terminal screen from behind? That's impossible—the distance effects would render text impossible to see beyond a short distance, and you couldn't possibly miss a person being that close to you."

"What if they used a scope or binoculars? Someone I know claimed to have spotted someone punching in a security code using a simple mirror. Is it possible to nullify the distance effect using an item?"

"That would be crazy. If you used binoculars in such an obviously public place, you'd get reported to the GMs and banned. This is an American game, so they take player harassment very seriously."

But Kirito was expecting that response. He leaned in even closer and whispered his theory, the words just barely audible.

"What if...what if the cape Death Gun's wearing...can make use of the Optical Camo ability in town? It was very gloomy in the regent's office hall. If he went invisible in the shadows, nobody would notice him. If he used large binoculars or a scope while hidden, and watched the terminal screen...couldn't he also read the address and real names that players were entering on the form?"

"..."

Invisibility and long-distance sight tools. It might be possible with that particular combination. In-game menu windows were invisible to other players unless you enabled it, but because the touch panel monitors on the terminals could sometimes be used by a group of people at once, they displayed to everyone by default. In both this tournament and the previous one, Sinon had entered her address and name with the screen set to visible. Had someone...had that leering reaper in the tattered cloak actually been watching her from behind? So he could copy her name onto his murder list?

She desperately searched for reasons to discount it, unable to accept the ramifications of this theory.

"But...even if they knew the real address...how would they get inside without a lock? What about the victims' families?"

"Both Zexceed and Tarako lived alone...in old apartment buildings. They probably had real outdated electronic locks with weak security. Plus, they're guaranteed that any target logged in to GGO will be completely unaware of their presence. Even if breaking in proves difficult, they don't have to worry about being detected."

She took another deep breath. It was only in the last seven or eight years that home locks had followed car locks in transitioning to keyless electronic models. It made lockpicking impossible, but she felt like she remembered reading about the early models having "master signals" like master keys, that were cracked and rearranged into unlocking devices that were traded on the black market. Since then, she used not just an electronic lock, but a physical one and a keypad as well. That reassurance did not eliminate the cold crawling up and down her back, however.

Death Gun was not a vengeful spirit from the past, or an avatar with mysterious powers, but a normal, real-life killer.

As the theory took on more and more weight in her mind, a different kind of fear settled over her body. Urged onward by a sense of resistance that she didn't understand, she came up with the last possible rebuttal.

"Then…what about the cause of death? You said 'heart failure,' right? Can they stop the heart using some method the police and doctors can't detect?"

"They probably inject some kind of drug, if I had to guess…"

"But…wouldn't they find that? Like the injection mark, or—"

"The bodies were apparently discovered after a significant amount of decomposition. Plus…sad to say, it's not that uncommon for VRMMO players to die of heart attacks. After all, they're just lying around all day without eating or drinking…As long as the killer isn't ransacking the house or stealing anything, the authorities are going to assume it was a natural death. Still, they took a close look at the state of the brains, but from what I understand…if they didn't expect that the victims were drugged, they wouldn't detect something like that."

"…No way…"

She clutched Kirito's jacket, shaking her head like a child having a tantrum.

Killing for the sake of killing, using such incredibly thorough means…The mind of someone who would do such a thing was beyond her understanding. All she felt was unlimited darkness, filled with tremendous evil.

"…It's insane," she whispered.

Kirito nodded. "I know. It's crazy. But…while I can't understand it, I *can* imagine it. He was willing to go to those lengths to stay a 'red player.' I know that…because there's also a part of me that still feels like the swordsman who fought on the front line of Aincrad…"

The name was unfamiliar, but she soon processed that he was referring to the castle floating in the sky that was the setting of Sword Art Online. For just an instant, she forgot her fear.

"I think…for whatever reason, I understand, too. There are times when I think of myself as a sniper…but then, what about the other one, not the player in the cloak…?"

"Yes, I think it's likely that they're another SAO survivor. Possibly even a fellow survivor of Laughing Coffin…You can't pull off a murder like this without significant teamwork…Oh, wait. Maybe…"

She gave Kirito a quizzical glance, prompting him to explain.

"Oh, it's nothing serious. I was just thinking about the cross gesture. It could be both a sign for the audience, as well as camouflaging a chance to check his watch. After all, he's got to coordinate things with the accomplice in the real world in a very tight window. And he can't just keep checking his watch every time he shoots—it would stick out."

"I see…If he hid a small watch on the inside of his wrist, he'd be able to see the time when he touches his forehead."

Sinon couldn't help but be impressed at the ingenuity of the idea. Suddenly, Kirito grabbed her by the shoulders. His face was more serious than ever as he slowly asked, "Sinon…do you live alone?"

"Y…yes."

"Do you lock up? What about a door chain?"

"I have both an electronic lock and an old-fashioned cylinder lock…The lock itself is one of those early electronic types. And the chain…"

She stopped, frowning as she tried to recall what she did before diving in.

"…might not be on."

"Okay. Listen carefully, then."

There was deeper concern on Kirito's face than she'd ever seen before. Her body went as cold as if ice had been poured into her chest.

No, I don't want to hear what comes next, she thought, but his lips didn't stop.

"Death Gun tried to shoot you while you were paralyzed next to the ruined stadium. In fact, when he was chasing us on the robot horse, he *did* shoot at you. That must mean…his preparations are complete."

"Prep…arations? What kind of…"

Her voice was barely audible. Kirito paused for the slightest of moments and whispered back.

"I think it's possible that…at this very moment, *Death Gun's accomplice is in your room back in the real world, watching the tournament and waiting for the moment you get shot.*"

It took quite some time for his words to penetrate her mind and form a tangible meaning.

The sights around her faded as the familiar sight of her room came to her mind. She stared down at the small room from a height, like some kind of out-of-body experience.

There was the tile flooring that she vacuumed regularly. The pale yellow rug. A small wooden table. The black writing desk on the west wall, next to a black pipe-frame bed. The plain white sheets. On top of the bed, dressed in loose sweater and short pants, was herself—eyes closed, a double-ringed metal device around her forehead. And…

Standing at the edge of the bed and watching the sleeping Shino, a dark figure. Its form was blacked out into a simple silhouette, but one thing in its hand was clearly visible: a cloudy glass syringe with a silver needle extending from the end, filled with a fatal substance.

"No…no…"

She turned her tense, creaking neck, moaning. The vision disappeared, replaced by a sandy cave, but the glinting of the intruder's syringe still flashed in her eyes.

"No…it can't be…"

It was more than just "fear" at this point. A seething impulse to reject the idea raced through her, sending her entire body trembling. A stranger was standing right next to her, looking down at her helpless, unaware body. In fact, it might be worse than that. He could be touching her…looking for the right spot to inject the needle…

She felt something block her throat. She couldn't breathe. Her back arched, squirming in search of air.

"Ah…aaah…"

Her vision faded. A rushing roar filled her ears. Her soul was ripping away from this temporary body—

"No, Sinon!!" bellowed a voice in her ear, deafeningly loud. Someone clutched her arms. "It's too dangerous to disconnect on your own! Hang in there…try to calm down! It's all right, you're not in danger yet!!"

"Ah…ah…"

Her eyes were wide open, but focused on nothing, so she reached out blindly, clinging to the source of the voice. Her arms circled around the warmth of the body, clinging desperately.

A powerful arm reached around her back and enfolded her, holding her tight. His other hand tenderly, softly stroked her hair.

The whisper again: "The intruder can't do anything to you until you're shot by the Black Star, Death Gun's pistol. That's the rule they created. But if your heart rate or internal temperature causes the unit to log you out automatically, you'll see the intruder's face, and that puts you in danger. So you need to stay calm."

"But…but, I'm scared…I'm scared…" she pleaded like a child, burying her face into Kirito's shoulder. She squeezed harder and eventually felt the faint but regular rhythm of Kirito's pulse.

Sinon focused with all her might on the pulse, trying to blot out the terrifying image hanging over the back of her mind. *Tump, tump, tump.* About once a second, his heart beat, the pulse blending into her body. Like matching a metronome, the wild allegro of Sinon's pulse slowly synchronized with his.

As though she had become one with Kirito's mind, the symptoms of her panic faded. The fear was still there, but she could tell that the reason and rationality to control it was returning to her mind.

"...You feel calmer now?" Kirito asked quietly. He started to remove his arm from her back, but Sinon shook her head.

"Stay...just like this, a bit longer."

He didn't respond, but she felt the solid warmth return. With each stroke of her head by the delicate hand, she felt the ice at her core melt a little. Sinon took a deep breath, shut her eyes, and let the tension flow away.

After most of a minute, Sinon mumbled, "Your hands feel like my mom's."

"Y-your mom's? Not your dad's?"

"I don't know anything about my dad. He died in an accident when I was a baby."

"...Oh," he said simply. Sinon buried her face in his chest.

"Tell me what to do," she said, her voice much firmer than she expected.

Kirito stopped stroking her hair and answered promptly, "We beat Death Gun. If that happens, his accomplice in the real world will have to disappear. In fact, you can just stay back here. I'll fight. He can't kill me with that gun of his."

"Are you sure...it'll work?"

"Yeah. I didn't write my name or address on my entry form, and I'm not even diving from my own home. There's someone watching over me, as well. So I'll be fine. I'm just going to beat him according to the rules of the game."

"But...he's still really tough, even without the Black Star. You saw him dodge my Hecate shot from just a hundred yards, didn't you? He might be your equal when it comes to dodging."

"True, I'm not perfectly confident in my chances...As far as other options, like you said earlier, we can hide out here until there are only three players left, then commit suicide, but..."

He glanced at his watch. Sinon looked at the numbers as well:

9:40 PM. They'd already completely passed the nine thirty Satellite Scan. Nearly twenty-five minutes had passed since they had entered the cave.

Her eyes traveled from his watch to his face. She slowly shook her head. "I don't think I can just keep hiding in here. Pretty soon, the other players will realize that we're hiding in the desert caves. There aren't that many to choose from, so they could toss in a grenade at any time. In fact, we're pretty lucky to have survived nearly half an hour in here."

"Oh, I see…" Kirito murmured, biting his lip and glancing at the mouth of the cave.

She told him, "We've been working as a team for this long. Might as well fight together to the end."

"But…what if he shoots you with the pistol…?"

"It's just an old-fashioned single-action handgun," Sinon claimed, surprised at how easily the statement slipped out of her mouth. For years, the Type 54 Black Star had been The Gun—the very image of terror that plagued Shino.

But it wasn't that the fear was gone. If it was coincidence that Death Gun had chosen the Black Star to be his symbol, then The Gun really was the very curse that haunted Shino's life. But the one thing that she could say was that as an item in this game, the Type 54 was not very powerful. If she feared the gun more than the threat it actually represented, she would be passing up her chance to fight back.

"Even if he shoots it at me, you can use that sword of yours to knock it away with ease, right? Its firing rate is barely a tenth of a proper assault rifle, after all," she noted, suppressing the trembling of her voice.

Kirito grinned, a combination of worry and relief. "Yeah… I won't let him shoot you. But in order to ensure that, I think it's best if you don't expose yourself to him."

She started to argue, but he held up a hand. "Trust me, I'm grateful that you're offering to fight alongside me. But you're a sniper, Sinon. Long-distance shooting is the entire basis of your style, isn't it?"

"Well, yes, but…"

"Tell you what. When the next scan comes, I'll jump out into the map to expose my location and draw Death Gun's interest. My guess is that he'll hide in the distance and try to shoot me with his rifle. You use that information to detect his location, and shoot him back. Deal?"

"…So you're going to act as a decoy and spotter?" she asked, shocked by the reckless bravado of his plan, but based on the combination of their builds, that was probably the most effective plan they had. It was clear that in a combination of extreme close-range and long-range fighters, one of the two would be ineffective.

She took a deep breath and nodded. "Deal. Let's do it. But you'd better not die on his very first shot."

"I-I'll try…but his rifle is silent, and there's no bullet line to detect."

"And who was it that bragged about predicting the prediction line?"

Sinon noticed that the fear hanging over her back was fading as they teased each other, still holding each other tight. In truth, she was just trying not to think about the horrifying possibility that a murderer was inside her apartment at that very moment. She had no choice but to cling to Kirito's notion that defeating Death Gun would render him helpless. In fact, perhaps it wasn't his words that she clung to, as much as his virtual body heat. When they left the cave and she split off from Kirito to find a sniping position, she wasn't sure that she'd be able to maintain her current state of mind. So she leaned against him one last time, feeling the warmth of his avatar while she still had the chance.

Kirito murmured suspiciously, "Um…anyway, Sinon, I can't help but notice that some weird red circle has been blinking in the bottom right corner…"

"Huh?"

Her eyes glanced over and saw the indicator he was talking about. For a moment, she had to remember what it meant—then her eyes shot up. She found what she expected to see on the ceiling and was about to leap up from his legs before she realized it would be pointless after that much time. She sighed, "Oh…crap, I didn't think about that…"

Floating up in the air was an odd, pale blue group of concentric circles. It was not a tangible object, but a symbolic glowing light effect. Kirito had spotted it, too, and he was quite confused.

"Umm…what was that thing, again…?"

Sinon shrugged and answered, "It's a livestream camera. It usually only follows players engaged in battle, but since we're running low on combatants, it's had to come after us."

"Uh…crap, do you think it heard what we've been discussing?"

"Don't worry, it doesn't pick up voice unless you really shout at the top of your lungs. Go on, give it a wave," she suggested, her tone of voice presenting a cool challenge. "Or is there someone you'd prefer not to see this?"

For a second, Kirito's face went cold with fear, which was quickly covered with a nervous, stiff smile. "Uhh…no…well… wouldn't that be you? Besides, wouldn't most people watching this just assume we're two girls?"

"Uh…"

He had a point there. In either case, it seemed that Sinon would be required to make some uncomfortable excuses. But that could wait until they had survived the current crisis.

She snorted and said, "It would be more pathetic to freak out the moment you see a camera watching you. And I don't mind… If people want to start rumors about my tastes, at least it will cut down on the number of times I get hit on."

"Does that mean I have to pretend I'm a girl from now on?"

"Don't tell me you've conveniently forgotten that you pretended to be a girl to get me to guide you around town…Oh, it's gone."

Just as it occurred to Sinon that no one watching could possibly guess that they were having such a witheringly sarcastic conversation, the visual effect that indicated the presence of a camera left in search of a new target.

She sighed with relief and finally sat up. "So…it's time. Only two minutes until the next satellite pass. I'll stay down here and you'll check your terminal outside the cave, right?"

She got to her feet and offered a hand to her human chair, helping him up. When she took a step backward, the chill of the desert embraced her body, causing her to wince. She picked up her rifle and clutched the cold steel, feeling the faint core of warmth within it.

"Oh, by the way," Kirito prompted. She looked up to see that the lightswordsman's fine brows were furrowed in thought.

"What is it now? We don't have time to change plans."

"No…the plan is fine. What I'm thinking about is…Death Gun's real name, or official character name. It was Steven, right?"

"Oh…right, that was it. I wonder what the meaning of that was…"

"If I do come into close range, I'll have to ask. Well, time to dip outside."

The black-haired swordsman gave her a resolute nod, turned and started for the entrance of the cave. Sinon couldn't tell if the chill on her skin even with the Hecate in her arms was from the tension of the imminent final battle, the peril that threatened her in real life—or the loneliness of being separated from Kirito.

She hunched her shoulders, drew in a deep breath of dry desert air, and called out to the back of the man walking away.

"…Be careful."

His answer was an upward thumb, visible over his shoulder.

13

Asuna battled with the dread that welled up endlessly from within her, awaiting the moment.

She logged out from the virtual apartment in Yggdrasil City and returned to the second floor of the Dicey Café in the real world. Three minutes ago, she had called a cell phone number. She accosted the person who'd answered and demanded a meeting in ALO at once, then jumped back into virtual space to rejoin the others. It had been less than a minute since she dove back in, but each second felt like an eternity.

"I don't suppose it would do any good to tell you to calm down, Asuna," Lisbeth said from her spot next to the virtual sofa.

Asuna let out a small breath at last and answered tensely, "Yes…I'm sorry. But…I just get this bad feeling. The only reason Kirito would convert to that game without telling us about the Laughing Coffin connection is because of something very serious…Perhaps even some kind of real-life danger."

"Sadly, I can't tell you you're overthinking this. Not after what we just saw," Lisbeth said, referring to the eerie event they'd witnessed on the stream of the Gun Gale Online tournament.

The player in the tattered cloak had shot his opponent with one measly pistol bullet. But the target disconnected and vanished. Then the cloaked player turned to all of the people watching the event and announced, "It's not over. Nothing's over. It's showtime."

As soon as he heard those words, Klein announced with shock that the cloaked man had to be a former member of the SAO red guild Laughing Coffin.

Asuna had experienced many large-scale battles during the two years she'd spent in that floating castle, and easily the worst experience of them all was the battle of the front-line players to eliminate Laughing Coffin. No other battle of player against player ended up with over thirty fatalities.

In all honesty, the fine details of the battle were lost from her memory. The most vivid detail in her mind was the back of the black swordsman who fought like a demon when their group was ambushed and in danger of falling apart. If it weren't for Kirito's efforts, the entire vanquishing party could have perished.

The battle was far, far shorter than any floor boss encounter, and it left about ten dead from the party, and over twenty dead from Laughing Coffin. All of the survivors of the killer guild were sent to the prison in Blackiron Palace, and the dead were briefly mourned. Since then, no one had spoken of the battle. Asuna, Klein, and Kirito each forgot about what happened in their own way. They forgot everything…she had thought.

But she was shocked to find that bloody event of the past coming back like this, a year after everyone had been freed from SAO.

Silence settled over Asuna, Klein, Lisbeth, Silica, and even the unrelated Leafa. They simply waited for the arrival of someone who knew more about the situation than they did.

The knock on the door came about a minute after Asuna logged back in. He had probably dived in as soon as humanly possible after receiving the summons, but Liz gave voice to everyone's honest opinion when she greeted him with "You're late!"

"I…I flew as quickly as I could from the save point. If ALO had a speed limit, I'd have my license revoked," quipped the visitor, a mage of the undine race like Asuna. His slender form was wrapped in a plain robe, his marine-blue hair was styled in a simple part, and his thin, pleasing features were outlined by round, silver-framed glasses.

His character name was Chrysheight. Four months had passed already since he began playing ALO as a companion of sorts to the group. Only Asuna and Kirito knew that his alias came from a combination of *chrysanthemum* and *height*, two of the kanji characters in his real name.

In the real world, his name was Seijirou Kikuoka—member of the government's Virtual Division and onetime agent of the SAO Incident Rescue Task Force. After Kirito returned safely to the real world, Kikuoka had offered all kinds of help to Kazuto, and even helped him rescue Asuna. As for why such a person would bother to have his own ALO character, he had claimed it was "to better get along with you and your VRMMO friends," but Kirito himself claimed that it was just a facet of his information-gathering duties. Asuna herself felt that Kikuoka was a rather fishy character, but she didn't have a good reason to refuse him, so they had adventured together on a few occasions as partners. Until today.

Chrysheight—no, Seijirou Kikuoka—closed the door behind him and strode forward much more comfortably than he had four months ago, when he first dove into the game.

Asuna strode over, boots clicking, until she was right in front of him, stared into the soft eyes that he shared with the real Kikuoka, and asked, "What's going on?"

When she called him on the phone from Dicey Café, all she said was that she had a question about Kirito's conversion to GGO, and she wanted him to come to her place in Ygg City. As he was a bachelor and government official on a Sunday night, she knew this request was a big one, but he was fortunately home at the time, and she didn't need to twist his arm any more than that. For being "home," his reception sounded poor, and there was some kind of rumbling sound coming over the call, but she didn't have time to ask about that. He was there in barely two minutes, so if anything, she ought to apologize for calling on him so suddenly, but the feeling of haste urging her on cut that short.

Chrysheight's narrow eyes blinked several times behind his humorous round glasses. Asuna knew Kikuoka well enough to realize that it was not an act of surprise, but a defense mechanism to allow his high-speed mind enough time to think of an answer.

The mage cleared his throat and began to lecture in the tone of a professor. "It might take some time to explain everything for you. And where to even begin…?"

Asuna was about to round on him for dodging the question, but she was cut off by the appearance of a tiny figure who emerged from among the glasses and cups on the table, who looked up at Kikuoka and said, "Then I shall do it for you."

It was Yui, of course. Her normally lovable little face had taken on Kirito's serious look. In a clear, ringing voice like a tiny bell, she stated, "The first appearance of a player in Gun Gale Online claiming to be called 'Death Gun' was late at night on November 9, 2025. He fired his gun at a TV monitor in a tavern zone within GGO's capital city of SBC Glocken…"

For the next two minutes, Yui ran through the situation to a frightening level of detail. Death Gun made two meaningless gunshots within the crime-controlled zone of town where all attacks were nullified. But they were immediately followed by a disconnection that seemingly *had* to be a result of those shots. The two players who were shot hadn't logged in again since. And there were two strange deaths that fit the time of the shootings.

"…No media outlet went more in-depth than to say that the deceased were logged into a VRMMO at the time, so I cannot be certain if they were playing GGO. But based on the extreme similarity in the cases, I do not need to hack into the network of the coroner's office to make a good case that the victims were Zexceed and Usujio Tarako. Therefore, I have come to the conclusion that Pale Rider, the player who was forcefully disconnected by Death Gun six minutes and forty seconds ago, is already dead in reality," Yui finished. She leaned against a nearby glass. Asuna reached out and scooped up the little pixie, cradling Yui to her chest.

The ability of Yui's AI to sift through media reports and individual testimony and process them into a logical conclusion, then phrase it into a grammatically proper statement, was nothing short of stunning. The flip side of that was the fragility of her emotional circuits. When she was still a mental-care counseling program in SAO, she was unable to process the overflow of fear, desire, and malice from the player population, and was most of the way to a total breakdown when they found her.

To Yui, compiling and selecting from all the information regarding Death Gun had to be a terrible burden. Asuna leaned down and whispered, "Thank you," even as she reeled from the enormity of the information she had just learned.

That shock extended to Leafa, Lisbeth, Silica, and Klein as well. No one spoke.

It was Chrysheight's gentle voice that broke the silence. "This is quite a surprise. I'd heard that little fairy was an ALO Navigation Pixie…but I didn't know they could compile and analyze so much information in such a short time. Do you feel like taking a little job in Ra…er, in the Virtual Division?" the mage joked.

Asuna shot him a dirty look. Kikuoka raised his hands in surrender. "Sorry, sorry. I have no intention of playing dumb at this point. Everything the little one just said…is true. Zexceed and Usujio Tarako died of heart failure right around the point that Death Gun shot them."

"All right, Chrys. You're the one who hired Kirito for this, right? So you're sayin' you knew about the murders, and you still sent him into the game anyway?!" Klein demanded, hopping down from the bar counter to accost Chrysheight. The mage held up a hand to stop him in his tracks. The light glinted off of his glasses, hiding the expression in his eyes.

"Just a moment, Mr. Klein. *This is not a murder case.* That was the conclusion that Kirito and I came to, after a lengthy discussion about the two incidents."

"What...do you mean...?"

"Just think about it. How would he kill them? The AmuSphere is not a NerveGear. You should know that better than anyone. The AmuSphere was designed with every possible safety measure, and no matter how hard you try, it can't put a scratch on anyone's brain—and it certainly can't stop the heart, over which it has no direct influence whatsoever. Kirito and I met last week for a long debate, and that was our ultimate conclusion. There is no way to kill a player's real body with a gunshot from within the game," Kikuoka explained, calmly and logically, like a teacher lecturing an overexcited student. Klein grumbled, but returned to his stool.

Next it was Leafa's turn to break the following silence with a hoarse murmur. "Then why did you ask my brother to go to GGO, Chrys?"

The shapely legs extending from her bright green skort pounded the floor. The sylph warrior got to her feet and slowly crowded in on Kikuoka, as if she were in a kendo bout. "You felt it too...In fact, you can feel it now, can't you? Just like us. There's something to this. Whoever Death Gun is, he's hiding some terrible, horrifying secret."

"..."

Kikuoka fell silent at last. Sensing that even he didn't know what they knew, she offered him their shared secret. "Chrys, Death Gun is...Well, he's an SAO survivor, just like us. And he was a former member of Laughing Coffin, the horrible killer guild."

The tall mage froze, sucking in a sharp breath through thin lips. Even the cool, elite agent couldn't hide his shock this time—his normally soft, narrow eyes bolted wide for an instant. Two seconds later, his voice was subdued.

"...Is this true?"

"Yes. We can't remember his name, but both Klein and I took part in the battle against Laughing Coffin. That means it's not the first time Death Gun killed someone in a game. Are you going to continue claiming that this is all a coincidence?"

"B...but...what are you stating, Asuna? That ESP and curses are real? That Death Gun's had some abnormal power since SAO, and is using it to kill people again?"

"...Well..."

Asuna bit her lip. She had no answer for that. A moment later, Lisbeth broke in.

"H-hey, Asuna? Does Chrysheight know about SAO? I thought he was some kind of government employee involved with networks in real life, and was playing ALO as a way to study VRMMOs..."

Surprisingly, it was Kikuoka himself who confirmed this first. Perhaps he had no intention of hiding this from the start. He explained, "Lisbeth, that is essentially correct, but I was doing a different job before it. I was a member of the SAO Incident Rescue Task Force...not that we ever managed to develop any kind of plan to counteract it. Our team was all name, no results..."

Lisbeth's eyes went wide, and she looked conflicted. Chrysheight was being self-deprecating, and selling himself short. The task force worked quickly after the start of the SAO Incident in November 2022, promptly transferring all ten thousand victims to hospitals around the nation. There was difficulty in acquiring funds for the beds and hospital costs, but according to Kirito, it was Kikuoka himself who had negotiated hard to gain the cooperation of the appropriate government ministries. Every SAO survivor today knew how hard the task force fought, and were grateful for it, not bitter.

Liz, Klein, and the others were, in fact, stuck between their anger at Kirito's dangerous job and their debt to Kikuoka for helping save their lives, and they couldn't take him to task.

Instead, Asuna stepped in and quietly said, "Chrysheight, I don't know how Death Gun is killing people, either. But that doesn't mean that I can just sit back and watch Kirito battle this figure from the past on his own. Isn't it possible for you to figure out the real address and name of whoever is playing Death Gun? I'm sure it's not easy, but if you consult the list of the Laughing Coffin survivors and cross-reference it against all the Internet providers for whoever's connected to the GGO servers…"

"H-hang on. First of all, I'd need a court warrant for that, and it would take hours just to explain the situation to the investigation office…"

Kikuoka held his hands out to placate Asuna, but he seemed to notice something as he spoke and trailed off, blinking. He shook his head.

"No, in fact, that wouldn't be possible to begin with. All the SAO player data the Virtual Division has is real name, character name, and final level. Guild names and number of kills are completely unknown. So just knowing that someone was a former Laughing Coffin member won't help us track down their real name or location."

"…"

Asuna bit her lip hard. She was sure she remembered Death Gun's way of speech and actions. She was certain that she'd come face-to-face with him at some point between the big battle and the aftermath. But she couldn't remember the name. In fact, maybe she'd never even tried to learn it. She just wanted to forget everything she knew about the group as quickly as she could…

"I think my brother is in the midst of that battle now, so he can remember that name," Leafa suddenly mumbled. In a way, she was the closest to Kirito—Kazuto—in real life. She clutched her hands together. "When he came back home last night, he had a terrible look on his face. I think he must have realized that Laughing Coffin was in GGO during the preliminaries last night, and that this person was actually killing again, somehow. So I'm positive he went to settle the score. He went to figure out the player's name, and stop them from PK-ing again."

Asuna held her breath when she heard this. Though it pained

her a bit to admit it, Leafa's guess had to be right. In fact, Kirito had to feel that it was his responsibility. As a member of the group that came together to vanquish Laughing Coffin, he felt a duty to ensure their wicked deeds were eradicated once and for all.

Oh, Kirito. You always have to...You just can't help yourself...

"You...goddamn...fool!" Klein bellowed, pounding the bar counter. His scruffy jaw twisted into a howl. "Don't just leave us outta the loop! If you'd said one damn word about this...I woulda converted without even askin' what game we were goin' to..."

"Indeed...but Kirito would never say. If he felt there was any danger, he would try his hardest to keep us out of it. That's just what he's like," Silica said, wearing a tearful smile.

Leafa smiled and nodded. "Yes...that's right. He's always been like that. In fact, I bet he's even found some enemy combatant in this tournament to protect, right about now."

Out of habit, everyone looked over to the huge screen on the wall. Here and there in the multiwindowed display was the bright flash of gunfire. But as usual, Kirito's name did not appear, and the player who called himself Death Gun in the tattered cloak hadn't shown up since his last exhibition.

Then again, no one present had seen Kirito's GGO avatar, so if he had been the target at any point, rather than the character named as the viewpoint player, they might not have recognized him. Still, KIRITO hadn't disappeared from the player list on the right edge of the screen, and he was still listed as ALIVE as more and more combatants' status shifted to DEAD. Somewhere on that vast island battlefield, he was locked in a subtle, secret struggle with Death Gun.

Even if Asuna converted to GGO right at this moment, she couldn't enter the tournament or help Kirito. But she wanted to do something. She needed to support him, protect him, encourage him.

Filled by this sudden emotion, Asuna turned to Leafa and asked, "Leafa, you said Kirito's not diving from his own room, right?"

"Yes. But all I know is that he's coming from somewhere in the center of Tokyo."

Asuna had already heard as much—that was why she was diving into ALO from Dicey Café in Okachimachi rather than her home in the more distant Setagaya Ward, so she could meet up with Kirito sooner once the tournament was over. She nodded and turned to Kikuoka.

"Chrysheight, I'm certain you know the answer. Where is Kirito diving from?"

"Uh…well, that would be…" mumbled the robed mage, his sea-blue hair waving. Asuna took a firm step forward, and this time he answered in the affirmative. "Yes, I know. I set it up, in fact. The security is airtight, and he's being monitored. There's someone with him, so I can guarantee that his physical body is in no danger…"

"Where is he?"

"…Uh, well, that would be…at a hospital in Ochanomizu, Chiyoda Ward… But don't worry, just because he's in a hospital. It was only chosen because they have heart monitors there, not because we anticipated any bodily harm," Kikuoka said, trying not to make it sound like an excuse. But Asuna waved her hand and cut through his chattering.

"A hospital in Chiyoda?! You mean the same one that he visited for physical rehab?!"

"Well, yes…"

That's close. Dicey Café in Okachimachi and Ochanomizu are only separated by Suehiro in between. It might take five minutes if I can catch a cab, Asuna realized. Her mind was set.

"I'll be going now. To Kirito in real life."

14

When I separated from Sinon and left the cave, the red of the sunset was almost entirely gone, with only a purple brushstroke across the sky to mark the dying of the light.

I'd been under the impression that GGO was stuck in a perpetual twilight, so it was a surprise to me that night could actually fall. I looked up at the sky. Then again, it was nearly ten PM in the real world, so it made sense that it would be dark here.

There were hardly any stars in the sky. In this world, a large-scale space war in the distant past had doomed civilization, leaving humanity to scrape by on the technological remnants of its former glory. Obviously, they hadn't destroyed the stars in their war, but the emptiness of the sky almost made it seem that way.

A small light cut across from the southwest, splitting the infinite darkness.

It was not a shooting star, but a satellite—launched by the old civilization, still mindlessly sending information without anyone to manage it anymore.

It was nine forty-five PM, which made this the seventh Satellite Scan since the start of the Bullet of Bullets final competition.

I turned away from the vast sky, pulled out a thin terminal from my pouch and touched the screen. The panel lit up and displayed a map of the area. Nearly the entire northern half of the island that served as the battleground was desert, and aside from the occasional rocky outcropping and oasis, the terrain was flat. Not a place that suited snipers—or so I thought.

I put my back to the side of the rock I'd just emerged from, taking care to hide myself as much as possible so I could study the terminal in peace. A few seconds later, a little blip appeared in the center of the map without a sound. I didn't need to touch it to know that it represented me. As Sinon was lying in wait in the nearby cave, she didn't appear on the map, of course.

To my surprise, in the desert zone there were no other dots for living players within five kilometers. It made sense that Death Gun—or 'Steven'—would not appear, thanks to his Optical Camo, but I had been expecting a gathering of enemy players who had figured out our hiding spot, ready to toss their grenades into the cave.

Instead, there was a scattering of dark gray blips throughout the desert. They were the players who had already been eliminated, but it was eerie to know that so many bodies were lying around, yet we hadn't heard any sounds of battle whatsoever.

I zoomed out. There was one dot about six kilometers to the southwest. Tapping the dot told me that it belonged to Yamikaze. That name was familiar.

Farther to the south, in the ruined city, there were two dots approaching one another and a host of gray spots. The survivors were No-No and Ferney. A further zoom-out showed the entire island on the panel. But to my surprise, there were no other lit dots. Even the dot that had set up shop on the peak of the southern mountain at the very start of the game, the one Sinon had derisively called "Richie the Camper," was now gray. There were two blips of the same color nearby, which suggested that he'd been teamed up on.

That meant, if you included Sinon and Death Gun, who

wouldn't show up on the screen, there were currently six players left on the vast island.

Naturally, I couldn't deny the possibility that other players were hiding in caves or water, but unless they had a special ability like Death Gun, they wouldn't be able to receive the satellite information, either. Not many could afford to sit through the climactic stage of a battle without knowing what was happening…

"…Ah!"

As I stared at the terminal, lost in thought, something changed significantly on the screen. It wasn't more dots, but the opposite. The two blips clustered in the city both went dark at once.

My guess was that until the scan started, neither of the two knew the other was there. Perhaps they were surprised to see on the screen that an enemy was just beyond the wall, and they each threw a desperate grenade at the other, blowing themselves up. If that was the case, it had to be a bitter end for contestants who had fought hard to get this far. I just barely resisted the urge to say a brief prayer in their memory.

At any rate, this meant that only four players were left out of the original thirty. But out of those, only Yamikaze and I showed up on the map. Finally, I did a quick count of lit dots and shaded dots on the map. When I was done, I gasped.

"Wha…"

I had to recount. Then again. But the number did not change. There were two white dots on the terminal screen for survivors. And twenty-four in gray for the losers.

The numbers didn't add up. Even if you added the hidden Sinon and Death Gun, that only made twenty-eight. With Pale Rider, who didn't show up because he was shot by the black pistol and disconnected, that was twenty-nine. One short.

Were my assumptions incorrect, and one more person was hiding?

Or had Death Gun managed to "erase" another combatant?

The possibility of the latter was slim. After all, Death Gun's real-life accomplice had to be either in Sinon's house or in her immediate environment. I didn't want to think of her as bait, but as long as Death Gun was going after her, his accomplice couldn't leave to travel to a different target.

No, wait... Maybe I'm missing something huge here...

No good. I couldn't be waffling about this. I squeezed my eyes shut and shook off the chill settling in on me.

When I opened my eyes again, the dots on the screen were blinking—the satellite was nearly done with its pass. It was possible—no, likely—that there wouldn't be a next scan. I offered the satellite a silent thanks for its work, then looked at my surroundings. Nothing moved or shone in the gloomy desert. I returned the terminal to my pouch and headed back for the cave.

The sniper with her massive rifle was waiting for me just around the curve, rather than in the very back with the buggy.

"How was it? What's the situation?!" Sinon demanded, her tied-up hair waving on either side of her face.

I gave her a concise but accurate account. "In the middle of the scan, two players knocked each other out, which probably leaves just four. You, me, Yamikaze, and Death Gun, who didn't show up. Yamikaze's about six kilos to the southwest. Death Gun's probably somewhere in the desert, on his way here. And there might be one other person hiding in a cave, like us."

I couldn't bring myself to say that the missing person might possibly be a second victim of Death Gun's. Sinon didn't seem to pick up on it.

She muttered, "Only four or five left," but accepted it at once. "It's already been an hour and forty-five minutes, though. Last time it took just about two hours, so the pace fits the prior pattern. It's almost a mystery to me that no one came by to toss a grenade into the cave, though..."

"Yeah. Maybe Death Gun was wandering around searching for

us, and he picked everyone else off with that rifle of his. There were plenty of gray dots in the desert."

"In that case, he's going to wind up with the Max Kills prize," she said unhappily, then switched topics. "The problem now is Yamikaze. The only other survivor that appeared on his screen would be you, so he's got to be on his way over."

"I recognize the name...Is he good?" I asked.

Sinon gave me an exasperated look. "He was the runner-up of the last tournament. Plays an extreme Agility build; they call him the Run and Gun Demon."

"Run and...Gun?"

"Just what it sounds like—a playstyle where you run around and shoot. He uses an ultralight Calico M900A submachine gun. He came in second to Zexceed's rare gun and armor, but some say Yamikaze's actually the better player when it comes to skill."

"So...he might be the best on GGO's Japanese server...?"

It made sense that someone who had lasted this long would be very good. I frowned, wondering what to do.

Sinon spoke up, her voice resolute. "Listen...if your conjecture that it's actually an accomplice doing the killing in real life is correct, then Death Gun can only kill me right now. After all, the accomplice has to be staked out at my place to do it."

"..."

I was more than a little surprised. I stared at the little, catlike face across from me.

An unfamiliar killer had his sights on her unprotected body in real life. The horror of that situation was, in a way, even greater than the shackles of the NerveGear and game of death that I endured. But Sinon's dark eyes, even with her fright, showed a will to face that threat directly.

I was at a loss for words, so Sinon calmly continued, "That means we don't need to seriously worry about Death Gun killing Yamikaze. So, while I mean no disrespect to him, perhaps we could let Yamikaze be our decoy? If Death Gun shoots him with the L115, we'll know his location. That's a more solid plan than having you be the bait. Plus...depending on how you think of it, that's kind of what I'm doing now."

I took her last sentence to mean that she was using her real body as a lure to keep Death Gun's accomplice present. While her voice did quaver a bit at the end, the willpower needed to say it at all was impressive.

"...You're real tough, Sinon," I murmured. The sniper blinked, then her lips pursed a bit.

"No...I'm just trying not to think about it. I've always been good at shutting my eyes to scary things," she remarked ruefully. "At any rate, what do you think of the plan? I think we ought to make use of whatever we can at this point."

"Yeah...you're right, I agree. For the most part, I'm in...but..."

I bit my lip, then elaborated on the concern that had been eating away at me for the last few minutes. "The thing is...there's one thing that worries me. I counted up all the survivors and losers in the last satellite scan, but there were only twenty-eight. Even if one is Pale Rider, that leaves us one short."

"...You mean...Death Gun might have killed someone else?" Sinon's eyes went wide, but she promptly shook her head. "Th-that's impossible! I mean, his accomplice is after me, right? It's not virtual reality—he can't just teleport anywhere he wants. Unless you're trying to say that one of the other contestants just so happens to live in my apartment building!"

"Right...that's the point...But if you think about it, it's a bit unnatural..."

I glanced at my watch to see that two minutes had already passed since the scan. I tried to explain what was on my mind in as short a time as possible. "Only thirty minutes passed between when Death Gun shot Pale Rider at the bridge, and when he tried to shoot you near the stadium. That means that in the real world, Pale Rider's home is within thirty minutes' travel from yours. Maybe it's not impossible, but it seems awfully convenient to me."

"But...that's the only possibility, isn't it?" Sinon asked, her brows furrowed.

I revealed the thought that had plagued me since the Satellite Scan. "No, it's not. What if...*Death Gun has more than one accomplice?* If he has a strike team with multiple members, he could have one of them on standby, ready to kill you, at the same moment he's busy killing someone else. That means we can't deny the possibility that Yamikaze might be another target."

"...!"

She sucked in a sharp breath and clutched her sniper rifle tighter. The pale face floating in the gloom shook slightly.

"N-no...You mean there are three or more people working together to commit these horrible crimes?"

"...I know there are at least ten surviving members of Laughing Coffin. And they were locked in the same prison for half a year in SAO. They easily could have traded real-life contact information...even planned out this whole horrible strategy in all of the time they had there. I doubt that all ten of them are in on this...but there's no proof that there's only one accomplice."

"...Why would they...Why would they go to such lengths to keep PK-ing...? Why, when they were finally released from that horrible game...?" she whimpered.

I wrung the answer from my dry, painful throat. "Maybe...it's the same reason I decide to be a swordsman, and you decide to be a sniper..."

"..."

I thought she would be angry, but Sinon only bit her lip. Her skinny body stopped trembling, and her navy blue eyes turned hard and resolute. "If that's the case...we can't let them win. I just said they were PK-ing, but I take that back. There are plenty of people who PK in this game, and I've joined squadrons who did that, but PK-ing has its own pride and determination. Poisoning an unconscious victim while they're in a full dive isn't PK-ing. It's a sickening crime…It's murder."

"Yeah. That's right. We can't let them keep getting away with this. We'll beat Death Gun in here, then make his accomplices pay for their crimes."

That message was to myself as much as to her.

Yes, it was my primary duty. I had to start over from there. I killed two people on that night of madness, then another one later, and I had to atone for those stolen lives.

Normally this would be my battle alone, but now I'd involved the sniper girl in my sins. I stared at her.

If I was prioritizing her safety, I'd let Yamikaze and Death Gun fight, then when one of them was victorious, we'd both commit suicide, ending the tournament immediately. The worst possible scenario would be if the one person missing from the map wasn't one of Death Gun's victims but had been hiding in the river or caves after all. The tournament would *not* be over, and after defeating Yamikaze, Death Gun could appear and shoot Sinon's temporary body before my eyes. Plus, if Yamikaze happened to be one of Death Gun's targets, we'd only be increasing the number of his victims.

I had to fight. I had to protect Sinon, eliminate Yamikaze, and defeat Death Gun. It wouldn't be easy, but it all had to be done…

Sinon herself interrupted my thoughts with her own offer: "I'll take out Yamikaze."

"Huh…?"

"He's very good. Even you won't be able to wipe him out instantly. And while you're fighting, Death Gun will go after you."

"Um…okay, but," I mumbled. Sinon took her hand off the gun and slapped me lightly on the chest.

"Knowing you, you've probably got some idea in your head that you need to 'protect me' or something."

I had no response; she was right on the money. A smile appeared on the sniper's lips, followed by a grimace.

"Well, that's crap. I'm the sniper, and you're the spotter. If you help me out by revealing their location, I'll take care of Yamikaze *and* Death Gun."

I wasn't sure what she called me, but I smirked and nodded anyway. "Okay. It's up to you, then. They should both be real close by now. I'll zip out in the buggy, and you pop out behind me and find a good sniping location."

We were back to the original plan. Sinon nodded her agreement. She stared right back at me, her eyes serious once again, and said, "Let's do it, partner."

―――――

Sinon pressed her right eye to the scope of the Hecate II, which had been switched to night-vision mode.

Nothing moved on the vast desert for now. But Yamikaze was approaching from the southwest, and Death Gun would be converging from wherever he was hiding, she figured.

For her sniping position, Sinon chose the top of the rocky structure that housed the cave she'd been hiding in. She was hard to see from the ground, and she had a good vantage over the area. But there was a risk, too. Though it wasn't particularly tall, the stone outcropping was over thirty feet off the ground at its peak, which meant that with her low Vitality stat, Sinon couldn't just hop down safely. There was only one way up to the top, so if an enemy got close, she'd be shot before she could escape.

But this was the time to abandon any negative thoughts. She kept her mind flat, panning the rifle to her right.

In the center of her view, right at the top of a large dune, stood a silent figure. The occasional breeze rustled his long, back-length hair. The black fatigues covering his slender body melted into the night, making him look less like a gun-toting soldier than a fairy swordsman presiding over the desert of a fantasy realm.

Beyond Kirito was the trusty steed that had taken them into the desert from the ruined city—the three-wheeled buggy. There was hardly any gas left when he took it out of the cave, so it was probably done for good. But the buggy had performed its final task admirably. Thanks to the cover of its large chassis, Kirito could be seen easily, but would be difficult to snipe from the north.

To the south of him was the rock where Sinon hid, and her vision was equally limited. That meant that if Death Gun shot with the L115, it would be from the west or the east. Given that Yamikaze was most likely approaching from the west, he would be coming from the east. Kirito had already come to the same opinion, as his girlish face was turned to the pale moon appearing through the thick, trailing clouds.

Death Gun would probably shoot Kirito with the .338 Lapua Magnum, rather than the electric stun round. If the shot landed on his head or heart, he would die instantly. If it hit one of his limbs, he would lose half his HP from the impact. But evasion would not be easy, either. Not only would Death Gun's first shot not give away a bullet line, the enemy's Metamaterial Optical Camo meant that he could get into sniping position while invisible. He couldn't get too close, as he'd still leave visible footprints in the sand, but it was clear that he held an overwhelming advantage at this point.

But if anyone can do it, it's you. You beat the Untouchable dodging game on your first try, and you cut my point-blank Hecate bullet in two. You can dodge it, Kirito, Sinon thought, setting her rifle back in position.

Her job was to give Kirito all the concentration he could muster. In order to do that, she had to eliminate the incredibly agile attacker Yamikaze as he approached from behind, as soon as she could.

If she had enough time and a safe way to do it, she could explain the situation to Yamikaze, and perhaps convince him to evacuate or assist them. But it would be very difficult to convince anyone that real murder was taking place during the BoB final. Even Sinon would have laughed off everything that Kirito had told her, if she hadn't come face-to-face with the chilling sight of that black pistol pointed at her face-first.

So she had to shoot now. In a tournament without Zexceed, she had to take down the player everyone agreed was the most likely champion, with a single shot.

...Am I even capable of that?

Sinon fought off the encroaching hesitation and fear as she scanned the desert with scope and naked eye alike.

Her attempted shots atop the buggy while they were escaping the city were pathetic. She had missed the cloaked player by a mile, and it was sheer coincidence that she had hit the truck's gas tank at all. All the pride she had built up in the game had evaporated in that instant.

As Sinon the sniper, if she racked up kills, honed her craft, and one day won the BoB, then Shino Asada, real-world girl, would find the same strength. She would shed her fear of guns, no longer remember the events of her past, and finally have a normal life. That had been her belief ever since Kyouji Shinkawa had invited her to play GGO.

But perhaps that desire was just a little bit off-target.

At some point, she began to think of Sinon and Shino as separate people within her mind. There was strong Sinon and weak Shino. But that was a mistake. Sinon still had Shino's weakness within her. It was why she trembled in fear at Death Gun's Black Star and missed her shot.

Both of them were her. She only noticed this once she had seen the mysterious boy named Kirito. He had to be the same way in real life. He had to resist his own weakness and fight every day to be strong—even without a lightsword at his waist.

In that case, Sinon's strength had always been inside of Shino.

I'll fire this bullet as Shino. The same way I did in that incident five years ago.

She'd been running from that moment this whole time. She tried to forget, to erase it, to shut her eyes, to paint over the memories.

But that's over now. I'll face my memory, my sin, head-on. I'll go back to that moment so I can start walking from there. That's the moment I've been waiting for all this time, I think.

If that's the case...then this is that moment.

Through the scope, Sinon's right eye caught sight of a figure moving at high speed: Yamikaze.

Her finger touched the trigger. No pressure on it yet. This would be a one-chance shot. She didn't have time to move and reset her locational data.

If she missed, Yamikaze would charge on Kirito first. Even Kirito couldn't handle Death Gun and Yamikaze together. He would fall from one of their attacks. If Death Gun downed Yamikaze, the reaper would turn his Black Star on Sinon again. The 7.62 mm virtual bullet would hit Sinon, and the accomplice waiting in the real world would see it on the stream and administer the fatal drug to Shino's body, stopping her heart.

That all meant that Shino's actual life depended on this shot. Just as it had once before.

Oddly enough, her heart was calm. Maybe it was just because she couldn't fully process the situation. But that wasn't the whole story. Something, someone, was giving her strength. The warmth she felt in the fingertips of her freezing, numb hand belonged to...

...the Hecate II. Her indispensable counterpart, the weapon that had pulled her through countless battles.

...Oh, right. You've always been here with me. Not just in Sinon's arms...but by Shino's side as well. Even when I couldn't see you, you've been there, encouraging me.

Please...I am weak. Give me your strength. The strength to stand, and walk again.

Through the weeks and months of battles in the late Aincrad, the front-line warriors developed and mastered a number of extra-system skills.

There was *reading ahead*, the ability to predict an opponent's first move in a duel, based on his sword position and center of weight. There was *discernment*, to predict the attack trajectory of long-distance monster or human attacks based on eye location. There was *hearing*, pinpointing locations of approaching enemies out of the midst of the ambient sound mix. *Misleading* was taking advantage of the monster's AI patterns to put them at a severe disadvantage. Then there was the *switch* tactic, which allowed for a group to heal individual members at the same time it attacked.

Out of all these skills that you'd never find in the player menu, the most difficult to master, and thus the one treated like some kind of occult magic, was *hyper-sensing*—the ability to detect spirit.

It worked quicker than eyesight or hearing to detect the presence of hostile enemies. In short, it was the ability to sense ill intent focused on the user.

Those who denied that this ability existed claimed that a person's "killer intent" was physically impossible in the virtual world. After all, anyone in a full dive was perceiving the world solely through the digital signals the NerveGear passed to their brain. All information had to be represented as code, and there was no way to program something as dubious and imaginary as ill will or sixth sense.

Their argument made perfect sense. I certainly wasn't going to argue that some kind of extrasensory skill really existed.

But over the two years I spent in that floating castle, on multiple occasions, I experienced what I could only describe as sensing bloodlust. Without seeing or hearing anything, I sensed that I was being targeted by someone, and hesitated from proceeding in the dungeon. As a matter of fact, I had saved my own life doing that.

I tried telling my "daughter" Yui about the experience this year. Yui was once a low-level subroutine of the Cardinal System that ran SAO. She assured me that in SAO and its replica system

The Seed, there was no means of informing a player about the presence of other players or monsters outside of the standard five senses.

Therefore, it wasn't possible to detect a foe waiting in perfect silence out of the line of sight, she said. I tried explaining something I'd secretly imagined for many years.

While diving into a VRMMO, a player is always connected to the version of himself that exists on the game server as data. While alone in the wilderness or a dungeon, only the player can observe that data. But if something else was waiting in ambush, it required twice as much data to be accessed from the server. Perhaps this extra processing, an infinitesimal lag in the data transfer, could be interpreted by the player as killer intent...

Yui put on an extraordinarily skeptical face and suggested that any server that lagged over a load that tiny ought to be put out to pasture for good. But she did add that theoretically, she could not state with 100 percent confidence that it was impossible.

In the end, chalking it up to ESP might have been a more convincing explanation.

But at the current point, the reasoning did not matter.

For the first time in my long history of VRMMO playing, I had nothing to rely upon other than this Hyper-Sensing skill.

Beyond the very last traces of light left in the sky, a hazy disc of pale white rose. The moon was full. But thanks the presence of heavy clouds, it was much darker than a full moon night in Alfheim. The curves of the dunes melted partially into the night sky, making it difficult to tell if the occasional jutting shadow was a cactus or a rock formation.

If someone was hiding at the foot of such an object and pointed a gun at me, I might not be able to detect the movement with my eyesight. To make matters worse, the foe who had to be watching now had the unbelievable advantage of invisibility. The only visual clue I could use was footprints in the sand. At a distance of over half a mile, such an effect might not even be displayed.

It was a waste of time to try to spot it. Similarly, the sound of such an approach would be completely lost in the howling of the wind.

So just shut your eyes. Turn off your ears.

I closed my eyelids, shaking off my fear. One by one, I purged the whistling of the wind, the dry chill, and the scraping of the sand beneath my feet from my mind.

From the very far distance came a barely perceptible vibration. Someone was running at a very high speed. That would not be Death Gun. The distance was southwest. It had to be Yamikaze.

I withstood the urge to turn and look for him. Yamikaze was Sinon's target; she would stop him. I eliminated even those footsteps from my mind. I focused all of my senses forward, utilizing them for nothing more than picking up any kind of change in the environment.

Oh...that's right. Now I remember. On the night of the Laughing Coffin battle, it wasn't movement or sound that tipped me off to their ambush. It was just "the willies." I turned around on instinct alone to spot the silent, creeping shadows in the side branches of the cave.

What was the name of the man who led the ambush charge? It wasn't PoH, the leader of the group. He probably wasn't there at all. So it was one of the lieutenants. The man wielded an estoc, a very long, pointy sword. It had no blade, only a point for stabbing. The tiniest little glimmer of that deadly prong, snaking forward...

Did I kill him? No, I didn't. When his HP got down to half, he switched with a comrade, drawing back to lick his wounds. As he retreated, he hissed something at me. It wasn't some cocky boast. It was a halting, unpleasant hiss.

"...Kirito. Later, I will, kill you."

That way of speaking. That attitude. The two reddened eyes that seemed to glow beneath his hood...

Something prickled between my eyebrows.

It was that feeling. The inorganic, clinging, freezing bloodlust—coming for me.

I opened my eyes.

Across the desert, at the foot of a cactus just a shade north of east, a tiny light glimmered.

The point of an estoc. The firing of a rifle.

I leaned to the right. But in fact, by the time I was starting the lean, a tiny mass of pure compressed damage bore down on my forehead. The flow of time shifted. It turned heavy, so heavy, freezing the air itself—

The tip of the rotating bullet barely grazed the temple of my tilting face, clipping my hair as it passed by.

"Aaaahhh!!"

I let out a roar, launching off the sand and leaving a lock of black hair floating in the wind.

He's fast!!

Yamikaze's speed through her scope exceeded Sinon's imagination. His maxed-out AGI and extreme dashing skill produced a pace that matched his name: dark wind.

He wore a dark blue combat suit with a minimum of protection covering his small frame. He had no sidearm, and only a single plasma grenade on his belt. He didn't even have a helmet on to cover his pointed, stern face. The thin M900A was cradled in his arms as he leaned forward into his sprint, and even at full speed he hardly shook at all. Only his legs appeared to move, a furious blur beneath him. The sight made him less a soldier than a ninja, and he showed no signs of slowing.

Even the quickest player normally ran a bit, then found cover, checked his surroundings, and ran again. For a sniper like Sinon, that brief pause was her best chance to attack.

But Yamikaze, though he used cacti and rocks as cover, never stopped behind them. He knew that a player with his level of agility was actually safest on the move at max speed.

...What to do? She could try to read ahead and fire in front of him. But Yamikaze didn't sprint in a straight line. He circled around the dunes and occasionally over one, randomizing his movement so that predicting his course was impossible. She could also intentionally put the first shot at his feet, making him panic and giving her a chance to hit him when he dove for cover. But it was unlikely that such a plain, familiar trick would work on a hardened veteran like him. And once she used that first shot, he would have her bullet line to make use of. Perhaps it wasn't a good idea to waste the sniper's greatest opportunity like that...

Sinon couldn't decide. But unlike when she was on the buggy, this indecision was not caused by fear and hesitation. Her mind was cold and clear. She had strength from the smooth wooden stock of the Hecate against her cheek, and the boy who kept his back to Yamikaze out of his faith in her.

I shouldn't just fire a desperate shot at Yamikaze while he's sprinting, she finally decided, letting her trigger finger relax just a bit.

That wasn't sniping. When she shot, she needed absolute confidence. Yamikaze would stop just once before he got Kirito into the firing range of his M900A. That was her chance. She would wait for the final moment, when that opportunity presented itself.

The navy blue ninja was already within a kilometer of Kirito. As long as Kirito kept his back to the man and did not move, Yamikaze would assume that he hadn't noticed his presence yet, and move to the hundred-meter range that AGI types preferred best.

I can wait until then. You hold out too, Kirito. Trust in me.

There were no communications items in the battle royale, so all Sinon could do was send her message mentally. But she felt like her thoughts reached him. That was the last thought she had. Her whole existence fused with the Hecate, her vision becoming the scope; her touch, the trigger. Even her breathing and heartbeat faded away. All she sensed was the speeding target and the cross-hairs trained over his heart.

She didn't know how long that state lasted.

Finally, the moment arrived.

A white light shot across her view from the lower right to the upper left: a bullet. It was not from the Hecate, obviously. It was a .338 Lapua bullet, shot by Death Gun from the east end of the desert. Kirito dodged the bullet, and it reached all the way near Yamikaze to the west, thanks to the L115's incredible range.

Yamikaze clearly wasn't predicting a massive bullet to come bearing down on him from the other side of Kirito, whom he assumed wasn't aware of the racing pursuer. He didn't hit the deck entirely, but he did crouch down and put on the brakes, swiveling over to a nearby rock.

This would be her one and only chance to snipe.

Her finger began to pull the trigger, largely following the will of the Hecate. The light green bullet circle appeared and shrank to the size of mere pixels in an instant. The point was centered on the middle of his chest. The trigger clicked, the hammer struck the firing pin, the .50 BMG cartridge exploded in the chamber, and a massive bullet instantly rocketed out at super-sonic speed.

Through the scope, Sinon's right eye met the wide, shocked gaze of Yamikaze as he noticed the Hecate's muzzle flash. There was surprise, frustration, and a certain element of admiration there.

A bright flash erupted from the chest of the championship con-tender ninja. The avatar flew several yards into the air, tumbled onto the sand, and came to a stop, facing upward. At his side, his M900A and grenade fell, rattled loose by the impact. The DEAD tag began to rotate over his stomach, but Sinon did not see it—she was already turning 180 degrees with the Hecate.

Kirito!! she cried, a silent scream.

The swordsman in black was running straight for the pale moon rising beyond the horizon. His running form was not at all like Yamikaze's compact machinery. His chest was puffed out and his chin was tucked down, legs pumping in a wide stride like some kind of dance. His right hand flashed and unhooked the lightsword from his belt. The violet-blue blade crackled and shone in the darkness.

Ahead of Kirito, an orange light momentarily flickered. Gunfire.

The curve of the lightsword's swing intersected the bullet. Then again. And again. Now that he'd dodged the first shot, Kirito could see the bullet lines. No matter how many times he fired that bolt-action rifle, Death Gun could not break his target's ultraquick reaction speed.

Sinon flipped the scope's night-vision on and raised the magnification level to maximum, pinpointing the source of the gunfire.

There he was. Below a large cactus. She saw the recognizable sound suppressor poking out from the tattered cloth, as well as the cleaning rod affixed to the barrel. It was Death Gun, a true murderer, with his "Silent Assassin" L115A3.

She kept her eye open in the scope, battling the fear that suddenly welled up at the sight of him.

You're not a ghost. You killed many people in Sword Art Online, and you're sick enough to have plotted and carried out this ghastly plan after regaining your freedom—but you're a human being who lives and breathes. That means I can fight you. I can hold to my belief that the Hecate and I are more powerful than you and your L115.

She pulled the bolt handle and reloaded the next bullet as she swung the crosshairs into the darkness of the cloak's hood.

She could see flickering red eyes in the darkness. But it was not the hellfire of the dead. It was simply the lens of a full set of goggles. The only thing behind them was the face of an ordinary in-game avatar.

Sinon brushed the trigger and squeezed very slightly.

The next moment, Death Gun's head twitched. He saw the bullet line. Thanks to her shot on Yamikaze seconds earlier, Sinon's location was officially revealed. But that only meant they were on equal footing.

You're on!!

Through the scope, Sinon saw Death Gun swivel his L115 toward her. A bloodred line extended from its black maw and chillingly caressed her forehead. Sinon didn't wait for the circle to contract; she pulled the trigger.

The gun blasted at the same moment that Death Gun's rifle spit a tiny flame. Sinon pulled her head away from the scope, catching sight of both her own bullet and the oncoming projectile with the naked eye. Their trajectories seemed to be perfectly aligned.

For a moment, she thought the bullets might collide, but that miracle did not happen. Instead, they very nearly touched in midair, throwing each round just slightly off course.

She heard a high-pitched *kwang* right next to her ear—the scope on the top of the Hecate vanished without a trace. She'd have been dead if her eye was still pressed into it. Death Gun's .338 Lapua brushed Sinon's right shoulder and passed behind her.

Meanwhile, the Hecate's .50 BMG missed its mark as well, colliding with the L115's receiver.

In GGO, each major gun part had its own durability rating. In normal use, only the barrel suffered degradation, which could be recovered with maintenance. However, if a bullet struck any part, it would suffer massive damage. Even then, it rarely resulted in total destruction, and repair was possible if some HP was left—just not when the delicate receiver got hit by a high-caliber blast. Such as in this case.

A small fireball erupted in Death Gun's arms, and the center of the L115 burst into a mass of polygons. The stock, scope, and

barrel all collapsed into the sand. Those parts could be reused, but the receiver was gone forever. The Silent Assassin was dead.

...*Sorry*, Sinon mentally whispered to the rare, powerful gun—*not* its owner—and pulled the bolt handle again. The next bullet slotted in with a reassuring clank, but without her scope, Sinon couldn't pull off any more long-distance sniping.

"It's up to you now, Kirito," she murmured to the racing light-swordsman's back.

There were less than two hundred meters between Kirito and Death Gun now. Even if he activated the Optical Camo, escape was impossible in this terrain. His footprints would remain, plainly visible.

The cloaked player slowly emerged from under the cactus and stood up, apparently not in any hurry. The lengthy barrel of his L115 still hung from his hand. He began to slide forward. Was he going to use it as a club? Kirito had cut a Hecate bullet in two with his lightsword; the man wouldn't last a second.

The distance between them closed rapidly. Kirito charged forward, kicking up huge waves of sand. Death Gun scraped out footprints, practically dragging his feet. Thanks to her Eyesight skill, Sinon could see them both clearly, even without her scope.

Kirito drew the sword up over his shoulder as he ran, holding his free hand out in front of him. It was the stance for the astonishingly powerful thrust attack that she'd seen him do several times during the preliminary tournament.

Meanwhile, Death Gun moved the gleaming barrel to his left hand, brushing the mouth of the gun with his right. They would intersect in five seconds.

Sinon could see a live camera behind each player. None of the people watching the stream in GGO's pubs or the outside world had any idea about Death Gun's crimes or Kirito's mission, but they had to be holding their breaths nonetheless. Sinon had forgotten everything in the world but what she was seeing with wide eyes.

Kirito raced onward, stomping the desert in half during his charge. Death Gun held the barrel level with both hands. A sharp light glinted there.

"Ah!!" Sinon gasped.

Death Gun spread his arms wide. The barrel flew out of his left hand behind him, detached and spinning. And in his right hand was a narrow metal pole that he had removed from the barrel—the cleaning rod. Was *that* his final weapon? The rod was just a maintenance tool. It didn't even have offensive value. You could whack someone with it and not take down a single pixel of HP...

No...wait. That wasn't a tool for cleaning out the barrel of his gun. The point of such an implement was supposed to be expanded with a little hole, but this was as sharp as a needle. A sword? But the base of the blade was barely a fraction of an inch across. Could he even do any damage with it? And more important, there were no metal blades in the world of GGO aside from combat knives.

But the lightswordsman did not stop, thrusting his glowing energy blade before him. Even atop her rocky outpost, Sinon could hear the jet-engine roar of the sword. The deadly point of its blade plunged toward the chest under the cloak. It lunged, reached out—but did not connect. Death Gun bent over backward, his upper half entirely level, as if he knew exactly when and how Kirito was going to attack.

All the force of Kirito's thrust did nothing more than singe the air, vanishing harmlessly behind the target.

After his grand attack was evaded, the lightswordsman's body froze for an instant. He moved again just as quickly, trying to leap forward to his right, but Death Gun's right hand, still tilted parallel to the ground, snaked forward like it had a mind of its own. The two-foot metal rod plunged forward...

And sank deep into the black fatigues over his left shoulder.

"...Kirito!!" Sinon screamed, as a crimson visual effect splattered into the darkness like blood.

—◠◠◠—

Just a second after pressing her phone to the payment pad to bring up the cashier sound, Asuna Yuuki was out of the taxi, shouting a hasty "Thanks!" over her shoulder

Facing the roundabout was a large building entrance that still had some of its lights on, despite being nearly ten o'clock. The automatic doors were off, naturally, but there was a small glass door nearby for nighttime entrance. She ripped open the door and plunged through.

Asune strode through the chill air of the lobby that smelled like disinfectant, and headed for the reception counter. Seijirou Kikuoka had already contacted the hospital, so when the nurse looked up, Asuna had the right message to deliver: "I'm Yuuki, meeting scheduled for Room 7025!"

She pulled her student ID from her pocket and slapped it on the counter. As the nurse took it and compared the photo to the real thing, Asuna busied herself studying the floor plan on the back wall.

"Asuna Yuuki. Here's your visitor pass. Don't forget to turn it in on your way out. You can reach the room via the elevator on the right…"

"Got it. Thank you!"

Asuna snatched the pass, bowed briefly and rushed off to the elevator, leaving the bewildered nurse behind. Kirito—Kazuto Kirigaya—was entered into the system as a routine checkup, not treatment or hospitalization, so she had to be wondering why Asuna was in such a hurry, but that wasn't Asuna's problem.

There was a turnstyle gate before the elevator, much like the kind at a train station. She swiped her pass and pushed through as soon as the metal bar rose. Only once she'd hit the UP button and jumped through the open door did she take a short breather.

Kazuto must have felt the same way a year earlier, when he was rushing to see Asuna after he'd freed her from the birdcage in

ALO. He should be fine. Nothing had happened. She knew these things with her rational mind, but she couldn't stop her heart from pushing her onward.

Ding. Ding. With each floor passed, the elevator rang pleasantly. It was only a seven-floor ascent, but it was taking an eternity.

"It's all right, Mama," a young voice echoed suddenly from the speaker of the cell phone she still clutched in her hands.

It was Yui, her AI "daughter" with Kirito. Yui's core program was contained in a desktop machine in Kazuto's bedroom, and when needed, she could dive into ALO as a Navigation Pixie, or speak to them through the phone in real life. She couldn't stay present all the time or she'd drain the battery, but she'd been connected since Asuna left Dicey Café.

"Even the strongest foe can't stop Papa. After all, he's Papa."

"...Yes. You're right," she whispered back into the mic, practically kissing it. At last, it felt like her freezing-numb fingers were thawing, but the nerves hadn't left her yet.

Kirito had gone into GGO on Kikuoka's request to investigate the mysterious "Death Gun." Whoever was controlling his avatar was once a member of SAO's killer guild, Laughing Coffin. And two people shot by Death Gun in the game had died in real life under mysterious circumstances.

Something was happening—that much was clear. Kikuoka claimed that Kazuto was in no danger in middive, but even he did not fully believe that the two deaths were a mere coincidence.

Ding. The elevator passed the sixth floor and gently slowed, coming to a stop on the seventh floor with another pleasant sound. As the door opened, Yui pointed out that he was fifty feet to the right, then after a left, another twenty-five feet. This time, Asuna ran at full speed through the empty halls.

She noted the metal plates to the sides of each spaced-out sliding door along the walls. 7023...24...25! She pressed her pass to the plate, the indicator turned from red to green, and the door opened.

It was a personal room coordinated in off-white. Right in the center was a density-adjusting gel bed of the kind that Asuna herself had once depended upon. The room's partition curtains were drawn. Right in front was a menacing monitor. The various cords extending from the machine split apart here and there, ending in electrodes on the exposed chest of the boy lying on the bed. Around his head was a familiar silver crown: an AmuSphere.

Kirito! she was about to shout, sucking in a huge lungful of the warm room air. But before she could let it out, someone else's voice echoed off the walls.

"...Kirigaya!"

Asuna nearly fell face-forward. She craned her neck right, noticing a simple metal-frame chair to the far side of the bed, previously hidden by the monitoring equipment. Someone was sitting on the chair.

She was wearing a white uniform and a nurse's cap, and featured braided hair and fashionable glasses. It was the nurse. Now that she thought about it, Kikuoka had mentioned that someone was watching over Kazuto.

But she couldn't resist an unhappy grumble at the fact that his security was a young and very pretty nurse, who was leaning over Kazuto's shirtless form on the bed. That only lasted a moment, however. When the nurse looked up to see Asuna's entrance, her face was a mask of nerves.

"Oh, are you Miss Yuuki? I heard you'd be coming—have a seat," the nurse chattered huskily, getting up and motioning to the left side of the bed. Asuna hadn't bothered to wait for the offer, already racing over and bowing briefly before she got a good look at Kazuto's face.

His eyes were closed, naturally. But he wasn't sleeping or unconscious. All five of his senses were isolated from the real world by the AmuSphere and taken to a far-off, alien realm. Meanwhile, the device intercepted all of the signals from brain to body, so his face and limbs were utterly still. Yet the moment

Asuna saw Kazuto's face, she could tell that what was happening on the inside was far from peaceful tranquility.

"What's going on with Ki…Kazuto?!" Asuna asked, raising her head. The nurse, who had a name tag reading AKI, frowned and shook her head quickly.

"Don't worry, he's not in any physical danger. But his pulse just shot up to 130 a moment ago…"

"His pulse?" she murmured, and looked over at the heart monitor. The LCD panel featured a classic cardiogram graph of the kind you'd see in movies, and a readout that said 132 BPM. Right before Asuna's eyes, the graph shot into sharp peak after peak.

It was not abnormal at all for the heart rate to rise while playing a VRMMO. After all, a player faced with a huge, terrifying monster while in a full dive was bound to get nervous, sending the pulse racing. In a way, that was what the games were meant to do.

But this was Kirito. The solo conqueror of Aincrad, the man who had risked death more than any other in a game chock full of it. What circumstances in a safe, normal game could cause this reaction in him? In the year they'd been playing ALO together, Asuna had never once seen Kirito lose his cool.

What's happening in there?

Asuna bit her lip, tracing a drop of sweat on his forehead with the tip of her finger. Suddenly, Yui's voice rang out from the phone in her other hand.

"Mama, look at the touch-PC on the wall! I'll patch the live footage from MMO Stream onto the screen!"

Asuna raised her head with a start. There was indeed a forty-inch flatscreen monitor on the wall facing the bed. Yui had somehow managed to connect to it wirelessly from Asuna's phone, then activated the screen and set its browser to full-screen mode.

It was the exact same thing they were watching from the apartment inside ALO. In the top left was the rough logo of Gun Gale

Online. Next to it, a narrow strip of text announcing that it was the exclusive livestream coverage of the third Bullet of Bullets battle royale final.

On the right side of the screen was a list of player names. But most of the screen was taken up by a multiangle, multipicture visual feed. At this point, there were only two large windows left.

Both pictures showed a nighttime desert presided over by pale moonlight. It looked like a single, close-range battle, with cameras positioned behind either player. In the left window was a short, small avatar, clad in black fatigues darker than the night, long hair flapping in the wind. The player held a glowing purple sword in one hand, while the other dangled below. Dark red damage effects spilled out of one shoulder. The player's name was listed in a small font below: KIRITO.

"That's…Kirito…?"

The avatar was far different from the "black swordsman" of SAO and the spriggan he used in ALO. From behind, his delicate form looked exactly like a girl's. But the stance and the way he held himself were undoubtedly Kirito.

On the other side of the bed, Nurse Aki wondered, "Does that mean that's Kirigaya's avatar, there? So while he's right here, he's controlling that character in real time?"

"That's right. He's in battle… I think that's why his heart rate is so high," Asuna replied immediately. But some things she couldn't explain so easily. That Kirito had already suffered severe damage to his left shoulder—and that the person who did it to him was probably a murderous SAO survivor. On top of that, that the man might have actually killed two players from within GGO.

She turned to look at the right half of the screen, dreading what she would see.

As she expected, it was the back of the tattered cloak facing the camera. From behind he looked lifeless and lax. But Asuna could tell from experience that he had the stance of someone very familiar with virtual reality. She watched the cloaked player thrust out his hand, holding her breath.

"Wha…" she gasped, involuntarily.

He wasn't holding the huge rifle she had seen earlier, near the bridge, nor the black pistol. It was just a narrow metal rod…

No. No, it wasn't. It was tapered down from the bases, and pointed as sharp as a needle at the end. It was a sword. A weapon much like Asuna's rapier, sharp at the end but without a cutting blade, meant for thrusting only.

"An estoc? Oh…oh…"

Asuna didn't even realize she was speaking aloud. It was as though the estoc was jabbing right out of the screen and prodding her distant memories. There was…There was a major member of Laughing Coffin who used an estoc. But his name.., What was his name?

Naturally, the person in the tattered cloak was not going to use the same alias as in SAO, the way that Kirito did. But Asuna couldn't help but glance at the avatar's feet.

Like Kirito's, the player name displayed there was written in the Western alphabet.

STERBEN.

She stumbled over the name, not sure how it was meant to be pronounced.

"St…Ste…ben? Is that a typo of 'Steven'…?"

"No…not quite, Mama," Yui answered from her phone, at almost the same time that Nurse Aki said, "No," herself. Asuna looked over in surprise to see the nurse's fine eyebrows knitted in concern, her face more worried than before.

"That's German. I know it because it's a medical term. It's pronounced more like *shter-ben*."

"Shter…ben."

Asuna had never heard the word before. After a moment's hesitation, Nurse Aki rasped, "It means…'death.' In hospitals, it's used…when a patient has passed away…"

All the hairs on Asuna's arms stood on end. She tore her gaze away from the screen and over to the face of the boy lying on the bed.

"Kirito…"

Her voice was trembling so hard that she barely registered it as her own.

———

GGO was built and managed using the free VRMMO tool package known as The Seed.

The Seed was a very versatile and easy-to-use system, but there existed certain "black boxes" that even an administrator could not tamper with. Any title that had been open to the public for three months was automatically and irrevocably set to allow the conversion system that made it possible for players to bring over their characters from other games. In a similar fashion, while it was possible to fiddle with the settings of the pain-absorption system that prevented players from receiving pain signals, there was no way to disable it entirely.

Meaning that no matter how many bullets you took in GGO— even if they blew off an arm or a leg—the worst you would feel was numbness.

Which meant the pain in my shoulder, like a needle of ice penetrating it, was an illusion. In fact, the pain absorber even canceled out illusionary pain, so it wasn't real at all. It was a memory, the return of a sensation I'd suffered in the same spot from the same weapon, in a different world.

Death Gun stood about fifteen feet away, the gleaming point of his estoc waving back and forth as if keeping some kind of rhythm. He would thrust from that stance without any warm-up. Just watching the sword wouldn't help me dodge it.

I had to have thought the same thing in Laughing Coffin's cave hideout. Back then, I must have noted the rarity of his weapon. But the midst of that battle was no time to remark on it.

A year and a half later, I finally said what I hadn't then.

"That's an…unusual weapon. In fact…I thought there weren't any metal swords in GGO to begin with."

A hissing laugh emerged from the depths of Death Gun's hood. Next came his halting voice. "That's very, poor study, for you, Black Swordsman. The Bayonet Creation skill, an offshoot of, the Knife Creation skill, lets you, make this. This is the, longest and, heaviest, I can do."

"…Sadly, I doubt you can make my kind of sword, then," I snapped back. He hissed again.

"So you still, like those, high-STR swords. Then you must, be unhappy, with that toy."

The Kagemitsu lightsword in my hand did not like being referred to as a toy. It crackled with a few tiny sparks.

I shrugged and spoke up for my weapon. "It's not that bad, really. I always wanted to use one of these things. Plus," I continued, bringing the point up to midheight with a buzzing growl, "a sword's a sword. As long as I can cut you and take down your HP bar, I'm happy."

"Heh, heh, heh. You've got, spunk. But can you, pull it off?"

The red glowing eyes blinked unevenly. The metal mask, fashioned into a skull, seemed to smirk somehow.

"Black Swordsman, you have breathed, too much, foul air, in the, real world. If the old you, saw that clumsy, Vorpal Strike, he would be, disappointed."

"…Yeah. Maybe. But the same goes for you. Or do you still think of yourself as a member of Laughing Coffin?"

"Ahh, so you, remember now."

Hiss, hiss. Death Gun breathed like an exhaust vent, lazily waving his hands in a mock clapping gesture. The scraps of cloth he wore as a glove around his right hand shifted, exposing the symbol of a laughing coffin on the inside of his wrist.

"Then you, should know, already. The difference, between me, and you. I am, a true, red player, but you, are not. You only killed, to survive, out of fear. And you tried, not to think, about the meaning, to forget. A coward."

"…!!"

For a moment, I had no words. He had struck me right in the most vital, central point.

How? How is he able to say that? When from the night I crossed swords with him, to our reunion in the dome yesterday, I never made contact once with him. Does he…does he have some kind of psychic power? Was my brilliant uncovering of his killing methods just nonsense in the end…?

As my eyesight began to warp, it took all of my concentration to stay standing. It was a miracle that I kept the lightsword from wavering. If I had, Death Gun would thrust from a standing position again, piercing me through the chest this time.

I let out a breath through clenched teeth and growled, "Maybe you're right. But you're not a murderer anymore. I've already got a very good idea of how you killed Zexceed, Usujio Tarako, Pale Rider, and possibly one more. It's not because of the black pistol—not even because of you."

"Oh? Then tell me, what it is."

This was the showdown.

I glared in the enemy's eyes with all of the power I could muster, putting the truth as I believed it into words.

"You used that camouflage cloak to hide in the regent's office, watching the contestants enter their addresses into the BoB form. You had an accomplice sneak into their homes ahead of time and administer an injection timed to your shooting, making it look like you caused the resulting heart failure. That's the truth."

"…"

Finally, Death Gun was silent.

The red eyes in the darkness narrowed. I couldn't determine if that meant my conjecture was right or wrong. I let his thick, choking hatred flow through me as I explained further.

"Though you might not know this, the Ministry of Internal Affairs has a database of all SAO players' character names and actual names. When we find out your old handle, we'll know your real name, address, and the methods of your crimes. Put an end to it all. Log out, and turn yourself in at the nearest police station."

Again, silence.

The dry night wind caught the front of the tattered cloak, making the tendrils squirm like little insects. The live camera, REC symbol active, rose slightly in impatience. Nearly three minutes had passed since Death Gun and I faced off. The audience couldn't hear us talk, so their confusion and irritation had to be reaching a peak. But for now, all I could do was continue our battle of words. If Death Gun backed up my assertions, there would be no need to cross blades.

But a few seconds later, all that came from his hood was the usual hissing laughter.

"That is, a very interesting, idea. But, it's too bad, Black Swordsman. You cannot, stop me. Because you, will never, remember my, old name."

"Wh…what? How can you be so sure?"

"Heh, heh. You've even forgotten, the reason why, you forgot. Listen…when the battle, was over, before you sent me, through the portal, to jail, I tried, to name myself. But you said, 'I don't want, to know your name, and I, don't need to. I will never, see you, again.'"

"——!!"

I stared, wide-eyed. Death Gun hissed at me again. "You don't, know my, name. That's why, you can't, remember. You cannot, do anything. You will fall here, sprawled into the dust, and have no choice, but to watch as I kill the girl…"

There was a sharp whistle of air being cut. A silver curve glittered in the darkness.

"You can, do nothing!!"

Death Gun suddenly thrust out the estoc, like a spring-loaded puppet. Before I even realized what I was doing, my arm was moving the lightsword to intercept the needle aimed for my heart.

The energy blade growled, and the tip just barely intersected with the estoc's trajectory. The pale plasma cut into the underbelly of the metal weapon.

It should have cut it in two. The Kagemitsu had sliced Sinon's rifle bullet in half, after all. How could it not slice that slim piece of metal, too? I swung my sword up, prepared to cut right through Death Gun's shoulder.

A very, very nasty sound came from the inside of my avatar.

My eyes went wide with shock as I stared down at the piece of metal piercing my solar plexus.

Death Gun's estoc was slightly charred in one spot, but otherwise completely whole. The supposedly extreme power of the energy blade had passed right through it. But how was that possible?

The enemy plunged in further, pushing the estoc in to the hilt. With each inch of the metal, my HP gauge dropped precipitously. I gritted my teeth and put as much power as I could into a backward leap. The blade popped out and spilled bloody red effects in an airborne line.

Twice, then thrice, I hopped back, putting distance between us. Death Gun brought the estoc up to his mouth and waved it about, as though he were going to lick it.

"…Heh, heh. This is made, of the best, metal you can get, in the game. Battle cruiser, armor plating. Heh heh, heh."

He tossed the cloak back and charged, done with the conversation. His right hand moved so fast it blurred, the little point of light leaving countless afterimages in the air. It was the first time he had showed off a combo attack. I recognized it as Star Splash, an eight-part, high-level, thrusting-sword skill…

Unable to parry with my sword, and prevented from adequate footwork by the shifting sands, I was helpless to stop the sharp needle from gouging me, over and over.

———〰———

Kirito!

Sinon fought with all her self-control not to scream his name aloud, or squeeze the trigger.

Nearly half a mile away, the black-clad swordsman was knocked off his feet, spraying blood effects. To Sinon, who had never used a weapon that wasn't a gun, his opponent's sword proficiency seemed tremendous. She held her breath, wondering if that combination attack had finished all of Kirito's HP, but fortunately, Kirito leapt backward, doing a backflip and pulling further away. There was no DEAD tag floating in the air.

Meanwhile, Death Gun needed no regrouping. He trailed after his prey like a ghost. The automated cameras seemed to sense an impending conclusion, as they were multiplying in number. Nearly ten cameras spread out around the two in a circle, turning the desert stage into its own little coliseum.

If only the Hecate's scope was still there, she could snipe to assist Kirito. But at this distance, even Sinon couldn't control the bullet circle with the naked eye. Even worse, if she fired wildly, she might hit Kirito.

You can do it. Hang in there, Kirito, Sinon prayed, forgetting the danger that her real body was in as she kneeled on the rock and clutched her hands together.

Kirito had killed people in the legendary Sword Art Online, even if it was to protect himself and others. That experience was shockingly similar to the past Shino bore. In that sense, his own mental anguish had to resemble Shino's.

Kirito said that you couldn't overcome terrible memories by compartmentalizing them and hiding them somewhere. You had to face them, accept them, and think about them.

At this moment, he was trying to turn his words into action. He was trying to stop the criminal named Death Gun, who brought the darkness of SAO with him.

It wasn't Kirito's strength that made him capable of this. It was his drive to be strong. He was a person who could accept, anguish, and suffer over his own weakness, and face his foe anyway. Strength was not a result—it was the process of aiming for something.

I want to talk with you right now. I want to tell you about what I've noticed, what I've felt. Is there anything I can do? Descending this rock and coming closer would have the opposite effect. The instant the Black Star gets pointed at me, Kirito will be helpless. On the other hand, sniping without a scope is just gambling. I don't have nearly enough range with my MP7 sidearm. There must be something…some other way to help him…

"…!"

Suddenly, Sinon's whole body shook.

There was. One kind of attack that she could actively attempt. She didn't know how effective it would be—but it was worth a shot.

Sinon took a deep breath, clenched her jaw tight, and watched the distant battle.

—⁓—

Kirito!!

Asuna was just barely able to keep the scream trapped in her throat.

Although it didn't have the same visual effects, the combination that Death Gun whipped out was clearly the eight-part Star Splash, a high-level sword skill that Asuna the Flash had once made good use of. It was a rapier skill that contained no slashing movements, which made it available to the estoc, an offshoot weapon of that category.

On the wall screen, she watched Kirito dash backward over and over, trying to maintain distance. But the cloaked player stayed right on him, gliding eerily over the sand. Kirito kept pulling away, just barely out of the estoc's reach.

The tempo of the beeps coming from the heart monitor rose, causing Asuna to glance over. His heart rate was already up to 160 bpm. She tore her eyes off the screen and looked at Kazuto's face.

Beads of sweat hung on his forehead, and it seemed to her like his expression was pained. His parted lips made way for short, quick pants. Nurse Aki had noticed this as well; her eyes were clearly worried behind her glasses.

"I make sure he gets plenty of water before he dives...but it's been over four hours already. With how much he's sweating, dehydration is a concern. You don't suppose we could have him...temporarily disconnect, do you?" the nurse asked.

Asuna bit her lip and shook her head. "Nothing we say here will reach Kirito...and this is a PvP tournament, so I don't even know if he's capable of logging out..."

Based on ALO tournament events, she was familiar with the practice of temporarily preventing players from intentionally logging out, to protect against desperation log-outs by losing players—one of the cardinal sins of VRMMOs.

"But the AmuSphere does monitor blood flow in the brain, and it will automatically log him out if it detects dehydration is about to occur," Asuna added.

The nurse nodded back. "I see. We'll monitor him a bit longer, then. We can't go giving him an IV when he isn't even technically a patient, after all."

"Ah...of course."

Her voice stiffened against her will. If he had to be hooked up now, he might as well be back in SAO.

But there was one major difference between then and now: Kazuto wasn't wearing a NerveGear with its deadly trap installed, but a guaranteed-safe AmuSphere. So there shouldn't be any danger if she just reached down and yanked the silver rings off of Kazuto's head. Kirito would disappear from the desert footage and instantly return to the hospital bed—and Asuna's side. The sword of the terrible foe bearing the name of death would not reach him.

It took all of Asuna's willpower to resist the impulse to do this.

Kirito/Kazuto was fighting with all of his swordsman's instincts. She could not interfere with that process.

But there had to be *something* she could do. Some way she could reach him where he fought in that far-off world, from his side right here.

"Mama, his hand," came Yui's little voice from the cell phone speaker. "Take Papa's hand. The AmuSphere's physical signal interrupt isn't as complete as the NerveGear's was. I'm sure he'll feel the warmth of your hand. My hand can't touch him in the world he's in now, but…you can do it…for me…"

Her voice quavered and stumbled toward the end. Pierced through the heart, Asuna shook her head briskly. "No…that's not true, Yui. You *can* reach him. We'll cheer Papa on together."

She put the phone into Kazuto's limp hand and squeezed it between both of hers. Despite the considerable warmth of the heating, Kazuto was cold as ice. She had to be careful not to squeeze too hard, so as not to set off the auto-disengage feature. So it was that Asuna tried to subtly warm him up as much as she could.

She closed her eyes, shutting out the images on the screen, and prayed.

Hang in there, Kirito. Keep trying, for the sake of what you believe in. I'll always be at your side. I'll always be behind you, watching your back and supporting you.

Faintly, but certainly, his cold hand twitched.

———

He was tough.

In speed, balance, and timing. He was a master of all. Very few of the front-line players could boast of such considerable, polished skill.

So why? When he was a lieutenant of Laughing Coffin, the man who now played Death Gun was barely able to keep up with my sword. Otherwise, it wouldn't have been so easy for me to knock him down to half HP and send him scurrying off to lick his wounds.

Which meant he had changed after that, probably during the half a year that he spent in Blackiron Palace's prison. He'd honed his skills, living off his burning desire for revenge against me and the others who brought Laughing Coffin to ruin. There was strength to be gained by practicing sword skills over and over, even if it didn't result in more col or experience. How many thousands, how many millions, of times did he practice these moves in that gloomy, chilly prison? The exact movements necessary to pull off the estoc's attacks had been burned into his nerves.

But I knew that when it came to the number of swings, I was at least his equal. The problem was that the photon sword I carried now was far lighter than the swords I was familiar with. It felt entirely different. A single attack like Vorpal Strike was one thing, but it would be very tricky to pull off a combination attack. On top of that, Death Gun was not going to give me enough time to execute a major attack. He maintained close proximity, overwhelming me with a variety of moves. While I dodged as best I could, that sharp point caught my avatar from time to time, taking chunks of HP with each bite. I was down to barely a third of my health.

Of course, even if his pointed weapon took the rest of my HP and knocked me out, I wouldn't die if he shot me with that black pistol. I never typed my address into the terminal in the regent's office, and he had no way of finding out the location of my real body.

Maybe I'd been leaning too heavily on the truth of my safety. I was so concerned with the black pistol that I failed to notice the true power of the player holding the gun. If that was the case, I'd earned this outcome. He was still in the game of death, and I had drifted away from it in body and mind.

It was far too late to realize all of this now.

But that didn't mean that accepting defeat was an option. I wouldn't suffer a single wound in real life. But as he swore to me earlier, Sinon was within the firing range of his black gun, as she waited on the boulder in the distance. If I went down, he would attack Sinon. If she took a single bullet from that handgun, his accomplice would do his dark duty on her real body.

One moment. I just needed one moment. Just one chance to break through his onslaught.

As far as attack power went, my lightsword was far more potent than his narrow estoc. If I landed a heavy critical blow, I knew it would eradicate all of his HP. I just couldn't get enough space to do it. He wouldn't fall for any half-executed feints, and his estoc could pass right through my energy blade, so I couldn't keep him at bay with a powerful swing. What to do, what to do…

Tist-tist-tist. Three quick thrusts hissed at my right cheek and one caught it, sending my HP bar into the red at last.

The stream of light from my cheek turned my vision crimson.

And Death Gun's red eyes flickered fiercer than before, certain of his victory.

Red…The estoc fencer in Laughing Coffin had red eyes, too. My memory creaked and groaned. A crack ran through the heavy lid that kept it down.

That's right…I had refused to hear his name. I didn't want anything to do with him ever again. I just wanted to forget that night of madness, blood, screams, and hatred, and not a second too soon.

But in reality, I couldn't do it.

I didn't forget everything. I just pretended that I did. I was fooling myself, nothing more. I'd shut down the neural pathways to a whole chunk of memory, and convinced myself that something that did exist was invisible to me…

Death Gun pulled back the estoc, preparing for the finishing blow. The cold gleam in the tip caused discrete images to flash out of my distant memory.

Just before the vanquishing party left, we held our final meeting at the base of the Divine Dragon Alliance. At the meeting, we went over all the information we had on Laughing Coffin again. The abilities of PoH, their leader. The weapons and skills of his trusted lieutenants. Their descriptions—and names.

It was mentioned that two of the officers had their own distinctive colors. One was black. He liked to use a poisoned knife, and his name was...yeah, it was Johnny Black. Klein turned to me and said in all seriousness, "Don't fight him. We won't know which one of you is which."

The other was red, but not all over. The estoc-wielding fencer had customized his eyes and hair to be crimson red, and wore a gray, hooded cloak with an upside-down red cross on it. Asuna the Flash, vice commander of the Knights of the Blood, did not appreciate this unsubtle play on the guild's colors and crest. He was the one I crossed swords with right at the start of the battle, the man who swore he would kill me one day and tried to tell me his name as we cleaned up after the fight.

Now, a year and a half later and into an entirely different virtual world, the man with the estoc and the tattered cloak had come to make good on his promise. His name was...

"Xaxa."

The short little word that tumbled out of my mouth, pronounced like *Zazza*, threw off the course of the metal rod that plunged toward my heart. Instead, it grazed my chest and lurched past me, but I barely even registered the sensation.

"Red-Eyed Xaxa. That's your name."

A number of things happened after that point in quick succession.

A red line flew in from behind me and pierced the center of Death Gun's hood without a sound.

It was not a bullet, but a bullet line—Sinon. I understood her intention in an instant. She was attacking him with the bullet line itself. A last attack, wringing out all of her experience, intuition, and will to fight. A phantom bullet.

With the instinct of an animal sensing a predator, Death Gun leaped backward. A growl of rage escaped his skull mask. He must have noticed right away that Sinon would not risk the danger of shooting me by accident. But the shock of me dropping his real name had dulled that realization. So his body reacted to the phantom shot and took evasive maneuvers before his mind could stop it.

This was my last chance. The bullet line feint wouldn't work again. I couldn't let Sinon's opportunity go to waste. I lunged forward, chasing after Death Gun.

But there was a cruel fate in store. He began to disappear—the Optical Camo. I could follow the footprints to track his location, but there was no way to ensure my lightsword would hit his crit point with any accuracy. I had to finish it with one strike, or his counter would knock out my remaining HP.

Then, an even more surprising phenomenon:

My left hand moved on its own, as if guided by someone else. My freezing, nervous hand was enveloped, warmed, and guided by the familiar hand of another. It moved to my left waist and grabbed something tight. It was the other weapon whose existence I had completely forgotten: the Five-Seven. The moment it slid out of the holster and its weight registered on my arm, a single thought etched into my mind and burst into flame.

"Rrraaaaahh!!"

I howled. Leaped. Twisted left, then bolted forward in a spiral like a bullet.

Before me, Death Gun was in the process of disappearing entirely. I swung my left hand at the outline of the wavering silhouette.

In my normal dual blades configuration, my left blade would jump up from ground level to break the enemy's defense, but I was holding a pistol now, not a sword. But who decided that a gun couldn't execute a sword skill? I held the trigger down, in the same way I would slice the sword upward.

The bullets flew in a diagonal line, striking the invisible object and erupting with sparks. Death Gun's body reappeared from their midst. His camo was exposed, his avatar open to my attack.

With all of my inertia and weight in a clockwise spin, I struck downward from the left with my lightsword. It was the Dual Blades charging attack, Double Circular.

The energy blade bit deep into Death Gun's right shoulder, severing diagonally through the torso until it passed out his left flank. The black pistol was holstered there, and it too was split down the middle by the blade's precision, exploding in a burst of brilliant orange.

The severed avatar, ripped cloak, and arc of flame danced beneath the full moon.

The long, long flight finally came to its end...

And with a series of heavy thuds, Death Gun's upper and lower halves landed a slight distance away. A half second later, the long, narrow estoc plunged into the sand between the two of us.

As I slumped to my knees, I caught a very faint whisper.

"...It's, not...over. We won't...let it end... He will...ensure..."

The DEAD tag that floated over the severed halves of Death Gun's avatar brought a premature end to his statement. I slowly rose and looked down at the "corpse" below me.

Now that Death Gun had lost his tattered cloak that was more a symbol of his avatar than his actual body, there was very little to distinguish him, aside from the skull mask. I gazed into the lens without their signature red color and murmured, "No...it is over, Xaxa. We'll find your accomplice in no time. This is the end of Laughing Coffin's bloodshed, once and for all."

I turned around and dragged my wounded, battered body west through the desert.

How many hundreds of steps, how many hundreds of yards

did I trudge? Eventually, a pair of small, booted feet came into view, and I lifted my head at last.

It was a small sniper girl with a scopeless rifle in her hands, and a gentle smile on her face.

—◦◦◦—

Sinon opened her mouth to say something, but no words emerged.

She couldn't even state for certain what emotions were running through her. Waves of heat roiled in her chest. She clutched the Hecate even harder.

At last, Kirito cracked a slight grin. He put his Five-Seven back into the holster, clenched his fist, and held it out. Sinon raised her own and bumped it to his.

"...It's over," the lightswordsman mumbled, lowering his fist and looking straight upward. Sinon followed his gaze.

The clouds had drifted away at some point, replaced by a curtain of stars that all competed to outshine the others. It might have been the first time she'd ever seen stars in this game.

The sky of GGO was always covered in thick clouds, owing to the effects of the apocalyptic war that caused it to collapse. The gloomy sunset coloring stayed constant throughout the day, and even the night sky was a clouded, bloody red.

But according to a prophecy by a wise old NPC in town, one day the poisons of the earth would be purified, the sands would turn white again, the clouds would dissipate, and the light of stars and starships would return to the night sky. No players took that boilerplate background setting seriously, but perhaps this desert was not the wasteland the players normally traversed, but the promised land of the future.

Sinon silently watched the glinting of the brilliant night sky, and the wreckage of the spaceships that flowed between the stars like a river.

Eventually, Kirito said, "We should probably put an end to the tournament now. I doubt the audience is very happy about this."

"…Yeah. Good point."

Here and there in the night sky, the pale blue cameras blinked in impatient annoyance. Kirito smirked at the sight, then got serious and took a step closer to her. "That eliminates the danger of this tournament. Now that we've beaten Death Gun, his accomplice should be leaving you alone. Remember, their goal is to create a legend that anyone shot by his black pistol in GGO dies in real life, not to just murder anyone willy-nilly. So there shouldn't be any danger with logging out now…but just in case, you should call the police."

"But…what am I going to tell them? How in the world do I convince them that there are people plotting simultaneous murders inside a VRMMO and outside?"

Kirito bit his lip for a moment, then nodded. "Good point… I was hired by someone in the government, so I could have him take care of it…but I can't just ask for your name and address here…"

The swordsman's glance shifted away. He understood that asking for someone's real life details in a VRMMO was the worst, most boorish of faux pas.

But it only took Sinon a second to make up her mind. "It's fine. I'll tell you."

"Huh? B-but…"

"Seems pretty stupid to get hung up on that now. I mean…this was the first time I actually opened up and told someone about my past on my own…"

Kirito's eyes widened a bit, but he soon agreed, "I guess you have a point. Now that I think about it, the same might go for me…"

If she hesitated now, the shy part of herself would appear and decide not to go through with it, so Sinon hoisted the Hecate onto her shoulder and took a step forward. She put her lips up to Kirito's ear and whispered, low enough that no one could hear, "My name is Shino Asada. I live in Yoncho-me in Yushima, Bunkyo Ward of Tokyo…"

Once she had listed her apartment building and number, Kirito turned to her in surprise. "Yushima?! No kidding...I'm diving from Ochanomizu in Chiyoda Ward."

"Wait...what?! Then we're right next to each other," Sinon nearly shouted, flabbergasted. The only things separating Kirito from her home were Kasuga Street and Kuramae-bashi Street. Kirito's eyes narrowed a bit, and he grunted.

"In that case, maybe it would be quicker if I just run over as soon as I log out..."

"Wha... You're..."

She was nearly about to ask, *You're coming over?* but held her mouth shut in time. She cleared her throat awkwardly and resumed, "N-no, it's fine. There's a friend nearby who I can trust..."

Kyouji Shinkawa, aka Spiegel, the boy who invited her into this game, lived in nearby Hongo, the second son of a medical practitioner. He'd come right over if she called, and he had to be watching the tournament from start to finish, so she knew she'd have to explain why she had been working so closely with Kirito.

"Plus, he's the son of a doctor, so he can help in an emergency," she added as an excuse.

Kirito noted seriously. "Don't even joke about that. But...it is a bit of a relief to hear. Anyway, once I log off, I'll contact my supervisor and have him explain the situation to the police. Even at the latest, they'll send a car around in fifteen...no, ten minutes."

"Hmm, all right. Hopefully they'll catch the accomplice..."

"Yeah..."

He looked a bit worried. Sinon glared at him. "So, you're going to make me expose my information, and just walk away?"

"Oh, er, s-sorry. My name is Kazuto Kirigaya. Like I said, I'm diving from Ochanomizu, but my home is Kawagoe, in Saitama Prefecture," he babbled. Sinon pored over his statement and couldn't help but giggle, despite the seriousness of the situation.

"'Kazuto Kirigaya.' *Kiri* and *to*, combined to form 'Kirito.' You're right, that *is* cliché."

"H-hey, look who's talking," he said, grinning slightly. He looked up at the cameras overhead and changed the subject. "We'll need to finish the BoB if we want to log out, though... What's the plan, Sinon? Do we settle this with another duel, like yesterday?"

Sinon realized that she had completely forgotten about the rematch with Kirito that had burned such a hole in her. She looked at the beautiful face across from her and thought for a second.

"Strength comes...not from results...but the process of what you aim for..."

"Huh? You say something?"

"N-no, just talking to myself. Listen, you look like hell. I won't get any enjoyment or bragging rights for beating someone in your condition. We can save the duel for the next BoB final," she smirked. Kirito's eyebrows rose in surprise, and he grimaced.

"Meaning I'm not allowed to convert back to my original game until the fourth tournament happens?"

"Hey, you can convert as many times as you want. Just don't assume you can waltz in and beat me that way. Anyway...let's wrap this one up."

"But how? It's a battle royale, so one of us has to go all the way to zero, or else there's no winner, right?"

"Well, it's rare, but you can have two winners—the first BoB on the North American server was a dual championship. The person who was supposed to win got cocky and fell victim to a grenade from the grave."

"Grenade from the grave? What's that?"

"When a person who's about to lose rolls out a grenade, hoping to take down the other person with them. Here, take this."

Sinon reached into her pouch and pulled out a black sphere, placing it in Kirito's upturned palm. She found the detonator timer, sticking out from the top like the stem of a fruit, and set it to about five seconds.

It was the plasma grenade that she'd rushed to pick up from

Yamikaze's side, once she confirmed that Kirito had killed Death Gun. She'd been ready for this ending since that moment.

Kirito finally realized what he was holding. His eyes bulged, and he nearly tossed it away on sheer instinct. Sinon put her arms around him and held him tight to stop him from doing so.

A blinding light erupted between them, melting Kirito's grimace and Sinon's grin into a screen of white.

The total time of the match was two hours, four minutes, thirty-seven seconds.

The battle royale final of the third Bullet of Bullets was over.

The result: simultaneous victory for Sinon and Kirito.

15

Sinon was teleported off of ISL Ragnarok, the island on which the event happened, and returned to a temporary waiting zone. She stared at the results board before her, complete with log-out timer, and tried her best to cool down her racing mind.

The event was over at last, but the Death Gun incident was not. His accomplice might still be lurking nearby when Shino returned to reality. Kirito said that he would have the police dispatched to her place at once, but given that he was logging out at the same time she was, and then had to contact his employer, it would easily take more than ten minutes. She would have to defend herself in that time.

First she'd check the safety of her apartment, then call Kyouji Shinkawa and have him come over. He might encounter the accomplice, but their weapon in the scheme—according to Kirito, at least—was a syringe full of poison, not guns or knives, so they wouldn't possibly try to jam a needle into a conscious person in the middle of the street. Still, she would tell him to be careful on the phone, of course.

The large countdown ticked away with astonishing speed. Only ten seconds until she was logged out.

She checked the results screen one last time. At the top, Sinon's and Kirito's names were sparkling. It was the ultimate goal of any GGO player to be listed in that spot, but sadly, she was certain that the honor would be stripped from her. Too many fishy things happened to reach that point. She'd have to wait until the fourth tournament to reach her goal.

Stuck in third place was Death Gun's registered name, Steven. Oddly, he spelled it "Sterben," which perhaps meant it was supposed to be pronounced slightly differently. The cloaked man's true identity, of course, was "Death Gun," and his character name was nothing but a piece of camouflage.

In fourth place was Yamikaze. No doubt many players had bet on him to be the champion, which meant the betting market had to be in a state of chaos now. A list of famous names stretched down from fifth place onward, including Dyne and Xiahou Dun—ending with twenty-eighth place.

At the very end were two players who'd been disconnected: Pale Rider and Garrett.

So Death Gun had claimed two victims after all. That probably meant he had two accomplices. What kind of a group had to come together in a VRMMO, and what did they need to go through, for three people to undertake such a horrifying crime spree?

When the countdown reached zero, Sinon was feeling not the elation of victory, but a deep, freezing chill.

A momentary floating sensation came and went, and Sinon was Shino again, lying alone on her real bed.

But in fact, she might not *be* alone. She reminded herself not to open her eyes or move all of a sudden. She kept herself utterly still and her eyelids closed, trying to sense her surroundings through other means.

There were a few different sounds she could hear. First, her own breathing. Next, the quick thumping of her heartbeat.

The low thrum near the ceiling belonged to the heating cycle of her air conditioner. The dripping was from the tank of her humidifier. Outside the window, the gentle rumble of street traffic. A stereo subwoofer from some other apartment in the building.

That was it. No other sources of unfamiliar noise in the apartment.

She took in a slow, long breath. The only smell her nose picked up was the gentle scent of the herb soap on top of the dresser she used as an air freshener.

Nobody else is in my room, Shino thought, but she couldn't open her eyes quite yet. She couldn't eliminate the fear that someone might be standing just on the left side of the bed, staring down at her.

In fact, it didn't even need to be in the room. There was the kitchen, the bathroom…the veranda…Even in her tiny apartment, there were plenty of places one could hide if they wanted. In fact, he might even be hiding under her bed. It was awful. She didn't want to move.

Meanwhile, Kirito—Kazuto Kirigaya—should be calling the police through his government contact. In another fifteen minutes, she'd hear the police siren. If that was the case, it might be smartest just to stay put and wait.

She had just shut her eyes tight, prepared for the long wait, when her old-fashioned heater ran out of juice and spit out a burst of unheated air that brushed Shino's exposed thigh. A chill ran across her skin, and she suddenly felt an ominous itch deep inside her nose.

She was only able to resist for two seconds. The space between her eyebrows and the bridge of her nose crinkled up, and her traitorous respiratory system emitted a small but undeniable *achoo!* Shino froze up, waiting for a reaction from somewhere else in the room.

Still, nothing moved.

Shino slowly, carefully lifted her right eyelid. The dimmed room glowed dully from the streetlights coming in through a crack in her curtains. She checked the state of the room, first within range of her eyeball, then with the turning radius of her neck.

For now, she didn't see any human figures. She gingerly, silently took off the AmuSphere and placed it next to her pillow. She sat up with nothing more than her stomach muscles and took a quick look around the room.

It seemed like everything was exactly as she'd left it when she full-dove a few hours earlier.

The mineral water bottle was on the table. Next to it was a large stereo. Her schoolbag was on the floor. None of them had been moved.

Shino pushed off the sheets and moved to the edge of the bed, swallowed, then leaned over to look under the bed. Nothing there, of course.

She looked up through the crack in the curtains to confirm that the lock on her window was firmly in place.

Next, Shino set her feet on the floor and craned her neck as far as it could to peer into the kitchen. But it was far too tiny of a space for anyone to be hiding in it.

She stood up and walked over to the wall, stifling her footsteps without realizing it, and hit the light switch. The room was suddenly full of white light that spilled down to the entranceway on the other side of the kitchen.

If she squinted her eyes, she could see that the lock on the door was still horizontal. She stayed right where she was, trying to sense anything from the one place in the apartment that was separated by a wall—the bathroom. There was no sound coming from it. She tiptoed from the main room to the kitchen.

The door to the bathroom across from the sink was shut tight. It wasn't locked, and the lights were off. Her sweaty hand gripped the aluminum doorknob.

With a deep breath, she flipped the light switch with her free hand and opened the door.

"…"

Shino stared at the interior.

"…I feel *really* stupid," she muttered. The beige interior of the bathroom was, of course, empty. At long last, from her neck to her shoulder and further on down, she felt the tension drain away. She made a half turn, leaned back against the wall, and slid down to a seated position.

There was no one else in the apartment. Nor were there any signs of a break-in so far. Naturally, that did not preclude the possibility that someone had hacked her old electronic lock, watched the progress of the GGO tournament on a cell phone, then left just after Death Gun's defeat.

If that was the case, the intruder should still be in the area. As long as the possibility of a return visit was greater than zero, she ought to call Kyouji Shinkawa for help at once—but Shino didn't have the strength to stand at the moment.

She glanced up at the kitchen alarm on top of the refrigerator. The digital readout said that it was 10:07.

What an incredibly long three hours that was. Eating the yogurt out of this empty container here before I dove in feels like ancient history at this point.

She felt like something inside of her had changed, and also that nothing had changed.

But at the very least, the hasty panic that Shino felt dwelling within her for a very long time seemed more distant now. Perhaps she had learned that the haste to be strong, to get stronger, was an empty thing. It all started with a single step.

"All…right!" she told herself, then realized that she was ravenously thirsty. Shino walked over to the sink, filled a glass with tap water, and drank it down in one go.

Just as she was about to fill up another cup, she heard the old-fashioned *ding-dong* of her doorbell.

She tensed up, staring at the door. Her breath caught in her throat as she imagined the lock turning all on its own.

Perhaps it was the police already. But when she looked at the clock, it had only been three minutes since she logged out. It was much too quick for them.

She stood there long enough for the doorbell to ring again. Stifling her breathing, she approached the door without making a sound. She reached out hesitantly to put the chain on the door, but just as her fingers were about to touch it…

"Asada, are you there? It's me, Asada!" came a familiar, high-pitched boy's voice through the electronic lock's intercom.

She felt the tension drain out of her shoulders and stood on her sandals as a footstool to look through the peephole, just in case. Through the fish-eye lens was the very person she was just about to call—her former classmate and GGO friend, Kyouji Shinkawa.

"Shinkawa…?" she asked through the intercom.

He immediately responded, though he didn't sound quite sure of himself. "Um…I just wanted to celebrate with you…I bought this for you—sorry, it's just from the convenience store."

She looked through the peephole again to see him hold up a small box that looked like it contained a piece of cake.

"Th…that was really quick," she blurted out. Even counting the time she spent in front of the results screen, it was less than five minutes since the tournament ended. Perhaps, instead of being at home, he'd been watching in a nearby park and rushed to the store on the way here. That hastiness was appropriate for the AGI-heavy Spiegel, she had to admit.

But at least it saved her the trouble of having to call him. She breathed a sigh of relief and put her hand on the knob. "Hang on, I'll open up."

She looked down as she reached over and noticed that she was still wearing the baggy sweater and short pants, which wasn't much, but she didn't feel in the mood to change. Shino turned the knob ninety degrees.

The door opened to reveal Kyouji Shinkawa, grinning away. He was heavily outfitted with jeans and a fleece-lined military jacket, but it was cold enough outside that even that seemed inadequate.

Shino hunched her neck at the chill against her bare legs and said, "Ooh, it's freezing. Quick, come in."

"Uh, sure. Thanks."

Kyouji bowed and stepped into the foyer, squinting as he looked at Shino, as if she was glowing.

"Wh-what? C'mon, shut the door before it gets cold inside. Oh, and make sure to lock it," she said, feeling a bit self-conscious about Kyouji's gaze. As she turned back into the apartment, she heard the heavy click of the door lock behind her. Back in the main room, she picked up the remote off the table and turned the heat on higher. With a heavy groan, warmer air flooded into the room, driving away the chill.

Shino plopped down onto the bed and looked up to see Kyouji standing at the edge of the room, looking uncomfortable.

"You can sit wherever you like. Oh, need anything to drink?"

"Uh, no, I'm fine."

"Listen, I'm tired, so unless you *really* don't need anything, speak up," she teased.

Kyouji finally smiled weakly, set the cake box down on the tea table, and sat on the nearby cushion. "Sorry for barging in like this, Asada. But...like I said earlier, I wanted to help you celebrate as soon as possible," he said, clutching his knees like a child. "Um...congrats on winning the BoB. It was incredible, Asada... Sinon. You're finally the greatest gunner in GGO. But...I always knew this would happen someday. You've got true strength, the kind nobody else has."

"...Thanks," she said, hunching her neck at the ticklish feeling the compliment gave her. "But my victory was only a tie at the top...plus, as I'm sure you noticed watching the feed, there was a bunch of weird stuff that happened in this one...I have a feeling that the entire tournament might get nullified."

"Huh...?"

"Um...listen..."

Shino wasn't quite sure how to bring up the topic of Death Gun to Kyouji. She herself didn't know enough about the incident to explain it all logically; plus, at this point, it almost felt to her like all of those events were some kind of strange hallucination.

Perhaps...

Could this all have been the product of sheer coincidence? Was it even possible to have someone poisoned at the same time they were shot in the virtual world? The only thing Shino actually saw was the scene of Pale Rider losing connection. If he and the other victim really did die, then Death Gun and his crimes were real, but nothing about that was certain until this was revealed.

In either case, the police would arrive within another ten minutes. She could explain it all to Kyouji then. Shino made up her mind and changed the topic.

"No, never mind. Just some weird players involved. Anyway, you really showed up here quick. It was barely even five minutes after the event finished."

"Um, well…the truth is, I was watching on my phone nearby. So I could congratulate you as soon as possible," he said hurriedly.

Shino smiled. "I had a feeling that was the case. You'll catch a cold in this weather. Maybe I should make some tea after all."

But Kyouji shook his head and stopped her. The smile was waning from his face, replaced by an expression more of desperation. Shino blinked in surprise.

"Um…Asada…"

"Wh-what?"

"I saw you…inside the cave, in the desert…"

Together with the look in his eyes, Shino understood what he was trying to say at once. She recalled what happened in the cave and felt heat burst along her face from cheek to ear.

"Oh…That was, uh…"

She'd completely—perhaps intentionally—forgotten about how she'd laid down on Kirito's knees and cried and wailed. Kyouji had witnessed the whole thing. It was so careless of her that she hadn't considered this possibility.

She looked down in sheer discomfort, while Kyouji continued. She was sure that he was going to ask what the connection was with that man, but his statement took her by surprise.

"He was…threatening you, wasn't he? He blackmailed you into doing that stuff, right?"

"H-huh?"

She looked up, stunned. Kyouji was leaning forward in a slight crouch, an odd look in his eyes. His lips trembled irregularly as he gasped, "He threatened you, and forced you to snipe his target...but in the end, you caught him off guard and blew him up with that grenade. But...that's not enough, Asada. Like I told you before, you need to make him pay..."

"Uh...err..." Shino was at a complete loss for words. She scrambled around for something to say. "Listen...no, he wasn't threatening me or anything. I realize it's not something you're supposed to do in a free-for-all competition...but I nearly had one of my spasms while in the dive. I lost control, and I...I took it out on Kirito. I said some horrible things to him."

"..."

Kyouji's eyes were wide as he listened raptly.

"But...while I did find him obnoxious, I thought...he was like my mom. Maybe that was why I cried like a little girl again...It's embarrassing, really."

"But Asada...it was because of the spasm, right? You wouldn't have done it otherwise? He doesn't...*mean* anything to you, does he?"

"Huh...?"

"You told me to wait, remember?" Kyouji said, eyes full of desperation as he leaned forward on his knees. "You did. You said that if I waited, you would be mine someday. So...so I..."

"...Shinkawa..."

"Say it. Say he means nothing to you. Say you hate him."

"Wh-what's going on...?"

She did remember telling Kyouji to wait before the tournament, in the nearby park. But that was meant in the sense of *wait for me to overcome my obstacles*. Only when she did that could she be a normal girl.

"But...you won, Asada. You're strong enough now. You won't have any more attacks. So you don't need him. I'll be with you forever. I'll...I'll always be around to keep you safe," he mumbled, getting to his feet. He stumbled a few steps closer—then suddenly threw his arms wide and embraced Shino with all his strength.

"Wha…?!"

Shino was too stunned to do anything but tense up. Her arms and ribs creaked, and the air leaked out of her lungs.

"Sh…in…ka…wa…"

The shock and pressure drained her breath away. But Kyouji only squeezed harder, pushing heavily enough to knock her backward onto the bed.

"Asada…I like you. I love you. You're my Asada…my Sinon," he croaked, less a passionate confession than a chanted curse.

"Stop…it…!'

Shino thrust her arms against the bed to support herself. She put her strength into her legs, leaned her shoulder her against his chest, and…

"Stop it!!"

It came out as nothing more than a desperate whisper, but she was able to knock Kyouji back. She gasped for air.

Kyouji, stumbling backward, fell onto his bottom when his leg hit the cushion behind him. The cake box fell off of the table and splattered wetly onto the floor. But the boy barely noticed. He just stared at Shino in pure surprise, unable to believe that she would reject him.

His round eyes eventually faded, and his lips trembled harder and harder. "No, Asada. You can't betray me. I'm the only one who can save you. You can't look at any other men."

He stood up slowly, approaching again.

"Sh…Shinkawa," she mumbled, unable to recover from the attack.

It was true that when she invited him in once before for dinner, and when he hugged her in the park, there had been a glimpse of this kind of impulse within Kyouji. But she figured that as he was a boy, this kind of action was somewhat of a given, and that weak-willed, reserved Kyouji would never lose control of himself like this.

But as he stood silently over Shino, who sat helplessly on the bed, there was something insane that gleamed in his eyes, something she'd never seen before.

Shinkawa isn't actually...going to...

The fragmented thoughts crossed through her brain bit by bit, until fear spread over her, greater than her shock. But Shino's imagination, while working in the right direction, was woefully inadequate in predicting the measure of his response.

Mouth parted, panting restlessly, Kyouji reached into the front pocket of his military jacket. He grabbed something inside of it. When the hand emerged, it was holding something strange: a shiny, plastic, cream-colored object about eight inches long.

The tapered tube was about an inch wide on average, with a grippable protrusion sticking out diagonally, which Kyouji used to hold it. There was a green button where the grip met the main tube, and he had his index finger placed against it.

A silver-metal part was affixed to the very end of the tube, a bit spiked, with a hole at the very end. All in all, it looked like a child's toy laser gun, but the very lack of any decoration gave it the look of a tool, a device designed for a specific purpose.

He slowly and simply moved the tip to Shino's neck. The chilly touch against her skin made all the hair on her body stand on end.

"Shi...k...wa...?" she gasped, but he cut her off before she could say anything further.

"Don't move, Asada. Don't speak. This a high-pressure needleless syringe. It's got a drug called succinylcholine inside. If it gets into your body, it'll render your muscles useless and stop your lungs and heart at once."

If her mind could be said to have an outer shell, this shock would have caused the bottom of it to give out. Even Shino couldn't keep track of how many times that had happened today.

The chill at the nape of her neck spread to the tips of her limbs, and as she felt them throb with numbness, her brain worked overtime to put the words that Kyouji said into an understandable thought.

Kyouji had just said that he would kill Shino. If she didn't listen to what he said, he'd use that toylike injector to pump her full of a drug with a long and confusing name, stopping her heart for good.

But in parallel to this thought, a voice in the corner of her mind kept stating, *This is a joke, right? Shinkawa wouldn't do something like that, would he?* But her mouth was now as immobile and brittle as dried-out wood. And the sensation of the metal tube pressed a few inches below her left ear was chillingly, mercilessly cold, a phenomenon that brooked no possible humor.

Shino was unable to see Kyouji's face due to the reflection, but she stared at him all the same. His young, rounded chin moved, emitting a voice devoid of feeling or inflection. "It's all right, Asada. There's nothing to be afraid of. We're about to become one. I'm about to give you the feelings I've been saving up ever since we first met. The injection will be very soft and gentle…It won't hurt a bit. Don't worry. Just let me handle everything."

Shino had no idea what he meant. It sounded like Japanese, but it might as well have been a foreign language. Two phrases stood out, echoing over and over in her head.

This is a high-pressure needleless syringe. I'll stop your heart at once.

Syringe. Heart. She'd just heard those two words very recently…somewhere else.

At this point, it felt like something from an imaginary fantasy. On a moonlit desert, in a tiny cave, from the mouth of a boy with the face of a girl. Zexceed and Usujio Tarako had been injected with some kind of drug, and their hearts failed…

But did that mean—could it be?

Her lips trembled and spasmed, and she heard her own voice leak out like it belonged to someone else.

"Then…are you…the other…Death Gun?"

The tip of the syringe pressed to her neck twitched. She saw Kyouji's mouth take on the admiring smile that she so often saw when she spoke with him.

"Wow...incredible work, Asada...You figured out the secret of Death Gun. That's right, I'm part of Death Gun. But in fact, until the BoB started, I was the one playing Sterben. I hope you saw that video of me shooting Zexceed in the pub in Glocken. But for today, I got to play the real-life role. After all, I can't have any other man touching you, Asada. Even if it *is* my brother."

Her body stiffened.

She had only once heard him mention that he had a brother. But aside from the fact that he'd been sickly since birth and in and out of hospitals, Kyouji said nothing about him, so Shino never bothered to ask further.

"B...bro...thers? So the one in the killer guild in SAO years ago was...your...brother?"

This time, Kyouji's eyes bugged out in true shock.

"Wow, you knew? I didn't think Shouichi would reveal that much during the tournament. Maybe he decided he liked you, too. But don't worry, I won't let anyone else touch you. In fact, I wanted not to inject you with the drug today, though I knew my brother would be mad...I mean, in the park, you said you would be mine."

He stopped briefly. The drunken smile on his lips faded, replaced by another empty expression.

"But...then you were with *him*...You're being fooled, Asada. I don't know what he said to you, but I'll drive him away. I'll help you forget him."

He clutched her right shoulder, still pressing the syringe to her neck with his other hand. He pushed her down onto the bed, then got onto it with her, straddling her thighs, mumbling as he did.

"...Don't worry, I won't let you be alone. I'll come with you very soon. We'll be together, just like GGO...No, let's do a more fantasy-themed one. We can be reborn in that world and live together as husband and wife. Going on adventures…having kids…It'll be a blast."

Kyouji was completely off the rails now. Somewhere in Shino's paralyzed brain, she was able to cling to just one thought: The police will be here soon, so keep him talking.

"But…without his partner, your brother will be at a loss… a-and…I didn't get shot by Death Gun in the game. So if I die, then everyone will start to doubt the legend of Death Gun you spent so long crafting," Shino said, taking great pains to keep her desiccated tongue moving. Kyouji pressed the tip of the syringe under her exposed collarbone, a twitching smile on his face.

"It's fine. We had three targets today, after all. My brother brought in another helper to carry it out. A guildmate from SAO, he said. So he's already got a replacement for my position. Plus, I'd never let you get lumped in with scum like Zexceed and Tarako. You belong to *me*, not Death Gun. We'll go somewhere on vacation…I'll carry you all the way into the mountains where nobody is, and then I'll follow right after you. So wait for me once you're there, okay?"

Kyouji's left hand touched her midsection through the sweater, as timidly as if he were frightened of her. He tapped a few times with his fingertips, then slowly began to rub her with his entire hand.

Shino tried her best to ignore the revulsion that crawled along her skin and keep talking. If she made any sudden moves or shouted, the harmless-looking boy with her would press the button on the syringe without hesitation. Sadly, there was something in Kyouji's voice and face that made that very clear.

As quietly and gently as possible, Shino continued, "Th-then… you're saying you haven't used that syringe before in real life? Then, we…we can still do it. We can start over. You shouldn't think about dying…Aren't you going to take the high school proficiency test? Aren't you going to a cram school? Aren't you going to be a doctor…?"

"Proficiency…?" Kyouji repeated, as though he'd never heard

that word before. After a moment, he murmured in understanding, and his hand lifted off of Shino and went into his jacket pocket. He pulled out a long, thin sheet of paper. "Want to see?"

He thrust it into Shino's face with a sardonic smile. The printout was something very familiar to Shino: the results sheet of a mock exam. But all the scores, in every subject, were almost unbelievably poor.

"Sh...Shinkawa. How...?"

"Isn't it funny? Bet you never thought people actually got percentile scores this low."

"B-but...your parents..." she said, unable to believe that Kyouji's parents would allow him to keep using his AmuSphere with grades like that. He picked up on what she meant.

"Heh...as if I couldn't make a sheet like this in any old printer. Besides, I tell my parents that I get online tutoring through the AmuSphere. Sure, they wouldn't let me set up an autopay for the GGO subscription, but I was able to earn that much in the game...I could have managed..."

Suddenly, the smile vanished from his face. The bridge of his nose wrinkled, and he bared his teeth in a snarl. "I decided... I don't care about this stupid reality anymore. My parents... the people at school...They're all idiots, every one of them. If I'd become the strongest in GGO...I would have been happy. And I should have been. That's what should have happened with Spiegel..."

Shino felt the tip of the syringe trembling against her neck and held her breath, expecting him to push the button at any time.

"And then...that piece of crap Zexceed...lied about the AGI build being the best...and thanks to that cheating coward, Spiegel can barely even equip an M16...Dammit...dammit!"

The loathing in Kyouji's voice completely surpassed the bounds of a mere video game.

"Now I can barely even make back the subscription fee...GGO was everything to me. I sacrificed everything in real life for it..."

"And that's...why you killed Zexceed?" Shino asked, shocked

and horrified. He clamped his eyes shut for a moment, and the drunken smile returned.

"That's right. Is there any better sacrifice to make to create a legend about Death Gun being the greatest player in GGO—no, in all of VRMMOs? I killed Zexceed, Tarako, and now Pale Rider and Garrett. Even the idiots playing this game have to realize that Death Gun's power is real now. I'm the greatest alive..."

Kyouji's entire body shook with uncontrollable pleasure. "Now I have no need for this worthless reality anymore. Come, Asada...Come with me to the next stage."

"Sh-Shinkawa," Shino stammered, shaking her head. "You can't do this. You can still turn back. You can start over. Come with me to the police..."

"..."

But Kyouji only shook his head, staring off into the distance. "Reality doesn't matter anymore. Now become one with me, Asada," he said emptily, bringing his hand up to brush her cheek and run it through her hair. "Oh, Asada...You're beautiful. You're so beautiful..."

His fingertips were scaly and dry. Each time the cracked skin at the base of his nails scraped the fine skin around her ear, an unpleasant pain ran through her face. But she made no show of it, and Kyouji continued absently.

"Asada, my sweet Asada...I've always, always loved you. Ever since...I heard about what happened to you...at school..."

"...Wha...?" Belatedly, what Kyouji said registered in Shino's mind, and her eyes went wide. "Wh...what do you...mean...?"

"I loved you. I wanted to be like you...always..."

"Then...you..." she squeaked, praying that what he was saying wasn't true. "You mean...you only talked to me...because of what happened to me in the past?"

"Yes, of course," he stated, stroking her head like she was a little child, nodding fervently. "You won't find another girl in Japan who got to shoot a bad guy dead with a real gun. It's incredible. Didn't I tell you that you have true power? That's why I picked the

Type 54 to be central to Death Gun's legend. You're what I want to be. I love you...I love you...more than anyone..."

"You...can't..."

What an incredible gulf. What an incredible separation between them.

She had once believed that this boy was the only human being not related to her by blood whom she could trust. But his mind did not belong to the same world as hers. From the very first step, he had been incredibly, unfathomably distant.

At last, Shino's heart was full of black, deep despair. Sight, sound, hearing—all of her senses began to lose meaning, and the world slowly faded away from her.

Shino lost all strength.

In her faded, unfocused vision, Kyouji's two eyes floated like black holes. Like passageways connecting her to a world of darkness.

They were that man's eyes.

He had returned at last. The man who had bided his time, lurking in the shadows—in the gloom of the night streets, between the furniture, within the hood of Death Gun.

The warmth drained from her fingers. The connection between her body and consciousness began to peel away at the edges. Her soul was contracting. In the warm, cramped darkness at the very center of her mortal shell, Shino shrank into a little ball. She didn't want to see anymore. She didn't want to feel.

The world she'd lived through for sixteen years was too cold, too cruel. It stole the father she'd never recognize, stole her mother's mind, and with great malice, took away a part of Shino's soul.

The stares of adults, reflecting the curiosity of viewing some rare creature in a zoo, and even more ill-concealed loathing. The merciless taunts of the children her age.

The world decided that wasn't enough, and wanted to take more from her now. She didn't want to accept this as the one and only "reality" that existed.

That was right—it wasn't reality. It was just one particular combination of events, out of the countless worlds that existed and overlapped. Somewhere out there was another world where none of this had happened.

Somewhere out there was a world in which Shino Asada didn't meet Kyouji Shinkawa, the post office wasn't attacked, the accident that killed her father never happened, and she lived an ordinary, happy life. As she curled smaller and smaller into a compressed, inorganic ball, Shino's soul sought a version of herself that was smiling in the warm sunlight.

In what little rationality remained to her, Shino caught a tiny whiff of irony. In her inability to withstand the cruelty of life, she was escaping into the realm of dreams, which made her just like Kyouji Shinkawa.

Kyouji was bullied at school, pressured by his parents' expectations, and flattened by the difficulty of tests, so he abandoned reality and sought salvation in the virtual world. If he could earn the title of the strongest in the virtual world, that would have more than enough value to fill the emptiness of his real life, he believed. But when that hope was taken away from him, he fell apart.

Shino, too, sought the same kind of strength in Gun Gale Online. And at one point, she thought she had realized something, had found her way. But the chilly hand from the swamp of memory had caught Shino, dragged her back with it, and she never tried to resist. She couldn't even open her eyes. It was all pointless in the end.

As the thoughts trickled up, bit by bit, like tiny bubbles from the bottom of the sea floor, she wondered, *What about that other boy?*

He had been trapped in a virtual prison for two long years, and ended up taking the lives of several people. He probably lost others who were important to him in that long, long battle for survival. Did he regret that, too? Did he hate the virtual world that stole so many things from him?

No, he probably didn't. No matter what challenges came his

way, he wouldn't abandon the things he bore. He seized that desperate, unlikely victory from Death Gun because that was what kind of person he was.

You are strong, Kirito, Shino muttered from the deep dark. *You went to the trouble of saving me...and now I've let it go to waste. Sorry...*

Kirito said he would send the police over as soon as he logged out. She didn't know how many minutes had passed since then, but it was clear that they wouldn't arrive in time. What would he feel when he learned that she'd been killed? That was the only thing that weighed over her mind...

Then, like a chain reaction, another fear lit up within the darkness of her heart.

Would Kirito just call his employer and call it a day? Or would he rush over to Shino's apartment himself, just to be sure? He would still be late, she figured, but what would happen if he came here and encountered Kyouji Shinkawa? Would Kyouji run away, give up...or turn his syringe on Kirito next? The last option was quite possible, after the way he seethed in hatred of Kirito earlier.

She might be able to accept her fate, to acknowledge that she was meant to die here. But getting him involved, that innocent boy...

That was a different matter.

But it won't change a thing, young Shino said to herself, curled into a ball on her side, blocking her eyes and ears.

Kneeling at her side, hand on the girl's slender shoulder, Sinon whispered through her sand-yellow muffler, *We've only ever watched ourselves. We've only ever fought for ourselves. That's why we didn't notice the voice coming from Shinkawa's heart. But while it might be too late for us now, we can at least fight for someone else, here at the very end.*

Shino slowly opened her eyes in the darkness. Right before her was a white, fragile, but somehow powerful hand. She timidly reached out and grabbed it.

Sinon grinned and helped Shino to her feet. Her pale lips opened, speaking briefly but clearly: *Let's go.*

The two leaped off the floor of darkness and began to rise up to the light far above, glimmering like the surface of water.

Shino blinked hard, connected again to the real world.

Kyouji was trying to pull the sweater off of her, keeping the syringe pointed to her neck with one hand. But with only one hand to work with, the process was not going easily, and he was visibly frustrated. He started pulling on the fabric as hard as he could, attempting to rip it off of her.

Shino leaned to the left with the momentum of his pulling, pretending that he yanked her too far. The tip of the syringe slipped off of her neck and landed on the bedsheet next to her.

She did not miss the opportunity. She grabbed the syringe cylinder with her left hand and struck upward at Kyouji's chin with the heel of her right.

He grunted and lurched backward. The weight on her body lifted. She smacked him over and over, pulling desperately on the syringe. If she couldn't wrest it away from him, she would never get another chance.

But the tug-of-war between Kyouji's hand on the syringe handle and Shino's hand on the smooth barrel did not favor her. When he had regained his balance, he pulled hard, screeched, and swung his free hand.

"...!!"

The fist pounded Shino's right shoulder. As the syringe came free from her grip, she toppled over the head of the bed, hitting her back hard against the writing desk. One of the drawers jarred loose with the impact, spilling its contents onto the floor.

Shino gaped, trying to will the air back into her lungs. Kyouji was clutching his bruised chin atop the bed, but he recovered and stared at her straightaway. His eyes were wide, and his lips quivered, shining with saliva. She could see a trail of blood from his bitten tongue.

Eventually those lips parted to croak, "Why...?"

His head shook slowly, clear disbelief on every inch of his features. "Why...would you do this? You don't have anyone but me, Asada. I'm the only one who understands you. I've been helping you all along... Watching over you..."

Shino recalled what happened several days ago, when Endou's group ambushed her on the way home from school. They demanded money, and Kyouji coincidentally happened by and scared them off...

But that wasn't a coincidence.

Kyouji must have followed her home from school for days in a row, watching to ensure she got home safely, then turned to go home and log in to GGO to wait for her there.

It was nothing short of obsessive delusion. She had a hint of his dangerous nature, but no idea of its true depth. Even in her endangered state, a part of Shino couldn't help but feel a bitter element of punishment for not taking him seriously.

"Shinkawa," she said, her lips tense, "I know it's been nothing but pain...but I still love the real world. And I think..I can love it more. So I can't go with you."

She put a hand on the floor to push herself up, and her fingers touched something heavy and cold. Shino instantly sensed what it was. It was what she kept hidden within the drawer that just fell out: the real-life symbol of all her fears. The Procyon SL model she won for participating in the second BoB.

She found the handle by touch, lifted up the heavy gun, and pointed it at Kyouji. It was as cold as if it had been carved directly from a block of ice. The feeling in her right hand began to drain away as the numbness crawled up her arm.

Even she knew that this sensation was not actual cold. It was her mental rejection of it that caused it to feel that way, but understanding how the sensation worked didn't make it go away. A fear she couldn't describe began to well up in the depths of her heart, like black water.

The spotless white of her wallpaper began to waver, like the surface of water, and cracked gray concrete floated up from behind. Her floor tiles turned to faded green linoleum, the window to a wooden counter. Shino was back in the rickety old postal office.

Kyouji's face, caught in her crosshairs, suddenly warped and melted as well. His skin turned oily and ashen, deep lines appeared, and crooked, yellow teeth jutted from his cracked lips. The syringe in his hand had turned into an old-fashioned automatic pistol, gleaming dully. And so had the gun in her hand.

Shino shrank, predicting the scene she would see next. Her stomach convulsed, leaping into her throat, and all the muscles in her back stiffened.

No. I don't want to see. I want to toss aside the Black Star and run away.

But if she ran now, everything would go to waste. She'd lose both her life and something else just as important. Perhaps fighting the terror of the spasms as Shino, or fighting countless powerful foes as Sinon, would never bring her the results she sought. But...all strength was found in the process.

Shino clenched her teeth hard enough to crack them and clicked the hammer of the gun with her thumb. The hard, dense sound tore through all of the illusion at once.

Kneeling on the bed, Kyouji shrank back slightly at the sight of the Procyon SL pointed right at him. He blinked rapidly in terror, rasping, "Wh-what do you think you're doing, Asada? That's just...a model gun. Do you really think you can stop me with that?"

Shino put her hand on the lip of the desk, putting as much strength into her quavering legs as she could to stand up. "You said it yourself. I have the true power. There's no other girl like me who's shot someone with a gun."

"..."

Kyouji's face went as white as a sheet. He scrambled back further.

"So this isn't a model gun anymore. When I pull the trigger, an actual bullet will come out and kill you," Shino said, inching backward toward the kitchen with the gun still pointed at Kyouji.

"Y…you're going to…kill me…?" he mumbled, slowly shaking his head. "Asada's going…to kill…me?"

"Yes. You're the only one going to the next world."

"No…no…You can't do that to me…"

The willpower drained out of Kyouji's eyes. His absentminded features stared into space, and he took a proper sitting position on top of the bed.

When she saw his hand relax and the high-pressure syringe start to slip out of his fingers, Shino was briefly arrested with the choice to snatch it away from him at that exact moment. But she had a feeling that if agitated, he would lose all reason whatsoever and attack her. She continued her steady retreat into the kitchen instead.

The moment Kyouji disappeared from view, Shino bolted back for the front door. It was only five yards, but it felt unbearably long. She raced with wide strides, trying to keep her footsteps quiet.

But right as she reached the big step down into the foyer, the mat slipped beneath her feet, and she fell. When she swung her hand to regain balance, the model gun flew out and landed in the kitchen sink with an incredible clatter.

Though she hadn't fallen completely, Shino's left knee hit the floor painfully. Still attached to the ground, she reached out as far as she could and snagged the doorknob.

But the door didn't open. She noticed the lock was horizontal and frantically twisted it vertical, her teeth clenched. At the same moment that the lock clicked open, a cold hand grabbed her ankle from behind.

"…!!"

She turned back, breath stuck in her throat, to see Kyouji's soulless face. He was down on all fours, clutching her leg with both hands. She didn't see the syringe.

She shook her leg wildly, trying to break free, even as she

lunged to get the door open. But while she could reach the knob, she couldn't get a grip on it. Kyouji was pulling her back with astonishing strength.

He dragged her backward a few feet into the kitchen, but Shino resisted by grabbing the lip of the foyer step and clinging to it.

She tried to scream, thinking that it might be audible from outside, but her throat was constricted, unable to suck in air. All that emerged was a weak rasp.

Kyouji's strength defied understanding. He was the same height as her, so where was he getting so much power? She lost her grip on the step as he continued pulling, and slid quickly through the kitchen.

His weight was immediately pressed onto her. She clenched her fist and tried to aim for his chin again, but only grazed it before he caught her wrist. The bones creaked as he squeezed like a vice, setting off sparks of pain in her head.

"Asada-asada-asada," he rushed, the sounds only recognizable as her name after several seconds. Excited, bubbling white froth spilled from the corners of his mouth, and his eyes were unfocused. His mouth opened wide as he leaned in, teeth exposed as he made to bite her skin. She tried to push him back with her free hand, but he easily caught that one as well.

Though her hands were immobilized, she could still use her own mouth. Her jaw tensed as she prepared to bite at his throat.

Suddenly, cold air rushed over her shoulders. Kyouji looked up with a start over Shino's head. His eyes and mouth went wide.

Somehow, the door was open, and something—someone— rushed through like a black gale of wind and kneed Kyouji in the face. Shino stared in shock as Kyouji and the mystery intruder tumbled past her, further into the apartment.

Kyouji was being pressed down to the floor by an unfamiliar young man. Blood was flowing from his mouth and nose.

The boy had longish black hair and a riding jacket of the same color. At first she thought he might be another resident of the apartment building, but the identity of the man—no, boy—became clear to her when he turned and shouted, "Run, Sinon! Call for help!"

"Kiri…" she mumbled, then bolted upright. She wanted to get to her feet, but they wouldn't listen. She was only able to rise at all by pulling herself up against the side of the sink. He really had come from wherever he was diving in Ochanomizu. That meant the police should be coming soon. She lashed her weak legs into motion, hopping the few steps to the door.

But then she remembered something crucial.

Kyouji had a lethal weapon. She had to warn Kirito.

She turned around to shout, and saw Kyouji roar like an animal, all self-control lost. Kirito's body flew backward, and the two switched positions.

"It was you…it was *youuuuu*!!" Kyouji screamed, so deafening that she practically heard speaker feedback in her ears. "Stay away from my Asadaaaaa!!"

Kyouji's fist thudded heavily into Kirito's cheek. His other hand went into the jacket pocket and pulled out the horrible gun-shaped syringe.

"Kirito!!" Shino screamed, right as Kyouji howled, "Dieeee!!"

The high-pressure, needleless syringe stuck in the T-shirt between Kirito's jacket and chest and made a small, sharp, but unmistakable *pshht!*

Terrifyingly enough, it was strikingly similar to the sound of a gun with a high-quality silencer attached, though Shino only recognized it by virtue of Gun Gale Online, not from a real-life experience. But no matter the source, the sound represented a threat that needed to be dealt with. The next thing she knew, she was racing forward.

Shino crossed the kitchen and went into the room, searching for the most effective weapon without consciously realizing what she was doing. She chose the stereo atop the table, picking it up by the handle with her left hand. It had served her quite well, but it

was old and much larger than the newer wall-mounted stereos—a block of metal weighing well over five pounds. She hauled it with her waist and swung it around backward.

The half turn of her body and the momentum of the heavy stereo carried it straight into the left side of Kyouji's head, the drunken smile plastered across his face once again. She barely even felt or heard the impact. But she *did* hear the sickening thud of Kyouji's head slamming backward against the corner frame of her bed.

Battered on both sides of his head within the span of half a second, the boy groaned and flopped forward. His grip loosened and the syringe started to slip out.

She didn't know if the device was made for administering multiple doses in succession, but she clawed it out of Kyouji's hand regardless. Its owner's eyes were rolled back into his head and he kept groaning, but he wasn't likely to move anytime soon.

Shino thought about getting a belt or something to tie up his hands, then remembered that there was something more important first. She turned and shrieked Kirito's name, then crouched over his fallen form.

There was a softness to the boy's face that she thought she recognized from his online character. He gazed up at her with barely-parted eyes and grunted, "He got me...I didn't realize... that was a syringe..."

"Where? Where did it get you?!"

She tossed the syringe aside and tore down the zipper of Kirito's jacket. Her thoughts were a jumble of half-formed impulses: Call ambulance—emergency care before that—but how to remove the poison? Her fingers trembled.

There was an ominous dark stain right above the heart on his faded blue T-shirt. She didn't know how strong the piercing power of that syringe was, but it didn't seem likely that a thin cotton shirt would have stopped it.

"Don't die...You can't die like this!" she shrieked, yanking the bottom of his shirt out of his jeans and pulling it upward. The skin of his chest and stomach was white and scrawny, as if someone had carved it down from its proper size. Just to the right of the center, in the very spot where the stain had been—something was stuck to his chest.

"...?!"

She stared at it, confused.

It was a small circle, about an inch across. There was a thin silver disc, surrounded by what looked like a yellow rubber suction cup. A socket-like protrusion emerged from the metal disc, but it wasn't connected to anything.

The whole surface of the metal was wet; a single drop hung from it. The clear liquid had to be the fatal "succinylcholine" Kyouji had spoken of.

Shino looked around the floor for her tissue box and pulled two out, carefully wiping the liquid away. She leaned in closer to examine the skin around the odd patch to ensure that the high-pressure stream hadn't broken into his flesh.

No matter how hard she looked, she couldn't find any marks on Kirito's skin. The tip of the syringe must have hit this inch-wide metal disc through his T-shirt and been absorbed by the stiff object. She touched the skin above the patch just to be sure, and felt his pulse racing away healthily.

Shino blinked a few times and looked up at Kirito. His eyes were closed and he was moaning and groaning.

"Um...hey."

"Ugh...it's too late...It hurts to breathe..."

"Hey, can I ask you something?"

"Dammit...now that the moment's finally here...I don't have any good final words..."

"What's this thing stuck to your chest?"

"...Huh?"

Kirito's eyes opened again, and he glanced down. His eyebrows furrowed and he brought up a hand to trace the metal disc.

"Are you saying...the injection went into this?"

"Um, I think so. What is it?"

"Uh...I'm pretty sure it's...an electrode from the heart monitor..."

"H-huh? Why would you have one of those? Do you have a bad heart?"

"No, not at all...It was a safety measure against Death Gun... Oh, I get it. I was in such a rush to get disconnected, I must have pulled the cord out of this one by accident," he muttered, sighing heavily. "Damn...You really had me going, there."

"That's—" Shino started, grabbing him around the neck with both hands and squeezing violently "—what I was going to say! I...I thought you were dead!!"

All of the tension and nerves suddenly drained out of her, and her vision darkened. She shook her head to clear the cobwebs and looked back at the collapsed Kyouji.

"Do you think...he's okay?" Kirito asked. She reached out and picked up his limp wrist. Fortunately, there was a pulse there, too. She wondered again if they ought to tie him up, but with his eyes closed like that, Kyouji's face was too innocent looking. She had to turn away. She didn't want to think about him right now. Her chest was full, not of rage or sadness, but plain emptiness.

For several seconds, she just stared over at the high-pressure needleless syringe—the true "Death Gun," in a way. Eventually she opened her mouth and said simply, "Thanks...for coming to help me."

Kirito gave her a familiar one-cheeked smirk and shook his head. "Nah... I didn't end up doing anything for you in the end... Plus, I'm sorry I was late. Kiku—my employer wasn't getting the picture fast enough. You aren't hurt, are you?"

Shino shook her head. Suddenly, she noticed something was flooding out of her eyes. "Ah...what the..."

Her head was as fuzzy and useless as if it were stuffed with cotton, but the tears streaming out of her eyes only picked up momentum, dripping off her face.

Shino closed her mouth, stayed still, and let the tears flow. She knew that if she tried to say anything, she would only start bawling at the top of her lungs. Kirito didn't move, either.

Eventually, she sensed the howl of distant sirens approaching, but her tears were not going to dry up anytime soon. Secretly, as the big drops fell one after the other, Shino understood that the source of the void that filled her heart was deep, deep loss.

16

The sky above was so vast and distant that she could feel the space beyond it.

No VR world could recreate that feeling of empty sky. Within the deep, pure blue that was a forgotten remnant of the past autumn, little tufts and streaks of clouds formed a hanging blanket. Two sparrows perched on a thin electric line, and a military plane far above glinted with reflected sun.

Shino gazed endlessly into the tremendous depth of this combination of layers without tiring, feeling her mind being sucked into it.

The breeze was warm for mid-December, and the bustle of the students after school did not reach this spot behind the building. The sky at the center of Tokyo, usually a dull gray, looked like the sky over her hometown to the north on this rare occasion. Shino had been staring up into the endless sky for nearly ten minutes with her schoolbag clutched on her lap, sitting on the edge of the dreary planter with its bare, black soil.

Eventually, giggling voices and numerous footsteps intruded on her peace and quiet, and Shino was returned to the Earth at last. She craned her stiff neck and pulled up her white muffler, waiting for the offenders.

When they emerged from the path between the northwest corner of the campus and the large incinerator, Endou and her two cohorts noticed Shino and smirked sadistically.

Shino picked up her bag and stood. "Don't call me out and then keep me waiting."

One of the two followers blinked her heavy eyelids at high speed. The smile was gone from her lips. "Is it me, or are you gettin' a little too full of yourself these days, Asada?"

In nearly identical form, the other one followed up, "Yeah, who talks to her own friends like that?"

They had all stopped about six feet from Shino, and were throwing her menacing stares from what they believed to be intimidating angles. Shino decided to stare back at Endou in the center, looking directly into her predatory insect's eyes.

The silence lasted only a few seconds. Endou smiled and jutted her chin out. "Aw, whatever. Friends can handle anything you say. 'Cuz you'd still help us if we needed it, right? And we, like, *really* need it right now."

The two followers snorted.

"Let me see 20,000 yen, for starters," Endou said, in the casual tone of one asking to borrow an eraser.

Shino took off the noncorrective NXT polymer-lens glasses she wore and put them in her skirt pocket. She glared with every fiber of her being, enunciating every word carefully:

"As I said before, I have no intention of lending you anything."

Endou's eyes narrowed until they were as thin as wires. There was a persistent, hungry glare exuding from them. She growled, "Don't think you can keep getting away with this bullshit. Just so you know, I actually borrowed it from my brother today. I can break you, Asada."

"...Do your worst."

Shino didn't think she would actually do it, but to her surprise, one end of Endou's mouth perked up into a smile. She put her hand into the bag.

In a way, a large black pistol emerging from a schoolgirl bag laden with clattering little mascot trinkets had some measure of black humor. Endou clumsily pulled the large pellet gun out and pointed it at Shino. "This thing can pop a hole in cardboard. He said I should never point it at anyone, but I bet you don't mind. You're used to it."

Shino's eyes were automatically drawn to the black muzzle. Her pulse suddenly jumped. The ringing in her ears started to drown out the other noise. Her breathing got fast and short, and a chill crept into her fingertips.

But she clenched her teeth, and using all her willpower, tore her eyes away from the darkness of the gun's interior. She followed Endou's hand on the grip up her arm, to her shoulder, her bleached hair, and then her face.

Endou's agitation caused the capillaries in her eyes to float to the surface, making the irises dark and cloudy. They were ugly eyes. The eyes of one drunk on violence and power.

It wasn't the gun that was truly frightful. It was the person holding it.

Endou frowned, unhappy that Shino wasn't giving her the reaction she expected. "Cry, Asada. Get down on your hands and knees and apologize. Or I really will shoot you."

She pointed the model gun at Shino's left leg and smirked. Shino noticed her shoulder twitching, the movement necessary to twist her finger and pull the trigger. But no bullet emerged.

"What the hell?"

Again, then again, Endou pulled the trigger, but the only sound was the squeak of plastic. Shino took a deep breath, summoning strength to her stomach, then dropped the bag and reached out. Her thumb pressed hard on Endou's wrist, weakening the grip, and she snatched the gun away with her other hand. Shino slipped her index finger into the trigger guard and squeezed the handle with her palm. For a plastic model, it was quite heavy.

"A 1911 Government, huh? Your brother's got classic taste. Not my style, though," she said, pointing the left side of the gun toward Endou. "The Government's got a grip safety in addition to the thumb safety. You can't shoot it unless you unlock both spots."

Click, click. She removed the safety devices. "Plus, it's a single action, so you have to cock it yourself to start with."

She used her thumb to raise the hammer, and the trigger rose slightly within her grasp.

Shino ignored the dumbstruck girls and looked around. About six yards away was a line of blue plastic buckets next to the incinerator. Her eyes stopped on an empty juice can sitting atop one of the upturned buckets.

She propped the gun up with her free hand and took a basic isosceles stance. The can lined up along the axis of her right eye and the sight of the gun. After a moment's thought, she raised the weapon a hair, held her breath, and squeezed the trigger.

It made a weak *shump* sound, and she felt a very slight recoil. The gun's blowback system did work perfectly, however, and a little orange bullet popped out.

She figured that without knowing the finer control of the model, she would miss, but to her surprise, the shot landed luckily right near the top of the can. It twanged and spun like a top before eventually tumbling over and rolling off the bucket.

Shino breathed out and lowered the gun, turning to look at Endou.

Her sardonic smile was gone. She was completely stunned, at a loss for words. As Shino maintained her direct stare, Endou eventually quavered and took a half step backward.

"N-no...don't," she squeaked.

Shino let her gaze soften at last. "...You're right. This isn't meant to be pointed at people," she said, decocking the hammer and reactivating the safeties. She offered Endou the gun handle-first, and the other girl tensed in fear before eventually reaching out to take it.

Shino turned, picked up her bag, and tugged her muffler up again. She cast a brief good-bye over her shoulder and started

walking. Endou's group did not move. The three stood in paralyzed silence all the while it took Shino to round the corner of the
building and put them out of her sight.

The moment she was safe, the strength drained out of her legs,
and Shino nearly slumped to the ground. She put a hand to the
wall to stay upright.

There was a howling in her ears, and she felt the pulsing of
blood in her temples. Sour bile burned at the back of her throat.
She was in no condition to repeat what she'd just done.

Still, this was the first step.

She willed strength into her wilted legs, forcing them to
resume walking. The cold weight of the model gun was still stuck
to her palm and refused to disappear, but as the cold, dry wind
blew on her hand, the effect slowly faded. When her fingers were
ready to move again, she took out her glasses and placed them on
her face.

Shino crossed the walkway linking the west entrance of the school
to the gymnasium, and a short while later, cut across the corner of
the athletic field. She walked past the members of the sports clubs
running around the track, then passed through the small copse of
trees to the south, putting her at the front entrance of the school.

She weaved her way quickly through the milling groups of
students departing for the day, then stopped when something
caught her eye. Several groups of female students within the high
walls of the school had stopped nearby, speaking softly among
themselves and glancing at the gate.

Shino spotted two classmates who weren't totally hostile to
her, and walked over to them. The one with long hair and black-
rimmed glasses noticed her and waved with a grin. "Are you
leaving now, Asada?"

"Yeah. What's going on?"

The other girl, who had brown hair tied into two tails, shrugged
and chuckled. "There's a boy with a different school uniform on,
waiting at the gate. He's on a motorcycle and has two helmets,

so we figure he has to be waiting on someone. We were all wondering who the lucky girl is. I know it's gossipy, but who do you think it is?"

Even as she heard it, Shino felt the blood drain from her face. She checked her watch, furiously denying that it could be true.

It was true that they had agreed for him to wait for her around this time, and she had demanded he give her a ride on his bike to save the train costs. But who would be so bold and so daring as to park his motorcycle right in front of the main gate of the school?

...He *would. He absolutely would.*

She leaned timidly against the wall and glanced at the driveway turnaround on the other side of the gate, then slumped her shoulders. There he was, leaning against the flashy-colored little motorcycle with kickstand deployed, helmet in both hands, gazing absentmindedly up at the sky, dressed in an unfamiliar uniform. It was undoubtedly the boy she'd met just two days earlier.

The thought of walking over to him and hopping onto the back of his bike with over a dozen people watching made the tips of her ears burn with embarrassment. Shino wished with all her heart that she could just log out of this scene. She summoned up what courage she had left and turned to her classmates.

"Um...well...that's, uh...an acquaintance of mine," she said, her voice barely audible. The girl with the glasses went wide-eyed.

"Huh... It's for *you*, Asada?!"

"H-how do you know each other?!" the other girl shrieked. Shino felt the growing attention from others around them and squeezed her bag tight, trying to shrink into as small a ball as she could. She started to race off, stammering an apology for some reason.

One of them demanded an explanation tomorrow as she raced through the old-fashioned bronze gate and into the turnaround.

The brazen intruder continued to stare absentmindedly into the sky, even as she approached right next to him.

"...Excuse me," she said, right into his ear. He blinked in surprise and looked down. The lazy smile returned.

"Hi, Sinon. Nice afternoon."

Now that she got a better look at him in the light of day, the real Kirito had a slightly transparent, out-of-place air about him. His longish black hair, extremely pale skin, and surprisingly scrawny body contained a whiff of all of those girlish features that she remembered from his virtual self.

That fragile atmosphere he carried around—if she was being uncharitable, she might describe it as "sickly"—put Shino in mind of the two years of imprisonment he had suffered. She hastily held her tongue before she hurled any more snark his way.

"...Hi. Sorry about the wait."

"Nah, I only just got here. By the way...it seems like..."

He looked around the front entrance of the school, noticing all of the students who were watching the scene unfold.

"...we're drawing a lot of attention..."

"Okay, listen," Shino said, annoyed, "anyone who parks their motorcycle at the front of a school they don't go to is gonna attract attention."

"Oh...I guess you're right. Well," he said, suddenly showing off that cynical, cheeky smirk she saw him make often in the virtual world, "if we hold out a bit longer, maybe the guidance counselor will show up and tell us off for being a bad influence? That could be fun."

"N-no, that's not funny!"

It wasn't out of the question, actually. She automatically glanced back toward the gate and growled, "C'mon, let's go!"

"Yeah, yeah," Kirito smirked. He took a light green helmet off the handlebars and offered it to Shino.

She took the helmet, reminding herself that he was the same snot-nosed, arrogant jerk who had caused her so much headache in GGO, and that she shouldn't be fooled by his appearance. She swung the bag over her back and put the open-faced helmet over her head. She tried to put the chin harness on, but didn't know how.

"Hang on a sec."

Kirito's hand appeared and adjusted the strap under her chin. She felt her face grow hot again and lowered the visor to hide it. She had no idea how she'd explain this one at school tomorrow.

With his own black helmet on, Kirito swung over the seat. He paused and wondered, "Sinon…what about your skirt?"

"I have leggings on underneath, for PE."

"I-is that the only thing that matters?"

"Well, it's not like *you* can see anything," she shot back, then straddled the rear seat. She'd ridden on her grandfather's rusty old Super Cub C90 when she was a little girl, so she knew what to do.

"All right, then…Hang on tight."

Kirito turned the key and the old combustion engine growled to life, startling her. But the vibration through her hips and the smell of the exhaust reminded her of days gone by, and Shino couldn't help but grin as she put her hands around Kirito's bony midsection.

Traveling from Yushima in Bunkyo Ward to their destination in Ginza would be quite tricky using the subway, but it was actually quite close on surface streets.

After going down Chiyoda Street from Ochanomizu to the Imperial Palace, they puttered safely along the moatside. Fortunately, the mild weather gave them a pleasant breeze to enjoy. They passed the Ote gate, turned left from Uchibori Street onto Harumi Street, passed under the JR bridge, and found themselves in Ginza Yoncho-me.

It was a turtle's pace compared to the mad rush they used to escape Death Gun on the three-wheeled buggy, but it still took less than fifteen minutes to reach their destination.

Kirito showed Shino into a very expensive-looking café the likes of which she'd never been in. The instant she walked in the door, she was taken aback by the dignified bow of a water in a crisp white shirt and black butterfly tie.

No sooner had he asked if it was a party of two, setting off dire implications in Shino's head, than a rude bellow erupted from the rear of the establishment, destroying the chic atmosphere.

"Hey, Kirito, back here!"

"Um, I'm with...*that*," Kirito noted uncomfortably. The waiter nodded and bowed in understanding without missing a beat. Shino timidly walked down the sparkling floor, feeling extremely out of place in her school uniform in the midst of so many fancy ladies in the middle of their shopping day.

Standing at the other end of their table was a tall man wearing an expensive, dark blue suit, a regimental tie, and black-framed glasses. She knew that he was a government official, but while he did fit that white-collar vibe, there was also something scholarly about him.

He gestured to the chairs and sat down across from them next to the window. Within seconds, steaming hot towels and leather-bound menus materialized.

"Order anything you like," he offered. She opened the menu and glanced down, only to register sheer shock. The sandwiches, pasta, and other meals were expensive, of course, but even the desserts all had four-digit prices in yen.

She froze with indecision, but Kirito only snorted. "You might as well get whatever looks good. This is all on the taxpayers' dime."

She looked up and saw the bespectacled man smiling and nodding.

"W-well, then...I'll have the cheesecake with cranberry sauce... and Earl Grey," she said. On the inside, she was pale: *Oh my God, that cost 2,200 yen!*

Kirito followed by ordering an apple chiboust, a Mont Blanc, and an espresso. She didn't even want to imagine what the total cost was approaching now. The waiter bowed deeply and left.

The man across from them reached into his pocket for a black leather case and handed Shino a business card from it.

"It's nice to meet you. I'm Kikuoka, from the Ministry of Internal Affairs' Telecommunications Bureau," he said in a pleasing tenor.

Shino hastily took his card and bowed. "N-nice to meet you. I'm Shino Asada."

Kikuoka's mouth pursed shut, and he bowed deeply. "I am truly sorry that our lack of preparation led to your being put in danger."

"Um…it's all right now," she said, bowing back.

Kirito butted in, "You'd better get a proper apology out of him. If Mr. Kikuoka had done his research, neither you nor I would have gone through all of that."

"As to that, I can offer no defense," Kikuoka replied, hanging his head like a scolded child. "But you didn't predict everything yourself, did you, Kirito? You certainly didn't expect that Death Gun was a team."

"Well…you've got me there," Kirito replied, leaning back in the creaking antique chair. "You might as well tell us everything you've figured out, Mr. Kikuoka."

"Fine, but…it's only been two days since their crimes came to light. It's a long way until we know the full extent of the situation…"

He lifted his coffee cup and took a sip before continuing, "As I said, this team was three in all—at least, according to the testimony of their ringleader, Shouichi Shinkawa."

"And this Shouichi was the one in the tattered cloak who attacked me and Sinon in the BoB final?" Kirito asked.

Kikuoka nodded. "It's almost certain. The log from the Amu-Sphere we confiscated from his apartment showed that he was logged in to Gun Gale Online at the same time as the event."

"His own apartment…What kind of person was Shouichi Shinkawa? He was the one pulling all of the strings?"

"As for that, we'll have to start from before the SAO Incident in 2022. But before we get to that…"

The waiter brought a delicate cart by, bearing a number of

plates. Once they had been silently deployed onto the table and the waiter was gone, Kikuoka waved for them to tuck in. Shino was not in a particularly hungry mood, but she could probably eat a small piece of cake. She and Kirito said grace and picked up their golden forks.

She carved out a small corner of the wedge of cheesecake, drizzled in a brilliant red sauce, and brought it to her lips. A flavor like concentrated cheese filled her mouth, but to her surprise, it practically melted on her tongue. For an instant, she wanted the recipe, then realized that they would never give it to her.

Once she had gobbled down half of the cake, she set the fork aside and picked up her tea cup. When she had taken a sip of the hot, faintly citrus-flavored liquid, she felt the compressed parts in the very depths of her heart begin to relax, bit by bit.

"...It's very good," she murmured, which brought a smile to Kikuoka's face.

"Of course, the best time to eat delicious things is alongside more pleasant topics. You'll have to join me another time."

"Uh, s-sure."

Meanwhile, Kirito had decimated the tawny brown mountain of Mont Blanc. He joked, "I wouldn't do it if I were you. His idea of 'pleasant' topics is either stinky or creepy."

"Wh-why, I'm hurt. I'll have you know the story of my Southeast Asian gourmet tour is quite a riveting one...But before I get off topic, let's discuss the incident."

Kikuoka pulled an ultrathin tablet out of his business bag and began prodding at the screen with his long fingers. Shino sat still, nervously awaiting the teacherlike man's explanation.

She *did* want to know everything to do with the Death Gun incident, of course. But at the same time, something deep in her heart screamed out that it didn't want to know the truth.

She knew that in a way, part of her still trusted Kyouji Shinkawa. Even after he pointed that terrible syringe at her, she couldn't bring herself to hate him entirely. She couldn't just give up on her fondness for him altogether. She wanted to believe that what she saw didn't represent him, but someone else who had wormed their way into his mind. That was just how she felt.

About forty hours had passed since what happened late Sunday night.

At Kirito's suggestion, she had washed her face in the bathroom and changed out of her sweater, at which point the police arrived.

They arrested Kyouji Shinkawa at once, who was still only half-conscious after the battering his head had taken. An ambulance came, and he was transported to the police hospital.

Shino and Kirito were taken to a different hospital, for a few just-in-case tests. The doctor on duty pronounced them just fine aside from a few abrasions, at which point they underwent police questioning there in the examination room. Shino tried to keep her fuzzy mind working, telling them only what had happened in her apartment.

Though she didn't realize it, Shino had hit the peak of her mental stress, according to the physician, and he called an end to the police questioning at two in the morning. She spent the night there in the hospital and woke up at six thirty in the morning. The doctor recommended that she return to her apartment, and she decided to go to school.

She just barely made it through her Monday classes, nodding off here and there. She assumed that Kyouji's attack had already made it around school—though he hadn't attended for a while, he was still a registered student there—but no one was spreading any rumors about him.

When she returned to her apartment after school, ignoring Endou's usual summons, there was a police car waiting for her. She headed to the same hospital with a change of clothes, took a simple examination from the doctor, then underwent her second questioning. This time, Shino asked a number of questions, mostly about Kyouji, but learned nothing other than that he wasn't hurt too bad, and was mostly refusing to say anything to the police.

She was told to stay in the hospital again that night, for "security reasons." After eating, showering, and making a brief call to her grandparents and mother, Shino laid down in her hospital bed. She slipped into a deep sleep and remembered nothing afterward. When she woke, she had the sensation of coming out of a long dream, but didn't remember anything about it.

On Tuesday—this morning—she was taken back to her apartment in an unmarked police car. As she stepped out of the car, the detective informed her that her questioning was over for now. She was grateful for that, but she wondered how she would learn more about what had happened. She was slicing tomatoes for her breakfast before school when the phone rang. It was Kirito. Right off the bat, he asked if she had time after school, and she automatically said yes.

Now she was seated next to Kirito, hearing the briefing from the government official who was the boy's "employer."

Kikuoka looked up from the tablet and spoke in a low voice, mindful of the people around.

"Shouichi Shinkawa is the eldest son of the owner and director of a general hospital. He was sickly from a young age, in and out of the hospital until he graduated middle school. He was a year late to high school…and because of that, his father abandoned his hopes for Shouichi to inherit the family business, placing his hopes instead on his second son, Kyouji, who was three years younger. Kyouji had a home tutor while in elementary school, and would sometimes receive his father's lessons himself, leaving Shouichi completely to his own devices. The elder brother was pressured by the lack of hope, while the younger was pressured by the weight of that hope…according to the testimony of their father."

He paused, taking a sip of coffee to wet his tongue.

Shino looked down at the table and tried to imagine what parents' expectations must be like. But she couldn't get a good feel for it.

Despite how close they had been, she'd never sensed any of this pressure from Kyouji in person. She realized once again that she'd been so obsessed with her own issues that she never paid any attention to his. It was a painful reminder.

Kikuoka continued, "But despite the circumstances, the brothers still got along. Shouichi quit high school and sought solace in the online world, particularly in MMORPGs, and his brother picked the habit up from him soon after. Eventually, Shouichi fell prisoner to Sword Art Online, spending two years in his father's hospital in a coma, but once back, he became a sort of idol figure to Kyouji...a hero, if you will."

Shino sensed Kirito's breathing becoming a bit more tense next to her. But Kikuoka only paused his smooth, hushed explanation for a moment before continuing.

"After he returned, Shouichi never touched upon his experiences in SAO, it seems, but once his rehab was over and he returned home, he did tell Kyouji some things...about how many players he had attacked in that world, and the fear his murderous ways struck in the others. At this point, Kyouji's grades were suffering, and he was being extorted by upperclassmen, so in Shouichi's tales he found not disgust or fear, but exhilaration and release."

"Um..." Shino piped up. Kikuoka looked up and craned his neck, prompting her to continue. "Did Shinkawa...I mean, Kyouji tell you about this?"

"No, this is all based on his brother's statements. Shouichi answered everything the police asked him, including what he thought about his brother's state of mind. On the other hand, Kyouji has maintained total silence."

"...I see."

There was no way for Shino to know what kind of place Kyouji's soul wandered now. Though she knew it was impossible, she almost imagined that if she logged in to GGO right now, she would find Spiegel in the corner of the bar where they usually met, as if nothing had ever happened.

"Uh, p-please continue," she urged. Kikuoka nodded and glanced at the tablet again.

"We only have conjectures as to when the brothers reached the point of no return, but I understand that Shouichi started playing Gun Gale Online on Kyouji's recommendation. Shouichi didn't show the kind of VR rejection that many of the other SAO Survivors did, but he also didn't take to the game very enthusiastically. Rather than venture into the wilderness, he preferred to watch other players in town and imagine how he would kill them, he said. But that all changed when he got himself an invisibility cloak through a Real Money Transaction."

"An RMT," Shino muttered to herself. She suspected that the tattered cloak with the Metamaterial Optical Camo effect had to be an ultrarare drop from a boss monster. It could easily go for a higher price than her Hecate II on the open market.

"I would have to assume…it cost an incredible amount," she said.

Kikuoka affirmed her assumption, shaking his head in disbelief. "It apparently cost just over 300,000 yen. But that wasn't much, given that Shouichi had a 500,000-yen monthly allowance from his father."

"Which means…his huge rifle and rare-material estoc were bought with real cash, too…I'm glad SAO had no monetization or auction systems," Kirito murmured, his face deadly serious.

Kikuoka nodded and continued the story. "Indeed. Once Shouichi was able to hide himself using that cloak, he began working on his ability to stalk other players in town without being detected. At that point, he was simply enjoying following them around…but one day, he followed a target to the hall of the regent's office and noticed that they were using one of the game's information terminals. On a whim, he took out his binoculars and watched the screen from the shadow of a pillar. To his surprise, the screen showed the real-life name and address of the player."

"Meaning that he didn't buy the cloak in order to gain information, but the opposite...That he had the cloak before the idea came to him," Kirito sighed, leaning back in his chair. "Hiding has always been a core skill in MMOs, going way back. It would be strange for a game *not* to feature it. But...I think that in a VRMMO, the full range of its uses is too heavily weighted toward bad behavior. They ought to outlaw it in town, at the very least. Can you submit a complaint to Zaskar about that, Sinon?"

She was not expecting to have the conversation directed her way. "Wh-why don't you do it? Anyway...it sounds like it was the cloak that caused the birth of Death Gun," she said, directing the statement toward Kikuoka. The official nodded and looked down at his tablet. Something about his calm, pleasing face struck Shino as notable, but she decided that it didn't matter now.

Kikuoka's hushed voice traveled over the sunlit table. "That would be correct. Shouichi automatically memorized all of the personal information he saw, logged out, and wrote it down. But at the time, he had no intention of doing anything with it. It was the act of stealing their information that excited him, and so he spent the next several days camped out in the regent's office, waiting for players to enter their addresses. Ultimately, he gleaned the details of sixteen players over this stretch. That includes yours, Shino Asada."

"..."

Shino nodded. If it was in early September, that was just before the second BoB. Assuming there were at least five hundred players who registered for the tournament, and roughly half of them would have put in their information in the hopes of getting a model gun, stealing the info of sixteen of them seemed quite possible.

Kikuoka continued, "One day in October, Kyouji revealed to Shouichi that he had hit a wall with his character. He blamed it all on the false information spread by another player named Zexceed. Shouichi recalled that Zexceed was one of the very players whose information he'd stolen, and he told Kyouji about it."

That was it. That had to be the moment that the wall between Kyouji's virtual and real lives began to crumble and disappear.

"Shouichi claims that it wasn't solely the idea of either of them," Kikuoka said, his smooth voice passing right into Shino's ear. "The two of them discussed how they should use Zexceed's personal information to purge him, and thus the outline of the Death Gun plan came to be. Still, he explained that it was just a bunch of fun, imaginary games at first. Shooting a player in the game at the same time the player died in real life sounds easy when you say it, but in reality it is fraught with challenges. They debated for days, clearing hypothetical hurdles to the plan one after the other. It seems the biggest issues were getting the master code to undo the electronic lock, and acquiring the syringe and drugs..."

"A big hospital should have legal master codes they can use to unlock a patient's door in the case of an emergency. I would assume that goes for their father's hospital as well," Kirito pointed out.

Kikuoka pursed his lips in a silent whistle of admiration. "Very good. As a matter of fact, the government's support of keyless locks on residential homes was to strengthen control over the previously inviolable realm of private residences...but that's supposed to be a secret. At any rate, the two brothers did indeed plan to steal the master code, high-pressure syringe, and succinylcholine from their father's hospital. Shouichi claimed that up to this point, everything about the plan was just one big game— nothing different from the way they gathered info on a target party in SAO, scraped together the necessary equipment, then carried out an attack. It seems that he suggested to the detective who was questioning him that they must have felt the same way about their job. They listen to NPCs, gather intel, capture bounties, and turn them in for money. Being a police officer is no different than playing a game, he said."

"I wouldn't take that at face value," Kirito muttered.

Kikuoka's eyebrows rose. "Is that so?"

"Yeah. In a sense, Shouichi might think that way. But when he was Red-Eyed Xaxa, he convinced everyone around him that it was all just a game, yet the only reason he was so fascinated by what he did was the knowledge that the players' deaths were real. In either world, he just believes that whatever doesn't suit his ends isn't actually real. You might call it the dark side of VRM-MOs. It makes reality less real."

"Ahh. And…what about your reality?" Kikuoka asked.

Kirito was about to put on his usual sardonic smirk, but switched to a dead-serious look as he stared into space. "…There are absolutely some things I left behind in that world. And therefore, I'm currently lacking that much right now."

"Do you want to go back?"

"Don't ask me that. It's tasteless," Kirito said, grimacing. He glanced toward Shino. "What do you think about that, Sinon?"

"Uh…"

She wasn't prepared to answer that question. Shino was not used to the practice of putting her thoughts into words. Nevertheless, she tried her best to say what she had felt.

"Well…what you're saying now isn't what you said earlier, Kirito."

"Huh…?"

"You said there was no such thing as the virtual world. You said wherever you are, that's reality. There are lots of VRMMO games out there, but it's not like the players are all divided up between them. I mean, this around us…" She reached over and traced his arm with her fingers. "This world is the only reality. If it turned out that all of this was just another virtual world created by the AmuSphere, to me…it's reality."

Kirito's eyes went wide, and he met her gaze long enough for her to feel self-conscious. Eventually, he put on a smile that surprisingly held not a hint of cynicism.

"…I see. Good point." He glanced back at Kikuoka. "You

should jot down what Sinon just said. It might be the only truth with any value to this incident."

"Don't tease me," she said, bopping his shoulder with a fist. When she looked forward again, Kikuoka was staring at her, too. Feeling awkward, she examined the empty plate that had held her cake instead.

"No, maybe it's right. Maybe it was just the complete opposite for Shouichi. To him, reality was always the place where he wasn't."

"He often repeated the phrase, 'It's not over yet.' Perhaps he hasn't completely returned from Aincrad yet…Perhaps Akihiko Kayaba's goal of creating a world did not actually come about until the castle fell to ruin."

"That's scary. There are too many mysteries to the way he died…but that has nothing to do with this case. To bring us back on topic, once Shouichi had finished the preparations to make the plan a reality, he had essentially eliminated any mental barriers to the act of actually breaking into his victims' homes and administering the lethal drug directly. It was Shouichi himself who drugged the first victim: Tamotsu Shigemura, aka Zexceed. Around one o'clock on November the ninth, he used his master code to unlock the door and infiltrate the apartment. At half past the hour, while Shigemura was taking part in an interview on the MMO Stream channel, he used the high-pressure syringe to inject the drug into the underside of the man's chin. It was a muscle relaxant called suxamethonium chloride, or succinylcholine, which immediately shut down Shigemura's respiration and heartbeat and caused him to die. That would mean that the player in GGO who shot at Zexceed was his brother, Kyouji."

Shino's shoulders twitched when she heard Kyouji's name. Inside her head, she could hear his voice, full of loathing and hatred for Zexceed, as he straddled her in her apartment two nights ago.

It seemed that the false rumors leaked by Zexceed about statistical choices that caused him to lose out on his chance to be the strongest player in the game—though the existence of Yami-kaze, who was an incredible player with an AGI build like Kyouji, belied that conclusion—made for an even more unpardonable crime than those students at his school who bullied him and took his money.

Or perhaps at this point in time, reality for Kyouji was already that other realm...

"The one who carried out the actual deed against the second victim, Usujio Tarako, was again Shouichi. The method was almost exactly the same. They had chosen a final list of seven candidates who shared similar traits. They had to live in Tokyo, alone, with older electronic locks that didn't keep a log, or would have spare keys hidden nearby..."

"That had to be a lot of work to research," Kirito noted.

Kikuoka grimaced. "I've no doubt that it involved a great amount of time and effort. But it seems that even after taking the lives of two players, still no one took the rumors of Death Gun very seriously."

"Yes. Everyone thought they were just a stupid urban legend. So did I," Shino murmured.

Kikuoka nodded heavily. "And no wonder. Kirito and I brain-stormed a number of possibilities, but our ultimate conclusion was that it had to be the product of baseless rumors. Of course, it was the very approach of our conjectures that was wrong..."

"If only we'd noticed the truth just a day earlier...we could have prevented those two extra victims in the tournament itself," Kirito said bitterly.

Shino didn't even raise her head. "But you did save me."

"No, I didn't do anything. It was all you."

She threw him a glance, then realized that she hadn't properly thanked him for his part in it yet.

Kikuoka broke the brief silence. "If it weren't for your hard work, it's not hard to imagine that all seven people on that list would have been victimized. Please don't blame yourselves."

"I'm not, actually…I just think it would be a shame if this tarnished the reputation of VRMMOs again."

"You know the buds growing from The Seed are too strong to die out because of this. Now there's a gathering of countless little seedlings that will one day form a great World Tree of their own. What I want to know is, who could have planted such a thing?"

"…Who, indeed? On with the story," Kirito prompted, clearing his throat.

"Of course. Well, I think you already know what happens next. Upset that the threat of Death Gun was not being taken seriously, the two brothers decided a more dramatic demonstration was necessary. They put together a plan to shoot three different players in the final round of the third Bullet of Bullets tournament. The players they singled out were Pale Rider, Garrett…and you, Sinon."

"…"

Shino nodded. She already knew the name of Garrett, the fourth victim. He was a fashionable fellow who used an antique Winchester rifle. She thought of his trademark ten gallon hat and said a silent prayer in his memory, then realized something.

"Oh…by the way, maybe this is just a coincidence, but…"

"What is it?"

"I think there might be one more quality that all seven of the targets shared. All of them, including me, were non-AGI builds."

"Oh…? What does that mean…?"

"Shinkawa…I mean, Kyouji played a pure Agility build, and that caused him to hit a dead end. I think he probably felt conflicted about players who tried out a different build…especially if they had more than a little STR to work with."

"Aha…" Kikuoka stared down at his tablet in silence for a bit. "So you're saying…everything in the motive was rooted within the game itself. This will be a difficult thing for the prosecutors to use in court. But I don't know…" He shook his head in disbelief.

In a tone of regret, Kirito said, "No, it's quite possible. An MMO player's character stats are the basis for their essential values. I know someone who pranked his friend by pushing his hand and causing him to place a single point in the wrong stat, and it led to them killing each other for months...within the game, of course. But that's how big of a fight it caused."

Shino could relate to that. But Kikuoka's eyes went round, then he shook his head again.

"That would require the prosecutor, lawyer, judge, and jury to all experience a VRMMO for themselves to process. Perhaps it might be time to take the court's facilities into consideration... But in any case, that's not for us to worry about. Now, where was I?"

He prodded the tablet again. "Ah, yes. They chose three targets. But unlike the previous two cases, there was a big roadblock to pulling off the plan during the BoB—Death Gun and his collaborator in real life cannot be in contact. That made timing the shootings very difficult. It was technically made possible by the fact that the livestream was viewable from outside the game, but—"

"—it's still not easy. There's the matter of moving around," Kirito interrupted, his expression bitter. "That's where I missed out. I assumed there were only two Death Guns..."

"Yes, that's correct. They chose the three targets who were closest together. While Pale Rider's home in Omori and Garrett's in Musashi-Kosugi are fairly close, Asada is quite a distance away from them in Yushima. And it seems that the usual Death Gun actor, Kyouji, was quite insistent on carrying out the real-life act in this case. Shouichi has a scooter, but Kyouji cannot drive. So Shouichi proposed adding a new partner. He is—let's see... Atsushi Kanamoto, age nineteen. An old friend of Shouichi's. Or more accurately..."

He glanced at Kirito. "A fellow guild member from SAO. His character name was...Johnny Black. Does that ring any bells?"

"It does," Kirito said, closing his eyes. "He was the poison-knife guy who always teamed up with Xaxa in Laughing Coffin. They attacked and killed a number of players together back then, too. Dammit…If only I knew…If only I'd…"

Shino reached out and squeezed his hand to stop him from finishing his sentence. She stared into his eyes and shook her head from side to side. That was all it took to get her message across.

For a moment, Kirito's face scrunched up like a child about to cry, but he indicated his understanding with his eyes. Then he was back to his usual poker face. Shino pulled her fingers free of his chilly hand and faced forward. Kikuoka stopped watching the two of them and continued his report.

"Whether Kanamoto, aka Johnny Black, took an active role in this plan isn't clear from Shouichi's testimony. It seems that even to Shouichi, this Kanamoto fellow was hard to understand in certain ways…"

"So why don't you ask Kanamoto about all of this?" Kirito asked. It was a perfectly reasonable question.

Kikuoka only shook his head. "He hasn't been caught yet."

"Wha…?"

"We captured Kyouji Shinkawa at Miss Asada's apartment, and took his brother Shouichi into custody at his home forty minutes later, but when we searched Kanamoto's apartment in Ohta two hours later, based on Shouichi's statements, he wasn't there. They're still watching the place in case he returns, but I haven't had any reports of an arrest."

"…And you're positive that he carried out the murders of Pale Rider and Garrett during the tournament?"

"It's almost certain. We haven't found the high-pressure syringe and drug cartridge that Shouichi gave him, the same as Kyouji's, but we did recover some hair in the victims' apartments that was a DNA match for the stuff we found in Kanamoto's residence."

"Cartridge…" Shino repeated, feeling a chill at the coincidence with gun terminology. She remembered when Kyouji had the syringe pressed to her neck, claiming that it was the true Death Gun.

Kirito grimaced as well. "Did they use up all the drugs on the two targets?"

Once again, Kikuoka shook his head. "No...A full cartridge of succinylcholine contains well over a fatal dose, but Shouichi gave him three, just in case. He might still have one of them. That's why we had police escorts for you from Monday until this morning—particularly for Miss Asada."

"You're saying that...Johnny Black might still be after Sinon?"

"It's just a precaution. The police aren't giving it serious consideration. After all, their Death Gun project fell into ruin. He has nothing to gain by attacking her, and there's no history or hatred between Miss Asada and Kanamoto. We've already got the metropolitan automated security cam net in a trial run, so he won't be able to hide for long."

"...What is that?"

"We call it the S2 System. Computers automatically analyze camera footage to recognize the faces of wanted criminals...but the details are all classified."

"Well, *that's* not unsettling," Kirito opined sardonically, sipping his coffee with a grimace.

"I agree with you there. But I think we can agree that it's a good thing that Kanamoto will be caught soon. Back to the incident..."

Kikuoka traced the tablet and promptly shrugged. "I think you two probably know the details better than me after this point. Kyouji Shinkawa led an assault on Miss Asada's residence just after the tournament, but was fortunately caught before he could carry it out. Shouichi Shinkawa was arrested soon after, and now Atsushi Kanamoto is wanted. The brothers are held at Motofuji Police Station, where their interrogation continues...and that is the full report of what happened. At least, as far as I understand it. Do you have any questions?"

"Um..."

Shino didn't know if this was a question that could be answered, but she had to ask it anyway.

"What's going to happen to Shinka—Kyouji—after this?"

"Hmm," Kikuoka grunted, pushing his glasses back up the bridge of his nose. "Shouichi is nineteen, and Kyouji is sixteen, so they will be tried as minors. However, given that there are four fatalities in this mess, I think they'll probably get moved from the lower family court to a criminal prosecution. There, they'll be subjected to a psychiatric examination. And depending on the results of that…Well, I think it's likely they'll be sent to a juvenile medical institution, given their actions. After all, they seem to be living outside the bounds of reality…"

"No…I don't think that's true," Shino muttered. Kikuoka blinked and motioned for her to continue.

"I don't know about his brother…but to Kyouji…I think reality *was* on the inside of Gun Gale Online." She held up a hand and swiveled her fingers. "I think he decided that all of this in the real world was worthless, and the only truth was in GGO. Sure, everyone else might see that as simply an escape from the real world, but…"

Kyouji Shinkawa had tried to take Shino's life. The fear and despair he inflicted on her was massive. But even then, for some reason, Shino couldn't bring herself to hate him. All she felt was a deep, deep misery. It was the pain of that sorrow that moved her to speak.

"But the more energy you pour into an online game, the more it eventually turns into something other than just recreation. I mean, it's a boring pain to keep grinding experience and money just to get stronger. Sometimes it's fun just to mess around with your friends for a bit…but when you're like Kyouji, committing hours of grunt work every day just to be the best, I think it has to cause an incredible amount of stress."

"A game…causing stress? But isn't that completely against the whole point…?" Kikuoka asked, aghast.

She nodded. "Yes. Kyouji literally flipped his world upside down. He switched this world…for that one."

"But…why? Why would he need to go to such lengths to prove that he was the best?"

"I don't know the answer. Like I said earlier, to me, the real world and the game world had their own separate continuities... Do you know what I mean, Kirito?"

She looked to her right and saw Kirito leaning back against the chair, eyes shut. Eventually, he murmured, "He wanted to be strong."

Shino shut her lips, thought on the meaning of that statement, then nodded slowly. "Exactly. I was the same way. Maybe every VRMMO player is the same way. We just...want to be strong."

She turned back to face Kikuoka. "Um, when do you think I'll be able to see Kyouji?"

"Well, once the case has been filed with prosecutors, he'll be held for a while, so it'll have to be after he's moved to juvenile classification."

"I see. Well, I'll pay him a visit. I want to tell him what I've been thinking...and what I'm thinking now."

Even if it was too late, or her words didn't get through to him, Shino felt she ought to do that much. Kikuoka gave her what felt like a genuine smile for once.

"You're very strong. I highly suggest you do that. I'll send you the details of his arrangements at a later time." He checked the watch on his left wrist. "Pardon me, I ought to be going. For a dead-end post, there certainly are a number of duties to stay on top of."

"Sorry about taking your time like this," Kirito said.

Shino bowed her head. "Um...thank you. Very much."

"Not at all. It was our lack of foresight that put you in danger. This is the least I can do. I'll let you know if we learn anything new."

Kikuoka picked up his bag from the nearby seat and stashed the tablet away, then rose to his feet. He was about to reach for the check on the table, but stopped.

"Oh, and Kirito."

"...What?"

"Here's what you asked me for." He put his hand into his suit pocket and pulled out a small scrap of paper, handing it to Kirito across the table. "When the investigators told Death Gun...er, Red-Eyed Xaxa...that this was a question from you, he answered it at once. But only under the condition that he be allowed to send a message back. Of course, you have no obligation to hear him out, and of course, we can't go leaking messages from suspects in the middle of a case, so officially, this never left the department... What do you say? Want to hear it?"

Kirito made a face like he'd just tasted the bitterest coffee ever, but nodded. "Well, since you went to the trouble..."

"Very well. Ahem." Kikuoka pulled a second memo out of his pocket and looked down at it. "'This is not the end. You don't have the power to end it. You will realize this very soon. It's showtime.' That's his message."

"...He really is a crafty bastard."

Ten minutes had passed since Kikuoka left, waving good-bye. Kirito was grumbling on the walk back to where he had parked his motorcycle.

"Who *is* that man, anyway? He said he was a ministry official, but...he seemed more like..."

Shino thought he was a very hard person to get a handle on. Kirito shrugged.

"Well, I'm absolutely certain that he's part of the Ministry of Internal Affairs' department in charge of monitoring the VR world. For now, at least."

"For now?"

"I mean, it's only been two days since everything happened. Don't you think he's a little *too* in the know about the police information? Especially in Japan, where every government department sections itself off?"

"...What are you saying?"

"I think maybe his true affiliation is somewhere else. Maybe he's in the police department...or maybe—but it couldn't be..."

"...?"

"I met him here once before, and I trailed after him when he left."

Shino shot him an exasperated look, but the boy didn't seem to take any notice.

"There was a huge black car waiting for him in a nearby parking garage. The driver had short hair and a dark suit, and he looked like trouble. I tried my best to follow on my bike, but they might have noticed me... Kikuoka got off in front of Ichigaya Station, and I lost sight of him while I was looking for a place to park the motorcycle."

"Ichigaya? Not Kasumigaseki?"

"Right. The Ministry of Internal Affairs is in Kasumigaseki... but it's the Ministry of Defense that's in Ichigaya."

"Def..." Shino was speechless. "You mean...the Self-Defense Force?"

"That's why I said it couldn't be. I mean, the police are even more ornery with the SDF than the Ministry of Internal Affairs," Kirito said, shrugging, but something about this struck a chord in Shino's memory.

"Oh...speaking of him, I was noticing that the lens on Mr. Kikuoka's glasses seemed...very weak, maybe? Possibly even flat. I didn't notice any refraction through them."

"Ooh...interesting," the boy responded, clearly finding something of note in that revelation.

Shino asked, "But...let's say he is involved with the SDF. Why would he be doing investigations into VRMMOs? I mean, shouldn't that be completely out of their jurisdiction?"

"Hmm. Well, from what I've heard, the American military has a plan to use full-dive tech for unit training."

"H-huh?!" Shino exclaimed, stopping in her tracks. Kirito stopped with her and gestured with a hand.

"Yeah, like, for example...Oh, is it okay to...talk about guns?"

"U-um...as long as it's just talking."

"Good. Let's say you were handed a real sniper rifle right now. Could you load it, fire it, and all of that?"

"…"

She thought back to just hours before, when she shot Endou's Government model gun, and nodded. "I think…I can. If it's just firing. But I won't know if I can handle the recoil until I use it myself, and I probably wouldn't be able to hit the target."

"Well, I don't even know how to load a bullet. Think of how economical and safe it would be to learn the basics of operating a weapon in a virtual environment, without burning ammo or fuel."

"Um…I don't know…"

She dropped her eyes to look at her hand. What Kirito was talking about was so huge that she couldn't process it for herself.

"It's just a possibility. There are tons of different potential uses for full-dive technology that have popped up in just the last year. Anything could happen in the future. I'm just saying, it's worth keeping an eye out for him," Kirito said breezily, then approached his motorcycle and undid the U-lock on his rear wheel. He handed one of the two helmets to Shino and started to say something.

"Urm…so…"

"…What?"

"Sinon, do you have some time after this…?"

"I've got nothing going on. I'm not logging back in to GGO for a while."

"I see. Well, if you don't mind, I could use your help with something…"

"What's that?"

"Well, it turns out that our little scene in the cave during the BoB final was on the stream…and some of my old SAO companions saw it. They realized that 'Kirito' was the same Kirito they knew…so I'd really, really appreciate it if you could help explain to them that what we were doing wasn't romantic in any way."

"…Oh?" said Shino, who couldn't help but crack a grin. She did feel a bit self-conscious thinking about that moment, but it brought her more than a little savage pride to know that the endlessly selfish rogue was getting a taste of his own medicine, answering to what other people thought about him and her.

"I'm surprised they figured out it was you, even with the same name. Even if they *were* your old friends."

"Yeah…it was the sword style that gave me away."

"Ah, I see. Well, fine—but you owe me one. You'll have to buy me a slice of cake sometime."

Kirito's face sank pathetically. "You don't mean…at that same place?"

"I'm not going to be *that* heartless."

"Th-that's good to hear. Well…can you swing over to Okachi-machi with me, then? It won't take that much time."

"Oh, it's just next to Yushima. Right on the way home."

She took the helmet and stuck it on her head. As Kirito gave her chin-strap assistance again, Shino couldn't help but rue that she hadn't just gotten used to helmets in GGO like she ought to.

They went from Chuo Street in Ginza to Showa Street, then headed north for a while, coming across the redevelopment district on the east end of Akihabara Station. The looming silver high-rises brought the sights of Glocken to mind, but when they reached the boundary of Okachimachi, it turned into a very old-fashioned urban sprawl.

The bike puttered along, heading left and right down narrow alleys, before finally stopping outside of a small business. Shino got off the seat and removed her helmet. The dark gleam of the wooden exterior was a bit offputting, and the only thing that identified it as a café was the metal sign of two dice hung above the door. Below that was stamped the words DICEY CAFÉ, the name of the establishment, but the sign on the ugly door said CLOSED.

"…This is it?"

"Yep," Kirito nodded, extracting his key and pushing right through the door. The door jingled, and the strains of slow-tempo jazz drifted through it.

Shino stepped inside, guided by the fragrant scent of coffee. Though the interior was cramped, the orange-lit, shine-polished wooden interior was full of warmth that eased the weight she'd had on her shoulders.

"Welcome," boomed a smooth baritone from the counter. It was a large man with chocolate skin. His hardened warrior's features and bald head were imposing, but the dainty bowtie tucked under the collar of his white shirt added an air of good humor.

There were two guests already in the café, girls wearing school uniforms seated on the stools at the counter. Shino noticed that their jackets were the same color as Kirito's uniform.

"You're late!" complained one girl as she hopped off the stool. Her shoulder-length hair was curled slightly inward.

"Sorry, sorry. Our talk with Chrysheight went long."

"I ate two whole pieces of apple pie. If I get fat, it's your fault."

"H-how is that my fault?"

The other girl, whose straight, brown-ish hair hung to midway down her back, just watched their bickering and smiled. Eventually, she got to her feet and broke into the conversation with familiar ease.

"Well, are you going to introduce us or not, Kirito?"

"Oh, yeah…right."

Prompted by a hand on her back, Shino walked into the middle of the room. She bowed her head, trying to squash the little insects of fear that crawled on her whenever she had to interact with strangers.

"This is the third champion of Gun Gale Online, Shino Asada—aka Sinon."

"S-stop it," she protested, but he just laughed and continued the introductions. He pointed out the proactive girl who'd just argued with him.

"This is Rika Shinozaki, better known as Lisbeth, the rip-off blacksmith."

"Why, you…"

He nimbly evaded the attack of the peeved Rika and extended

a hand toward the other girl. "And this is Asuna Yuuki, the berserk healer who normally just goes by 'Asuna.'"

"Th-that's mean!" she protested, but never lost her smile. Asuna turned her beautiful, clear eyes toward Shino, and she made a smooth, floaty bow of her head.

"And that over there," Kirito said, jutting his jaw at the manager behind the bar, "is Agil, better known as Agil the Wall."

"Why do I have to be 'the Wall'?! Besides, I have a wonderful name that my mama gave me."

To her surprise, even the manager was a VRMMO player. He grinned and put a hand to his burly chest. "It's nice to meet you. I'm Andrew Gilbert Mills. The pleasure's all mine."

When he said his name, it was in perfectly native pronunciation, but the rest was all fluent Japanese, which caught Shino by surprise. She hastily bowed before it got too awkward.

"C'mon, sit down," Kirito said, pulling out a chair from one of the pair of four-seat tables in the place. Once Shino, Asuna, and Rika were seated, he snapped his fingers. "Agil, I'll take a ginger ale. Anything to drink, Sinon?"

"Uh…I'll have the same."

"He makes it spicy here," Kirito said with a smirk, then called out, "Make that two!" to the bar, and folded his hands atop the table.

"So… Liz, Asuna, we're going to explain exactly what happened on Sunday."

Even in a digest form, with Kirito and Shino taking turns filling in for the other, it took over ten minutes to go through the events of the BoB and Kikuoka's further reporting.

"…And the media hasn't announced anything yet, which is why we didn't mention any names or details, but that's pretty much the whole story," Kirito finished, sinking exhaustedly back into his chair and downing the last of his second glass of ginger ale.

"I don't know what it is about you…but you always get wrapped up into things that don't involve you," Rika said, shaking her head.

But Kirito only looked away. "No, that's not true in this case. I had a long-ago score to settle with this one."

"Oh…I see. Man, I wish I could have been there too. I've got plenty of things I'd like to say to that Death Gun jerk."

"And he's probably not the last one. I think there are more people out there whose souls were warped by their experiences in SAO."

A gloomy silence settled on the conversation, eventually broken by Asuna's gentle smile.

"But I think there are others whose souls were saved, like mine. I'm not going to defend SAO, and what the commander did… and many people died there…but I don't want to deny or regret what happened in those two years."

"Yeah, good point. If you hadn't been holding my hand during that last battle with Death Gun, I wouldn't have been able to pull off that move. It must have been a connection that only existed… because of the years I spent in SAO…"

Shino didn't understand what he meant. She gave him a confused look, and he abashedly smiled and explained.

"I told you I was diving from a hospital in Ochanomizu the night of the tournament, right? My location was supposed to be a secret, but Asuna here ran Kikuoka up the flagpole to make him give it up."

"I did no such thing!" she protested, cheeks puffed. He laughed mischievously.

"So she raced from her dive location right here over to the hospital, and…just at the moment I was fighting Death Gun in the desert, she squeezed my hand from the real world side. It's weird, but…at that exact moment, I *felt* her hand. That's the only reason I remembered to draw my Five-Seven, I think."

"…I see…"

The way he explained that made her wonder if the two were a couple, but she pushed that out of her mind instantly. No one else seemed to pick up on it, though, and Kirito moved on.

"And that's not all. After I logged out, Asuna taught me that Death Gun's registered name, 'Sterben,' was a German word meaning 'to die.' But she said it was only used in Japan by doctors and nurses, and it hit me…You said you were going to contact your friend, the doctor's son, and I just got a bad feeling about it. I didn't think the cops would make it in time, so I hopped on my bike and raced to Yushima…though ultimately, I wasn't able to help…"

This revelation filled Shino with a strange, quiet shock.

"…Sterben. So it wasn't 'Steven'…" she whispered, shutting her eyes for an instant. "And in medical terminology, it means 'to die'…I wonder why he would give himself a name like that."

"Maybe it was part of a rebellion against his father, the doctor. But I don't know if the reason is simple enough to sum up like that," Kirito lamented.

Seated diagonally from him, and directly across from Shino, Asuna said clearly, "You shouldn't search for anything more than a name in a VRMMO avatar's handle. It's more about what you're missing than what you're learning."

Next to her, Rika smiled. "Yes, that sounds very convincing from someone who just uses her real name."

"Hush!" Asuna said, jabbing Rika with her elbow. Her friend feigned terrible pain. Shino grinned at the lighthearted display, then noticed Asuna was looking right at her. There was a brilliant gleam in her bright brown irises which suggested an inner strength lay behind her reserved nature.

"So…Miss Asada."

"Er, yes?"

"It might be strange of me to say this, but… I'm sorry you had to be put through that horrible event."

"Uh…I'm fine," Shino said hastily, shaking her head. "I think part of this whole incident was something I brought upon myself. Something about my personality, or my play style…or my past.

And because of those things, I panicked in the middle of the tournament…and needed Kirito to calm me down. That's what you saw on the broadcast…"

Kirito shot upright again and quickly added, "R-right, I forgot the most important part. That was an emergency evacuation, you might say. We were being chased by a murderous madman. So don't get any funny ideas about it."

"…Well, we can leave it at that. But I'm not sure about what will happen in the future," Rika grumbled, throwing Kirito a very skeptical glance. Then she clapped her hands together and put on a big smile. "At any rate, it's great to meet another VRMMO girl in real life."

"That's right. I'd like to hear more about GGO, too. Can we be friends, Asada?" Asuna asked with a gentle smile, extending her hand across the table. Shino looked at the white, soft hand…and shrank.

The instant the word *friends* sank into her heart, she felt a burning craving well up there, as well as a painful sense of unease.

Friends. That was something that she had desired countless times since the incident, only to be horribly betrayed, and swear that she would never seek them again.

I want to be friends. I want to take the hand of this girl named Asuna, who exudes mercy and benevolence, and feel her warmth. I want to be around her, talk about silly things, and do whatever normal girls do.

But if that happened, at some point she would learn that Shino had once killed a person. She would see the blood that stained Shino's hands. The disgust that would appear in Asuna's eyes terrified her. Touching others was something she could not experience. Not now, not ever.

Shino's hand was frozen hard beneath the table, immobilized. Asuna's eyes grew questioning, inviting an explanation, but Shino just looked down. She thought of just leaving. For the moment, she could at least keep her heart warm with the offer of being friends. She would just apologize and be on her way.

"Sinon."

The whisper jolted Shino's frightened, timid wits. She flinched and looked over at Kirito. When their eyes met, he gave her a brief, but clear nod. His eyes were saying it was okay. She turned back to Asuna.

The girl's smile never wavered, and neither did her outstretched hand. Meanwhile, Shino's arm felt like it was tied down with lead weights. But she fought against the shackles and slowly, slowly, raised her arm. For the first time since the incident, she decided she would rather bear the pain of trusting others than the bitterness of keeping them at bay so they couldn't betray her.

The distance to Asuna's hand was unfathomable. The closer she got, the more dense the wall of air became, as if it was actively repelling Shino's hand.

But at last, their fingers touched.

The next instant, Shino's hand melted into Asuna's. The warmth of it couldn't be put into words. The gentle conduit of heat passed through her fingers to her arm, shoulder, then her whole body, melting her frozen blood.

"Ah..." Shino gasped, without realizing she had done so. It was so warm. She had forgotten that the human hand could shake one's soul in this way. In that moment, she felt reality. No longer was she running away from the world in fear, but was connected with true reality at last.

She stayed that way for seconds. Nearly a minute.

Shino noticed that even as she kept smiling kindly, there was a bit of hesitation and uncertainty in Asuna's expression. She started to automatically pull her hand away, but Asuna squeezed even harder. The other girl spoke slowly and carefully, finding each phrase as it came to her.

"Listen, Asada...Shino. There's another reason that we had you come here today. We thought you might find it unpleasant... that it might make you angry, but we just...wanted to tell you something."

"Another reason? That would...make me angry?"

It made even less sense now. To her left, Kirito spoke up in a surprisingly tense voice.

"First, Sinon, I need to apologize to you." He gave her a very deep bow, and caught her gaze through his bangs with the black eyes he shared with that feminine avatar. "I told Asuna and Liz... about what happened in your past. I needed their help with this."

"What...?!"

She didn't even register the latter part of his statement.

They know?! About what happened in the post office? Asuna and Rika already know what I did when I was eleven years old?!

This time, Shino tried to pull her hand out of Asuna's with all her strength.

But she couldn't. Asuna gripped her hand with a power that seemed impossible from those delicate arms. Her eyes, expression, and body heat were trying to tell Shino something—but what? What could she possibly want to tell her, knowing about the blood that could never be washed from those hands?

"Shino, as a matter of fact...Liz, Kirito, and I took school off yesterday and went to the city of..."

"——!!"

It wasn't even shock. For several seconds, Shino couldn't even process what Asuna had said to her.

The girl's plump, shining lips pronounced the name of a place. The very town that Shino had lived in through her middle school graduation. The place where the incident happened. The place she wanted to forget and never visit again.

Why? How? How?

The questions swirled around her head and escaped her mouth at last.

"But...why would...you...?"

She stood up to escape this place, shaking her head back and forth all the while. But before she could get all the way to her feet, Kirito held her shoulder down. His voice was stern, desperate.

"Because Sinon, you haven't met someone you ought to meet... You haven't heard something you ought to hear. I thought it would probably hurt you—I knew it would—but I couldn't let you stay the way you are. So I went to study the newspaper database about your incident…and I knew the post office wouldn't understand if I called them, so I went in person to ask for someone's contact information."

"Someone I ought…to meet…? I ought to hear…?" she repeated, dazed. Rika caught a look from Kirito and stood up, walking to a door in the back of the room with a PRIVATE sign on it. She opened the door and a person walked out.

It was a woman of about thirty years. Her hair was semilong, her makeup was slight, and her clothes were relaxed. She looked more like a housewife than an office lady.

Little footsteps behind her bore that impression out. A little girl of preschool age trotted out after the woman. They bore a strong resemblance—clearly mother and daughter. But this only increased Shino's confusion. She had no idea who these people were. She hadn't met them in Tokyo, and not even in her hometown.

The woman looked at the stunned Shino, beaming with that strange crying look, and bowed deeply. The little girl next to her bowed, too.

It stayed that way for a long time until, prompted by Rika, the family crossed the room to the table where Shino sat. Asuna stood up and allowed the woman and her daughter to sit down on the other side of the table. The bartender, who had been watching the entire scene in silence, swiftly brought out a café au lait for the mother, and a glass of milk for the girl.

Even up close, Shino still didn't recognize them. Why had Kirito claimed this woman was someone Shino ought to meet? Was he mistaken somehow?

No.

Somewhere deep in her memory, a little spark flashed. This woman was a stranger, so why…?

At that moment, the mother bowed again. She spoke at last, her voice trembling slightly.

"It's nice to meet you, Miss Asada…Shino, is it? My name is Sachie Oosawa. This is Mizue, age four."

Once again, the names were unfamiliar. There was no connection between Shino and this family. But her memory continued its faint prickling.

She couldn't bring herself to respond, or do anything other than stare. Sachie took a deep breath and began to explain.

"I didn't move to Tokyo until after she was born. Before then, I worked in the city of…"

And then, Shino understood everything.

"…at the Sancho-me Post Office."

"Ah…"

That was *the* post office. The place it happened. The little, unremarkable, completely ordinary local post office that Shino and her mother visited five years ago, where she encountered the event that completely changed her life.

The bank robber shot and killed the male employee at the window first, then hesitated, unsure whether to shoot the two female employees behind the counter next, or her mother. Shino interrupted him in a mindless, desperate rage, yanking his gun away and pulling the trigger.

That's right… Sachie was most definitely one of the two women working in the office at the time.

So that was what it meant. Yesterday, Kirito, Asuna, and Rika went to the post office. They found the address of this woman, who had quit her job and moved to Tokyo, called her, and set up this meeting with Shino today.

She understood that much. But the biggest mystery was still left: Why? Why would they skip school to do this?

"…I'm sorry. I'm so sorry, Shino," Sachie blurted out, the corners of her eyes getting teary.

Shino had no idea why she was receiving an apology. But her voice trembling, Sachie continued, "I'm so, so sorry. I…I should have met you sooner. But I just wanted to forget about what happened…and when my husband got a transfer, I took the opportunity to leave for Tokyo… I should have known that you would be tormented this whole time…and I never apologized… or thanked you…"

The tears fell now. Next to her, Mizue looked up at her mother with concern. Sachie stroked the girl's braided hair.

"When it happened…I was pregnant with her. So you didn't just save my life, Shino…you saved hers, too. Thank you…thank you so much. Thank you…"

"…I saved…your lives?" Shino repeated.

Eleven-year-old Shino had pulled the trigger three times in that post office, and took a life. That was all she had done. That's all she ever thought she'd done. But now, at long last, this woman had given her a different answer.

She had saved her.

"Sinon," came Kirito's uncertain whisper. "Sinon. You've always blamed yourself. You've punished yourself. I'm not saying that was a mistake. But at the same time, you have the right to think about those you saved. You have the right to forgive yourself because of that. That's…what I can give you…"

He shut his mouth tight, unable to find anything else to say. Shino looked away from him and back at Sachie. She knew she ought to say something, but the words would not come. In fact, she didn't even know what to think.

There was a small tap of feet.

The four-year-old girl hopped off of her chair and came walking around the table. The braids Sachie tied for her shone in the light, and her puffy little pink cheeks and huge eyes were filled with the greatest innocence to be found in the world.

Mizue reached into the pochette slung over her kindergarten uniform blouse and rummaged around for something. It was a piece of drawing paper folded into quarters. She awkwardly unfolded the paper and gave it to Shino.

It was a crayon drawing. In the center was the face of a woman with long hair, beaming. That had to be Sachie, her mother. To the right was a girl with braids—Mizue. The man with glasses on the left was obviously her father.

And at the top, in letters that she'd probably just learned recently, was written "To Miss Shino."

Mizue held the drawing out with both hands, and Shino accepted it the same way. The little girl smiled and took a deep breath. In an awkward, halting way, she delivered a message that she'd clearly done her best to memorize.

"Miss Shino, thank you, for saving Mama and Mizue."

Everything she saw was full of rainbow light, blotted and blurred.

It took a bit of time before she realized she was crying. She had never known that there could be tears so gentle and pure and cleansing.

Shino held the drawing tight, big tears dropping from her cheeks one after the other. Suddenly, a tiny, soft hand reached out, hesitantly at first, then eagerly, squeezing her right hand, right on the very spot where the traces of gunpowder had left a permanent mark.

It'll take a long, long time for me to fully accept everything in my past. But I still love the world I live in now.

Life is painful, and the road ahead is treacherous.

But I can still keep walking down it. I'm sure of that.

I know this, because this hand in mine, and the tears on my cheeks, are warm enough to tell me so.

AFTERWORD

Hello, this is Reki Kawahara. You've just finished *Sword Art Online 6: Phantom Bullet*, my final book of 2010.

Since February 2009, I've had an alternating schedule of *SAO* and *Accel World*, publishing a new book every other month, twelve books in total. Of course, the only reason this insane plan was even possible was the fact that the *SAO* series already had been written. If all I did was just some minor retouching of what I had previously published on my website, that shouldn't be too hard, I thought.

However, upon rereading the material, I found not just tweaks to make, but entire passages to rewrite. For the first two volumes, I was able to keep it to just "fixes," and for the next two, it was more like "additions." The fifth volume ended up being more of a "rewrite"…and for this sixth volume, it was essentially "written from scratch." *(laughs)* Not only that, it ended up being far longer than any of the previous books…it's actually a slight miracle that I survived (debatable) to write this afterword. I can't help but scream at myself: *Why! Did this! Happen?!*

So with the help of that inexplicable effort, I managed to put together a book that I hope readers of my published edition and web version alike will find fresh and new and exciting. The next volume should be focused on Asuna instead. I hope you're ready for our main heroine, after she barely appeared in the fifth and sixth volumes! (I won't be rewriting it—I think.)

And now, for this year's final apology section...

As I'm sure some of you know, in October of this year, I attended a signing event in Akihabara called the "Dengeki Bunko Autumn Festival 2010" with my illustrator, abec. And yes...I showed up late! Extremely late! Thirty minutes after the event began! Due to a data block malfunction in my brain, I processed "12:30" as "2:30"!

From what I understand, in the four-thousand-year history of Dengeki Bunko, I was the first writer to ever show up late to his own autograph signing. I don't even know how to apologize to those people who applied to the event and waited in line for long hours...I'm so sorry. I won't do it again. (Then again, maybe they'll never ask me to do another signing event after this!)

So, to my editor, Mr. Miki, who I troubled so very much with my lateness in both events and manuscripts, and my illustrator, abec, I hope the next year will be a good one. And to you readers, if you've read this far, I hope you have a good 2011! And to me— stop being late!

Reki Kawahara — October 2010